Dangerous Waves
Amanda Taylor

Published by Northern Heritage Publications
an imprint of Jeremy Mills Publishing Limited

113 Lidget Street
Lindley
Huddersfield
West Yorkshire HD3 3JR

www.jeremymillspublishing.co.uk

First published 2013
Text © Amanda Taylor

The moral right of Amanda Taylor
to be identified as the author of this work has been asserted.

ISBN 978-1-906600-94-5

Publisher's Note

Dangerous Waves was originally published under the title *The Chinaman's Bastard* in August 2009. It was re-visited by the author and substantially revised before re-editing and re-publishing under its new title.

Cover Illustration
Safely into Harbour
Frank Wasley
© Private Collection

To Sara and Clifford for keeping the faith

The past is but the beginning of a beginning, and all that is and has been is but the twilight of the dawn.

Lecture given to the Royal Institute on 24th January, 1902, by H.G.Wells

Chapter One

The winter of 1879. A comet, a ball of brilliance, arced high above the captain's house on the main street of Staithes – it passed over unseen – there was no reaction from the dull glow in an upper storey window.

The room's poor illumination was provided by a few dying embers in the hearth and a single candle burning low in a corner. In this angle of flickering candlelight, a Friend sat reading on an upright chair, an actress waiting on stage for the performance to begin. Under her Quaker bonnet she yawned from time to time. Her vigil had already been hours long.

'The day is not good,' whispered a voice from the bed in shadows.

'The day is not good to be out at sea,' elaborated the Friend, no more than a girl. A gust of howling wind drowned out the response from the bed. 'The men have already taken ten of the yawls out into open water in the hope they'll be safer there.'

'May the Lord protect them.'

'And those aboard the *Daniel*.'

'There is no word of them yet?' The figure in the bed wriggled to free itself from restraining covers – a moth from the cocoon – weakened, disconsolate it fell back beaten. The Friend shook her head regretting she had mentioned the *Daniel*.

'I have heard tell that the Queen was taken so badly during birthing, noxious gases were given to aid delivery,' she said, changing the subject.

'That is apparent from the results.'

''Tis a blessing that those with inner light are not tempted by such wicked stimulants.'

'No, not even a smidgen of gin in caudle.' Tempted, the figure in the bed licked her dry lips.

'Dr Allanby has promised to return soon,' reassured the Friend with forced optimism, snapping her book shut.

Flora Robertshaw didn't want to think about the doctor who equated with cold rough hands and unrelieved pain. She didn't want his stale brandy breath blowing into her face. She wanted her husband, who smelt of the sea, by her bed.

She groaned once more. There was a storm going on outside and inside her. The child was thrusting to quit her belly but her mind wasn't at peace, wasn't ready for its arrival yet.

It shouldn't be like this, she told herself. She didn't feel right about this. Although how could she know what it should be like, this being her first time. Her husband, who was part of the life within her, should be here, had promised to be here. Flora tossed about thinking these things but stoically holding her tongue from the young girl.

The spasms again like waves running in from the sea. Sweat ran down the slight elevation of her cheeks. Then the spasms stopped – a brief respite between contractions – the bliss was unimaginable. She relaxed further and further back into the bed, as far back as she could get. Until another billow hit her. The strongest contraction yet. The child was tearing her apart. Another, and Flora could no longer bite back her scream.

The young Friend lent forward in alarm, the discarded book in her lap slid to the floor as she tilted her charge's face towards a glass of water. Flora could not swallow. The water gushed obscenely down her nightgown front. She grasped at the girl's sleeve desperately. The girl took this as an apology for the jettisoned water until Flora mumbled that more intimate waters had broken.

'Do something or send for help, Susannah,' gasped Flora.

Susannah Mott had no choice, Dr Allanby must have been delayed by the storm. She had seen other women bring her blood brothers and sisters into the world. She had carried warm water and cloths for them. Now she must act midwife herself.

'See, the little crown is already here,' she told Flora encouragingly. Flora didn't know how she was supposed to "see" but she was prepared to believe. 'Push, sister, push gently now.'

Flora would do anything to rid herself of this burden. She heard a primeval scream that seemed to come from somewhere else other than from her own mouth.

'He is come,' she sobbed, a minute or two later.

'Not quite, sister, push but do not rush.'

'He is here, I tell thee,' said Flora, with such conviction that Susannah peered gamely into the pudenda for any emerging sign as to sex.

'The head is only just visible. There is not enough exposed at present to know for certain if the child is male or female. Push, push harder, sister, I beg thee,' coaxed Susannah.

'No, no, I do not mean the child,' objected Flora fiercely.

'Who is come then?' asked Susannah in bewilderment.

'My man has come. He is standing next to thee.'

Whoosh! A lull in the storm and Flora was vaguely aware of the sound of rushing air. She did not see the second distress rocket travelling across the night sky. But she saw Susannah appear to levitate from her bedside – no, more probably a trick of the flickering candlelight.

There is always a beginning. Some beginnings are more difficult than others. Some beginnings are almost impossible to comprehend.

Susannah paced the lying-in room. Flora Robertshaw's naked man-child gurgling and cuddled in her apron. She felt nervous, on edge, it seemed no time at all since she had tied off the white umbilical cord in two places and cut in between with hurriedly obtained dressmaking scissors. This had been the worst part. She had steeled herself to sever this original bond between mother and son.

One. Two. Three … The grandfather clock struck out the next day in the parlour below.

Thump! *Thump*! *Thump*! Came up from the street door as if part of the same mechanism. It cannot be the captain returned or he would have just walked in. If it was Dr Allanby that was just too bad, he was too late.

She looked enquiringly across to Flora who had sunk back onto the bed in a state of exhaustion. Thank goodness the storm outside had abated. Perhaps they all could get some sleep at last. What a night it had been.

She bundled the funny wrinkled creature into a towel. Gurgles had been replaced with strange little squealing noises as he stretched and writhed in her embrace. He reminded her of one of her uncle's piglets.

'Is all well with the child?' asked Flora, one eye winking open.

'He is perfect, sister.'

'All his fingers are there?'

'All there, sister.'

Whoever had been at the door was still there, hammering louder.

'The street door,' appealed Flora in a whisper, all one with the white sheets.

'Don't fuss, sister, everything is in hand.' But it wasn't, nothing was as it should be the night of the big storm.

The shutters downstairs were closed against the threatening sea, leaving the parlour in darkness. Susannah shivered – the entire ground floor felt cold, neglected during the hours of birthing upstairs. She could still smell the faint whiff of tobacco lingering in the air from the captain's long clay pipe. Amazingly, as he had been away for months. She let out a small startled cry as she knocked her leg on something hard. She would have to be more careful. This was a substantial house full of stout mahogany furniture. What if she stumbled and anything befell the child? More demanding banging, hit with increasing desperation.

'I'm coming, I'm coming,' she called, treading more carefully, holding the captain's son tighter to her chest. Although she was from a village a few miles up the coast, she had met the older widowed Captain William Robertshaw once or twice at the Friends' Meeting House in Whitby. She liked him, liked his clay pipe, found him manly, age could not erase that. Pity he'd not got back in time for his second wife's confinement.

It wasn't Dr Allanby waiting out on the street. It was the last person on earth Susannah would have expected abroad at this hour.

'Thought thou would never open the door, lass.' Nathaniel Nab, another of the Friends, raised his cap. Nathaniel had a long face on him and a pallor to match the woman upstairs. 'Bad news. Can I come in?' he asked, absorbing the new born child in Susannah's arms without comment.

'What bad news?' Susannah was unable to contain the quiver of apprehension in her voice.

'The *Daniel* has gone aground beneath Boulby Cliffs.'

'Art thou sure?'

'Ay, it was impossible for her to make port here safely. She fired two rockets as she ran along the harbour wall.'

'I had no idea it was the *Daniel* in distress.'

'We followed her progress from the cliff top. Captain Robertshaw tried to turn and anchor off White Stones. The wind was too fierce, blowing her further in.'

'And the crew?'

'All feared drowned,' affirmed Nathaniel, who had had one or two trips out in the *Daniel* himself. 'We Steers lads watched on and could do nothing.'

The fisherman hung his head. The two of them sat in a state of shock at the bruising mahogany table. Susannah remained sitting there long after Nathaniel had gone, willing Captain Robertshaw to materialise out of his stale tobacco residue. How was she going to tell Flora? And Flora imagining him by her bed like that only an hour ago. She, herself, could still feel the presence of the man in this house. Could such a strong man be really dead just like that? "All feared drowned" that is what Nathaniel had said.

'Thou forgot,' Flora chided her as soon as she walked into the lying-in room.

'Forgot?' asked Susannah preoccupied.

'It is the custom in Staithes always to take a new born up to the attic before taking him downstairs. The belief is he will then go up in the world.'

'I didn't know there was an attic in this house. I've seen no stairs.'

'There isn't. Captain Robertshaw had it walled up some twenty years ago because of the smuggling.'

'Smuggling? Here in a Friend's house?'

'No, no, Susannah. The smugglers would often leap from roof to roof to escape the pursuing Revenue men. Sometimes this roof, sometimes neighbouring roofs. And occasionally they would break in through the attic window to hide and avoid capture.'

'So how without an attic can I meet the custom?'

'Thou can stand on a chair with the baby and that will have to suffice.'

With dawn light streaming through the bedchamber window, Susannah mounted the chair in the middle of the plain lime-washed room. She felt terrible and ridiculous performing these antics before a woman blissfully ignorant of her probable widowhood. But the fifteen year old miner's daughter was willing to fall in with any superstition rather than tell this woman that her husband and stepson might be dead. By giving expression to Nathaniel's news, Susannah felt she would bring poor Flora's new status closer to becoming fact.

Flora passed the child up to her. 'That's right, now lift his head above thy head,' she continued enthusiastically.

The ritual completed, Susannah returned the child to Flora to nurse. He had hardly made a sound in the last half hour as if his tiny mind had sensed something was very wrong.

'The distress rocket we heard was from the *Daniel*, was it not?' asked Flora, cooing baby talk.

Susannah stared at Flora speechless. How did she know?

'She is lost, is she not?'

Susannah's eyes sought the floor. She had just managed to cope with birth, how could she be expected to deal with death?

'Then God has given thee to me in compensation,' pronounced Flora over her scowling son. His face already puckered against a difficult world.

Chapter Two

The spring of 1897. It was two days after Oscar Wilde walked out of Pentonville Prison. The local Friday newspaper was full of the writer's release. At odds with the vitriolic sentiments of the paper, I hoped that Wilde might at least be able to rebuild part of his life, hoped it wasn't too late for him, such a gifted fellow when all was said and done. Disturbed and angry at the hypocrisy in society – a society that is outraged by the goings on of Wilde and his consenting renters, yet turns a blind eye to the endemic public school bullying and worse of minors – I lowered the paper from my flushed face. If I had not been so taken up with my own thoughts on the Wilde controversy, lifted only by glimpses of lush flowering countryside and the flat infinite seascape bordering the railway line between Whitby and Staithes, I might have returned to the paper and delved deeper into its pages, full no doubt of preparations for the Queen's Diamond Jubilee celebrations in a month's time.

Eventually, becoming sated with so much natural beauty, I turned from the window to examine the hard sour faces of my fellow passengers and wondered how many of them would share my sympathy for Wilde – none, I suspected – certainly not that scowling chap across from me, an ironstone miner, at a guess.

'That bloke should have been 'anged,' said the miner, jerking one calloused finger towards the newspaper in my lap.

'Really,' I shrugged.

'Yes, *really*,' he sneered. I shook my head, reluctant to enter into this conversation.

'Yes, blokes like that should be drowned at birth.'

'I understand it is impossible to tell "blokes like that" at birth.' I intended my remark to be taken as a slight witticism, a courtroom aside, but from the miner's thunderous expression I realised I was stepping onto dangerous ground here. And was the miner really a miner? Maybe he was an undercover police officer who happened to have filthy nails. Although, confusingly, he had used the term "bloke", the passive partner in a homosexual relationship, or so I had been told by my more instructive Navy friends.

Yes, I thought, I've got this chap placed now. He must be an engineer on one of the new steam trawlers, perhaps pressed into the senior service as a boy and sexually abused below decks into eternal ponce hatred.

'Um,' grunted a bowler-hatted man seated next to him, examining the stock market reports in his salmon pink *Financial Times*. He glared up at me, obviously feeling my conversation with the engineer had gone far enough with a lady present in the compartment. I did my best to smile him out of his hostility. I doubted the credentials of the lady anyway. Squashed by the door, she was absent-mindedly picking her nose as she appraised the bulge in the steam engineer's trousers. I turned back to the window and a more pleasant view. Under no circumstances was I about to let these people spoil my day – thankfully not far to go now.

I consoled myself in the knowledge that I had several weeks to look forward to in Staithes, weeks of freedom in which to indulge my passion, plus a special mission to perform. I patted the vellum envelope in my breast pocket, nervously checking it was still safe. Daniel would be pleased with this, his mother more so. Nine months had passed since my first encounter with the child/man of Staithes.

'What's your name?' I had asked him, my hammer reluctantly paused.

'Robertshaw, sir.'

Twing, ping, thud, my chisel bit satisfactorily into the cliff at the north end of Brackenberry Wyke, glanced off the shale, was hit again. The child, for I do not know what else to call him, laughed excitedly.

'What is that?' he asked.

'Come, take a look for yourself. I'm hoping to extricate this specimen in one piece. What would you say it is?'

His tongue lolled forward vacantly.

'A rock snail,' he offered.

'Almost right.'

'Thou cannot eat them though, Mister. A boy once got me to try and it broke my tooth.'

I chuckled half-heartedly, half-listening, engrossed with what I was doing. My fingertips probed for any smooth edges lifted from the grit. I was revelling in the primitive smell of clay, of sea in the air, of freeing something that had remained dormant and tethered for millions of years.

'Still there?' I asked, without turning round.

'Still there,' the boy replied.

Twing, ping, thud, he jumped back as I brought the hammer down on my excision's outer margins with increasing determination and crusts of shale splintered everywhere. He was not the only one to be startled, as we were eclipsed by a mass of screeching feathers. Old and fledgling herring gulls must have decided enough was enough, perhaps this wasn't the best place to enjoy family life after all.

'Those are your original dinosaurs,' I told the boy, nodding up towards the huge birds. He stared into the sky at the everyday gulls, unimpressed. 'Do you know what a dinosaur is?' I asked. He shook his head.

'Don't like puzzles,' he said. 'They make my head ache.'

Twing, ping, thud, flakes of lower Jurassic spiralled down. This was what the boy liked best, I could tell. Not fancy names, not explanations, he liked the ringing echo that had brought him here in the first place.

Boy and man alone on a beach. I sensed him watching on intently as I worked.

'Nearly out,' I said, wishing he would just move along, go away, so I could fully concentrate on the stubborn ammonite.

'Mister!' Unexpectedly and rather alarmingly he tugged at my jacket.

'Careful,' I warned. 'One slip of the chisel and I'll spoil it.'

'Seen a different one.'

'What do you mean?'

'A better one than this.'

'Where exactly?' I asked with growing irritation.

'Other side of Cowbar Nab.' Retaining his limpet hold on my jacket, he insisted there and then I follow him across the rocks, across the sand, and past the village. It was as if a memory had been triggered somewhere in his mind where things were not simple but tangled, and if the idea was not acted upon immediately it might return to that twining undergrowth to be lost forever.

Just below the cliffs beyond the Nab, he started kicking out with his boots at the free rocks. Hardly a scientific approach, I thought, about to voice an objection, when he announced, ''Tis here.'

A severed alum rock, as large and shaped like a cathedral gargoyle, rested against his toe.

'I don't believe this,' I whispered, crouching so low my nose was almost nuzzling the rock's split surface.

'Fish,' he suggested, apparently made uncomfortable by my enthusiasm.

'If this is what I think it is, it is very rare.'

'Yes, fish.'

'No,' I told him. 'This is a fish-lizard, a fossilised ichthyosaur.' I pointed to the tail, the snout. 'See, it shares the features of both a crocodile and a dolphin.'

'Dolphin?' repeated the boy. Like dinosaurs the concept of a dolphin was obviously beyond his understanding and his location.

'It's a very young one, little more than a baby, but the definition of the vertebrae is perfect.' He watched on apprehensively as I traced the impression of the ichthyosaur's spine. 'Difficult to date with any accuracy, must have been washed or mined out of its original fossil zone. Nevertheless, I've often dreamt of finding a specimen like this, in this condition. Do you realise men spend their entire lives trying to find something like this?'

The boy nodded, happy for me, though no doubt for him this etching in stone was little more than a poor representation of leavings on his plate after a herring supper.

'How old are you?' I asked.

'One decade and seven,' he recited parrot-fashion.

'And your name again?'

'Robertshaw, sir.'

'Your full name?' I insisted. He looked surprised, suspicious.

'Have I done something wrong, sir?' he asked hesitantly.

'Not at all.' I smiled reassurance.

'I'm the second Daniel Robertshaw. Son of the late Captain William Robertshaw.'

'What happened to the first?'

'A brother, drowned along with my father over there beyond White Stones.' He pointed vaguely towards the sea.

'Well, Daniel, I thought you were much younger.' What else could I say confronted with such tragedy.

'I was taken down the stairs instead of up.'

I decided to ignore his superstitious Staithes reference, saying instead, 'We have a great discovery here.'

'A discovery, like Australia?'

'Older than Australia.'

'Mister,' he paused thoughtfully, 'art thou a friend?'

'A friend?' It was my turn to hesitate, wondering if he meant was I a fellow Quaker or did he mean "a friend" in the straightforward secular sense.

'Ay, will thou be my friend?' He puffed out his chest boldly.

'I most certainly will,' I told him, warmly shaking the hand that had just made one of my greatest palaeontology dreams come true. 'James Cairn of York, barrister and amateur fossil collector at your service.' I made a small bow and Daniel laughed with such gusto I feared he would burst a gut. But it was not so much his gut at risk, there in his open mouth I glimpsed the remnant of a perfectly good molar.

'Staithes.' I jumped in my seat, the station-master's tin megaphoned voice breaking into my reverie.

STAITHES, proclaimed the smart new sign.

I struggled to retrieve my luggage from the overhead shelf. The engineer bounced up as well, opening the compartment door. My heart skipped a beat – was this his stop too or did he intend me harm?

'I'll give you an 'and with those,' he offered, as I struggled with my bags. 'You get off and I'll pass 'em down to you.'

'Well, thank you,' I said. With the bags safely delivered on the platform at my feet, I looked up into the engineer's face. Deep wrinkles ran like webs from his eyes. In his expression there was something unfathomable – tension, teasing perhaps?

'You some sort of expert on Wilde then?' he asked testily, leaning through the open carriage window as the train began to move off.

'No,' I laughed. 'I wish I had half his talent though.'

'Takes all sorts.'

Was that an insolent wink he gave me as I waved goodbye? – or had I imagined it? – a trick of steam.

'There goes another one down the line.'

'I beg your pardon?'

'Another train down the line, sir,' said the station-master, proud in his uniform jacket. 'Can we help with your bags?'

My second offer in a matter of minutes. After being beckoned forward by the station-master, a decrepit porter, who looked as if he had been standing there longer than the station, regarded my huge portmanteau doubtfully. To give the veteran some credibility, he sported an old fashioned guard's shoulder strap complete with silver buckle and a large embossed railway badge, no doubt at his sartorially minded boss's insistence.

'I'll manage, thank you,' I reassured the station-master.

Down the steep hill towards the High Street again. The Gladstone bag filled with indispensable tools tucked protectively under one arm and my portmanteau of clothes dangling from the other. All the while the gulls screamed and screeched overhead – those bloody gulls, I'd almost forgotten about them – I had never visited anywhere in the world with such a profusion of gulls.

* * * * *

'Mrs Shaw? James Cairn,' I raised my hat.

With aching muscles and a great sense of relief, I deposited my luggage in the hall with a rather flustered landlady. She explained that I was a little earlier than expected and that she had not got round to putting the finishing touches to my rooms yet. She gratefully accepted my refusal of a cup of tea, agreeing to move the portmanteau upstairs herself once my accommodation was ready.

Clutching my Gladstone bag, I could hardly contain myself. The success of my ichthyosaur find, our ichthyosaur find, Daniel's and my baby ichthyosaur find, had made me more ambitious than ever. Now I was back here in Staithes, I was impatient to dirty my hands in historical clays and escape the petty misdemeanours of others. Forget the career of my esteemed fellow professional – "The Great Defender" – Edward Marshall Hall, I would rather emulate the multitude of discoveries made by my boyhood hero the great palaeontologist George Young. Over the next few days I intended to systematically search Brackenberry Wyke for other fossils, comb the thin ironstone cliffs of Penny Nab where the Whitby museum's curator had told me one or two good samples of *Amaltheus* could still be found. It would be dangerous work examining the ironstone layers there, as they were often high and inaccessible and I would need to be suspended down the cliff face over the crumbling top surface by a pegged rope. Like an addict the thought of this additional danger only served to exhilarate me more, and who knows somewhere deep in that hardened Jurassic mud there might be an even bigger find waiting to be exposed. I might even chance upon a small headed, long necked plesiosaur like the one I had initially seen as a student displayed in the Fitzwilliam Museum in Cambridge. I remember to this day staring down on the remains of that giant beast entombed in its glass display case. The beast's amazing paddle feet splayed out beneath an interlocking chasm of rib cage. It must be a mock-up, I had thought, unable to believe that something so exotic could ever have roamed and swam the lagoons of earth. For me that initial vision of a plesiosaur had acted like magic on my senses – from an early age I had known lessons could only be learnt from the past, the future was for God.

Bathed in sunshine, I started to arrange my tools on the shoreline beneath the cliffs of Brackenberry Wyke. In eerie contrast a heat haze hung over the land and the sombre moors beyond. Somehow I had been drawn back to this east coast village. I loved the simplicity of sand and sea, hammer and chisel – the undemanding loneliness of it all.

And there it was the same stubborn fossil still in situ, all those months later, the fossil I had been working on when Daniel first interrupted me.

Frowning over the memory of that unlikely beginning, I set about removing the ammonite, this time with the resolve not to be distracted under any circumstances.

A strange sensation crept down my back. Chill rather than thrill ran the length of my spine as I approached the final delicate manoeuvre of releasing the prize from its aeons of anchoring silt. I became convinced someone was watching me again like Daniel had. This anonymous spectre was beginning to cast a long shadow that made me shiver. But I kept to my resolve of not being interrupted this time, certainly not at such a critical stage, not even for another ichthyosaur. The extricated pebble finally resting in the palm of my hand, I turned to see if anyone else was really there – nobody, an empty beach, sea and an infinite horizon. I smiled self-consciously at my foolishness.

Taking up my chisel and hammer I gently broke open the pebble below the give away tiny wavering line. I marvelled at nature's perfection – the rounded venter, the separated whorls, the rather straight ribs – *Dactylioceras*, a beauty.

Chapter Three

The natives had seemed friendly at first.

'Dan, Dan, your mam's been with a Chinaman.' But there they were again, those few stark words plaguing his life out, shouted with such hostility and he didn't know why. His boots continued their relentless stomp down the cobbles, trying to drown out the taunts echoing on either side of him. Down, down, through the main street of tall houses, the sun glinting off their red pantile roofs more in keeping with a Scandinavian than an east coast morning. And all the while the grey amorphous North Sea below licked at the land, sucking away all permanence. Most of the villagers were too young or ignorant to appreciate the instability of their position. In Daniel's own strange way, he knew more than most about vulnerability with his regular run of the bullies' gauntlet.

'Dan, Dan, the bastard man.' Were the children really shouting at him this time or was it simply a bank of word memory imprinted and buzzing in his head like emerging bees after hibernation?

Left right, left right, his awkward limbs tried to pick up a service rhythm as he approached the site of the haberdashers where Captain Cook once worked. The original sea-front building had been badly damaged by a storm and rebuilt in its new safer location at the bottom of Church Street long before Daniel's time. Nevertheless, he stopped and flattened his already puckish face against the new building, trying to conjure up an image of the great man against the rough stone.

His tormentors forgotten now, soon forgotten, forced out like the bucking mares of night. He would be *deaf as well as daft.*

Aunt Alice who came every Sunday in the trap from Whitby, Aunt Alice who had hair on her chin like a man and who never smiled at him or had fun but always cast long disapproving frowns in his direction, Aunt Alice, whom he hated so much, said he was deaf as well as daft, so he was doing nothing more than was expected of him.

His bobbing cap askew, his arms and feet marching, a frustrated landlocked Captain Cook.

What he wouldn't give to sail away right now, escape this street of shadows which always remained cold to him even on the warmest of days. But his mother wouldn't hear of it. His mother said he was too old to play with other children – those few children who were willing to play with him anyway – while maintaining all in the same breath that he was too young to go to sea, and hadn't the sea already taken his father and elder brother. No, his mother swore she wouldn't give up another of her men to the sea. So here he was hobbled to the land, like the beast in the field up the road, but only for as long as it took his imagination to switch back onto the *Endeavour*.

Left right, left right, he was by the sea where he liked to be most of all, his feet bouncing pleasingly along the wooden harbour front. He really was Captain Cook now walking the deck of the *Endeavour*, saluting his crew. Nathaniel Nab, an old fisherman and friend of his father, grinned baccy-blackened teeth and returned his salute. Not everybody in Staithes was unkind.

Up and down, up and down, on the rolling open sea. His men were rowing him ashore. On a narrow strip of Hawaiian sand, Captain James Cook stood and took stock of his surroundings. He sensed the many hidden primitive eyes observing his every move. Swinging round he tried to glimpse a crop of unruly black curls – there was nothing. He felt uneasy at his blindness before what he guessed must be a collective resentful stare. He had come to reclaim his stolen boat.

That is when he saw it. A grey seal lay on the exposed flat rock shelf beyond the shoreline. He had seen other seals sunning themselves on this exact spot before. Although all tidal subtlety was lost on Daniel, familiarity and instinct told him that the sea would be going out just long enough for him to make a brisk investigation.

Leaving his boots on the sand, he started to wade through the canal of water between shore and shelf.

'Gah! Gah!' An orchestrated heralding of spring began echoing behind him. Soon his feet hit a reassuringly harder surface. Wiggling his toes, barely visible through the still receding film of water covering the rock floor, he glanced back over his shoulder to one of the highest sea cliffs in the whole of England. The cliff was a bloom of brown and white feathers.

Daniel sighed, not because of the gulls – if you lived in his village you were conditioned to ignore this annual breeding frenzy – no, Daniel sighed in the knowledge that not even his imagination was fertile enough to conjure up the whole of England. How could he realistically be expected to know anything of his country of birth when he had only ever journeyed out of his native valley as far as Saltburn to the north and Whitby to the south? Mam and his aunt thought him incapable of travelling on his own the length and breadth of the land. But if they were so clever themselves, why didn't they realise that he thought nothing of land? He would sail up and down her coasts to know England. Why couldn't they grasp that his soul belonged out there with that sad endless expanse of lonely sea? – and his body longed to follow, longed to wriggle out beneath the waves like the Scarborough woof.

At his approach he expected the seal to flap and honk and back away but it did nothing of the sort, it remained perfectly still, maybe it was sick. Two yards off, he saw that the seal wasn't a seal at all. It had feet, legs and long silver hair. He gawped over the face-down doll in disbelief, so convinced had he been that this was a seal. The hairdresser sea had tangled the doll's ringlets, and her dress, he'd never seen such a pretty dress, it was as if it belonged to another age, it wasn't anything like the black and brown woollen dress he was used to seeing his mother wear all summer and winter through. This dress appeared to be soft and fine, the faded sweet pea material clung to her bottom, outlined her legs. Her hands reached from tattered frilled sleeves, forwards above her head like a breaststroke swimmer frozen in action. Her skin was the colour of his mother's best China cups, the ones with little green shamrocks on them, brought out only for those special Sunday visits of Aunt Alice's.

Bending closer over the doll, Daniel wrinkled his nose in disgust, she didn't smell quite right. He had expected there to be a light young scent about her hair but the smell rising up was disappointing, she smelt sickly-sweet, slightly fishy. Perhaps she wasn't a doll at all but half fish like the Staithes mermaids or the merman the Skinningrove fishermen had hauled into their boat a century or two back. Perhaps they were related.

'Kee-yow!' The gulls were yelping, chuckling, mocking him now. He remembered his friend James had once told him they came from something called "dinosaurs" but Daniel hadn't really believed that. All the same, he'd not forgotten James, James whose swirl of reddish brown hair reminded him of wind-driven grasses on Roxby moor, James whose strong rugged features could flash into a perfect smile, handsome James who he wished was here now to explain and smile away this.

Daniel screwed up his eyes, something was glinting above the gull's nesting site back there on the cliff. The reflection of a glass bottle perhaps or some sort of signal – a signal Daniel was unable to decipher.

The sun suddenly dropped behind a dark cloud. He felt goose bumps running up his arms. He struggled up onto wobbly feet that wanted to run but could not move. Here was a creature unlike anything he had ever seen before. Here was something he did not understand.

'Hello.' No response. He poked his toe gently in her side. No response. He wormed his whole foot under her. She remained stiff and cold, the icy material of her dress stuck to the top of his foot. She did not move, he could not move her.

Withdrawing his foot in horror, flapping his arms, seal-like himself, he finally noticed four dark figures slowly taking shape, getting closer, wading the rising miserable expanse of water between him and them.

It was at that moment Captain Cook somehow knew he was in great danger.

* * * * *

Daniel was humming to comfort himself when the men reached him.

'Shut that noise for God's sake,' a man shouted at him. Daniel jerked as if asleep but did not stop humming, could not stop his tuneless requiem.

'What are you doing messing about with a young girl out here?' asked another man. 'We've been watching you from the cliff over there.' Daniel saw out of his eye corner that the man was shaking some kind of brass pipe thing threateningly at him. 'Where is the lass now?' The man looked about him as if expecting to see Daniel's companion close by and knee deep in water. Daniel pointed out to sea. 'You don't mean …?' The man did not finish.

'He's let her float out to sea,' muttered a third man in disbelief.

'Launched her out to sea more like, to cover up what he's done,' said the posh man holding the brass pipe.

'We're too late.' Daniel finally recognised Job Lane beneath the sou'wester and realised it had been his voice shouting for him to stop humming.

All the men fell silent now.

'Doll,' explained Daniel.

'What shall we do?' asked Lane.

'Who was she?' Another man asked Daniel.

'A mermaid,' offered Daniel hopefully. The men had not seemed to like his explanation of the doll.

A jolt of superstitious fear passed between three of the men before being quickly dampened by the fourth.

'It's no good asking that idiot anything, Jackson,' said the posh man.

'Cold,' announced Daniel, taking exception to being called an idiot and hugging himself in the middle of the circle of grave-faced men.

'She'll be cold out there,' snarled the posh man, pointing accusingly out to sea.

'What have you done?' asked Lane, raising his fist towards the quivering Daniel.

'Go easy, Job,' warned the man called Jackson. 'The lad's as pale as a ghost.'

'Looks as if he's seen one too,' said the posh man, splashing around in his ridiculous ill-fitting waders.

'That's right,' snorted Lane. 'He's finished her off and floated her out to sea, I'd say.'

'There's no proof of that,' suddenly came in the more liberal voice of Nathaniel Nab.

'You were the one who first raised the alarm, saw him with her from across the water,' pointed out Lane fiercely.

'Yes, but I saw him walking along the staithe alone only minutes before.'

'He could have arranged to meet her out here. God help him if it's one of mine,' said Lane.

'Shut up, you two, with your idle speculation,' intervened Jackson. 'None of this is for us to decide.'

'Not doll, not mermaid?' asked Daniel incredulously.

'See, the lad doesn't understand a thing,' put in Nab again, appealing to the other men.

'Or so he's making out,' sneered Lane, gobbing towards the approaching sea.

Big fat tears rolled down Daniel's cheeks. He had never liked Lane. Lane was well-known in the village for his bullying and brawling. Daniel's feet felt like icebergs, the sea around them was rising rapidly.

'We'd best get a move on,' said Jackson, nodding towards the rising water.

'Jackson's right. It was hard enough coming across.'

Jackson swung round to find this surprising piece of endorsement came from Lane who had already set off towards the shore and was calf deep in the channel of water. Lane, the man he had nearly beaten to death seventeen years before.

'Where's thy boots, Dan lad?' asked Nab, once they had got safely back to shore. Daniel forlornly surveyed the meagre remnant of beach. His mother would kill him, his only pair of boots had gone.

The sea had given and the sea had taken away. The local constable, who lived on the top road, was sent for. Bare-footed, Daniel was rushed back through the higgledy-piggledy streets and across the old footbridge straddling the beck which at high tide ran deep and river wide. He was too frightened now to cry. Wiry Job Lane, whom he dwarfed by several inches, dug his fingers roughly into Daniel's left arm controlling his every movement. Daniel felt his nose running but did not dare wipe it.

Soon they reached the village's outskirts where poorer cottage dwellings clawed with desperation to an insubstantial hillside hefted from the sea. The entire coastline was indented by small "wykes" or bays all the way down to Scarborough. Settlers as far back as the Bronze Age had toiled to perch and pitch their homes and livings on this doubtful ground, struggled to keep safe what was theirs from an inherent thieving neighbour – the sea. And this too was where Daniel and his mother had been forced to find a home after the storm had taken everything from them.

Daniel's heart filled with dread when he spied above his escorts' heads the pig-tail of smoke wriggling from his mother's chimney on the hillside. His mother kept a fire going day and night, whatever the season. She had a fiery incessant temper to match. Daniel was sure he was about to die and all for a pair of boots.

'What the devil is this?' Crossed armed Mrs Robertshaw stood guarding her property.

'There's been an accident,' Jackson told her. 'On the rock.'

'On the rock,' repeated Mrs Robertshaw in bewilderment. 'What sort of …?' Since her husband's and her stepson's passing, the widow could not abide the word "accident".

'A young lass has gone missing off the rock.'

'And your lad was the last to be seen with her,' Lane interjected.

'Ay, they were seen together with this,' said Fletcher Warrington, brandishing his telescope.

'We have arranged to meet the constable in the top pub,' explained Jackson more calmly.

'The top *pub*!' Mrs Robertshaw exploded. 'He'll not set foot in that godless place and if he does it will be over my dead body.'

'Could be,' sniggered Lane cruelly.

'He's lost his boots, missus. He needs footwear,' said Nab.

In line with local custom, the four men waited patiently outside the widow's door. When it was time to leave, a clinging Daniel buried his face in his mother's apron as she stroked his hair. Job Lane would later boast that he had to prize the two apart like a scallop from its shell.

'Can I not go part way with the lad?' Mrs Robertshaw pleaded.

Jackson shook his head saying, 'Knowing you, if you go part way you'll go all the way.'

'But he's no more than a bairn,' she objected.

'Look at the size of him, missus. He is a man,' said Lane, shuffling aggressively below his charge.

Heartbroken, Daniel's clogged feet clattered resentfully over the slats as the party walked back over the footbridge dividing the village. A spot he usually stopped at to watch the sea water mixing with the fresh stream. There was no stopping today.

On passing, Jackson too regarded the swirling water below with some regret. It was an especially good tide and most of the boats that were usually anchored there in the mud had already gone out. He could see his own crewless mule moored directly below.

Hell's teeth, he thought, gone is the chance of much needed fishing for today.

Apart from those already out at sea, gossip about the girl missing from the rocks had already permeated every nook and cranny of the village. But for once the village was deathly quiet as Daniel and the four men trudged up the main street.

Chapter Four

'Spick and span, that's how I like things to look,' said the landlady on my return from Brackenberry Wyke. The excised *Dactylioceras* already triumphantly placed on the mantelpiece.

'These rooms are just perfect for me.' I strode approvingly from one room to the other past a thousand wallpaper flowers.

'I do hope you'll enjoy your stay with us, Mr Cairn.'

'I am certain I will. Might I trouble you for a pot of tea, Mrs Shaw?'

'No trouble, no trouble at all, Mr Cairn. You'll try some of my special spice cake as well I hope.'

'That would be lovely.'

The landlady hovered, her fierce brown eyes fixed on the *Gazette* discarded on top of my empty portmanteau. No doubt in my absence she had already gorged herself on the depravities of Oscar Wilde.

'Is there anything else, Mrs Shaw?' I asked; thirsty, famished and impatient for sustenance.

'Have you read through your newspaper yet, Mr Cairn?'

'I only got as far as the first page on the train.' I reddened, hoping I had not to listen to another vilification of Wilde's character.

'A young lass's body was washed off those rocks this afternoon.' Mrs Shaw pointed out of the bedroom window towards the exposed low tide Jurassic pavement, close to where I had been working only an hour before. 'They've not found her yet.'

'How awful. Do they know who she was?'

'Nobody seems to know.'

'The story will have been too late for the *Gazette*,' I pointed out.

'I realise that. But I just wondered if any local lass has been reported missing earlier.'

'You are welcome to borrow it and see.' I thrust the newspaper into her reluctant hands.

'My grandson, Samuel, is good with reading.'

'Right,' I said, embarrassed at my uncharitable suspicion that she had already read this issue end to end.

'I don't suppose you noticed anything this afternoon, sir?'

'Now you've drawn my attention to it, on my way back here there did seem to be something going on down by the slipway. I merely thought they must have brought a big catch in.'

'Maybe they have already found her then.'

'Maybe,' I agreed. 'Why don't you go down there and see for yourself?'

'I'm too busy preparing dinner and besides ...'

'Besides?' My stomach rumbled.

'I don't like anything like that,' she replied quickly. 'They are always bringing drowned seamen in. There's not one family in this village that hasn't lost a man at sea, the death toll here is terrible. And there's something else ...'

'Yes, what might that be?'

'I'm not from these parts. My family were farmers up in Esk Dale. Folk here don't like strangers meddling in their affairs. You'll soon find that out for yourself, Mr Cairn, if you stay in Staithes long enough.'

'I see,' I said, suddenly feeling not quite so at home.

* * * * *

'Who was she, lad?' The man dressed dark and strangely asked him.

Daniel moved his head slowly from one side to the other, an unsure child, an uncooperative child, a child who knew all his previous explanations of dolls and mermaids had met with disapproval. Why should this man be any different from these others? If anything this man with shiny silver buttons looked harder to please.

'You can tell me.' His voice was coaxing. His embossed buttons flashed in the limited light filtering through the ale-house's paned windows as he took a seat at one of the round tables. Daniel fixed on those buttons, was fascinated by them, found them a reassuring mesmeriser in his present distress. 'Tell the truth, lad, now, and if you are innocent of any indiscretion you'll have nothing to fear. I give you my hand on it.'

Embarrassed by the uncertainty of what he was supposed to do next, Daniel ignored the constable's proffered hand. Instead he slowly began to take in his surroundings. He wasn't sure he liked this place at all. The walls were a peeling yellow-brown that made him feel sick. He sniffed: the air was bitter with ale and tobacco, smells which would occasionally waft through tavern doors as he rushed past them down the High Street. His mother had warned him to keep away from such places as this, warned him about the dangers of men and women in drink. And hadn't he seen it for himself, only recently, when public house people had flooded out onto the street reeling and uncertain and had nearly stoned an innocent man to death mistaking him for a gypsy.

'Answer the constable.' Daniel winced as Job Lane stamped his boot onto the exposed instep of his clogged foot.

'No call for that, Job,' cautioned Jackson.

'No,' agreed the constable. 'Just answer my questions, lad.'

Daniel watched as the man opened out his notebook on the pot-ringed table top. If he had owned such a fine leather book, a book of empty crisp white paper like that, he'd not have dumped it down among sticky slops of ale. He'd have taken care of it. What's more, he would have polished those silver coat buttons till they shone like waves in moonlight.

'Come on, lad, Nathaniel saw you with the lass.' The man waited, the large hand now in possession of a thin pencil.

'So did I,' put in Fletcher Warrington quickly, just as Nab was about to oppose the constable's lack of accuracy. 'With this.' Again Fletcher Warrington drew the telescope from his jacket pocket to add weight to the authenticity of his claim.

I wish the bloody fool would stop waving that big fat wand of his about as if it's a symbol of his manhood, seethed Jackson. Anyone would think Warrington's the only man in Staithes to own a telescope. He's making a farce of this whole sad business.

'See,' said the more socially impressed constable. 'Mr Warrington, here, saw you with her too.'

'I did indeed,' confirmed Fletcher Warrington. A second large oval brandy glass was already set before him, a brandy flush suffused his face.

'We didn't actually see him *with* her,' said Nab, finally getting his objection in.

'How do you mean?' asked the constable, a little annoyed at this lone voice of dissent. 'Mr Warrington says you did.'

'We saw him stooping over her but not with her in the proper sense,' insisted Nab.

'Puh! "Proper sense",' puffed Fletcher Warrington. 'How much "proper sense" do you need, Nab?'

'We didn't see her with him walking and upright, I mean. At least I didn't,' added Nab, his colour rising to match Fletcher Warrington's.

'Stooping over the lass sounds almost more incriminating.' The constable's irritability was growing by the second.

'No, no,' disagreed Nab heatedly. 'Dan could have just found her out there on the rock.'

'Well, you would say that, wouldn't you?' scoffed Fletcher Warrington.

'Meaning, sir?' Nab's eyes bulged out of his head with indignation.

'Meaning, you are both of the same faith.'

'I deeply resent that remark, Mr Warrington.'

'Do you indeed?'

'And I demand thou retract it and immediately return the waders I was good enough to lend thee for the crossing.'

'Gentlemen, gentlemen, please,' appealed the despairing constable. 'This is not the issue. This is getting us nowhere.'

'Well, I just want things to be right,' pouted Nab.

'We all do, Nathaniel,' agreed the constable soothingly.

'Some more than others,' muttered Nab down into his grizzled beard.

'See what you have done with your silence.' The constable turned impatiently back to Daniel. 'You have caused rancour between these two good gentlemen.'

But Daniel could see nothing beyond the dark-blue conical helmet with its silver badge of authority now placed strategically next to the notebook on the stained table top, the tip of a truncheon peeking above the seated man's black leather belt. Daniel saw no future beyond these actual things and his overriding fear. He started to cry again.

'Playing the baby now,' suggested Lane contemptuously.

'Pretending,' chirped Fletcher Warrington.

'But the lad is … never has been … you know.' Jackson sought a delicate description that would not be too offensive.

'Ei'pence to t'bob is what you're seeking,' supplied Lane ruthlessly.

'I …' Jackson was appalled at Lane coming out with it like that in Daniel's presence.

'Gentlemen, I'm really getting tired of this,' announced the constable angrily. 'I'm in the middle of a serious inquiry,' he added with all the *gravitas* he could muster. Not until he had established that a semblance of order was restored, did he turn back to Daniel. 'Look, lad, we'll find her you know. The lifeboat is already out there searching for her, and Dr Allanby is standing by on the beach.'

Daniel turned to marble at the mention of Dr Allanby – the Allanby name – another name strongly connected with the woes of his family. Flora Robertshaw had never concealed from her son that she despised the Allanbys, told Daniel frequently how Dr Allanby senior had failed to rouse himself from his bed to attend her during his difficult birth on the night of the storm. And then, during her early weeks of grief for a lost husband and stepson, how she had never received one word of commiseration or support from the good doctor. So, the mean old sot is no more, had been Flora's uncharacteristic, non-Christian comment on hearing of old Dr Allanby's death. And now here was the Allanby name again – a son to haunt a son – rolling off the tongue of this threatening man in the dark blue coat.

'You know why Dr Allanby is waiting down there on the beach, don't you, lad?' the constable asked him.

'To attend the dead,' Fletcher Warrington filled in out of turn.

'Please, Mr Warrington, let the lad answer.' Beads of sweat formed on the constable's forehead.

'We can't afford the doctor,' Daniel told him inappropriately.

'So it can talk after all,' grunted Lane.

'That's not what I'm asking you, lad,' the constable told Daniel.

'I done nothing.' Daniel's bottom lip quivered.

'So why not tell us who you were with out there on the rock?' pleaded the constable.

Chapter Five

The lifeboat found nothing. Dr Allanby returned home. The search was called off for the night. Flora Robertshaw refused to let her restored son out of her sight, out of their cottage on Cowbar Nab, all that evening and most of the next day.

Bang! – a slam on the door in the late afternoon. A scuffing of feet outside, a commotion suddenly and shockingly within. Indifferent to local superstition, the self-elected Fletcher Warrington rushed across the widow's threshold – across her parlour floor – hair flying askew towards the petrified mother and son.

'We've found her,' he shouted. 'The lass, we've found her.'

Again Daniel was torn from Flora Robertshaw's bosom; again she was warned not to follow; again she cried for her confused scowling son. The waiting men outside escorted Daniel back across the clattering wooden bridge, but this time he was not frog-marched up to the pub but down hill to the staithe. No father, no friend, no James Cairn at his side, Daniel feared he would never see his mother again.

His mermaid – it was terrible, terrible to see. Daniel's heart was pounding so hard he feared it would jump out of his chest. A small silent group of men and women had gathered in a half circle round her. She was spread out on the staithe, displayed, lost of all dignity. One or two of the women were stooped in prayer, the men stood around exposed and powerless without a task to perform. Dr Allanby emerged from the rest when Daniel's party arrived.

'She's dead then?' The constable asked him.

'I'd have thought that was apparent,' snorted the doctor irritably.

Dead, that was the word they used – so she *was* dead – they were talking dead. She was as dead as his father and brother, never to return. But she was still here to be seen, skin and flesh to be seen like the fish they sold from this very spot in the season. Couldn't she somehow be made to live forever in stone like the fish-lizard he and James had found? – the stone James had caressed as if it were living flesh, the stone he seemed to love more than any living thing – then Daniel's mermaid could be made pure and odourless the same. Daniel did not want to take a step further, wanted to be fixed in stone himself, this life was too painful.

The man on Daniel's right blundered to a stop, held back too, his delicate senses reluctant to risk the slightest whiff of death. Rotting fish, over-ripe game, rotting anything come to that had never been Fletcher Warrington's forte either.

'Move.' Lane's voice hissed in Daniel's other ear. Lane's fist slyly pummelled the small of his back. 'Move forward and see what you've done.'

'Plosher over yonder found her and brought her in,' an old man told Jackson, nodding across to where a coble was being swilled out. Several men had formed a line from a large butt beneath a roof spout and were diligently passing along brimming pails of fresh water towards the landed boat. All the men still wore their high-necked guernsey patterned pullovers, leather waders on their legs, sou'westers on their heads, they cannot have been ashore long. The old man examined his own gnarled and idle hands, humiliated.

'Someone ought to send for the minister,' suggested another fellow.

'Which one?' laughed the constable dryly. 'You've three at least to choose from down here, haven't you?'

'Well, we don't want no Hinderwell priest, that's for sure,' croaked a drawn mouth beneath a Staithes bonnet. 'Official Church has never done nothing for the likes of us.'

'You make Staithes sound like Hell.' Fletcher Warrington guffawed nervously until he noticed all the sullen faces fixed on him. No one else was laughing, not even the more sophisticated Dr Allanby.

'I think the coroner is the man we should send word to at once,' Allanby told the constable, turning his back pointedly on Fletcher Warrington.

'Mind if I take a closer look first?' The constable's question was rhetorical.

'Be my guest,' motioned Allanby.

The half circle round the body straightened and parted like the Red Sea. A minute or two later, the constable sank back from the dead girl onto his haunches trying to collect himself before rising to his feet and stepping to one side. His face was ashen. He began whispering with Allanby. Jackson thought he overheard them mentioning the name of the Whitby magistrate, Matthew Wilder.

Nothing could have prepared even a tough seaman like Jackson for what he saw next through the space created by the constable and the doctor. A fine-meshed herring net with its decorations of green weed lay beneath a girl's body, a long boat hook rested at her side like Britannia's trident, pale ringlets fell limply about her head. He stared in horror at empty, fish-eaten orbits which he guessed must have once housed girlish playful eyes. There was no smile here for anyone. Jackson turned away. He could not stand that awful distorted face looking skyward any more, those terrible eye-sockets seeing nothing and yet appearing to see straight through him.

For most people this was their first unimpeded view of the corpse, though of course not for Daniel himself. He had closed his eyes and tried to pretend it wasn't really her, prayed that his mermaid had actually dissolved back into the sea like the two legendary ones. But there was no mistaking it, she *was* his mermaid right enough.

Daniel could hear Fletcher Warrington puking somewhere behind him. But he could not move forward or backwards or sideways for the men pressing against him. He could only lower his gaze from the awful scene laid out before him. The label "dead" had finally made his vivid, make-believe mermaid colourless.

'See, how he looks away,' snarled Lane.

'Look at her, man, for God's sake,' screamed the constable, losing all his previous self-control. 'Did you play any part in this?'

Daniel whimpered that he certainly did not. How could they think he would put her on display like this? 'Her head's all wrong,' he burst out loudly. 'Thou's got her head pointing to the sea.'

'There's no getting through to the lad,' moaned the constable.

'Dan's only referring to our way of always having the heads of market fish turned from the sea,' explained Nab protectively.

'Bring the Bible and let him swear on it,' suggested someone else briskly.

''Twill have to be a Friend's Bible,' joked the drawn-mouthed old crone malevolently.

'Do any of you know who this poor lass is, anything about her at all?' The constable politically changed the crowd's focus. In the past, he had already had a belly full of trouble and violence from this community of religious dissenters.

Shaking of heads; mutter mutter; 'Not from around here,' general hubbub of agreement.

'And you, sir, have you ever had occasion to visit a female such as this?' The constable next addressed himself exclusively to Allanby, thinking here was the best hope of identification.

'Well,' Allanby pondered. He was a medical practitioner in his middle years with a wispy fuzz of adolescent growth under his chin, this he now stroked thoughtfully. 'There is a likeness … something in the features … no, no, I cannot say I know her exactly.'

'What do you mean by "exactly", Doctor?'

'I mean *exactly* that.'

'Are you sure you don't know this lass?' The constable took another deep intake of breath: even the Staithes doctor was a simpleton.

'Sure?' repeated Allanby abstractedly, regarding the eyeless creature with concern. God damn it, he wanted to help the police but all this could involve him in a lot more work. And what right minded fellow would enjoy recognising a sight such as this? But there was something … the bleached delicate material of her dress, a fine silk material, pulled down to her ankles a moment ago by straight-laced village women. Ah yes, acknowledged Allanby cynically to himself, the decorum of the age had to be protected at all costs even though, only a few minutes earlier, he had had to remove a crustacean from the corpse's left eye-socket about to work its way up into her brain. Allanby smiled to himself. The human condition was still a great mystery to him, it certainly wasn't an exact science, it hadn't the controls of an exact science. He had witnessed it in all its most absurd manifestations but nothing he had previously experienced had ever prepared him for this.

'Dr Allanby,' prompted the constable, disconcerted by the smiling doctor.

'For a moment I thought there was something about her, some distant memory I am unable to recall. But no, I think not.'

'How old do you think she is?'

'From her skin tone I suspect she is much older than her style of hair and dress. Then again, she might have been in the water for some time making it hard to say.'

'Can you make a rough estimate of how long she's been dead?'

'See she is bleached. Death has been and gone a good while ago,' uttered Allanby ambiguously.

'Can't you be more precise, Doctor?'

'If you want precision then you must call an expert in the field. I am a medical practitioner not a pathologist or an undertaker come to that. This I will say, she is well beyond the state of rigor mortis.'

'And are you willing to hazard a cause of death, sir?'

'Officially, no.'

'Perhaps an unofficial guess then.'

'Drowning most certainly could be the main factor of course. But see, there, those slight abrasions round her throat worry me.'

'Are you suggesting foul play might be involved?' pressed the constable. The rest of the gathering held its breath.

'I am saying that some ligature or simply a strong hand might be the culprit here,' replied Allanby grimly.

'And here is that hand.' A jubilant Lane grabbed Daniel's unprepared left hand, raising it high into the air.

'Not necessarily,' disagreed Allanby, alarmed now at the possibility of a developing situation. 'A scarf, say, can get tangled in a mooring cleat if someone happened to tumble overboard.'

'Strangled, that's how I see it.' Lane hawked a globule of phlegm at Daniel's feet. 'Look at him. Guilt written all over his witless mug.'

'Stop trying to work up these good Christian souls into an unlawful act they would regret all their days, Job Lane,' boomed a God-like voice.

'Who sent for you?' Lane swung round on Ranter Pope, an unfortunate surname for the community's senior Methodist.

'That's my business not yours.'

'And this is mine.' Lane poked his pipe-stained finger into Daniel's chest.

'And mine,' boomed the Ranter, 'is to stop evil in all its wicked forms.'

'I never realised Primitives and Quakers bedded together,' sneered Lane.

'A blasphemy,' someone shouted out. No doubt a fellow member of the Primitive Chapel as Quakers in Staithes had long been conditioned to fight their corner through less overt means.

'The lad has his rights, same as we all do,' continued the Ranter firmly.

'"The lad" – they were talking about him again. Daniel sensed the crowd round him was growing restless by the minute. He tried to wriggle free of Lane's reapplied grasp, once more the deck-hand dug his fingers deeper into the soft flesh of Daniel's upper arm.

'She'd rights too.' Lane's free hand waved angrily towards the dead girl. 'She'd the right to live and now she's the right to be revenged.'

Waspish agreement, wasps about to swarm, Daniel trembled anticipating the sting. These were the mothers and fathers of the children who threw stones at him. These mothers and fathers were capable of frightening cruelty themselves. Daniel had seen for himself what they had done to that unfortunate man who had chanced upon the village with his shining armour of pots and pans. A knight of the road was what he must have been, his mother later explained, but Daniel had known that as soon as he had set sight on him.

Knight or no, the fathers had snarled that they knew the man's game, the mothers had screamed that he was a gypsy about to steal their bairns. Daniel learnt that day that it wasn't only children who threw stones. He felt guilty remembering the crouching man trying to shield his face as best he could, his pots and pans scattered on the ground, the hatred of his drunken aggressors. Cut and bleeding, the man had made a bolt for it back up the hill past the hobbled beast's field, otherwise they would have killed him, Daniel was sure of it.

'Are you going to kill me?' he whispered, only the Ranter's honest gaze seemed willing to meet his own.

'We'll have no talk of unlawful killing in my presence.' The constable stepped between Daniel and Lane and the more raucous elements in the crowd.

'Eye for eye.' Despite the constable, Lane managed to manoeuvre Daniel a fraction closer to the dead girl, tugging on his jacket collar as if controlling the strings of a puppet.

'Philistines!' declaimed Pope. 'The lad's harmless, you can all see that for yourselves.' One or two of his followers nodded their passive agreement but the awareness of being in the minority had subdued them.

'What are you going to do about this?' Allanby asked the constable. In response the constable took out his pencil and notebook, Allanby's frown deepened, he had thought the constable's truncheon might be more in order.

'Do you know this lass?' the constable asked Daniel. Daniel slowly shook his head, too frightened to expound on his mermaid theory yet again and certainly not for the written word. 'Did you have anything to do with her death?' Again Daniel shook his head. 'Have you anything further to add regarding this matter?' Again the disaffirming shake. 'The coroner must be sent for then,' announced the constable to the crowd. 'And reinforcements from the nearest militia,' he muttered for Allanby's ear alone.

'And what's to be done with him meanwhile?' bellowed Lane, prodding the terrorised Daniel.

'He will enjoy the full protection of the law until a time ...'

'You call this justice?' interrupted Lane.

'You, Lane, obviously prefer the lynch law of the Americas,' suggested Ranter Pope. 'Perhaps we could still find a boat to take you there.'

'Up you!' Lane gestured crudely to Pope.

'That's enough, both of you,' said the constable.

'Not for me, it isn't,' persisted Lane.

'Jackson, Nab, Pope, you take the lad home and keep watch outside his door until relieved,' ordered the constable.

'What about me?' gawped Lane.

'Any more threats of insurrection from you, I'll lock you up.'

Chapter Six

He knew she was there before he crossed the threshold. A horse and trap waited outside, dominating the small cottage. The horse was funereal black and restless, shuffling its hooves in agitation from time to time, impatient to be off.

Jackson, Nab and Pope examined the fine beast and its matching black leather tackling in wonder.

'Aunt Alice's,' moaned Daniel.

'All t' horse needs now is a feather in its cap and we're ready for a wake,' joked the Ranter.

'There might be one if the body of that lass on the staithe is not claimed,' muttered Jackson.

'I wouldn't feel at ease riding around in a morbid contraption like that,' rationalised Nab. Despite experiencing the full force of God's Inner Light, he was nonetheless pliant enough to participate in the superstitions of the village.

'Chance would be a fine thing,' laughed Jackson. 'How could any of us ever hope to afford such a rig?'

The three men rested thoughtfully on their weapons. On their way from the staithe to the Cowbar, Jackson and Nab had picked up a short oar each, the Ranter a heavy stick. Daniel asked them if they would come into the cottage with him, each man shook his head insisting they would keep guard outside.

'In case of trouble,' explained Jackson.

Daniel's mood was rock bottom, he swore he had never felt so weary, and after all he had been through he still had to face Aunt Alice.

The atmosphere in the cottage was dense, heavy, he felt it immediately. The cottage always smelt of boiled cabbage. To someone like Fletcher Warrington this was the unmistakable sickly reek of poverty, to Daniel it evoked the reassurance of at least one sustaining warm meal a day. But today the hanging pot had not been placed over the fire, the unattended fire was flickering its last, and there was something more oppressive than boiled cabbage permeating the air. Daniel sniffed deeply, whenever his aunt visited he smelt stale violets.

Through the gloom he saw her seated upright in her preferred upright chair, his mother bent forward and weeping on another. Aunt Alice always swooped down for family bad times, to share, to do her duty. His mother, Daniel reasoned, must have got word to her through their mysterious Quaker network – Quaker telegraph or telepathy or some suchlike. Used to the slow pace of rural life, Aunt Alice's town speed inevitably took Daniel's breath away. He began to hyperventilate.

'Thou can stop that for a start,' Aunt Alice snapped at him.

'Can't help it,' he panted.

'Look, see the grief thou's caused thy poor mother.'

Daniel bowed his head. He never felt comfortable with his mother's tears, not even her occasional happy tears, there was too much sad early memory attached to his mother crying.

'Look at her, I tell thee,' continued Aunt Alice mercilessly.

His mother raised a hand as if to censor her sister but it soon flopped back into the heaving mess of her. She seemed unable to talk.

Daniel swayed, distressed and bewildered by this outpouring of adult grief, aware that it all had something to do with him. At the same time, he noted slyly that the cup Aunt Alice lifted to her tight little mouth, small finger extended and rigid as always, was a plain cracked one. His mother's upset was genuine then: no shamrock cups and saucers for Aunt Alice's visit this time. Aunt Alice – dressed in her horse's colours, black from head to toe, the colour of fashion and her husband's trade which bought the horse and trap and dress and cape – sipped her tea and adjusted the sculptured pendant at her throat.

'What has thou been up to, tell us that? Thou must have been up to something, something to do with a lass. The constable wouldn't want to question thee over nothing, now would he?' Aunt Alice's tone was harsh. Daniel shook his head searching his limited brain for some expression of reassurance. 'Thy mam tells me she's warned thee time and time again to keep thy distance from lasses.'

'But she wasn't just any lass,' objected Daniel. 'She was a mermaid.'

'What gibberish is the lad talking now?' Alice asked her sister.

Again the raised hand in response, a sob and then another sob.

'Thou's brought shame on our family name again, haven't thee?' Aunt Alice frequently made statements in the guise of questions.

'Shame *again*,' repeated Daniel perplexed.

His aunt was not prepared to elaborate further on the shame of his birth and all that had followed it. Instead she puffed up her full bosom and for once kept a dignified silence. She was an imperious woman, proud of her position in Whitby society, the wife of a prominent jet manufacturer she had done well for herself, unlike her unfortunate widowed sister with this retarded son to keep. Nevertheless, a religious woman, she would not desert the vulnerable pair now, not in yet another of their crises. She would stand by them through thick and thin although she and her husband, Roderick, were firmly opposed to any free handouts under any circumstances.

'Son!' wailed Mrs Robertshaw, as if finally coming to life from some long mythical sleep. She had been so locked in grief it was as if she had not actually taken in his presence. Then again, she had never experienced a man returned once taken. 'Lord have mercy upon us!' A delayed action appeal, a rush of air and his mother was smothering him in wetness. 'I never thought I'd see thee again, thought this time they'd taken thee away from me forever.'

''Tis to be hoped they don't yet,' cautioned her elder sister acidly.

* * * * *

The day had not ended badly though the long night was yet to come. Alice had had the foresight to bring a skinned rabbit from Whitby market to stew. The rabbit was a young doe and the meat was still tender, unlike the occasional anonymous old buck that found its way into the Robertshaws' pot. Alice was a great one for seasoning all her dishes with herbs, dried out and powdered in the winter. After hours of slow cooking, with great diplomacy, she stepped outside to offer the three men guarding – or was it imprisoning? – her nephew, a bowl each of the rabbit, thyme and vegetable stew.

'Thank you, ma'am.' Taking one of the steaming bowls into his cold hands, Jackson nodded a grateful acceptance on behalf of his companions.

'Sorry, they've not enough spoons in there to go round,' apologised Alice, wishing to distance herself from "the spoonless ones" in the eyes of the men.

But the men did not give a damn about spoons. It had been many hours since particularly Jackson and Nab had enjoyed a square meal, eating had been forgotten through all the traumas of the day, now, with a little respite on their hands, the two men attacked their bowls ravenously.

'Good,' said Nab, dipping his long nose towards the contents of the bowl again and again.

'Just the job,' agreed Jackson.

Ignoring the queenly Alice's departure back into the cottage, the Ranter inspected his offering more dubiously and whispered the possibility of Quaker poison.

'Nonsense, Pope,' retorted Jackson, bowl to mouth, slurping up the stew with exaggerated relish. 'See, I'll act as taster. If I drop down dead here on the spot, you'll know not to touch yours.'

'We'll have two funerals then,' muttered the Ranter solemnly, before he too succumbed to the warm peppery aroma hitting his senses.

'Do you think there will be trouble tonight?' asked Nab; his mouth still full of stew.

'If there is,' replied Jackson, 'it will be after time's called.'

The Ranter took out his pocket watch. 'Not long to go then,' he told them; a worried expression clouding his face.

* * * * *

I was in an opium den, my terrible visions drug induced. I was confused about my exact location but guessed I must be down a ginnel off the Strand, or somewhere in the Haymarket perhaps, among whores and rent boys and disease. I could not breathe for it, wanted air, wanted keen pure air like that of Staithes. I thought I had left London far behind a long time ago.

Click, clack – high above in the canopy flexible limbs of trees knocked against each other, Lepidodendron prize-fighters, a hundred and thirty-five feet tall, hairy branched only at their very tops in the contest for sunlight, their bare stems scaled like the aquatic reptiles who at a future date would hunt off shore. Everywhere giant green ferns swished in the warm damp breeze, thousands of feminine parasols poised on the banks of braided rivers sweeping down from Scotland.

I rubbed the sweat from my forehead, out of my stinging eyes, walking on in time through a Mesozoic soup teeming with life. So much life that at first it was difficult to see, to distinguish one species from another.

Then I recognised her, her fleshy dorsal fin apparent through the cool clear water, the caudal fin driving her undulating towards me, her paddle arms steering her in my direction. Standing there on the hard ceramic beach I could hardly breathe for joy now. It was so blue out there in the lagoon I wanted to fling off all my clothes and rush to meet her, swim naked and free to join her. Her eyes were unbelievably large and her nostrils were pinned far back on top of her skull. She was approaching at high-speed, faster than any boat I had ever seen, faster than anything I had seen save for a bird, and in her wake rode the baby ichthyosaur – my – our baby ichthyosaur. The mother's head was long, she was twenty feet long in all, I saw her massive jaws were armed with numerous sharp teeth and finally I saw danger.

This could not be happening, no human being had ever been here before. White steam swirled across the marshes, huge shapes loomed out of the swamp, the watering-hole further down the evolutionary line. I felt thirsty but dared not drink, it was too dangerous to drink. A curdling scream rent the dank stillness, I jumped, trembled. Daniel, his mouth an open cave, the scream must have come from him then. The child/man of Staithes was suddenly thrown into shadow, dwarfed by a Jurassic monster. Daniel opened his mouth a second time, this time soundlessly, only pain.

In the distance a whistle blew – a signal that my dream was over.

Click, clack – I woke to find the shutter outside my window was rattling against its hook in the sea breeze.

* * * * *

'What's that?' Jackson asked Nab and Pope. They were slumped against the cottage wall, nervous and yet half-asleep. It had been a long day, and night had fallen quickly. They had begun to feel abandoned.

'What? Where? Where?' hissed Nab.

'I thought I heard something,' Jackson told them.

'Look, coming up towards us.' The Ranter pointed to the approaching dancing lights getting bigger by the second, far off stars changing into moons as they often did after too many hours out on the water.

Jackson rubbed his eyes in an attempt to rid himself of the illusion but this was no sea illusion.

'Perhaps it's our relief at last,' suggested Nab.

'About time too,' said the Ranter, who was particularly agitated knowing he had chapel to attend in the morning. 'They must have been waiting hours in Whitby for that devil of a train to come.'

Jackson said nothing, putting one hand behind his ear and the other to his lips.

It had started slowly those first signs that all was not well. The hollow clump, clump, of boots and then more crossing the wooden bridge; the muffled sound of leather pressed into earth coming up the bank; the distant flicker of approaching torches against the night. There was none of the satisfied talk of miners returning to their beds from a late shift working the jet holes, none of the drunken babble of lads swaying home after a night at the pub, whoever was coming up the hill they were moving in silence.

'Who goes there?' demanded Jackson, a minute or two later, towards the blinding line of flares strung out across the road only feet from them now.

'Step aside.' A slight figure inched to the fore.

'Job Lane, might have guessed,' said the Ranter scornfully.

Lane did not have a chance to respond. Someone behind him hurled the first stone bouncing against the Robertshaws' cottage, then another, then a hail of stones followed.

'Murderer! Murderer!' bayed the crowd, picking up rhythm and pitch. 'Give up the murderer.'

'In God's name,' implored the Ranter.

'What shall we do?' quivered Nab.

'This is an unlawful assembly and you know it, Lane,' warned Jackson, before raising his voice to the rest. 'Listen, please go home all of you before this gets out of hand.'

Nobody was listening, the mob already had its own agenda. Jackson, Nab and the Ranter were totally outnumbered. All their appeals were lost in a frenzy of hysterical screams.

'Send him out. Send out the killer. Send out the Chinaman.'

Jackson recognised the man leading the chant as a local Cowbar man called Carter. He could not stop himself imagining the Robertshaws cowering somewhere inside the cottage. How terrible and frightening for the widow to hear her poor son ridiculed in this way. And only he, Nab and the Ranter stood between them and these vengeful men.

'Don't I ... like this at all,' stammered Nab.

Jackson didn't like it either. He sensed this mob was capable of anything. He'd heard of mobs like this tearing people limb from limb.

'See up there under the thatch,' yelled Carter, pointing frantically. ''Tis a face, 'tis the Chinaman smirking down on us.'

A pale face surrounded by darkness had appeared in the attic window. Far from smirking the eyes were big with fear. Jackson tried to wave the figure back from the window but it was too late.

'Chinaman! Chinaman!' screamed the mob.

Jackson shook his head, knowing those big rounded eyes weren't Daniel Robertshaw's at all. The face at the window belonged to the woman who had provided them with rabbit stew only hours before, the same woman whose tethered black horse was stomping and pawing the ground only yards away. Unsettled by the screams and flaming torches, the horse's nostrils flared, its eyes rolled back from time to time – white with a fear to match its mistress's.

'We must do something.' The Ranter's voice had lost its preaching boom and squeaked with tension.

Jackson shook his head again, at a loss. How could they reason with mad men, men beyond reason? What could they do against this? Just as he was feeling completely useless, not up to the job, that's when the idea came.

'That's not him,' he jeered into Lane's face. 'You're wasting your time here, they took him away to Whitby hours ago.'

'How do you mean?' scoffed Lane. 'We've not seen or heard anything of his going.'

'That's because you've been in the Cod and Lobster all evening,' put in the Ranter.

'See for yourself, that's a woman's face up at the window,' said Jackson, jabbing his short oar towards the cottage.

Lane looked, saw, but wasn't prepared to agree with anything. 'So why are you three still here?' he asked instead.

'The constable thought it best we remain to look after the property.'

'Don't believe you, Jackson.'

'Nevertheless, be a good lad and call these men off.'

Lane stood his ground defiantly until one shrill whistle blast from down the hill broke the deadlock. The mob – many of whom were ex-navy men – stood stock-still, arms raised, stones locked in hands.

'It's the militia,' yelled Carter. 'They're coming for us.'

'You'll all get what's coming to you right enough.' Empowered, the Ranter started wielding his stick at them.

Lane and his men ran hither and thither, up the track, higher up the rough sides of the bank itself.

'Rat's deserting the sinking ship.' Nab spat his contempt towards the retreating backs.

Thwarted and spiteful, one or two in the mob paused in mid-flight, skipped a few yards back and deliberately threw their torches onto the cottage's thatched roof.

Jackson could hardly believe what happened next, the speed of it. Within seconds the whole roof was aflame, tongues of flames licking into the night sky out of a mist of smoke, until finally the whole structure began to collapse in on itself.

The tethered black horse was glistening with sweat as it frantically tried to free itself from the building, mouth foaming, writhing and bucking mad, screeching as the sparks from falling debris danced around its feet.

The constable, militia men, all looked on like petrified statues. Just as the horse was in danger of being scorched to death before their eyes, a figure in a hooded coat rushed forward out of the shadows with a curved bowie knife to cut him free. The horse galloped off up the hill into darkness.

The spell was broken. Men scurried around looking for buckets and water. Jackson remained rooted to the spot, knowing this part of the village's water supply still depended on lasses carrying skeels on their heads from the beck some way off.

'Are they still inside?' The constable picked Jackson out in the glow from the burning building.

'What do you think?' he growled back. 'That's what you wanted us to do, keep 'em inside.'

The situation was chaotic, the constable decided his best response was silence. Men's emotions were running high, particularly Jackson's, nobody had expected an outcome like this.

The constable's barrier arm was too late to stop Jackson hurling himself at the cottage door. Two militia men risked themselves by joining in. Shoulder barge after shoulder barge failed to break open the door. Tears of frustration rolled down Jackson's cheeks. Still that bugger of a door wouldn't budge.

'They must have barricaded themselves in,' he groaned, moving back a pace to weigh up the difficulty.

'Looks hopeless,' concluded one of the militia men, dodging a falling roof beam.

'Nearly!' joked his companion.

It was then that a really big lad pushed them all aside. He set about the door with an axe, making a hole through it. Jackson didn't know the fella, or where he and his axe came from, he could have been one of the mob for all he cared. The fella with the axe was the aunt's and the Robertshaws' only hope, a necessary hero in Jackson's eyes.

Jackson forced his body through the fragmented wood, his coat catching and tearing on the splintered edges, to be met by an unbelievable wall of heat inside. He couldn't stop retching and choking in the smoke filled room. Staggering on like a blind man, his arms flailing this way and that, willing his smarting eyes to see something alive, something human.

What was that? – a cough and then another – not from him, somewhere over there. He stopped and listened carefully. He could just make out a shape huddled at the back of the room, closing in he saw it was two shapes making one. A terrified Mrs Robertshaw was cowering animal-like on all fours on the floor, curled under her body was Daniel. Their faces were blackened with soot and smoke, they appeared to have given in, were preparing themselves for death.

'Come,' Jackson gasped through difficult breaths.

Mrs Robertshaw shook her head, the only part of her body which seemed capable of movement.

'Come.' He beckoned to them both. Still no response. 'They've gone, the bad men have gone. Come with me and I promise no harm will befall you.'

Still Mrs Robertshaw wouldn't move, shaking her head like one of those automatons they have on city fairgrounds. Jackson didn't believe this, didn't have time for this, it was his life at risk too. Stirred by this thought, he reached down and dragged Dan out from beneath his mother. She could follow or not, that was her choice. Coughing, stooping forward, he somehow trawled dead-weight Daniel from the mayhem.

'Well done.' A line of eager hands passed them along away from the burning building.

'You look like a bloody miner.' The big axe man slapped Jackson's back. He wasn't too sure if this was done in congratulations or to help clear his lungs.

'There are two women still in there, I've been told,' said the constable, looking up from attending to a crouching spewing Dan.

'Flora Robertshaw won't come out,' Jackson managed to splutter. 'But I for one aren't going back in there.'

'No one is expecting you to,' the constable told him.

'Mam! Mam!' His clothing almost burnt from his skin, half-naked, Dan suddenly lifted to his full manly height sending the constable sprawling.

Chapter Seven

Despite it being Sunday, I decided to risk the wrath of the locals and began work on the shale cliff close to the old disused alum quarry. The work was dangerous and I needed the security of an iron peg and a rope, even then the rock was of such poor quality the peg would sometimes jump out as it was hammered in. Each time I completed the process I could do nothing more than pray the peg would hold my weight. Despite these difficulties I was ecstatic. Here I was working in a location intimately associated with my great hero, Louis Hunton.

Louis Hunton had been born in 1814 at Hummersea House near Loftus. His father had been the head alum-maker at the Loftus and Boulby Alum Works. In his early twenties a sickly Louis had a short paper read to the Geological Society. Only two thousand words in length this paper was to be his life's work, his epitaph. His precocious insight and observations sinuously infiltrated the hierarchy of the new science of biostratigraphy as, tragically, the tubercle bacillus ruthlessly spread through his young body. Louis Hunton, the scientist, would die a poet's death in Nîmes in the South of France within three years of that first reading. But words and ideas can transcend illness, death, the grave, and, some sixty years on, here was I, his ardent disciple, exploring beds of fossils most probably last touched by his hand.

Louis, through his father, had access to many different layers of quarried rock. He started to notice that certain strata seemed to harbour particular fossils and these specimens could not be found anywhere outside them. He found the fossil most useful as an index for his new dating system to be the ammonite – the snakestone of Saint Hilda's coastline.

I knew it was always better to excise fossils *in situ* for dating purposes. I had not known, until informed by the curator of Whitby Museum, that it was Louis Hunton of Loftus who had originally advised this rule of procedure. So simple once thought of – but to be the one who first has the idea.

I could not resist a smile dangling there on my rope. Louis would not have been too impressed with the location of Daniel's and my ichthyosaur find – a gargoyle of a rock resting on the open beach. I had been aware that this austere fishing community only tolerated my presence among them, and I suspected that there were plenty of rogues about who might be tempted to spoil things for me just as they had spoiled my ingenuous friend's tooth. I had sworn Daniel to secrecy about the ichthyosaur find without being truly convinced he would honour our agreement. Daily, during the course of my business, I came across men with far greater intellectual capacity than he possessed who were incapable of maintaining a confidence. To date, I had found very few men in the world to trust.

So, for a disillusioned city barrister to return the following day and find the gargoyle rock still intact and undisturbed, and its original discoverer already hovering protectively over it at our prearranged time, served as additional fillips to the adventure. I had decided, if not Daniel's wits, I could at least utilise some of his apparent physical strength and I was not about to be disappointed.

Daniel, what would Louis Hunton have made of someone like him in the evolutionary process? – a domestic variation, distortion perhaps? When Louis's paper was read out to the Geological Society it was months before Charles Darwin had disembarked from H.M.S. Beagle. And, although he was restrained in the interpretation of his scientific findings – no doubt due to the religious intolerance of his age – he has to be considered as one of the earliest evolutionists. But *Fortis fortuna adiuvat*, fortune favours the brave – so it favoured Darwin ultimately.

'Hello there,' a light feminine voice rose a hundred feet from down on the foreshore.

'Back again?' I managed a reply.

'Back for at least six months.'

'I cannot afford to be away for so much time.'

'You're brave, aren't you, working on the Lord's Day? An artist friend of mine, Rowland Hill, got a basket of fish heads dumped on him for painting on the beach.'

I began to spin on my tethered rope.

'Careful,' came the artist's voice again, this time in warning.

I thought of struggling to raise my hat as I had done on our first meeting months ago, remembered mention of a fiancé, weighed up the risks of such bravado and thought better of it.

'Found anything?'

'Plenty of ammonites, nothing too significant.' I swayed a little less precariously on the rope, my words bouncing off the cliff.

'Daniel told me you were interested in stone fish.'

'As you can see that's what I'm doing up here, fishing.'

'Looks dangerous.'

'Indeed.'

'Did you hear there was some trouble on the Cowbar last night?'

'Really?'

'Yes, someone told me the militia had to be called out.'

'Drunks, I expect,' I offered briskly, eager to bring the conversation to a close.

'Mind if I make a quick sketch of you dangling there?'

'Be my guest.'

'I'll let you have a look at it later.'

'What will you call it?' I risked a glance down on the ribbons and bows.

'*The Fossil Collector*, of course.' The artist's laughter rang out beneath me more melodiously than any laughter I had heard before.

* * * * *

Where were the Robertshaws? Where was their home?

About five o'clock teatime – the vellum envelope stuffed into my jacket pocket – I had tired of waiting to bump into Daniel and decided to actively seek him out.

I was sure this was the spot up on Cowbar Bank where he told me he lived. Daniel had pointed the cottage out to me from Penny Nab on my last visit to Staithes. There was nothing left. I gaped in bewilderment at the empty space, a rectangular stain, a smouldering stain of ash. I must have stood there for several minutes in the late afternoon sunshine, unable to fully comprehend the disaster.

'Burnt down last night,' muttered a bandy-legged chap in passing.

'How?'

'Fire of course.'

'But what about the people living here?' I yelled after him.

'Don't know nothing about them,' he shrugged.

* * * * *

After enquiring unsuccessfully about the village regarding the fate of the Robertshaws, a warehouse-keeper finally told me a fellow called Jackson was the man to ask but unfortunately he was out fishing for the night. Early the next morning, the same warehouse-keeper, who seemed to know everything about everyone except the Robertshaws, directed me back to the footbridge between the main village and the Cowbar.

'Are you Seth Jackson?' The tide was out and a fisherman with dark bouncing curls was working on his boat. The black and yellow painted mule was beached at a slight angle on the mud flat to one side of the estuary below.

'Who wants to know?' came back the sharp reply. The fisherman remained absorbed in his task, did not look up for a second, enmeshed in coiling ropes and flattened nets.

Something indeterminate between a man and a Minoan snake goddess – this was my first impression of Jackson, for I was sure now this must be he. Jackson was most definitely out of the ordinary for Staithes. He was hatless for one thing, clean shaven, and from his colouring almost certainly not of Danish descent. He did not look like a man who would respond to God or Queen or any other given authority. But then Jackson himself seemed to command a great deal of prestige here in this village – people had spoken his name with reverence when I asked after him.

'James Cairn.' I gave a nod of introduction towards the indifferent Jackson, who did not falter for a moment in his complicated unravelling. 'I'm looking for the Robertshaws.'

'Why?'

'Daniel Robertshaw in particular.'

'What business could you have with the likes of him?' Jackson's arrow gaze finally flew up to the footbridge, pinioning me with its intensity.

'I've already seen … seen the Robertshaws' cottage has gone. I've asked a few people how it happened but no one has been prepared to tell me,' I rattled on awkwardly. Adding with some desperation, 'Or where they are now.'

'So why me, why search me out?'

'People have told me you know, you can tell me best,' I continued wearily; folk here could be so stubbornly bloody-minded if they chose to be.

Jackson slammed the ropes on top of his nets as if they suddenly disgusted him. Despite long waders, he jumped with great athleticism over the side of his boat to squelch in the mud below. I noted the man climbing the stone steps towards me moved with a willowy grace, yet for all his slenderness there was a latent power about him. Here was a very fit man, even Jackson's curls bounced health. In contrast I remembered Daniel's lank wispy strands of brown hair, still a child in mind but already displaying a man's receding hairline. A feeling of overwhelming sadness took hold of me, took me by surprise. What news was this bounding messenger about to deliver? God let Daniel be safe, the prayer of a father for the child.

'You one of those newspaper men?' Face to scowling face, Jackson was not about to reveal anything easily.

'No,' I sighed, the sense of weariness returning.

'Police, or legal then?'

'As a matter of fact I am a lawyer,' I admitted, very much taken aback.

'Who for?'

'Whoever I'm asked to act for.'

'Ever acted for t' other side?'

'The other side?'

'Police and suchlike?'

'It has been known,' I replied puzzled; a strange question for a man like Jackson to ask.

'Thought so.' Jackson's mouth clamped shut.

'We've never met, have we?' I queried. How could Jackson know that I was one of those very unusual beasts who, after representing the Crown, had returned to representing some of its more unfortunate subjects? An intuitive guess perhaps? Or had I prosecuted this man in the past? – perhaps Jackson was a man with a grievance, a dangerous man. Whatever, I soon realised this fisherman had no intention of enlightening me on the matter. 'I'm a friend of Daniel Robertshaw. He helped me out once and I want to know he's safe, that's all.' I decided on a little enlightenment of my own. The scowl subsided a fraction.

'Dan doesn't have any friends.' Suspicion next clouded Jackson's face. 'Not here in Steers any rate.'

'Well, I can assure you he has me.'

'How do I know you're who you say you are?'

So we hadn't ever met, I relaxed a little.

'You'll have to take my word for it,' I told him more confidently, 'as a gentleman.'

'A gentleman, eh. So what's a gentleman doing with the likes of Dan Robertshaw, can you tell me that?'

'I've already told you he helped me, helped with my fossil collecting, he's a good lad.'

'So where were you when he was in trouble, you a gentleman and lawyer?'

'In York, I live in York. I only found out about the fire yesterday evening. I went to visit him and found nothing, absolutely nothing left.'

Jackson stared at me long and hard as if he was attempting some sort of mental calculation. 'When you're poor everything has a use, charred beams, the lot, stripped within a day by neighbours. Some of them beams were still hot enough to burn the skin off your hand. And the fire was only half of it, Mister.'

'Half of what? And do call me Cairn.' A sense of foreboding began to inhabit the pit of my stomach.

'It's like this, Mister, a young lass was pulled dead from the sea a few days back and Dan Robertshaw was the last person seen with her on yonder rock.' Jackson gave a cursory wave towards the natural sea pavement. 'Afraid there might be trouble, the constable arranged for Nathaniel Nab, Ranter Pope and me to keep guard outside the Robertshaw cottage until the militia arrived.'

The names of Jackson's companions were meaningless to me, nevertheless I made a mental note of each of them – in my profession the irrelevant can often become relevant. With my sense of foreboding deepening by the second I willed him to go on.

'It was a miracle, Mister, that anyone could have survived such a blaze. I helped Dan out myself. His mother was paralysed like, refused to come. We all thought she was a goner. Then Dan started screaming and pointing like the crazy man he is.

We all looked on in disbelief as two hands appeared in the hole we had made in the cottage door. The hands moved a large box through the jagged space before the rest of a blackened body followed suit. It was Flora Robertshaw. She had emerged unscathed from Dante's inferno, cradling a scorched wooden crate as if it were a life.'

'She must be blessed.'

'I would never describe Widow Robertshaw as being blessed, Mr Cairn.'

'But they're safe?'

'Dan and his mother escaped the fire right enough, though his aunt, who had been upstairs, perished. Fell from the attic to the ground. Mrs Jeffrey she was called. They pulled out what was left of her yesterday morning – curled, black, unrecognisable. The only means of identifying her was the remains of a jet and silver pendant round her neck. She alus dressed in black in life and now she's died naked black the same. Pity though for she made the keenest rabbit stew I've ever eaten.'

'Poor woman dying like that. What a terrible fate.'

'Something else happened during the fire. Something that will haunt me for the rest of my days,' said Jackson, serious again. 'Mrs Jeffrey had a magnificent horse tied to the cottage fence. I've never seen such fear in an animal once the burning timbers started to fall. Thank goodness, someone had a knife and the presence of mind to cut it free before it burnt to death.'

'Where is it now?'

'No one's seen it since.'

'And Daniel and his mother, where are they?'

'She's gone to Grape Lane, Whitby. Her dead sister's husband has taken her in.'

'And Daniel, surely his mother hasn't deserted him?'

Jackson stuffed his hands into his pockets as if afraid they would give something away.

'Daniel?' I insisted.

'Arrested, I believe.'

'Arrested, in God's name why?' No answer, Jackson suddenly seemed preoccupied with the wooden slats of the footbridge. 'Did they think Daniel started the fire or what?'

'No, not him, as I've told you it was the mob out to get Dan that did that in revenge for the young lass's death.'

'You mean they believe he murdered her?'

'Yes, yes, done away with her. And the really terrible thing for me is, Mr Cairn, I promised both Widow Robertshaw and her son no harm would befall them once I got them out of that fire.'

'And do you think Daniel murdered the girl?'

'Don't really know.' Jackson thoughtfully appraised the bridge's slats once more before lifting his eyes to meet my interrogatory glare. 'I'd be very surprised if he did do it though. Dan has always struck me as a lad more sinned against than sinning.'

'Where can I find you if I need you in future?' I asked the fisherman, stony-faced.

Chapter Eight

'I'll not speak of mermaids until those two men in the corner have left,' whispered the old man. 'I am near the end of my journey, Mister, but those two men from the big house put the fear of God into me.'

'What men? Where?' I asked, taken aback.

'Never mind,' said the old man.

Despite the old man's warning, curiosity got the better of me and I turned to inspect the two figures seated behind us but they were obscured by the pub's alcove wall. Nevertheless, I could see their elongated shadows silhouetted by the fire light on the opposite wall, foreheads together like Siamese twins, they appeared to be engrossed in some intense conversation. The old man at my table retained his stubborn silence, until I heard a scraping of chairs and the two silhouettes on the opposite wall were no more.

The old man spat a ball of chewed tobacco into the spittoon by his foot. 'Imagine a story so improbable it could only be true,' he began with renewed confidence, a match-stick arm flung out to demonstrate his point, his grey head swivelling eagerly on its spindly neck now eager for a Cod and Lobster audience.

I settled back, happy to be here, uncomplicated and entertained. It did not matter if Jackson showed up or not. I was supposed to be on holiday when all was said and done. And for the price of a jug of beer I had ensured I would not be alone for the evening. Suffering badly from a lack of dental attention, my hired story-teller shrilled through more gaps than teeth. Nonetheless, any possible problems with translation did not deter him from whistling along at high-speed in the strong Staithes dialect.

'A long while ago two lovely sea creatures were landed at Steers. Ay, landed not many yards from this very pub.'

'Really?' I stretched lazily forward in my seat.

'They objected to being corralled like.' The old man raised his volume in the mistaken belief that this would make his meaning clearer. 'Didn't like folks staring and bothering 'em and such.'

I wriggled uncomfortably on my seat, wondering if "bothering" and "such" constituted some sort of sexual interference.

The old man looked round the room again, this time smacking his lips with satisfaction because others had started to eavesdrop. There was none of the incredulous jeering I would have expected from younger men standing at a bar, jeering the old fellow would certainly have received in most public houses in York if he had been talking about the reality of mermaids. No, here, everyone was wrapped with attention.

Yet, it was *here*, innocent *here*, that only days ago the Robertshaw cottage was destroyed and a woman was burnt to death. I quietly sipped at my pot and wondered how many of my fellow drinkers played a part in that crime.

'It wasn't long afore the two creatures made a bid back to the sea where they belonged.'

'That's the way of it,' chorused the men at the bar.

'Calling across to each other as they swam out of Steers Wyke. So much so that folk left their houses to see what was amiss.' The old man was really in his stride now, encouraged by stardom. 'Well,' he leaned conspiratorially towards me. 'There were some folk listening on the shore who could tell the meaning of the sea creatures' language, see.'

'That's right, Edwin,' shouted across the landlord. 'Josiah Skelton I heard tell was one.'

'"The sea shall flow to Jackdaw Well," one of 'em said. "You have not told all," said t' other. "No I have not," said the first. "I have not told them what egg broth comes to".'

'"Egg broth"!' I could no longer suppress a smile.

'Ay, sir, 'tis the truth, sir,' replied the old man forcefully.

'That's why we village folk throw out any water used for boiling eggs,' explained a florid fellow, propped against the bar a little way off from the rest.

'It's bad luck to use it again, you see,' confirmed the landlord. 'The prophecy.'

I stared across at him, a tough looking fellow but he was perfectly sincere. I looked back at the old man who was expressionless now, looked round the room for a spark of amusement in any of the other customers' faces, there wasn't so much as a flicker.

He's not really one of us was etched instead on every weathered face.

I focused my attention down towards my drink. Scepticism seemed to leap accusingly back at me from the creamy head of ale. In an attempt to hide my discomfort, I lifted pot to mouth with a shaking hand.

Suddenly a wiry little chap burst through the door bringing my silent stand-off with my fellow drinkers to an abrupt end.

'Have you heard? Have you heard?' he screamed. 'Police are about to move the Chinaman from Whitby to the Castle at York.'

The taproom exploded into cheers and applause and then just as suddenly returned to a deathly hush.

'Sit down, Lane.' The imposing figure of Seth Jackson towered behind the harbinger. Jackson hooked a free chair across with his left foot and pressed the astonished Lane onto it.

* * * * *

Two policemen sat at either side of Daniel on the train journey from Whitby to York. At first he had felt proud, an important person with an escort, and then he had begun to feel uncomfortable. They did not speak, no one spoke. The compartment was empty, quiet, apart from the breathing of the men and the running of the awake train over the sleeping track.

When the train did grind to a halt at the occasional station, gauping faces would appear through the compartment window from embarking and disembarking passengers on the platform outside. This did not bother him, life had already inured him to the stares of the curious.

Daniel had wanted to see England but not like this. He had not wanted to see York's ancient walls glimpsed with difficulty through the bars of a stinking, horse-drawn prison van, a trundling vehicle that seemed to stretch every nerve fibre in his body.

He heard rather than saw the iron gates of the Castle prison grind open and crash resolutely shut, and he feared this was one of those places that people never came out of.

* * * * *

Life goes on – a ripple of laughter broke into my room above the low tide beach the following morning. But both life and laughter seemed very removed from me in my present brooding siege mentality. The sad background ebb and flow of the sea had suited me better, whoever they were down there on the beach I resented them their happiness.

York, Daniel was going to the Castle at York, had been Lane's rallying cry. I knew the Castle prison well, knew a vulnerable person like Daniel would be frightened to death being incarcerated there, and surely his unworldliness would constitute a real risk for him among such brutality. How bizarre, Daniel would be locked up in the city I had just left to bring him some good news – now it was all bad news – my holiday in tatters.

Laughter again like a slap in the face, an insult. Laughter, insistent like the sea, familiar too. I strode across the room to the window. A déjà-vu – there on the beach below was the artist. She was painting side by side with a man I took to be her fiancé. The clear early morning light must have been perfect for them. Easels very close, they would be able to work on uninterrupted with no Daniel around to invade the scene. Not like that first time.

'Who is that?' I had asked Daniel as we struggled over the shingle with the boxed ichthyosaur between us, slanted very much lower at my end. Ahead a gracile figure sat before a small canvas and easel. Her skirt was dark. Her blouse as white as the cresting summer waves which caused her to glance up now and then away from her work, brush suspended thoughtfully, absorbed. She wore a dark bow at her neck and her hat was dressed with a similar ribbon. A true artist. No Staithes bonnet for her.

'That's Miss Laura Johnson,' muttered Daniel reverentially.

'She's a stunner,' I said, struggling to free one hand off the box and raise my hat in her direction.

The artist responded with a brief wave, her brush all part of the delicate action. How fine she was. I guessed she could be little more than nineteen years old. If she spoke I hoped her voice would be as refined and graceful as the fingers holding the brush. She said nothing.

'She don't like folk staring at her while she paints,' said Daniel, a possessive edge to his voice. The artist must have heard him for she flashed him a smile that seemed to be reserved for him alone.

'Where does she live?' I asked, when we had passed out of earshot onto the wooden staithe with its sweeping line of high-prowed moored cobles, works of art in themselves.

'She's spoken for,' snapped Daniel.

'I only asked where she lives.'

'Her aunt's got a cottage up in the village.'

'Where in the village?'

'Up there.' Daniel pointed vaguely towards Gungutter. 'Just for the summer. Her young man, Harold Knight, is staying there as well.'

'You like her very much, don't you?' I teased.

Daniel nodded, his expression fixed and serious. 'She's kind,' he said, as he helped me lift the ichthyosaur box into the hired cart bound for Whitby Museum.

Chapter Nine

I stood on one of the most fashionable streets in Whitby, although the door bell clunked rather than rang more in keeping with a curio shop. Regardless of this, Mrs Robertshaw had obviously come a long way in a short space of time from the hovel on Cowbar.

Dressed in a neat black and white uniform, a full-bosomed though starchy maid – fearing contagion – took my sweat stained, floppy tweed shooting-hat by the tips of her fingers. For this ritual, I was kept waiting in the porch before being allowed through into the hall with my new lighter valise specially purchased for the trip.

'Mr Cairn, I was intrigued to receive thy card this morning.' Flora Robertshaw was still a very fine woman in her middle years, her exacting Quaker diction only slightly corrupted by a Staithes intonation. And apart from her retained cotton Staithes bonnet, she was dressed in shimmering black satin from head to toe, by all accounts in the manner of her sister, no doubt still in mourning for her sister, and while perhaps not possessing her sister's culinary skills she seemed to have slipped with surprising ease into the role of matriarch in her brother-in-law's household. Expecting someone far more humble, taken very much off my guard, I held the widow's gaze perhaps a fraction too long. 'More sugar?' she asked.

'No, no, one is fine,' I coughed, trying to clear the small frog that had formed embarrassingly at the back of my throat.

'Captain Cook lived not a stone's throw from this very door,' she informed me with childlike pride. The silver teaspoon tinkled genteelly against the walls of her cup.

'From Staithes to Whitby, you have followed the great sailor's course almost exactly, ma'am.'

'He took up a formal apprenticeship with one of our brethren here, dust thou know? – a John Walker.'

I nodded politely, filling my mouth with cake and warm tea, undecided whether or not to admit I was well-versed in every aspect of James Cook's history.

'That was all such a long time ago of course. Nevertheless, it didn't stop my lad being obsessed by the man,' she added in a whisper.

'Because of the loss of his own father, perhaps?' I took a deeper gulp from the delicate cup.

'There was no indication upon thy card of how I can assist thee, Mr Cairn?' she asked, abruptly changing the subject.

'Indeed, indeed,' I agreed noncommittally, not quite ready yet to get down to the essence of my visit. 'What a lovely decoration this is.' My final gulp of tea had exposed an exquisitely crafted green shamrock at the bottom of the cup.

'There's a story attached to this tea-set.'

'Really?'

'Thou knows, Mr Cairn, I did not start out my life as a flither picker.' Flora Robertshaw gagged on the stifling, airless draped atmosphere.

'Well no, I'm sure … a flither picker?' I stared vacantly at my hostess.

'Ay, I never believed the day would come that I'd be forced to walk fifteen miles a day, alongside much younger lasses, in search of limpets to skane and bait the lines.'

I was unfamiliar with the term "skane" as well but guessed it must mean removing the animal from its shell. However, I was not prepared to reveal my naivety a second time before this handsome older woman.

'I didn't always live in penury on Cowbar Bank either, Mr Cairn. When I was married to Captain Robertshaw I lived in a big black and white house on Staithes High Street, the outside window-frames were etched in yellow. In keeping with local tradition the house was decorated in the same colours as my husband's boat.'

'The *Daniel*?'

'Yes, the *Daniel*. I see my lad must have told thee all about it then.' She did not wait for confirmation. 'I dare say that house might have been considered by some to be grander than this one.'

'I don't doubt it. Did you have many … ?'

Mrs Robertshaw did not appear to be listening to me, muttering more to herself, 'It took just the one big wave to change all that.'

'Yes, so Daniel said.'

'Ah, poor Daniel,' moaned Mrs Robertshaw. 'Daniel was born on the same night as the big storm. The moment he took his first breath was an omen of things to come. Nothing has gone right for me and the lad since then, since that storm sunk my husband's boat, nothing but this.' Mrs Robertshaw examined her own nearly empty cup against the window light. I could see her fingers playing through the fine porcelain like actors in a shadow play. 'This and the rest of the set was delivered to my door the very next morning after the *Daniel* went down, by a Friend, a young fellow called Nathaniel Nab, now an old fellow as decrepit as myself.'

'Nonsense, ma'am. Why you look as fresh ...'

'Packed in straw, in a wooden crate, it was the only item washed ashore undamaged apart from one cracked saucer,' interrupted Flora Robertshaw, oblivious to my flattery. 'Can thou imagine the force of the waves that night, Mr Cairn? The *Daniel* was broken up on rocks only yards off shore, and yet this set of delicate china survived.'

'Was every hand aboard lost, ma'am?'

'Survived the fire too. Nothing short of a miracle,' crooned Mrs Robertshaw, cup still in hand. Again she did not appear to have heard me but this time I felt no inclination to follow the question through.

'A wonderful story,' I said, suddenly realising that this must be the mystery box Jackson had told me Flora risked her life to retrieve.

'Hardly, Mr Cairn, I would rather have had my husband and stepson returned to me than fancy drinks of tea.'

'That goes without saying, Mrs Robertshaw.'

'They said my husband should have put in at Whitby earlier, certainly into Port Mulgrave.'

'Perhaps he was anxious to get home to you.'

'There are some in Staithes that still hold me responsible for what happened, for being pregnant, for sharing the captain's name so soon after his first wife died.'

'No, that cannot be.'

''Tis so, sir, that's why they always took it out on the lad. Now they've destroyed the roof above our heads. Those in Staithes have long memories. But I'll tell thee this for nothing, sir, if my husband did take the wrong decision that night, it was the first serious mistake he ever made in a lifetime at sea .'

'Maybe there wasn't a mistake to be made, maybe the conditions just suddenly turned from possible to impossible.'

'Shipwrecks wreck more than the lives in 'em, that's for sure. And we weren't alone in our grief, a hundred ships were lost along the north-east coast during that one night.'

For a minute or two, Mrs Robertshaw and I did not speak. In that interim a disconcerting speculation struck me. Was it possible that someone in Staithes with a grudge against the Robertshaws in general, rather than Daniel in particular, could be evil enough to try to deliberately implicate him in murder? But who and why? Someone insane, a religious fanatic perhaps. Then even more troubling hypotheses flashed into my mind: just suppose that "someone" was a victim of the loss of the *Daniel*, someone who had lost a loved one when the boat went down say, someone who perhaps held Captain Robertshaw responsible for the tragedy, someone who had been brewing resentment for years. Suppose that person actively encouraged Daniel to explore the rocks knowing the girl's body was there. Then there was the fire. I turned my attention back from Mrs Robertshaw's fireless grate to the woman herself.

'Strange to think the Queen was widowed a good eighteen years before me,' she confided meditatively.

'But aren't you happy now, here?'

'How can I be, Mr Cairn? Our cottage on the Cowbar wasn't much but it was a home. On top of that, they have taken my own poor lad from me.' I watched in horror as a tear dangled from the short lashes on Mrs Robertshaw's bottom lid. 'This visit has something to do with him, has it not? I expect thou's heard, they've locked him up in prison.'

'Yes, but I can hardly believe him capable of the terrible crimes imputed to him. He was always such a helpful chap.'

'I know. Thy name and Laura Johnson's were never off his lips.'

I felt myself blush at being linked with the artist. 'Did Daniel tell you about the ichthyosaur find?'

'He mumbled something about finding a stone fish, if that's what thou means, but I didn't always know how much to believe.'

'Well, Whitby Museum has paid me seventy-five guineas for the beast and, as Daniel found it originally, I would like you and him to have the money.'

'But he's away in York,' gasped Mrs Robertshaw.

'Do you not visit?'

A grimace creased her already strained expression. 'He will not have it.'

'Who will not have it? Daniel?'

'No, no.' Mrs Robertshaw shook her head vigorously from side to side. 'My brother-in-law,' she whispered. 'He says Daniel is a bad lot, always has been, and I am to wash my hands of him.'

'But he is your son?'

'Mr Jeffrey blames my sister's death on Daniel.'

'That's ridiculous as I understand it. It was the mob who threw their torches at your cottage.'

'All the same, Mr Jeffrey says he will put me out on the street if I don't disown Daniel for what he's done.' Mrs Robertshaw's words were now barely audible.

'Accused of doing,' I corrected forcefully.

Mrs Robertshaw put a finger to her lips in warning, rather than ingratiatingly at home she now appeared terrified. 'Do not think badly of Mr Jeffrey, sir. He is a good man, a strict religious man, he was kind to take me in. But things aren't as affluent as they seem here in Whitby anymore. Mr Jeffrey is a jet manufacturer and jet isn't as fashionable as it was, coloured glass and other semi-precious stones are replacing it, and, well, he was only telling me the other day that the business ...'

'Mrs Robertshaw, business worries are no excuse for inhumane behaviour towards you and your son. I will pay your train fare to York myself, if you wish to see Daniel.'

Mrs Robertshaw looked to the door and then to the floor and again in a lowered tone asked, 'Art thou a good friend, sir?'

'The faith or the state?' I remember facing the same confusion with her son.

'The state, sir. 'Tis obvious thou is not of the faith.' A faint glimmer of amusement travelled Flora Robertshaw's face and, almost before I could register it, it was gone. From the lines about her mouth, I guessed the captain's widow had once been a woman with a wonderful sense of humour. The tragic storm seemed to have wiped all that away too.

'Do I have to be a friend before you will accept the money on behalf of Daniel and yourself?'

'No, sir, but if thou's a true friend of Daniel's then thou might help my boy.'

'How?'

'The stone fish money thou's offering might buy someone to speak up on his behalf. Perhaps thou knows of such a person?'

I regarded her with incredulity. Disregarding their superstitious obsessions, the villagers (or in this case ex-villager) of Staithes seemed to possess an innate ability to pigeon-hole my profession.

'Things never go well for us, 'tis only fair to warn thee, Mr Cairn,' said Flora Robertshaw.

'You do know I am a legal man myself?'

'I didn't know, not for certain.'

'Suppose I were to offer you and Daniel my own service in that capacity?'

'That's why thou's called, sir.' The tension in Mrs Robertshaw's face finally relaxed, something that had been puzzling her was resolved.

'Here, I nearly forgot to give you this.' Reaching into my jacket pocket, I held out the vellum envelope containing seventy-five guineas towards her.

'No,' she told me fiercely. 'As I've said, keep that to help our Daniel.'

'You're really sincere about this?'

Mrs Robertshaw nodded, her intense gaze remained fixed on me.

Chapter Ten

I decided to stay in Whitby a day or two longer. I decided to do it in style and treated myself to a fine apartment on the Royal Crescent. It had a sea view bedroom upstairs and a sitting-room below. Watching the slow roll of the waves from my bedroom window that first morning, I thought how different the sea looked in this wide expanse of coastline from the one that tumbled between Cowbar and Penny Nab into Staithes. Perhaps Captain Robertshaw should have put his boat in here on the night of the storm. Perhaps it was his one fatal mistake in an unblemished career. Was I about to do the same thing? – take on a case where I had a slight involvement with the accused. The Robertshaws were obviously not a lucky family, as Flora Robertshaw had corroborated with such touching honesty, but would some of that ill-luck brush off on me? God! I was becoming as superstitious as the fisherfolk back in Staithes.

What the hell, all this was for tomorrow, work was for tomorrow. Today I was keen to see Saltwick Nab, famed for its plesiosaurus, ichthyosaurus and teleosaurus finds.

Unfortunately, before making Saltwick Nab I had to undergo further scrutiny from the Whitby landlady, Mrs Veazey. On my arrival in Royal Crescent, she had asked me (innocuously, I'd thought) what had brought me to the town. I had let slip that I'd just attended to some business in Grape Lane. Who with in Grape Lane, she had asked. Cornered, I acknowledged that I had visited Flora Robertshaw at Mr Jeffrey's house. Now here I was, some fifteen hours later, cornered again in Mrs Veazey's hall.

'Are you sure you don't require any breakfast this morning, Mr Cairn?'

'Quite sure, Mrs Veazey, I'm eager to make Saltwick while the tide is out.'

'It was Saltwick jet that made men such as Flora Robertshaw's "protector" rich men,' she said, tossing her head with obvious disapproval. I sensed that Mrs Veazey had been storing something up during the night that was about to explode in the light of day. 'There have been generations of Jeffreys in Whitby but I must say Roderick Jeffrey takes the biscuit.'

'I don't think this is appropriate …'

'He's taking advantage of his wife's sister and his wife in her grave less than a week and the nephew in gaol.' This was all said without a pause for breath. 'What a scandal, what a scandal.'

'Mrs Veazey.' I felt obliged to caution the landlady on the laws of slander but I had hardly got into my flow before she piped up again.

'But I have not said anything untrue, Mr Cairn.' Mrs Veazey folded her arms defiantly. I sighed, not for the first time this debater of the High Court had to give in to the superior verbal skills of womankind. 'Nothing the whole town isn't aware of any rate. And I must say, Mr Cairn, I am surprised that a gentleman like yourself would mix with people like that.'

Was Mrs Veazey right, I wondered, staring from Saltwick Bay up to the dark shales of the Nab. Was I really getting involved in a situation that perhaps I shouldn't be? Yet, how small my problems seemed against the weight of pre-history towering up there above me. It was in 1758 that two friends, Captain William Chapman and Mr Wooler, found some fossil bones embedded in the rocks above where I stood now. The unusual thing about their "alligator" find was that they each wrote out a formal report for the Royal Society which was published in its monthly journal, the *Philosophical Transactions*. Whereas before people would have just taken the bones home and perhaps forgotten about them in the bottom of a drawer or used them to scrape mud off their boots – these two men transformed themselves overnight from beachcombers into natural philosophers – after eighty-five million years the natural world was gaining academic credence.

I rubbed my hand across the gritty abrasive surface where history had been made, made and logged by Chapman and Wooler. Would I, myself, ever be regarded as an extraordinary man in years to come by my peers? Would the artist Harold Knight say? Would Harold be regarded as a run of the mill artist or was he destined for fame? I had a selfish reason for staying on in Whitby a little longer, I wanted to put some distance between myself and Laura Johnson and Harold Knight. Their obvious happiness together the other morning on Staithes beach seemed to encapsulate my own loneliness.

'I really think you should keep away from that Jeffrey family, a gentleman like you, Mr Cairn,' resumed Mrs Veazey, on my return to Royal Crescent as if I had never stepped out of the door. 'I can see how they are bothering you and they are nothing but bad news.'

'If only it was just they at the root of my trouble, Mrs Veazey.'

'Not worth it, not worth it at all,' chuntered on the landlady, oblivious to my denial.

'I hope you are not set against them because they are Quakers, Mrs Veazey?'

'That's nothing to do with it, nothing at all. Why, Mr Veazey himself had sympathies ...' She stopped short here and blew her nose on a large man's handkerchief. 'Wait here, Mr Cairn, and I'll get you the very thing to take your mind off all this nonsense with the Jeffreys.' Mrs Veazey soon reappeared with a book in her hand. 'I swear if you take this to bed with you, you'll not sleep a wink, I didn't.'

* * * * *

'An eerie tale indeed, Mrs Veazey.' I gave the book back to the hovering landlady on the morning of my departure from Whitby. She laughed at my theatrical shudder.

'And did you sleep well, Mr Cairn?'

'Not for two whole nights, Mrs Veazey. See the dark circles under my eyes. Do you frighten all your guests half to death by providing them with a little light reading?'

'You are the first, Mr Cairn. I've not had that copy long.'

'You're very lucky to have obtained one at all and so soon.'

Mrs Veazey looked smug at this. 'Friends in high places, Mr Cairn, friends in high places. They're already calling it a great success in London, I believe.'

'People love to be terrified.'

'They certainly do,' agreed Mrs Veazey, a wicked gleam in her eyes. 'And Mr Stoker seemed such a nice man.'

'You know Bram Stoker?'

'Of course, he stayed here with me for a while. His wife and son joined him for the last few weeks of his stay. Noel was a dear little boy.'

'And his wife?' I asked, picking up quickly on Mrs Veazey's omission.

'A neat little body, on the cool side,' admitted the landlady. 'In no way as warm and open-hearted as Mr Stoker, I'd say.'

'Where on earth did Stoker get all his horrific ideas from then?'

'Here, I wouldn't wonder.' Mrs Veazey lowered her voice confidentially. 'There were three ladies staying with me at the same time as Mr Stoker, from Hertford I seem to remember. I noticed him often watching them.'

'Lucy, her friend Mina and Mrs Westenra.'

'That's what I think. And there was the boat.' Mrs Veazey flapped her arms in excitement giving a fair impression of her Darwinian forebears.

'What boat?'

'The ghost boat. I told him about the ghost boat. The whole town was talking about nothing else.'

'Please, I'd love to hear about it too.'

'Just off shore down there.' Mrs Veazey waved her arms again frantically towards the unseen sea beyond her walls. 'A northward bound vessel rammed straight into a small fishing coble though the crew had screamed a warning to them. Smack! Like that.' The landlady startled me as she clapped her large ringed hands together. 'The mystery ship sailed on as if nothing had happened. There appeared to be no watch on board and its deck was completely deserted.'

'And the coble's crew?'

'Two men drowned and the rest were rescued by a nearby fishing boat.'

'A strange part of the book that, my favourite scene in fact, when the ghostly schooner leaps from wave to wave into the harbour between the two piers and a large black dog leaps ashore,' I enthused.

'There isn't much happening in this town that I don't know about including black dogs,' put in Mrs Veazey baldly.

'And Mr Jeffrey?'

'I was hoping you'd forgotten about him, Mr Cairn. He's still a powerful man in Whitby and mean into the bargain. If you take my advice he's better given a wide berth.'

'Like the ghost ship.'

'Ay, Mr Cairn, like Dracula's ghost ship.'

Leaving my bag with Mrs Veazey, I decided to take a final walk round Whitby, review the place through the eyes of Bram Stoker. Now where was it that the black dog had jumped ashore? The salt wind at my back, I flew to the end of the East Pier which helped form the narrow mouth of the harbour. East and West Piers were like crab pincers, I thought, as I turned back into the wind and crawled crab-like myself back up the Spa Ladder. This much repaired ladder was my sole access between the crumbling cliff and the pier. The whipped up sea swirled dizzily below me. The going was not much better crossing over the rough ground of the Haggerlythe, causing me to stumble once or twice. The shelter of Henrietta Street, running parallel to the cliff, proved to be an all too brief respite.

Breathlessly I counted each of the hundred and ninety-nine steps up to the church with the abbey beyond. It was still early morning and I was perfectly alone. Sitting on a form, as Bram Stoker must have done, surrounded by the tombstones of countless master-mariners and able-seamen, I contemplated the same grey sea below which had cost so many of them their lives. No human being with a smidgen of sensitivity could fail to be touched by the haunting aura of this spot, let alone a man with Stoker's vivid imagination.

Dong! Dong! Above and below me bells started ringing out – clappers struck mercilessly against their hollow vessels – I imagined the black widows shivering in the streets below, reminded of the mournful tolling for some personal disasters out at sea. And all the while, the brooding backdrop of the Yorkshire Moors seemed to absorb everything. I shivered too, conjuring up images of a sea-fret rolling in and the vampire Dracula rising from his tomb.

The noise of the bells travelled up the isolated coast as far as Kettleness, sucked into the wykes and longer bays as it went, weakened on its journey.

But this was not Sunday, I felt increasingly ill at ease, this was Friday. Apart from the rather stiff off shore breeze the waves below looked to be rolling in regularly enough. There couldn't really be another vessel out there in trouble, could there? Too much of a coincidence, surely, so soon after Mrs Veazey's talk of the disaster of the coble and the ghost ship. Nevertheless, my heart began to pound with every bell toll.

I quickly made my way back down the hundred and ninety-nine steps. Not until I reached Church Street and walked into the small market square did I realise that some sort of festivity was getting underway.

A kaleidoscope of bunting was draped here and there and performers had gathered to entertain those curious enough to stand and watch. I got particularly absorbed by one trickster. The man would spin his red deck of cards into the air and let a previously chosen card somersault to its amazed recipient's feet. My head moved from sky to ground with the rest of the gullible audience until I decided to keep my eyes focused on the trickster's hands. The man took in two more punters until I spotted the card slithering down the magical sleeve into the waiting cupped hand before being flung to the ground. Impressed but disappointed, like a child finally discovering that there is no such person as Santa Claus, I turned away. It was then that I saw them coming towards me.

Flora Robertshaw was slightly stooped on the arm of an upright looking fellow whom I presumed to be Mr Jeffrey. Flora did not move easily with the man, there was a tension to her movement, a reluctance. I was immediately reminded of all the prisoners I'd seen being hustled into the dock.

She lowered her eyes as she passed by. I wasn't sure at first that she had seen me. I raised my cap and no more. A flicker of relief appeared to cross her face. Life was tough for all widows but I suspected it had always been especially tough for the dead captain's second wife and more so now. How strange and unfair, I thought, in a period that has sentimentalised queenly widowhood more than any other.

Slowly, I became aware that I had become the centre of derision from those around me. People were actually booing me. The card trickster pointed to the toe of my boot. During my encounter with Flora and Mr Jeffrey, I had inadvertently stepped on the definitive card.

'Sir, pick up your Spanish sword,' the card man told me.

'I will.' With a flourish I lifted up the ace of spades to the applause of the audience.

Chapter Eleven

I never found out why the bells tolled that morning in Whitby. Whether or not it was for another fishing disaster or the festivities I had witnessed in the market square, even the literary Mrs Veazey was unable to enlighten me as I collected my valise.

I have to confess to having something of a contradictory character. Two days before I had itched to leave Staithes, now I was happy to scuttle back and wallow in low population peace.

I was aware that I was not the most popular man in Staithes, more a tolerant acceptance endured. The villagers sensed I was sympathetic to the plight of Daniel Robertshaw and they on the whole were not. But for my part I found them a fascinating tough breed of people. I was impressed by their robust strength, and the resilience they had to the harshness of their day to day existence made me feel slightly inadequate. Through gradual exposure, I had grown to love my visits to the Cod and Lobster where I would listen to their convoluted fishing stories.

Like its customers the Cod and Lobster itself hung defiantly out over the sea, a ridiculous and yet thrilling place in which to drink, every window filled with breaking waves. And those who drank in this warm, hop pungent atmosphere had a lot more to them than just the knowledge of how to bait lobster pots and the best grounds in which to fish. Though solid within themselves, they seemed to have an innate union with that sometimes lapping, sometimes brutal infinity out there.

Even the villagers' bizarre superstitions, going far beyond the mermaid story, began to intrigue me. Staithes seemed to be regulated by a mix of occult beliefs and religion – never say "pig" aboard ship or on a Friday, never wind wool after dark. It became apparent to me that some of these strange beliefs and the methods employed to ward off the evil eye gave the villagers a sense of control in a world usually out of control. Life in Staithes was never certain, always fragile.

'Hey, 'tis the piss man,' shouted the old man, the same old man who had regaled me with the mermaid tale. 'George, there's a gent over there who wants to know all about the *Daniel* sinking.'

George, a tall imposing figure blocking the doorway, appeared to be a smarter contemporary of the old man. In three strides he was across to my table.

'Why does he call you the piss man?' I asked him as he gingerly lowered himself onto a chair.

'The name's stuck from years back. I was the liquor man at the old Boulby Alum Works. The liquor man was responsible for overseeing the collection of the villagers' urine from a pair of padlocked tubs we had permanently set down on the street. Pee could be used as an alternative for seaweed in the alum making process. At eight shillings a ton even a bedridden old dame or the scruffiest street-urchin could watch their waste being transferred into glorious streams of gold.'

'The poorer the purer, isn't that right?' interrupted his old friend at the bar.

'What does he mean?' I asked.

'The poor couldn't afford strong drink, brandy and suchlike; urine containing too much alcohol corrupted the process.'

'Thy own piss would have been no good then, George Caplan,' tittered Mermaid-man.

'That reminds me,' I said, nodding to his pot. 'What will you have, George?'

George shook his head. 'Why do you want to know about the *Daniel* going down? I'd have thought all that is best forgotten.'

'Go on, George, you tell him. George is one of the few eyewitnesses still alive.' Mermaid-man indicated his empty pot. 'Wouldn't mind another myself, Mister.'

I nodded across to the landlord to fill the cheeky old fellow's pot up. 'I'm interested in the Robertshaw case,' I explained turning back to George, deciding honesty was the only policy in Staithes.

'Ay, I heard. Captain Robertshaw would turn in his grave to learn what has befallen his wife and son.'

'So what exactly caused him and his boat to perish the night of the storm?' I asked, keen to keep Caplan on track.

'It was one of those nights,' he began. 'I was watching the dark clouds banking on the horizon with a growing unease. You must have seen something similar yourself many times, thin rushing fringes of clouds sloughed off the main body by a lifting wind that increasingly begins to obliterate the moon. But the moon wasn't the principal source of light to silhouette me on that winter's night nor the rising wind my sole concern. You'll never have seen anything the like of this, Mister, several bonfires a hundred feet high glowed hot at my back in that gathering storm.'

'The volatile Boulby heaps?'

'The same. "A wild one, George. What do you think?" the work's manager asked me. I opened out my palms in a non-committal gesture, a barrier to any further enquiry, before continuing across the yard to check on the tools of my trade. I might be a magician but I certainly was not a fortune-teller.

Entering the smallest building on site, I was greeted with flying straw and feathers – a fox's reception – confirming my misgivings that my birds would run amuck with such high winds shaking their timber prison. Yet above the hens' frenzied squawks and my own dust induced coughing and the rattling of the roughly pinned shale roof, I still heard the explosion. Flinging back the hut door, I immediately ran back out.

I saw a rocket grazing the sky as I raced towards the cliff edge. My legs almost failed me as I stopped to look down the sheer six hundred foot drop onto unimaginable mayhem below. Drawn like a moth to our burning giants, a large fishing boat had come in too close. The impotent vessel was being spat towards the sharp jagged rocks bordering the coastline.

"She's dragging her anchor," muttered a man who had drawn up beside me.

Slowly, very slowly, I sensed others gathering around me – quarrymen from up the hill, alum workers, men and women from the fishing village down in the valley. One young woman, a limpet picker, whom I knew well from the quayside in Staithes snuggled up to me for warmth and comfort. I pushed her gently aside. Irrespective of a recently snatched moment beneath the slipway with the same young lady, I knew right then I had no comfort to give, not with the possibility of so much death about to be played out below.

We all watched in disbelief as the boat tossed about in foaming white skirts of sea like a petticoated dancer flung this way and that between deadly suitors,' said Caplan poetically. 'She was helpless, unaided, hopeless against such forces. Then the moon cleared again spotlighting her in detail. I saw the two masted lugger was painted black and white with a sharp yellow stripe running the length of her hull. Stunned, I tried to ignore the vessel's familiarity.

"It's the Daniel," whispered the limpet picker, clinging to me again.

"Wreckers," shouted a quarryman, pointing to a party of men struggling like ants along the lacerating rocks towards the stricken craft.

"God! The wreckers are out already," chimed his colleague.

"No, you fools, those men are from my village," hissed the limpet picker, angry now. "The boat's ours. You don't wreck what's yours in the first place."

The howling wind, the inseparable screams of rescuers and victims, the groaning elm beam, the grating strakes splintering and cracking – surely, I thought, this matchwood craft cannot stay afloat much longer.

She's breaking up, I thought to myself, bitter with resignation. The Daniel was going down and I knew every man aboard personally.

"No!" screamed a woman. The woman was Peg Thompson, the Daniel's mate's sickly young wife.

"She can't be going down," commiserated another woman desperately.

With emotions running high on that not so omnipotent cliff, I wiped the wind and rain from my eyes. I was the liquor man who possessed a secret that could hold half the world to ransom and cost a king his head; I, who timed the alum process to perfection with my floating hen's egg; I, who could turn stone and pee into gold, hung my head knowing there was no magic formula to break down this finite puzzle, no alchemy could settle this. Shaking the girl off a second time, I walked briskly back to where my escaped hens were foraging contentedly within the protective warmth of those dangerously flaming calcining heaps.'

'Do you think Captain Robertshaw should have put in before Staithes? – at Port Mulgrave perhaps? – as soon as Whitby even?' I asked him.

'Yes, but how could he have known he would be burnt off?' replied George.

'"Burnt off"?'

'Ay, the Staithes shore-men built a fire of tar and barrels on the beach to warn the *Daniel's* crew off. Robertshaw had only two options left then: to try and make an almost impossible turn given the weather conditions or seek some protection from Boulby Cliffs a fraction to the north.'

'And he chose the latter.'

'Ay, he chose the latter and the anchor failed to hold.'

'Tell me,' I asked him, 'what happened to your limpet picker?'

'Don't know,' he shrugged. 'Two months later I married the boss's daughter.'

* * * * *

'You do know why you are here, lad?' asked the governor.

Daniel shook his head. Perhaps this man was finally going to tell him.

'You are here for your own safety and protection. You are here until the law decides otherwise. This prison is run strictly in accordance with the Prison Act of 1865, do you understand?'

Daniel shook his head again. How could he understand anything? He shouldn't be here, didn't want to be here, wanted to be back home, the same home before the fire happened.

'Hard labour, hard fare, hard bed,' clarified the governor. 'You will only meet with hard labour if and when you are convicted, although for murder…' he hesitated, said no more and left.

'"Hard labour"?' Daniel asked a young warder. He had found the governor's visit more baffling than helpful.

'You climb the treadmill for six hours at a time, then there's the crank, then there's mailbags and picking oakum back in your cell.'

Daniel ruckled his nose in distaste. Why climb a treadmill when there were hills outside to climb? Oakum, he did know something about that at least. He had seen boat-builders in Staithes, their hands all blistered and bleeding, caulking up seams with the stuff.

'Still, you're only on remand at present,' reassured the warder kindly.

'Yes, remand,' repeated Daniel.

Chapter Twelve

Men rubbed the grit and sweat out of their tired inflamed eyes, hardly believing what they were seeing. Every muscle ached as they arched upright. This had to be a heat mirage or something, hadn't it?

'Down tools, men,' shouted the managers. The men, already resting on their pick-axe handles and spades, smirked to themselves. As always the managers' instructions lagged behind the men's own common sense and instinct.

Work completely at a standstill – workers frozen and gauping with a mixture of awe and fear – what was Union Pacific going to do about this little dilemma? It was not a hostile tribe of renegade Shoshoni about to launch a fresh attack on white progression that had halted work on the rail line that day. If not as mortally dangerous, it was something far more weird and out of the ordinary than that.

Hands on hips, the managers debated their next move. The men eventually squatted back on their haunches and shared tobacco among themselves, happy to puff on their pipes and discuss their amazing find and its possible origins, happy just to gain a little respite from their hard labour.

No one had ever seen bones like the ones gleaming out of the Morrison Formation rock there at Como Bluff. Only half exposed they were huge, must have belonged to some monster of gargantuan proportions, gargantuan and hidden before that first spade scraped against its massive femur.

One of the managers came up with the great idea of cabling Othniel Charles Marsh, a Yale palaeontologist, with news of the find. Birthday news as it turned out to be for Othniel. He quickly hired the railway workers to excavate the bones, crate them up, and send them by boxcar to him in New Haven. Marsh carefully examined them and then painstakingly reconstructed the complete skeleton. Brontosaurus became a household word in 1880's America. Western dinosaur fever rather than the latest exploits of the Sundance Kid hit the country's imagination.

The loose window shutter rattled once more in the gentle shush of air whistling through the building. I was vaguely aware that the wind was picking up outside. What the hell, I was comfortable enough in here by the fire with my glass of port and American scientific journal.

Cool Staithes seemed far removed from hot Wyoming where brontosaurs squelched on cushion-like feet through warm oozing Jurassic mud. I was so engrossed with the article on the Como Bluff find that, initially, I did not hear the commotion in the street under my window. Somehow, I had dismissed it as associated with the wind.

I suddenly realised that far from slow lumbering brontosaurs padding the marshes, human boots were clumping and clattering along the wooden staithe. I struggled to my feet to try and see what was going on through the salt-crusted window. The vague shapes of men and women with lanterns bobbed beneath.

'Turn out! Cobles!' The cry came from someone in the midst of the gathering crowd. The seagulls squawked overhead, the sky was darkening to the north-east, a storm must be brewing like the one George Caplan had recently described to me. Still in my slippers, I danced lightly down the steep staircase to join the rest on the staithe.

Laura Johnson and Harold Knight were already there. They did not register me at first.

'Ah, the fossil collector,' Laura finally acknowledged. 'Harold, I've told you about this mysterious gentleman, have I not? He swings ape-like from cliffs.'

'James Cairn.' I shook Harold's long fingered hand.

'And this is my dear friend Rosie Good.' Laura introduced me to a fair and dainty creature with a surprisingly firm and vigorous grip.

'What's going on?' I asked Laura's party as a whole. We seemed to be very much in the minority, tourists standing on the outer margins.

'The weather looked wonderful earlier in the afternoon. We saw the cobles putting out, didn't we, Rosie?' Laura sought her friend's confirmation but her eyes remained glued to the horizon. Rosie nodded, her attention fixed on the same ominous cloud formations. 'Their lugsails all set, looking so hopeful against the sun, the light shining through them as if through insect wings.' Rosie nodded her agreement once more wishing, no doubt, she could be as eloquent as Laura. 'Beautiful, they looked beautiful. But now …' Laura's voice trailed away.

Retaining the same impassive expression on his face, fair-haired Harold said nothing.

'I do hope they come home safely,' Rosie helped out.

'Rosie and I have set up a studio over there,' said Laura, collecting herself. She pointed towards a glowing room in the derelict darkness behind us. 'It isn't much but it will do for now.' Her face was flushed with wind and excitement, her eyes almost lavender in the light of her lantern.

'Look, is that something?' cried Rosie, waving one of her strong arms towards the north. Rosie Good had the musculature of an Olympian. My head, along with many others, turned and tried to follow her indication.

'Where? I can't see a thing,' complained Laura. 'All I can see is that a usually flat grey expanse of water has turned white from shore to skyline.'

The accurate eye of an artist, how right she was.

'I've never seen it like this before. Too many white horses to ride tonight,' remarked Harold dryly.

'How many cobles are actually out there?' I asked. ·

'Must be a dozen or more,' replied Laura.

The four of us fell silent, glad to be on the staithe and not out there ourselves. Harold's white horses were pounding the beach below us with increasing ferocity. How strange this all was, more boats like the *Daniel* in trouble again. But then, hadn't my landlady indicated that such terrible occurrences were not unusual for Staithes.

Wives watched and waited, huddled in small groups compatible with missing crews. They drew their shawls tightly round their heads and shoulders, arms wrapped across their chests in an attempt to hold something of themselves together. Their eyes never lifted for a moment from the stormy horizon.

'Who's that?' I nodded across to a woman standing alone. The long black cloak she wore emphasised the paleness of her skin. The emerald gown beneath it shimmered silk and rustled expensively as she twitched from side to side in an agitated manner.

'No idea,' shrugged Harold. 'Is she drunk?'

'She looks ill rather than drunk to me,' said Laura more charitably.

'Perhaps her husband's out there and she's sick with worry,' suggested Rosie.

'A fine woman all the same, eh James?' nudged laddish Harold.

I had noticed that all the women hereabouts held themselves exceptionally well, conditioned from girlhood to balance heavy weights on their heads, but this woman's bearing was positively regal. There was something very different about her as her eyes darted from wave to wave, scanning the darkening sea – there was a wildness in those eyes – a madness almost. If she really was a fisherman's wife like the others, why then was no one speaking to her, trying to comfort her?

'I'm sure I did see something over there, look just beyond Cowbar Steel. Yes, there's a boat coming in,' insisted Rosie.

I sighed with admiration. Not only was Rosie Good endowed with an enviable strength in that petite body of hers, she was, it seemed, also blessed with the keen eyesight of a child.

'Looks merely like a black dot to me,' I had to confess.

'Could be a bird,' conjectured Laura.

Just then a general scream rang out, others could see Rosie's boat too.

'Fletcher Warrington seems to know your mystery woman, James.' Harold pointed to a thickset man sidling up to the woman in the black cloak. The man appeared to be doing his best to engage her in conversation. The woman was ignoring him, keeping her attention fixed on the boat approaching Cowbar Steel.

'Who on earth is Fletcher Warrington?' I asked.

'Lives at Wykeham House. Keeps golden pheasants. The fellow's full of himself. A bloody nuisance, if you ask me. Always spying around when I'm out painting, a telescope invariably locked to one eye like Sinbad the Sailor.' Harold's sniff was dismissive.

'You must have see him before, James,' said Laura.

'Not that I know of.'

'They're not bringing her in across there,' exclaimed a man who had moved next to me.

'Why shouldn't they?' I asked him.

'That's Pot-a-Boiling, most dangerous piece of water around here, full of hidden holes and deep channels. If anything goes down yonder, it usually rises up days later from t' same spot.' The man pointed to a swirling ferment of white water.

'Keep larboard, keep larboard,' men screamed, their voices lost to the wind. 'Out! Out!' They gesticulated desperately.

The coble was almost upended as it tried to ride the waves beneath. One of the oarsmen was temporarily unseated until he fell back into place like a rag doll and immediately resumed pulling his oar hard against the thole-pin. The boat heaved and listed above the rush of water beneath its flat bottom. Again I was reminded of Harold's equine reference – a single bucking mare in fact – I kept the thought to myself, unwilling to push a flippant metaphor too far under these circumstances.

'Good,' said the man next to me, 'they're keeping out now, see?'

'But how will they get in?' I asked him.

'They'll begin to curve round like this.' The man demonstrated with his whole body.

'I hope they make it.'

'There's more of them coming now,' announced Rosie excitedly.

The men, who had been waiting anxiously on the shore, ran prematurely into the foam to meet the small fleet. Women, stronger Staithes women who were regular members of the coble launch parties, scurried down to join them. Long discarded lugsails remained heaped and sodden on boat floors as, oar and rudder assisted only, the first coble made the difficult turn stern to shore.

'Were she to try and land bow to shore, her sharply dipping forefoot would bury in t' sand and upset her,' explained my informant.

The first coble patiently held off for the right smooth – a wave that does not break – before surfing in. Long rudder and oars lifted, breaking water all around them, the exhausted seamen waited passively as many eager hands pushed against the bow and dragged forward the sloping stern to beach their coble safely.

Chanting "hurrahs" of encouragement came from those on the staithe to those down in the water struggling to catch ropes and push and pull the cobles ashore. Harold and I rolled up our sleeves and jumped down onto the beach to join the hauling parties. Large oiled coble oars and any available timber were thrust beneath the boats' own two drafts to act as runners and help slide them higher out of danger.

The man who had announced to the Cod and Lobster that Daniel had been moved to prison in York, the man called Lane, jumped from the boat I was hauling in. Lane seemed to recognise me. He nodded briefly before taking his place in the line of straining men somewhere behind me.

'Aaa-ah! Heave! Heave again!' I did my best to keep my footing on the coarse shale in my ridiculously flimsy slippers. I could feel the skin on my palms chafing from grasping the salty rope.

Cries came from further and further down the staithe as one after another the cobles made home. The slipway was jammed with them. Boats were being pulled over the staithe itself to protect them from the minute by minute rising stormy sea. One coble remained dangling vertically like a dead whale awaiting butchery.

'She'll break her back,' squealed her owner. More men and women joined in to lever her forward as gently as they could. A lost or badly damaged boat curtailed not just the owner's but several families' livelihoods in Staithes. Nobody needed to be reminded of that. The owner's frown eventually turned to a smile of gratitude as his coble was made safe for the night.

With a certain physical satisfaction I looked up from my raw and stinging hands to Laura and Rosie Good.

'I had all on to stop Rosie joining you,' shouted Laura.

I could not avoid noticing Rosie's skirt billowing up her legs in a sudden gust of wind, her girlish form momentarily silhouetted by the light from the studio behind.

Wheeling away, sweeping the hair from my eyes, I looked all the way down the staithe to the dark outline of the Cod and Lobster. The mystery woman and Fletcher Warrington were nowhere to be seen.

Harold and I were the last on the beach that night.

'I could have sworn I saw a light flash out there,' said Harold as we turned to leave.

'Yes, I thought I saw something too.'

'A light swooping down over Cowbar Steel. It's disappeared now.' We both peered harder into the far distance, the wind and saltwater stinging our eyes.

'A falling star perhaps?' I suggested hopefully. I had had enough drama for one night. Nevertheless, the two of us remained on the beach a good while longer, although it was well past midnight and we were ready to drop after our unaccustomed manual labour. But there was nothing more to be seen of the arcing light and we persuaded ourselves that we must have been mistaken.

Chapter Thirteen

I chose to lie-in the next morning. Snug and safe in the warmth of bedding, I relived the excitement of the storm. I could recall my smarting eyes and the pain of the coarse hemp rope as I helped drag the cobles up the beach. I remembered Rosie's skirt billowing up in the wind, my own arousal. But it was the memory of the mystery woman that unnerved me most. Who was she? – I knew I must find out. It was her succubine image that had haunted my dreams.

I was just thinking how quiet Staithes was after the storm when a piercing shriek split open the air – primitive, catlike, it lifted me out of the sheets. As I reached for my dressing-gown, I wondered if I was merely responding to something in my dreams. Until more shrieks came, real shrieks echoing round Nanny Nick and through the narrow ginnel of Gun Gutter. From my window I could see a tall woman stalking along the staithe, other women were tugging and pulling on the hem of her skirt as if attempting to tether her down. Confronted with this scene of female hysteria, men parted uneasily. They seemed at a loss whether or not to get involved.

The whole scene had the choreography of an opera: the heroine bent on her fatal course of action, her beseeching maids, bemused male hangers-on for once mute and in the background. Removed behind my theatre box window, I could have almost found the scene below amusing if it had not been so tragic.

Ashamed, I decided to do battle with the stiff sash-window and offer whatever help was needed.

'Are you all right down there?' Sticking my head through the open frame, I boldly addressed the woman amid her posse of followers. The woman made no response. Still shrieking, she continued her march down the staithe dragging the rest behind.

"Tis the death wail, Mister,' a young boy shouted up to me. 'A yawl left Middlesbrough yesterday, and she's not returned. They've found some gear in t' shallows of Cowbar Steel.'

I grabbed up my day clothes, heart racing as I hurriedly dressed. Maybe Harold and I had not been mistaken about seeing that light last night.

Making my way along the staithe, I saw the distressed woman was returning in the opposite direction without any definite purpose. 'They'll be home, just you see,' she muttered to herself over and over again. 'They'll be home.'

'Isn't it awful,' shouted Rosie Good, emerging from her and Laura's studio.

'Thought I'd take a walk towards Cowbar Steel,' I told her. 'See what's going on.'

'Wait, I'll get my oilers and come with you.'

Rosie took my arm. The wind of the previous night was beginning to pick up again. The bad weather fronts in this part of the world usually moved in from the North Sea. You could watch them pass by or come in from miles across the water.

'I find a high wind exhilarating, don't you?' Rosie flung her free arm out like a wing.

'Icarus' wing,' I laughed. 'To fly like Icarus.'

On cue the wind buffeted us harder. We joked and walked backwards into it, protecting our faces, turning and turning again – schoolchildren – the distraught woman and any possible tragedy ahead conveniently brushed aside. Leaning on the wind, step by step we fought our way forward.

Rosie smelt as fresh and good as her name. What more could a man wish for?

To others we must have appeared insensitive, callous even, but we were young with youthful optimism and it just wouldn't have been fair for things to turn out badly.

I almost forgot what I was expecting to see out there on Cowbar Steel if anything. I did not want to spoil the moment and tell Rosie of the light Harold and I had seen dropping into the dark abyss, tell her of my dread of finding some devastating tell-tale sign of our neglect the previous night.

The morning tide was well out. Foam, like soapsuds spawned on congealed city rivers, lifted into the air from the sunken reefs of Cowbar Steel.

Rosie and I saw them at the same time, our happy young mood immediately fell into melancholia and fear. A group of sombre men stood on the shore opposite the Steel, pointing to a black mass that was not usually there, that I had never seen there before during my fossil hunting expeditions along this part of the coast. Bladders bobbed, mocking heads round the shrouds of abandoned nets.

'Them nets is from Fines' boat,' a fisherman told us, his voice steady, emotionless, matter-of-fact. 'The rest o' t' gear might be sucked under Pot-a-Boiling, bodies too.'

'How many men are missing?' I asked him.

'Robert Fines and his two eldest lads.'

'Is there no hope for them at all?' Rosie asked, horrified.

The fisherman turned away, turned his face back to the nets and the sea. He considered her question irrelevant.

'Will they be found, their bodies come to the surface?' I dared to ask.

'Happen they'll be washed out later but I doubt it. See, it's like that young lass they found t' other day. If they reckon she was dead afore she reached the rock with the Robertshaw lad on it, I'd have expected her to be sucked down here first.'

Rosie and I moved along the water's edge searching for signs as to why and how. Other people joined in combing the shoreline. It all had the appearance of a continental promenade apart from the fact that it was conducted in a joyless silence. Every yard or so there was a relic from the missing boat: a piece of sail cloth, a battered bucket, part of an oar. Rosie stooped to pick up a broken thole-pin. She offered it to me in her open palm for scrutiny. The initials R.F. were burnt into the wood.

'Robert Fines, Laura knew him well. Painted one of his little granddaughters only recently.' With a shaking hand, Rosie put the thole-pin into the pocket of her oiler.

Confession time, I miserably acknowledged. 'Harold and I saw a falling light over this position last night, just one, we convinced ourselves we must have imagined it.'

'I know,' sighed Rosie. 'Harold told Laura earlier this morning. But suppose you had reported seeing something, by the time the rescuers got out here it would probably have been too late, impossible anyway,' she reassured me.

'All the same I feel so guilty.'

'We all feel guilty about something,' Rosie murmured to herself.

'What on earth do you have to feel guilty about?'

'Daniel Robertshaw. Perhaps we should be doing more for poor Daniel. I can't get him out of my mind. He worshipped Laura, you know, but then who doesn't. (This was said with an emotion I could not quite fathom.) You heard that fisherman just now, the whole village is against Daniel. Someone should go and see him. And this very place is where it all started to go wrong for him and his family. These same rocks wrecked his father's boat, he told me so himself.'

'He told me that as well,' I admitted, wondering whether or not I should tell her about my meeting in Whitby with Mrs Robertshaw. Until I had seen Daniel himself, interviewed him, I was not really sure of my own position in the matter. I decided to say nothing for the time being.

At that moment our attention was arrested by the scene ahead. More people were huddled round something on part of the beach known locally as Sandy Wyke. They retained a funeral silence as the wind howled and ripped at their clothing.

'What is it?' whispered Rosie. 'I hope it's not a ...'

'A boat. I think they've found the boat,' I assured her quickly, praying my eyes had not deceived me.

The yawl had come to rest upright on its keel. Stripped of all its contents it otherwise looked unscathed. A giant coffin without a body. And all the while the wind remained relentless.

I looked towards the unforgiving vastness of water. Three men were lost out there. I could only hope their ending had not been prolonged.

Rosie and I turned and scurried back towards Staithes, the wind behind us. There was no more arm-in-arm, not a word was spoken.

'I cannot work after this, not today,' pronounced Rosie, as we slipped and slid on the rocks beneath Cowbar Nab.

I heard her, nodded, but did not look at her. I was preoccupied with the sudden awareness of my own inadequacy against such forces – the fragility of man against the elements – and, mixed somewhere in there, there remained the clawing guilt that Harold and I should have done something about that falling light, told someone else about it at least. There was no way my hammer and chisel would be heard eking out the history of Brackenberry Wyke that day either.

If it were possible to see and feel grief that is what we saw and felt on entering the village. The whole of Staithes was at a standstill, stricken by the disaster.

'I'm going to see Harold and Laura,' announced Rosie.

I nodded, my mood deflated further. Rosie and I weren't even locked together by the tragedy – the experience of witnessing its detritus together – ultimately, she still wanted the friends she knew. I was alone as always.

'They'll be at Harold's lodgings, I expect.'

'I'll take you there.' My voice came out flat, a match for my mood.

'No.' Rosie lifted her hand, resting it on my shoulder.

'I want to,' I insisted, removing her hand from my shoulder and kissing it. The hand withdrew into her oiler too quickly to be encouraging.

Harold and Laura were waiting for news along with everyone else. I watched as Harold stooped to kiss Rosie. The kiss, though welcoming enough, was cool and restrained – a Harold kiss in every way. But it was the way Rosie looked up into Harold's face that really tortured me. Her expression was full of idolisation for the top boy in the life class. I reached for the door handle.

'Stay, James.' Unaware, Harold physically checked my departure.

'All right for just a little while,' I agreed, having no real wish to leave on this sour note myself, no real desire to confront the recent and terrible images of human mortality alone.

The four of us sipped tea, talked quietly and waited.

'By the way, James, I've just remembered, I know who your mystery lady is,' piped up Rosie, her irrepressible vigour suddenly restored.

'She's not my lady,' I snapped back, slightly irritated. 'I was curious about her, that's all. She had such a strange appearance.'

'But she is a lady though,' smirked Rosie.

'Not Mrs Fletcher Warrington?'

'Certainly not. Fletcher Warrington isn't married.'

'Who'd have him,' muttered Harold in an undertone.

'As soon as Rosie sets foot into a place, she gets to know all the eligible bachelors. Better watch out, James,' teased Laura, glad a little flippancy was breaking into the gloom.

'Who is she then?' I asked Rosie.

'That kind of information will cost you something.'

'A herring and toast tea,' I offered.

'What else here,' laughed Harold.

'She's Clarissa Parke, married to Sir Hugh Parke. They live at that huge castellated villa along the coast towards Mulgrave,' explained Rosie.

'How on earth have you found that out so soon?' asked Laura.

'One of Mrs Crooks' friends has worked for them for years. Mrs Crooks recognised Lady Clarissa as soon as I described her. Says she's a little odd.'

'Who is Mrs Crooks?' I asked Rosie.

'Laura's ex-landlady.'

'Odd how?'

'I don't know,' shrugged Rosie. 'Sir Hugh's always bad tempered and she's just odd.'

'Do they have any family?'

'Not that I know of. I didn't realise you wanted me to go into every aspect of their lives, James.' Rosie laughed petulantly.

'He is a barrister,' pointed out Harold, ruffling Rosie's springy hair before we all fell quiet again.

I began to pace to the window and back. Used to my own company I soon tired of other people. Long ago, I had acknowledged to myself that I am most at ease when alone. And what were we all actually waiting for anyway? As the fisherman at Cowbar Steel had explained it could take months, if ever, for bodies to re-emerge. A bell rang out midday. An hour must have passed since Rosie and I first stepped into Harold's lodgings.

Finally deciding to leave, I took a last look out of the window. It was then that I saw them coming. I beckoned to the others and we all bunched together to get a view of the slow procession coming over the flat, low tide rocks. A hundred men or more escorted the bearers of a horizontal ladder, a makeshift litter. It seemed an age before they made the permanent shore itself. Big strong men, they trundled up the slipway with great care and order. The marble effigy strapped to the ladder hardly moved – they were bringing home one of their own – but to whose home?

Along with the rest of the village, we crept out of our dwelling onto the street to see at which door the procession would stop. Behind the Cod and

Lobster, the bearers gently lowered their burden to the ground outside a small ironstone cottage with blending natural wooden shutters.

'Robert Fines' next to youngest,' murmured an old woman to Laura. 'Only just married.'

Robert Fines' next to youngest, no more than a boy asleep, was freed from the ladder and delivered indoors. The sound of breaking crockery could be heard by those of us outside as cups and saucers were hastily swished off the table with the tablecloth. The table now a catafalque, the cloth a shroud. The death wail shrieked out – younger this time but all the more terrible for that. The village watched on impotent and shocked.

'I'll never get used to this,' muttered Harold.

I looked up to the sky above the summer flowering Cowbar Nab. The wind had dropped. The seagulls seemed to be circling higher than ever out of respect. It *was* unfair – such tragedy on such a glorious afternoon.

'Not all bodies do get sucked down into Pot-a-Boiling forever then,' whispered Rosie Good.

* * * * *

'Seen it so many times afore, it never gets better,' muttered Nathaniel Nab, swinging his bandy legs over the staithe, seated next to one of his cronies in the late afternoon sun.

'Ye'll see it again afore too long, there's two more of 'em to come up yet.'

'Fines' nets were found exactly over t' same spot that took the *Daniel*.'

'Do you have to remind me of that?' Nab's companion folded one hand over the other in an attempt to keep them still.

Nab cleared his throat diplomatically, trying to ignore the other man's clasped shaking hands. 'Her ladyship was down here t' other night.'

'Really?' said the man with little interest, obviously still focused on the lost *Daniel*.

'Didn't think he let her out.'

'Don't ask me, I'm only the odd-jobman.'

'Thou must miss the sea, Carl. Odd-jobman, what calling is that for a fine mariner such as thee?'

'I vowed I'd never go out again, and I haven't.'

'It hasn't stopped thy son Martin from putting out any rate.'

'Martin was fortunate that illness prevented him taking up his place as second lad aboard the *Daniel* just afore we sailed. Otherwise, it might have been his *larl* body wrenched from me hands.' Carl Thompson shook his head at the memory – the one clear memory left to him of the disaster which his bruised mind ran and re-ran time and time again – Robertshaw's elder son planing away from him on the big wave. `

'And he'd not be out trawling everything up from t' seabed today.'

'What?' asked the still distracted Thompson.

'Martin, he'd not be trawling out of Scarborough,' repeated Nab in the same tone of disapproval.

'They say steam's safer than sail,' pointed out Thompson.

'Steers has had her fair share of misfortune with sail of late, I'll grant thee that. Someone must have failed to throw out the egg water or summat,' suggested a more conciliatory Nab.

'I don't believe in them things no more,' frowned Thompson. 'The days and nights afore the *Daniel* went down, we'd all been so careful not to cross the fates. When that big wave came and ripped the captain's lad from my grasp, the second before my own skull was crushed on Cowbar rocks, it was then, in a flash, that I realised there was no fate, no God, only the struggle to breathe.'

Nab gaped at Thompson. 'No God, Carl? We found thee, didn't we? More dead than alive, I'll grant, but thou alone lived.'

'Exactly. Why me? Why did a sinner like me live and a fine man like William Robertshaw drown?'

'Thou's lost me there, Carl.' Nab stroked his long curtain of beard thoughtfully. 'All these years I've know thee and I never knew thou felt that way. I guess thou could put forward the same argument of "why" about that innocent we found.'

'What innocent? What are you talking about now, old man?'

'The poor lass we saw on yonder rock.' Nab pointed towards Scar Shootings. 'Robertshaw's remaining lad standing over her.'

'Daniel? What was he doing out there with a lass?'

'Nobody knows,' shrugged Nab. 'But the lass's limbs were as white as those mannequins they have in fancy shop windows in Whitby. In fact, from a distance, I thought it was one of them mannequins laid out at first.'

'I've heard nothing of this.'

'How can that be?' Nab gaped again at Thompson, this time with complete incomprehension. 'Steers has talked of nothing else for a week until today. Police sniffing around everywhere, asking questions all the time. And now the hounds have sunk their teeth into a right simple doughy fox. But whether or no 'tis the right fox, that's another question.'

'What on earth are you blathering about?'

'Dan Robertshaw. Lane and the rest burnt down his house and then the police came and took Dan away.'

'Lane, he would be involved in this somewhere.'

'Ay, true enough,' pondered Nab.

'You say the police took Daniel away?'

'Yes, I've heard tell they've arrested him.'

'Why?' The colour drained from Carl Thompson's already pallid face.

'They think he killed the lass of course.'

'So where is he now?'

'He's away in York Castle as we speak.'

'How can they think that lad is capable of killing anyone?'

'Same way as thee and me, if we had a mind to it.'

Thompson fell silent, his brow puckered, he seemed to be puzzling over the news. 'Daniel, it's not possible,' he whispered more to himself.

'What's wrong, Carl?'

'Did you get a good view of this lass close up?'

'I most certainly did.' Nab puffed up with importance.

'What was she like? What was she wearing? How old was she?'

'Thou's so isolated up there at Brigham Hall, Carl. Thou might as well be out at sea.'

'Sea, sea, you people down here think of nothing else.'

'There is nothing else. 'Tis the sea that feeds us.'

'There's mining and suchlike.'

'And odd jobs,' jibed Nab. He remembered Carl's father well and knew that Thompson senior would be mortified to see his middle-aged son today.

'I asked you what was she like?' Thompson was well-known in Staithes for being short tempered. His friends put it down to the head injury he received when washed onto the rocks under Cowbar Nab, his enemies made no excuses for him and did their best to milk his shortcomings. Whereas, Nathaniel Nab was more inclined to forbearance with Thompson, someone like Lane was certainly not. Lane had no time for a man of sail whose son now steam trawled the sea and robbed line-fishermen of their catches. Lane despised the seaman turned odd-jobman. Should the odd-jobman occasionally, and perhaps foolishly, come down from Brigham Hall for the night to chance his luck in the Cod and Lobster, Lane would invariably call Thompson's (or his son Martin's) manhood into question before the entire gathering of seamen there to provoke a fight – a fight Lane knew he would win.

Nab shook his head sadly at the memories of all the odd-jobman's scrapes. 'Sometimes I think thou's thine own worst enemy, Carl.'

'I'm only asking what she was like,' said Thompson through clenched teeth.

'It took some time to bring her in once she'd floated away on the tide.'

'"Floated away on the tide",' hissed Thompson in disbelief, sure now Nathaniel was deliberately prevaricating.

'Ay, afore we got to her the sea had lifted her up and taken her away. A coble crew found her the next day. They stretched her out over there, poor wee bairn.'

'So what was she like?' Thompson felt his cheeks burning angry red.

'Fair, very fair, curls.'

'Ringlets?'

'Ay, ay, that sort of thing.'

'How old was she?'

'Young, very young.'

'About fourteen or fifteen say?'

'Could have been about that.'

'Anything else?'

'All these questions, Carl.'

'Go on.'

'Her dress, a fine dress, she wasn't a flither picker in my opinion, I'll say that much. Lasses round here never wear that quality of garment, not even for Steers fair. She'd no eyes left in her head though.' Nab watched Thompson's face pale again, he appeared instantly haggard. 'Why, dost thou think thou knows who she might be, Carl?' he asked with a mixture of alarm and excitement.

Thompson shook his head. 'How could I know who she is, me being up at the Hall all the time? I know nowt, I tell ye.'

'It's just that thou's gone the colour of a corpse thyself,' pointed out Nab calmly.

Chapter Fourteen

The tall carpenter – now smaller, older and lame – limped along the staithe towards the young widow's house. He had a job to do, measurements to take. His expression was practical rather than grave, tragedy was no stranger to a man whose own two good feet were once frozen solid to the deck of a whaler off Greenland. He was the resident coffin maker, death was his everyday business. But death was a new and terrible experience for Jacob Fines' eighteen year old widow. Kate had not taken off her clothes, left the house, gone to bed in days. She sobbed and belched in turns, and waited alongside her mother-in-law and sister-in-law for their men to "come in" too.

Back at his workshop, close to Rosie's and Laura's studio on the staithe, the carpenter began to beat in his nails. The reverberation from his hammer bounced back and forth between Cowbar and Penny Nab breaking the village's eerie stillness. Children were kept indoors. No one was out and about on the streets. Shore-bound fishermen no longer met and paced up and down the quay in pairs. Staithes had withdrawn, apart from men seeking solace in the Cod and Lobster on an evening they knew Jacob Fines would not be joining them.

* * * * *

Spray washed against the protective black tarred skin of the pub as I snuggled into a corner table and romantically schemed over a quiet whisky. Another storm seemed to be brewing out there in the ocean but tonight all Staithes boats were safely berthed.

Although the mood in the pub was sombre, I could not help looking up from time to time to see men with buttoned coats challenging the foul weather conditions outside to burst back through the pub's door drenched. Was this some sort of defiance in the face of the enemy or a masculine stunt to show how tough they were. From my table I could hear the howling breakers rolling in, crashing against the small quay – the only defence between pub and sea – a strange sport this for the locals.

'It's a real lipper again tonight,' announced a gruff voice above me and my cuddled whisky glass. I reluctantly lifted my gaze to meet a pair of cold blue eyes. 'I know you,' said Eyes.

'Could be, take a seat.'

'Job Lane.' Eyes stuck out his hand.

'James Cairn.' Job Lane's skin was rough in my smooth handshake.

'Saw you help haul in the cobles t' other night.'

'Did what I could along with everybody else.'

'Is it true that you're the fella that hammers open stones for a living?' chuckled Lane.

'Yes, I'm a fossil hunter but it's my hobby not my living,' I admitted defensively.

'Seen you walking along the staithe as I work the cobles.'

'I go that way sometimes.'

'Seen you walking along last year with the Chinaman.'

'Who?'

'Dan Robertshaw.'

'So why call him "Chinaman"?'

'Just do, we all do,' squinted Lane. 'It's the look of him. Seen you talking to Miss Johnson and Rosie too,' he quickly threw in.

'You seem to have noticed rather a lot, Mr Lane.'

'Job, please,' insisted Lane; a sly little gleam flickered for a second in the cold eyes.

'Pretty little thing, ain't she?'

'Who is?'

'Rosie, of course.'

I could see Job Lane did not just fish from cobles. I did not take to Lane at all. Lane looked more like a pirate or smuggler than a regular seafarer. My impulsive offer to socialise with this man had been a mistake and now I wished Lane would just take up his pot and go away.

'Shame that sister of Miss Johnson's isn't in such good health, isn't such a buxom wench, lovely in her own way though, delicate like,' continued Lane on a theme, rubbing his rough hand speculatively across his bristling chin.

'I wouldn't know, I've never had the pleasure,' I retorted sharply.

'Hair the colour of corn. And a pleasure it would be with any of 'em,' sniggered Lane, his hooded lids narrowing across the blueness. 'Why that...'

'I am not such a connoisseur of womenfolk as you appear to be, Mr Lane,' I interrupted, appalled at Lane's coarseness.

'Mr Knight's the lucky one, is he not? Though he returns to lodging with Tom Porritt of an evening, or so I understand, he's down at that studio place of theirs most days.'

'Aren't you forgetting their chaperone, Aunt West?' I immediately regretted getting drawn into this topic of conversation. Why should I have to justify the artists' behaviour to a man like Lane?

'Ha! Didn't you know the Frenchy's not with them this season? Them Frenchies have a different way of looking at things from us anyway.'

'I understood from my landlady that Mrs West isn't French, she just lives there,' I snapped back, committed to the argument now.

'Nevertheless,' sneered Lane. 'Womenfolk soon picks things up. No doubt the old matron taught them lasses a thing or two, eh?' He took out a tobacco tin and clay pipe from his breast-pocket, pressed a wodge of tobacco into the small bowl with his index finger suggestively, and without as much as a "by your leave" lit it. 'So you've been up to Ebor Cottage yourself?' he asked, wearing the same continuous leer, seemingly indifferent to my growing antagonism and not really interested in waiting for a reply. 'You'll know then it was because of the other Miss Johnson's health that Mr Barrett originally suggested they came here, apart from Steers being good for painting pictures like.'

'Mr Barrett? Who's Mr Barrett?'

'Mr Thomas Barrett. He's their teacher at Nottingham Art School, comes up here every summer himself.'

'How do you know so much about their affairs?'

'Just do.' Lane's hooded lids squeezed guardedly together again. 'Any rate, I'd have thought your friend, the village idiot, would have kept you better informed.'

'Don't call him that.'

'Close are we, sir?' He patted my hand ingratiatingly.

'Don't be ridiculous,' I said, pulling my hand away.

'You'll be able to meet up in York, I expect.'

'How do you know I come from York?'

'I wish those painting people would help me out touching up the cobles rather than wasting all their time on those picture things,' he said without answering.

'"Those picture things" are paintings and the people who paint them are artists. It's a profession like any other.'

'Not like mine,' sniffed Lane. 'Not like yours either by all accounts. Heard you do more than scratch around in t' mud cliffs, Mr Cairn. Heard you've been to Whitby scratching around in other folk's dirt.'

'And what's that to you?'

'What could happen to you is a better question.'

'Are you threatening me, Mr Lane?'

'Not at all, Mr Cairn, it's just good advice that's all. People around here prefer to keep their affairs private, within the family, within the village.' Lane cockily leaned back in his chair smiling, the pipe still balanced in the corner of his mouth. Slowly, he exhaled a cloud of smoke into my face.

* * * * *

The day of Jacob Fines' funeral was calm. The sea was calm. The white breakers far out to sea curled over lazily in the grey. The village in mourning knew the sea would give up nothing more today. Even the widow Kate seemed quiescent, spent of grief, waiting outside the ironstone cottage for her husband to join her for the last time.

Apart from the bedridden, everyone in Staithes gathered along the High Street. Parchment-skinned old folk, who had hardly ventured out of doors in years, shuffled like foreign migrants on neighbourly arms across the wooden bridge – some called the footbridge the trestle-bridge because of its braced framework – however it was known, this was the main border crossing between Cowbar and the rest of Staithes. A few proud old men still clung to their independence, refusing a proffered arm, their ancient black pilot-cloth coats hanging loosely over their withered frames as they dared themselves not to reach for the support of railings.

I had never seen such an array of funeral hats. There were the usual cloth peaks and one or two Icelandic sealskin caps, others looked like hand-medowns made of beaver, perhaps the result of some keen exchange conducted in Russian waters a hundred years before. And beneath various coats and jackets, men of all ages wore the customary guernsey for warmth though the day was not cold.

Reassurance in a life and climate of sudden change, I acknowledged, aware I was out of place in my holiday suit. I had not prepared my wardrobe for a funeral.

I was not alone in being slightly adrift, some of the village women stood a group apart as they watched on. They waited with an aloof upright grace dressed in smart black, black sashes girdling their bosoms, only the shawls slipping from their shoulders were white. According to my landlady, Mrs Shaw, these women were known as waiters and they would not be going to the service. Later, after it was all over, they would spring into action weaving between mourners with trays offering small cakes and glasses of wine.

I felt an arm reach under mine. 'Rosie. You gave me a start.'

'It's almost like the beginning of a party, isn't it?' she whispered.

'*Almost*,' I said, with little enthusiasm, as we watched Jacob Fines' coffin with its single tribute of a white flowered wreath being carefully manoeuvred out of the narrow doorway. Six bearers, a bow of matching white ribbon arranged in each of their buttonholes, lowered the coffin onto three poles before taking up the weight. Hollow-eyed Kate Fines – flanked by her mother, her tall mother-in-law – hair covered in a black scarf and her sister-in-law scarf covered likewise, fell in behind the coffin. I noticed poignantly that there was a dearth of menfolk at the head of the procession setting off at a slow walk up the High Street.

The white flowers in the wreath bounced like small waves themselves. People muttered how effective they looked there on their own.

'Hello.' Laura slid in next to Rosie as the procession broke into hymn singing. The singing seemed to act as a catalyst for the chief mourners to blow into their black edged handkerchiefs. Kate Fines did not cry. Her hunched worried mother looked up into her face. This wasn't as it should be at all. The timing of her son-in-law's death was unjust and not a bairn to be seen for all this pain.

'Where's Harold?' I asked Laura.

'He's too upset to come.'

'Not because of that business with the light over Cowbar Nab?'

'Harold always holds himself responsible for everything.'

'Shall I go and see if I can persuade him to come?'

Laura shook her head incredulously. 'I've told you, he's too upset,' she snapped. 'Why are you always so concerned about what Harold's getting up to?'

'I'm more …' I was about to say I was more concerned about the two ladies at my side but thought better of it. A funeral was hardly the occasion for flirtation.

'You won't find him anyway,' she snapped again. 'He's gone off painting somewhere with his old modelling master, Oliver Shepherd.'

'Gorgeous Pompey,' giggled Rosie, quick to try and lighten the growing tension between Laura and me.

'"Pompey", why Pompey?' I asked her.

'Harold nicknamed him "Pompus Iscariot".'

I turned to Laura again. 'Look, I was only trying to be helpful over Harold. I'd hate you to think I was prying,' I told her. She scowled more. Rosie flashed me a look of indulgent sympathy. At the rear of the cortège we filed past the railway station. If a train had been waiting there on the track, I was sure I would have run and jumped onto it. Why was Laura being so bloody abrasive about Harold? – and more importantly in front of Rosie.

Party had certainly turned to wake by the time the funeral reached Hinderwell Lane and the churchyard. Faced with an open grave, even Rosie was subdued.

'I am the resurrection and the life …' I hardly registered what the parson was saying, I was so aware of Rosie pressed up close to me. This closeness, that was not real closeness at all, irritated me.

Looking at Kate Fines' vacant expression, a soul emptied of all emotion, I realised I was being totally self-indulgent regarding my own unrequited feelings for Rosie Good. I did my best to concentrate on the service but "the hope of a better life in heaven once delivered from this sinful world" held out little hope for a confirmed Darwinist.

'Man that is born of a woman hath but a short time to live, and is full of misery. He cometh up, and is cut down, like a flower …'

I gazed at the white flowered wreath discarded on the grass by the waiting chasm and felt wretched. There was a strange sense of expectancy surrounding this graveside, one I had never experienced before. A funeral was usually a laying to rest of all expectation, not so here. I hated funerals and I hated this one more than most. Examining the expressions of those around me, the long looks towards the clear horizon, it soon became apparent what was fuelling the disquiet. No one had really forgotten for a moment that Jacob Fines' lost father and brother were still floating somewhere out there at sea. This was not the end of it. The Jacob now being gently lowered into the damp earth on taut straps might soon be followed by kith and kin.

'Earth to earth, ashes to ashes ...' I looked up from the uncomfortable thought, looked away from the soil pattering on the coffin from strangers' hands. It was then that I saw her again. She was standing on the opposite side of the grave wearing the same black cloak she had worn on the staithe the night of the storm. But today the dress beneath was black too, and her necklace was silver and jet, even the ring on her left hand was a large oval jet stone – Lady Clarissa Parke in the guise of Her Majesty Queen Victoria – and on this occasion it was not the flamboyant Fletcher Warrington at her side either but a taller, more quietly distinguished looking man. Lady Clarissa's eyes were fixed on the coffin, fixed on the bouncing soil. Her entire face writhed with emotion. Her mouth worked on some soundless lament. If I had not known better I would have sworn that it was she who was the grieving widow here. Clarissa Parke's grief seemed very personal indeed.

So that's bad tempered Sir Hugh Parke, I guessed, surprised. I ought to introduce him to Laura Johnson in her present mood.

Sir Hugh appeared to be trying to lead his distraught wife away from the graveside. But she would not be coaxed, holding her ground fixed and wooden, deaf to his appeals. A physical impasse seemed to exist between the two of them until Sir Hugh grasped his wife's arm more firmly and she reluctantly capitulated. There was no equivalence here, only battles, I was immediately reminded of Flora Robertshaw and the bullying Mr Jeffrey.

I could not resist smiling at my growing expertise on the lack of perfect unions – a bachelor's prerogative perhaps – until I realised where I was and that I in turn was being observed watching the Parkes.

'Who's that standing over there by the tree?' I muttered to Rosie.

'Kemp, that's Inspector Kemp from Whitby. He's the one that's been asking questions all over Staithes about the dead girl.'

'Rosie, you're a mine of information.'

Chapter Fifteen

There was a lot of hard drinking and bitter talk in the Cod and Lobster the next evening following Jacob Fines' funeral. For hundreds of years generations of Staithes fishermen had gone out in all weathers – risked their lives, often died – in the pursuit of fish. Despite the risks most of them would not have chosen any other way of life, the sea was a free and independent calling they were born to. Nevertheless, dissatisfaction was growing daily among their ranks: catches were down, some fishermen felt they were being squeezed out of their rightful and historical living. And who was responsible for this cancer in their midst? Trawlers, trawlers were the bane of line fishermen's lives.

'And now the bloody things are steam powered,' someone well in his cups shouted out.

'They think nothing of dragging off our lines,' objected someone else. 'Why only t' other day ...'

'Who knows it might have been a smacksman what pulled the Fines' boat down,' interrupted the drunk.

'Now listen up, lads,' shouted Ranter Pope, trying to impose some discipline into the proceedings. 'It's no good making wild accusations about what befell Robert's boat. We all know only too well how ugly the sea was that night. Though I agree with you, Isaac, them steam trawlers are destroying everything on the seabed, sprat, everything. Soon the sea will be as bereft of fish as this is.' The Ranter lifted up his glass of clear water by way of demonstration.

Ranter Pope hardly ever stepped inside public houses, and never, absolutely tee-totalling never, indulged in drinking any of their wicked brews. But, during Robert Fines' son's funeral, he had heard an informal meeting was to be held at the Cob and Lobster regarding the trawler threat to his community, and, despite his deep mistrust of the chosen venue, Seth Jackson had eventually persuaded him to attend as unofficial chairman.

'Nay, Ranter,' shouted a fisherman from the back of the taproom. 'Your sight must be failing for there's sure as hell a bloater in yon glass.'

'Lads, please,' appealed Jackson. 'This is a serious situation we find ourselves in and as such should be treated with according gravity.'

'That's good from a man who throws his lot in with t'law rather than his mates,' hissed Job Lane, hands on hips. Lane, who would have liked nothing better than to be regarded as the community's leader himself.

'For once, friend,' Jackson paused dramatically fixing Lane with a steely stare. 'We find ourselves irrevocably fighting for the same cause.'

The room exploded with applause. Lane's fists shot up in front of his chest.

'That traitor Martin Thompson better not show his face in t'village, that's all, because if he does I'll give you all a lesson in fighting.' Lane decided on diversionary tactics rather than a direct confrontation with Jackson, aiming his contempt at a spittoon and missing.

'That's all my eye and Betty Martin and you know it, Lane,' the Ranter shouted across to him, calmly pulling at the rift between his long white whiskers.

'No, *Martin Thompson*, Ranter,' corrected another joker.

'Whatever,' replied the pedantic Ranter without a flicker of amusement. 'Young Thompson's not been seen in Steers for years.'

'The Ranter's a poet,' screamed the original wit at the back of the room. The room fell into uproar again.

'I'll step outside with his father then,' insisted the equally humourless Lane, childishly stung by the room's disaffection. ''Tis all the same to me.'

'You can't fight a man who isn't here, Job,' guffawed the man most able of taking care of himself in the pub that night, the Cod and Lobster's landlord. 'Betty or otherwise.'

'Order,' shouted Jackson.

'Any more orders,' bellowed the teasing landlord. 'On the house for everyone.'

Jackson raised his hands palms forward, a helpless gesture. He had won the room over and scored another small victory over Lane but once the free liquor started to flow he knew he would have to content himself merely with that.

And so it was, the meeting soon dissolved into a heavy drinking session and any weighty discussion was forgotten. The Ranter left in disgust and Jackson sat back with a pot of ale and a convivial smile. Every meeting

Jackson had attended on trawling had ended this way, nothing ever got resolved. This was Staithes time, slow time, where the intention was always there to act but nothing ever got done. Perhaps, mused Jackson, Staithes was out of pace with the rest of the world. What could be done about trawlers anyway? There had been several Royal Commissions held on the subject. As far back as sixty-three, Jackson's own father had been called to give evidence, little good it had done.

'Government men are always for "progression" whatever the cost,' Jackson senior had told his son just before he died. 'Puh! "Progression", till there's nothing left in the sea to fish.'

'Time will prove the old man right,' muttered Jackson, blowing thoughtfully onto his flat head of ale. 'And I hope it's long after I'm dead and gone to see it.'

It was round the back of the pub after closing time, where vomit pooled with sea-water, that Jackson found himself rubbing shoulders with Lane of all people. Jackson self-consciously adjusted himself back into his trousers as Lane peed on.

'Had a skinful tonight.' Lane was first to break the deadlock. Since the Robertshaw fire the two men had avoided each other more than usual.

'Me too,' admitted Jackson.

'At least Jacob Fines got a good send off,' said Lane.

'He did that.'

'Same can't be said for his father and brother.'

'A sad affair,' agreed Jackson readily; thinking that he and Lane might at least be united in grief and adversity be it temporarily.

'That lass on Scar Shootings was a sad affair too, was it not?'

Jackson hesitated guardedly. 'Indeed.'

'That donnat standing all over her.'

'I didn't see that myself, that was something Nab and Fletcher Warrington said they saw.'

'And don't you believe them?'

'I …' Jackson hesitated again.

'You doubt their word, don't you?'

'They can only have seen so much.'

'How much more did you want them to see?' asked Lane, buttoning up his flies. 'Because from the way you talk, you sound as if you think the idiot is innocent.'

Jackson considered Lane's provocative remark. He decided to counter by asking a question himself. 'Has that Whitby peeler been round to your house?'

'Maybe he has.' Lane glanced up cunningly.

'Asking questions about the dead lass?'

'He could have done.'

'I had to make my mark against a statement t' other day.'

'Oh, ay.' Lane suddenly looked more interested.

'Have you had to do anything of the sort?' pressed Jackson.

'Ay, something of the kind,' Lane finally admitted.

'So what did you tell 'im?'

'That's my concern.'

'No it's not, it's *our* concern,' said Jackson, tiring of Lane's silly evasions. 'Yours, Nab's, Fletcher Warrington's and mine.'

'I'm not sure as I see it the same way.'

'Understand this, if we sing from a different hymn book once the thing gets to court them York barristers will make village idiots of us all.'

'Don't see why,' replied Lane sullenly.

'I think you do.'

'You can read my mind now?'

'For all our differences, I've known ye since we were lads together.'

'Too long, that's true enough.'

'And I tell you this, I've had some very difficult questions put to me by that peeler, very personal questions.'

'Really?' shrugged Lane.

'I was asked if I had any idea who that dead lass might be.' An expression of pain crossed Jackson's face.

'Kemp asked me the same.'

'Did you know her?'

'I told him I thought t' idiot did for her,' prevaricated Lane.

'No, how did you reply regarding who the lass might be?' Jackson struggled to see Lane's face in the darkness. As Lane mulled over his direct question, a terrible possibility struck Jackson.

'As it 'appens I do have my own idea as to who she might be,' admitted Lane.

'Who might she be?' Jackson's tone was measured.

'I've not forgotten how quiet you fell when we saw her spilled out of that net there on the staithe.'

'Who might she be?' repeated Jackson sternly.

'You were such a ladies man,' snorted Lane contemptuously. 'Couldn't keep your 'ands off 'em for a minute, could you Jackson?'

'What have you said to the police?' Jackson sucked in air, sucked in the smell of piss and shit rising up into his nostrils from the shore below. The women and children of Staithes used earth closets to relieve themselves, but their menfolk's favourite toilet was beneath the slipway on which he and Lane were now standing. Jackson looked at Lane and smelt shit. He was detestable and he had been right never to trust him. Lane was known as the most unreliable crewman in Staithes. Apart from washing out their cobles, few men would ever employ him to go out to sea with them unless they were absolutely desperate for a hand.

'Remember that Quaker lass over Loftus way, Seth?' jeered Lane. 'The one you courted and put in the family way. The one I told you I had afore ye and you took me seriously and half killed me for my piece of fun.'

'I remember.'

'And didn't that Quaker lass's father whip you within an inch of your life in turn? And later, didn't her mammy send her away with the child? – a girl child, I seem to remember.'

'Enough,' warned Jackson.

'Well, 'tis my opinion that your bastard daughter might have floated back to haunt ye. Maybe it wasn't that idiot Robertshaw who did away with her at all but your good self.'

'And why would I do a thing like that to my own flesh and blood?' snarled Jackson.

'Her turning up from the past could have proved an embarrassment to you, a costly embarrassment at that.'

'Who'll ever believe such blether? Certainly not the police, certainly not coming from your mouth. They already suspect you were involved in that woman being burnt to death at the Robertshaw cottage.'

'You'd better keep your mouth shut over that, Jackson, I'm warning you.'

'And I'm warning you to stop telling-the-tale about my private affairs.'

'I'll think about it.'

'Do. And while you're about it think about that poor Jeffrey woman burnt to a cinder up on Cowbar Bank. Where's your conscience over that, eh Lane? You're fortunate nobody in Steers has been prepared to blab your name as ringleader yet.' Jackson's face was distorted with rage, not purple but black with rage, if Lane could have seen better in the dark perhaps he would have desisted from a final taunt. But the myopic Lane could not, would not see, failed to remember history.

'At least I've never murdered my own lass in cold blood.' He gave Jackson a push, again pushing him to the extreme. 'Any rate, I bet that lass of yours is little more than a whore herself, wherever she is, like her mother.'

'Christ!' muttered a waking drunk, slumped and hidden behind a fish cart and Lane's and Jackson's call of nature. 'If they only knew the half of it.' The black minstrel of the night's teeth gleamed with pleasure at the image of the felled Lane.

Chapter Sixteen

Jackson sat in his cave-like room waiting for the knock on his door. He believed he had just murdered a man. A dog howled outside. He started up in his chair. The room was below street level and his window looked out onto people's feet – always onto people's feet – a difficult perspective for a proud man to contemplate. Out there on Weatherill Street big booted feet trod heavily across his difficult thoughts. Not those naked, free-spirited feet so worshipped by him, so imprinted in the sands of his consciousness.

Jackson had known nothing but Staithes and the sea, he had never wanted more than those two things from life. That is until the day he anchored his boat among the rocks off Cattersty Sands and saw her emerging water-sleek a little further down the shoreline, dressed only in her clinging undergarments, her long hair a halo of fire in the sun. Such grace, so womanly, startled by him she had begun to run up the beach towards a rock festooned with clothes.

She was flushed and healthy with the full ample figure of one of those ancient goddesses Jackson had seen in an old school picture book years before. During those formative years, or non-formative years Jackson would later maintain, one of his teachers had told his mam that he, Jackson, was predominantly interested in pictures rather than text. And, in truth, that teacher had been absolutely right, the adult illiterate Jackson remained more taken by the immediate vision than the story behind it – a plain instinctive man who took things at face value – and so it had been with the maid of Loftus that day.

'You been bathing in there?' he asked her. The rock a boundary of propriety between them. Beneath her dignity to answer the obvious, the girl reached for her bonnet instead – her Quaker bonnet – the first item to be plucked up from the dressed rock. Jackson felt the sun sink under a cloud on that hot, hot day as the girl attempted to stuff every damp strand of her hair out of sight. He rested his back against the rock. 'Why cover such beautiful hair?' He renewed his attempt at conversation, looking to the sea as he heard the soft rustle of drier cloth against skin.

'It is our way,' said the girl. Her voice was low and modulated and as wonderful and warm as her hair.

'You bathe everyday?' asked Jackson doubtfully. Jackson who did not swim and was conscious that his voice must sound harsh and abrupt in contrast to hers.

If the girl minded she did not show it as she sidled fully dressed but shoeless round to his side of the rock. Jackson looked down, looked to her small toes and surprisingly delicate feet. He could have kindled either of those feet in his mouth there and then.

'I love the water,' she said. 'I feel truly at peace in the water.'

'But it's so cold in there.' He acted a shiver.

'At peace and alive,' she insisted.

'Swimming is no use to fishermen. Should we fall overboard it only serves to make our dying slower.'

'Ah, a fisherman it is. The day's too fine for talk of dying, fisherman. I'd rather hear how successful the catch has been.'

Was there a hint of flirtation in her eyes, he wondered.

'Well?' She persisted.

'I have yet to cast my final line,' he told her, his mouth dry.

'Well, best make haste the day's almost at an end.'

'Will you be here tomorrow when the sun rises over the scaur?' he asked; his thumb pointing vaguely backwards, his gaze never leaving her face.

'Perhaps.' The girl raked the sand with her toes.

'Tomorrow.' Jackson turned, sensing the moment had passed for anything more to be said or done that day. The crash of the curling waves on the foreshore seemed to confirm the need of a cessation. He was not sure if he would ever see her again but knew he had to leave right then.

The next morning, Jackson waited on Cattersty Sands good and early. He waited an hour or more. And, as the sun rose even higher over Hummersea Scar, his hope diminished. He was about to clamber back into his boat and pull away when he saw her swaying towards him – naked feet on naked beach – and in her arms a bundle of driftwood as if she was already cradling a bairn.

Jackson could not believe his luck. He did not dare believe she liked him but he risked a hesitant kiss of greeting. He felt pressure on his waist, her hands on his waist.

'So, fisherman,' she whispered.

'So,' he replied. The lightness of the previous day gone.

With one hand Jackson carefully lifted her bonnet and freed her hair to the breeze and the sun. He kissed her again but this time on her mouth – locked unsure and testing on her mouth. His tongue became more confident and probing. He felt her heart rapid beneath his touch. Her heart reminded him of a plover he had once held in his hand with a broken wing – the plover had been all heart. But Jackson's rough hands had never known such softness as this.

'This is so right,' he whispered to reassure her, to reassure himself.

'Without words,' she put her finger flecked with sand against his lips.

The bundle of driftwood danced between their feet – dropped, discarded.

Job Lane had called her a whore, yet Jackson knew she was the purest creature that had ever touched his life.

Seated and preoccupied, he estimated he could have lost an hour or a whole day, he had lost all sense of time. His knuckles still ached from that one blow, the nerves in his hand remembering the sensation as his fist smashed into that mocking face. The thud of the other man's head hitting the ground was a sound ghost that could not be exorcised. Jackson had stood over him, briefly, watching his short matted hair mingling with the rain and piss from the overflowing gutter. Red hair concealed blood in bad light. Lane must be dead, pale dead now in a morgue somewhere. It was not so much a fight as an instant knockout.

There in his dim room, dim even in daylight, the unrepentant fisherman waited patiently for fate to call. How could he say he was sorry for something he had wanted to do most of his life? – ever since he and Lane were lads together arguing who could bait lines the faster.

Seth Jackson had no intention of making a run for it, of quitting a cottage that had been his father's and his father's before him.

* * * * *

'What do you find so fascinating about palaeontology?' Laura Johnson asked. She had invited me to call round to her studio on Wednesday morning, a morning I knew Rosie usually went out sketching and would not be there. Whether or not this was so Laura could make amends in private for her attitude towards me at the funeral, I had yet to find out.

'Detection, discovery,' I replied cryptically. Should I tell her in detail how I became fascinated with molluscs? – those early seashore days when my late father explained how oysters move with ease between sexes. Should I shock her with an insight into my own sexual ambiguity? – that I share the same sexual ambivalence with a hermaphroditic oyster. But then, perhaps she already suspected this with her comment about my preoccupation with Harold.

'And once something is discovered?'

'Then one moves on to the next layer of course.'

'You strike me as a man of many complex layers yourself, James.'

'Could be,' I admitted.

'And Rosie is such a simple creature.'

Simple, I winced. So this was what my visit here was all about.

'I also think there are many personal issues, James, that you haven't as yet addressed.'

'Such as?'

'Such as …' she hesitated. 'What do you exactly want from life?'

'Truth, honesty,' I suggested.

'Well, if it is honesty you're after,' she sighed. 'Rosie is already walking out with someone else.'

'Not Harold?' I asked wickedly.

'No, not Harold,' replied Laura. At least I gained the consolation of making her wince in return.

'I am sure if Rosie knew she would be grateful for your protection but is this the sole reason you've asked me here, to discuss her?'

'No, to give you this.' Laura handed me a flat sheet of heavy paper. I spread it across a nearby worktable to see the most exquisite charcoal drawing of a muscular me swinging against a vague outline of cliff.

'*The Fossil Collector*, but it's wonderful.'

'You sound surprised.'

'I'm totally astonished and very flattered.'

'I'm sorry about Rosie,' she said, her hand gently pressing my elbow. 'She really should have told you herself.'

'Yes, she should have.'

Laura cleared her throat, cleared away the subject.

'Have you heard any more about Daniel?' she asked. I shook my head. 'I don't believe for one moment he killed that girl. Daniel has always been a scapegoat for all the ills of this village.'

* * * * *

Down in the parlour below street level, Jackson shook his fist still painful from the previous night. This time he hoped he had killed Lane and his vicious lies once and for all. What if he did hang? – half of him had been dead for a good fifteen years now.

She was the only woman he would ever want. What did her religious history matter to him? And that was his downfall, her downfall, a tragedy in the making. Jackson was a handsome highly potent man, the Loftus maid overtly feminine with wide childbearing hips, and there was an end to it. But for Jackson it wasn't an end at all, it took only the once and it was the beginning of something ignorantly unforeseen and never to be forgotten.

Lane, for once, hadn't lied when he said the maid's father had whipped Jackson within an inch of his life. What Lane hadn't said, perhaps didn't know, was that he had done nothing to defend himself against what he considered to be a deserved punishment. And what was a flogging anyway to a man who suddenly realised he had lost his future? His woman had been separated from her child soon after birth and sent to some distant town to find the Inner Light again with righteous relatives. Jackson had wept when Nathaniel Nab told him his little girl, too, had been farmed out to a Quaker house far away. Jackson had never set eyes on mother or child again.

Surely, it can't really have been true what Lane had said about that poor eyeless creature hooked from the scaur being his daughter, his own flesh returned to torment him.

What if she was his daughter? What if Daniel had raped and murdered her? Could he have done? Jackson shivered by his empty hearth. His thoughts wandered on through his external and inner gloom, knowing his present uncertainty and turmoil could not have been far short of Daniel Robertshaw's own. Deep within himself, Jackson did not believe Daniel was capable of such a wicked act. But if Daniel hadn't killed her, who had? Did Lane truly believe that he, Jackson, might be involved? Had Lane actually suggested something of the sort to the police? Even if they'd originally ignored Lane's spiteful insinuation, what now when they find him murdered? Surely, this time it was a task completed.

The church clock chimed twelve times and still there was no constable's knock on his door. Maybe he should rally himself to go out and get a little legal advice. If the mountain will not come to Mohammed … Jackson guessed that lawyer chap, Cairn, was still in Staithes. He'd seen him with the two artist women at young Jacob's funeral only the other day.

* * * * *

'I'd like to see Mr Cairn, urgent.'

Mrs Shaw – dressed in deep regal queenly purple, never green, green only brought bad luck – looked Jackson up and down as if he were some apparition dragged up from the seabed.

'Do you know what hour it is, Seth Jackson?' Her eyes rested mistrustfully on Jackson's thigh length waders.

'I told ye, it's urgent,' repeated Jackson firmly.

'And I'm telling you, he'll see no one at this late hour.' She straightened her night-cap.

'Try him.'

'I'll do no such thing.'

'Try him, I tell you.' Jackson wiped his hand belligerently across his mouth.

'How dare the likes of you, Seth Jackson, be telling me what to do in my own house?'

'You'd best do as I ask, missus, for I'm in no mood for fancy shilly-shallying.'

'Threats is it now?' The landlady folded her arms defiantly across her ample bosom. Her bulk effectively guarding the passageway and staircase beyond.

'Just go and ask him,' sighed Jackson, weariness imbuing the request.

'What is going on?' I shouted down from the top landing.

Mrs Shaw pirouetted heavily on the spot. 'Don't trouble yourself with this, Mr Cairn. I'm taking care of it.'

'It's me, Jackson, Mr Cairn. I'm in a spot of bother.' Jackson pushed Mrs Shaw aside to get in his appeal.

'Come up, come up then, man, and we'll see what we can do.'

'Well, Mr Cairn, I never thought ...' Mrs Shaw slithered mawkishly back to allow Jackson passage.

Despite whatever problems Jackson was having, he could not suppress a quick grin at my dressing-gown. Although for Jackson it must have been a cultural shock to find a man wearing such a womanly thing. From what I had seen of the Staithes fishermen they often did not undress at all to sleep – they ate, worked, slept and went to funerals in their guernseys.

'Now what's this all about?' I asked, indicating an upright chair.

'If it's all t' same to you, sir, I'll stand.'

'Suit yourself,' I said, levering myself gently down into an upholstered chair.

'Last night I hit a fella,' Jackson told me bluntly, adding, 'very hard'.

'And who was he?' I feigned interest, supposing this to be just another pub brawl.

'Lane, Job Lane.'

'Oh, him, I wouldn't blame anyone for bashing him.'

'You know him then?' asked Jackson startled.

'Yes, nearly took a punch at him myself the other night. A crawling form of life, very disagreeable,' I concluded abruptly, hesitant to retrieve my own unpleasant memory of Lane.

'That's him.'

'Talked smuttily about some good friends of mine.' I frowned.

Jackson nodded sympathetically. 'That's why I hit him.'

'Sorry?'

'Lane insulted friends of mine too,' Jackson affirmed slowly, deliberately and with some effort.

'What friends?'

Jackson swallowed hard. 'We'd both had a skinful and I just played right into his hands and exploded.'

'Exploded how?' I studied the man standing before me with increasing alarm. Proud Jackson's shoulders had slumped, his head had sunk against his chest, and when he lifted his eyes again they were moist. Oh God, I squirmed, perhaps this was more serious than the usual drunken fracas.

'I should never have come here tonight, this is all a mistake,' he snuffled. 'How can a poor fisherman's troubles matter to a man like you?'

'They do matter. Come, things can't be that bad.'

'They are. I think I've really killed him this time.'

'This time?'

'Yes, I dropped him once before.'

'Do you know for certain he's dead?'

'He didn't get up after I hit him.' Jackson rubbed his elbow fiercely across his wet eyes.

'But do you know he's dead?' I persisted.

'If he's not, he should be. And I'll never be able to afford your fees to get me off for doing it,' moaned Jackson.

'Don't worry about fees now. Not until we've established the facts.'

'I can feel the rope round my neck already.'

'Can I get you a drink?' I reached up and briefly squeezed Jackson's limp hand, a hand, I suspected, that was usually very strong.

Jackson shook his head, saying with the flicker of a self-conscious smile, 'Things must be bad, I believe I'm too upset to swallow anything.'

'Tell me,' I asked soothingly. 'Who were these friends Lane maligned to make you so angry?'

'Both my sweetheart and my daughter,' he murmured. 'Lane said that dead lass on the scaur t' other day could be my lass. He said it could have been me that killed her, not Dan.'

'You're married then.' I was surprised having assumed Jackson to be something of a loner like me.

'No, no, I had a bairn out of wedlock many years past.' Jackson hung his head once more, projecting his confession to the floorboards. 'The mother was sent away afore I got a chance to put things right, not that her family would allow me to anyway. And I never set eyes on my bairn from that day to this.'

'How do you know the child was a daughter?'

'I was told.'

'Do you know where she is now?'

'Living a long way off.' Jackson let out the sigh of a beaten man.

'So why should Lane suppose the dead girl might be her?'

Jackson shook his head. He had already pondered the same question long and hard. 'Whether it was her or no, I've killed him for saying it.'

'You don't really know that for sure yet.'

'Twill be a miracle if he's survived such a blow, believe me, sir. What's more I think he told the police 'twas me what murdered the girl.'

'And did you?'

'Of course not. I doubt they would have taken much notice of Lane anyhow.'

'Oh, why is that?'

'He's not the class of person the police listen to,' shrugged Jackson.

'And I am, I suppose.' I smiled ironically, not bothering to wait for Jackson's reply. 'Have I got this right, it wasn't so much what Lane might have said to the police that made you hit him but the fact that he accused you, to your face, of murdering your lost daughter?'

'Just so,' nodded Jackson. 'And more.'

'What more?'

'He called them both whores.'

'Tell me, were there any other witnesses to this quarrel between you and Lane?'

'Not that I know of. Lane and I were taking a quiet piss round the back of the Cod and Lobster.'

'Some quiet piss.'

'Yes, indeed, sir.' Jackson's expression remained glum.

'Where does Lane live?'

'Corner house top of the Barris.'

'I'll tell you what we'll do, Jackson. I'll make some enquiries on your behalf in the morning. Meanwhile, you keep out of sight until I contact you.'

'You'll find me at the black and yellow cottage on Weatherill Street.'

'The colours of your boat.'

'You have a good memory, sir.'

'It is a vital requirement of my profession,' I laughed, springing up to show Jackson the door.

Jackson paused on the landing outside. He turned back and said by way of an afterthought, 'If and when I get out of this present predicament, sir, would you fancy a day's potting out in my boat?'

'Potting?'

'Ay, potting for crabs or maybe a gentleman like you prefers the taste of lobster.'

'Good, a lobster, my fee for a morning's work.' Lifting my hand I gave him a brief wave, never believing for a moment he was sincere in his offer of a boat trip, but, nevertheless, praying I would find some reassuring news for the fisherman the next day.

Chapter Seventeen

A jingling of keys, a grinding lock. The door opened. Two men stood silhouetted by the gas lit passage beyond.

Clang! The door closed as the two men walked from that world into his – into his slow uninspired world where even Captain Cook was becoming difficult to resurrect – he reacted slowly.

'Get to your feet,' shouted the warder, trying to kick him into activity. 'Governor's visit.'

'I have received a letter from someone who knows you,' said the governor.

Straw clung to Daniel's breeches and jacket, he stunk of piss and shit like a beast. An oily stain glistened beneath his armpits, the governor could smell the lad's fear. He seemed as surprised as the governor that anyone should know him.

'Stand up straight when the governor is addressing you.' The warder gave the shin on one of Daniel's bent legs another kick.

'That's enough, Goater,' the governor told the warder. That's enough, he thought, because unbelievably someone was taking an interest in this poor simpleton. He turned back to the prisoner and asked, 'Would you like this person who's written to visit you?'

Daniel stared ahead, he blinked at the small beam of light escaping from the sky into his cell through the high window.

'Answer the governor when he asks you a question,' snarled Goater.

'Mam?'

'No, this isn't a letter from your mother,' explained the governor, fluttering the white page in the air.

'Not Mam?' Daniel's face registered disappointment.

'No, this is a letter from a Mr Cairn,' continued the governor, pronouncing each word loudly and deliberately as if his charge were deaf. 'Mr Cairn is a man of law.'

'My friend.' Daniel's large puzzled forehead straightened a little.

'Yes, your friend,' sighed the governor. 'Would you like me to read out his letter?'

Daniel nodded eagerly, nodded like a grateful dog, he felt like a dog kennelled up in this place all day long. A dog among dogs. Goater savaged him like a dog. Goater didn't like him singing. Goater didn't like him talking to himself, telling himself stories about Captain Cook to wile away the hours. Goater didn't like anything human. Goater's face was as bitter as if he'd swallowed a mouthful of nettles.

'Calls me "dog", "no better than a dog",' Daniel told the governor.

'What on earth does he mean?' The governor appealed to Goater for enlightenment.

'No idea, sir, talks nonsense all day.'

The governor's spectacles glinted as he adjusted them round his large tufted ears.

'Dear Sir,' he began. The rich paper rustled in his hand once more.

My name is James Cairn and I am a barrister in chambers at York. I believe I already have had the pleasure of making your acquaintance once or twice during the course of my career.

According to his mother, Mrs Flora Robertshaw, you have a Daniel Robertshaw enjoying your protection at present. I understand that Mr Robertshaw is in the Castle at York for his own welfare as much as for anything else. I should be obliged if you would arrange a visit for me in the next few weeks, subject to Mr Robertshaw's agreement of course.

Your Obedient Servant,

James C. Cairn.'

The governor gave a schoolboy's self-conscious cough as if he had just read out a complicated piece of text before the whole class.

The tick, tick, of prison life hurt it was so slow. Never mind, James, his champion, would soon be striding in. And then surely his friend would take him home to the sea.

'Regrettably,' the governor was saying, 'Mr Cairn isn't fully up to date with your present situation. My advice is you'd do well to see him.' Daniel nodded, his expression mimicking the governor's seriousness. 'Get him cleaned up, Goater, for God's sake,' commanded the governor, turning from Daniel in disgust. Daniel blanched, knowing his mam and Aunt Alice would disapprove of the governor's blasphemy.

* * * * *

The sky was dark and heavy with clouds. Summer rain tumbled down on Staithes – not warm, tropical Captain Cook Queensland rain but cold, weighted northern hemisphere rain – this was nothing out of the ordinary for Staithes and people scuttled about their business as usual.

I hadn't to travel far in my quest for news of Lane. The smooth surface of Webster's steps glistened with wet as I made a precarious descent, almost stumbling into Lane ascending from the bottom. Lane was mounting one step at a time with great difficulty. He was cursing and swearing maniacally and both his eyes were circled in black like a racoon from the Americas.

'What's 'appened to you?' A fisherwoman, basket on head, shouted up to Lane from the High Street.

'Mind it, bitch,' growled Lane, turning to jab a finger crudely towards his nose. A nose that was bent, swollen and unmistakably broken.

'May the devil take you for the snivelling whelp that you are, Job Lane.' The fisherwoman gestured indecently back with one finger.

I could not resist smiling at these bestial references. I was not too sure about the woman but a "snivelling whelp" just about summed up Lane.

'What's so amusing?' asked Lane, reeling towards me on the slippery steps. 'I'd have thought any friend of the Chinaman had little left to smirk about now.'

'Watch where you're going.' I reached out to steady him, he was threatening to fall all over me. Was he drunk? – or was it the blow he'd received? – or both?

'Rudder smacked me in t' face, if you must know, Miss Busy-body.' Lane turned back to the fisherwoman, no doubt realising that his initial lack of explanation might cause more unwelcome curiosity on the street.

'Well, it's failed to knock any sense into your 'ead,' cackled the fisherwoman, readjusting the balance of her basket resting on its cloth roller ring.

'Sense is summat unknown to the likes of ye, daft tart,' persisted Lane, determined to have the last word.

By now I'd heard and seen enough of Lane.

'Been lying low, have you? Because I know what happened to you the other night,' I whispered into his ear, pushing him roughly against the wall of a house, my arms pinning his arms helplessly by his side.

'What the hell?' he gasped, completely taken unawares.

'You offended a friend of mine the other night.'

'What's that's to you?' jeered Lane gamely enough.

'It's everything to me because it's not the first time you've insulted someone I like. You even had the cheek to insult some lady acquaintants of mine, I seem to remember, and I let you get away with it then. But not this time, this time I'll let nothing pass.' I leaned my fourteen stone bulk harder into wiry Lane, flattening him against the stonework. 'Now listen carefully, Lane, do you know you can go to prison for slander?'

'You talk of slander when you're assaulting me.' Lane's black swollen eyes reverted to cunning swollen slits.

I pulled back a little. Lane might be one of the lowest forms of life but he certainly had a shrewd sense of self-preservation. 'Tell me, is there any truth in that story you told Jackson about the dead girl and his illegitimate daughter being one and the same?'

'Jackson, Jackson,' belittled Lane contemptuously. 'So, the African has finally won you over along with the rest of 'em.'

'Is that why you tried to upset him with a vicious lie?'

'How do you mean, *sir*?'

'You are purely and simply jealous of a better man.'

'"Better"?' sneered Lane, attempting to shake off my readjusted grasp.

'What other reason is there?'

'Truth. Maybe there was some truth in what I told him.'

'Only some?'

'You can try and twist my words as much as you like but I know what I know.'

'Did you tell the police you believed Jackson to be a murderer?'

'That's between me and the police and possibly a court of law, as you well know, Mr Barrister.'

I knew I would get no further with him, knew he had made his point perhaps better than I had myself. As I watched him shamble off up the steps, my fear was not that he would bring a charge of common assault against Jackson or even one of minor assault against me – no, he would lose too much of his already waning credibility locally for that – what he might have to say further afield regarding either Daniel, or Jackson, was a far bigger concern. Lane was a loose cannon, a man without principle, a resourceful and dangerous man with many real or imagined grievances.

If it had not been for the restraints of the law, I would have loved to emulate Jackson and do a little further damage to Lane's repugnant face.

'Good news. Lane is sore of head but intact and very much alive.' I told Jackson, a few minutes later, outside the door of the black and yellow cottage.

'That fella's head must be as hard as iron. How have you found out so soon?'

'I could lie and say it was through sheer professionalism but, in truth, it was purely a stroke of luck – I literally ran into him.'

'And you're sure he is well?'

'I have known of at least one delayed death after receiving a head wound. But, unfortunately, I think Lane's skull is so thick he would live on after being crushed under a herd of charging bull elephants.'

'That's good fortune for me though, Mr Cairn.'

'Indeed, but mark my words, Jackson, I wouldn't risk fate being kind to you a third time. There must be more subtle ways of dealing with Mr Lane.'

'Perhaps there will be no need. Perhaps he has finally learnt his lesson.'

'I doubt it very much with a man like Lane. He appears as spiteful and unbowed as ever.'

'Come in, come in, I'm forgetting my manners. Let's put Lane behind us for the present, sir.'

I was startled by the sensation of Jackson's arm engulfing me as I was hustled off Weatherill Street and down into his cottage dungeon.

Standing in Jackson's parlour, I was eye-level with the cobblestone street outside. As well as being badly lit the sunken room was sparingly furnished and had that musty damp smell of extreme age. Jackson indicated an upright chair. Suddenly feeling shivery cold I drew the chair closer to the low fire. Jackson said nothing, allowing me to adjust to my surroundings a minute or two longer. An old dresser in the corner displayed a few cracked crockery pieces; a modern seaman's telescope was edged in dust on an old rickety table; a clock on the wall ticked towards the correct hour. The only frivolous adornment in Jackson's entire living space hung from two faded ribbons secured to the wall close to the clock – a glass rolling-pin with a matt reproduction of Notre-Dame Cathedral painted on its reflecting surface – perhaps a memento of a long ago trip made to the gay city by some better-to-do relative.

'Nice.' I nodded to the rolling-pin.

'Father won that afore I was born for runner-up in the sacks.'

'Sacks?'

'Ay, sack race, run annually at Steers Feast in t' top field.'

'You live here entirely alone then?' I turned my attention awkwardly back to my host and away from the rolling-pin.

'Ay, Mam and Father are long since dead. And as you know I'm not wed, not yet anyways,' winked Jackson.

'Do you get lonely?'

'Do you?' shot back Jackson.

'Sometimes,' I admitted.

'You wouldn't be so lonely sharing a hearth with Miss Good, I dare say,' suggested Jackson. 'Seen you two about Steers together.'

'No, but I have many interests.'

'And I have the sea,' said Jackson, as if no further explanation for our mutual lack of marital status was necessary.

'The sea indeed.' I scrutinised Jackson's face partially illuminated by the firelight. The more our paths crossed, the more I found the fisherman intriguing. He was well-lined for his thirty plus years but these grids of concentration and emotion only served to add greater mystery to an already mysterious face. As I had previously noticed, when first setting eyes on Jackson from Cowbar Bridge, his dark looks stood out in Staithes where most men still walked tall and blond like their Viking ancestors. It had been fanciful of me to imagine Jackson's origins might be Minoan – Mediterranean at least, almond-eyed Mediterranean most certainly – but perhaps Jackson's forebears had cast off from the Barbary coast rather than a Cretan shore. Had there been something in Lane despisingly calling Jackson "the African"? Barbary pirates had virtually ruled British waters in the not so distant past, looting and carrying off whole villages as slaves, but this was not something a great empire wished to acknowledge.

'You are deep in thought, sir.' Jackson's very Yorkshire voice.

'Yes, I was thinking I came to Staithes to holiday and add to my fossil collection, yet somehow I have unwittingly become embroiled in a possible murder. One man is detained in prison, one man has been unofficially accused of the supposed crime by another, and still the alleged victim has not been named.'

'Have you had word of Dan Robertshaw, Mr Cairn?'

'I wrote to the prison governor a day or two ago enquiring about his well-being. On behalf of his poor mother, you understand?'

'And will you be helping the lad, sir?'

'It is for Daniel to decide who is to help him. There is one thing that is beyond doubt though.'

'What is that, Mr Cairn?'

'I cannot represent two men named in the same case.' I observed Jackson closely again. The fisherman appeared to be solicitous enough regarding Daniel Robertshaw's welfare but with some men it is difficult to tell. What if there was an iota of truth in Lane's allegation against Jackson? I could be staring into the face of a cool amoral murderer right now. I began tapping my iron heel cap on the flagged floor. There was something troubling me about this affair, some insignificant fact that was just out of reach but if retrieved would make matters clearer.

'Tell me, Mr Cairn, when you talked to Lane did he blacken my name further?'

'You could say that.' I felt the edges of my mouth twitching at Jackson's unwitting pun. Blacken, black, black African – my brow creased, hit by a sudden notion. 'Tell me, Jackson, did you see the dead girl when they brought her in?'

'Yes, why?' Jackson looked startled.

'Close to?' I asked. Jackson nodded. 'So, what was the colour of her hair?'

'Fair. Very fair.'

'And her general complexion?'

'Pale, I'd say, but it's difficult to tell in death.'

'Of course it is. But you said her hair was blonde, very blonde?'

'No, more white than blonde,' corrected Jackson. 'You are thinking it is doubtful she is my lass because of her colouring.'

'Indeed, indeed,' I murmured deep in thought.

'I did wonder about that myself.'

'Did you? That's interesting.'

'But it has been known for a bairn to skip a generation. My own mother was fair-haired.'

'Was she really? – and you're so dark.'

Jackson looked uncomfortable at this. 'I do intend honouring my debt to you, sir,' he said, changing the subject.

'Debt?' I was momentarily disconcerted.

'Remember, the offer of a potting trip out in my coble?'

'You have a coble as well as the bigger boat?'

'That I do.'

I wondered if I should insist on the mule. A mule seemed less vulnerable than her smaller cousin the coble. 'Yes, I …' Oh, damn, I thought, suddenly faced with the reality of Jackson's promised sea trip repayment. I could not swim a stroke and only recently I had seen how men die out there. 'You don't have to do this, this isn't really necessary.'

'Tomorrow night?' cut in Jackson.

'But I'm leaving the next day,' I protested.

'Tomorrow night at eight it is then,' confirmed Jackson, with a friendly thump that was enough to thrust my lungs through my rib-cage.

Chapter Eighteen

I was on the beach below the staithe promptly at 8 p.m. There was no sign of Jackson. I was relieved that the sea appeared calm and the light was still good.

One, two, three … I sat on the side of a coble in a uniform line of a dozen boats and wondered which was Jackson's.

Two merged figures were silhouetted at the edge of the sea. A man and woman linked arm in arm. A couple obviously enjoying an after-dinner stroll. My heart fell as I recognised the approaching athletic gait of Rosie Good. She said something to her older escort, who raised his hat politely in my direction. Somehow I knew this must be the "Gorgeous Pompey" Rosie had mention at the funeral. Giggling they continued past and I felt the same terrific sense of exclusion, the same stab of jealousy that I once experienced on hearing Harold's and Laura's laughter coming up to me from almost exactly the same spot on the beach. I felt disconsolate, disconnected, more than ever without connection to anything or anyone. It was at times like this that I became aware others might consider me very odd.

'I see you've found her then?'

I swung round to see Jackson standing behind me grinning.

'What do you mean?' I asked defensively.

'My coble, you're sitting on her.'

I bent over to look down the curving strakes of the vessel to see if any enlightenment was there. I saw nothing. 'It's through pure chance, I assure you, all these boats look exactly the same to me.'

'*My Friend*. Her name is painted aft, under your bum, sir.' Jackson's grin had widened.

Wriggling my buttocks off the improvised seat I saw the painted name now, saw the sad irony of Jackson's choice of name.

'Nice touch,' I told him.

'At least this is one friend that has never let me down.'

'No, and I hope she doesn't today.' I had a little irony left of my own despite my fear of taking to the water.

'You've not been out in a boat before, have you?' he asked, as the two of us struggled to inch the coble seaward.

'Not one this small although it's heavy enough,' I panted. 'I've sailed in bigger boats to Piraeus and then on to the Greek Islands.'

'Greek Islands, eh? Old Greece,' he remarked with passing interest.

'Yes, Ancient Greece,' I said, thinking some Minoan this.

The coble stuck in the lumpy shale half-way down the beach. Luckily, Nathaniel Nab, perched in his usual position on the staithe, saw our plight and summoned more youthful help to get *My Friend* afloat.

'Been sent for from Whitby. There's to be an inquest on the woman who died in t' fire. Have thou heard ought?' I overheard the old man asking Jackson. Nab had condescended to join in with the fun down on the beach without making much of a pretence at pushing.

'Ay, got word myself today,' replied Jackson.

'What will we say?' asked Nab.

'Only as much as we have to,' replied Jackson under his breath, elbowing Nab aside as the coble slid into the water and he boarded her effortlessly. 'Climb up quickly,' he shouted across to me as he took up the long oars. 'We've a fleet of creel pots to check.'

Feet, socks, boots drenched, I did my best not to upset the craft as I scissor-kicked over the side and fell backwards into her belly. The four young launchers and Nab doubled over with laughter.

'You've taken on summat here, Mr Jackson,' shouted one lad, his freckled cheeks as red as his mop of hair.

'That's enough,' retorted Jackson, pulling away through the breaking water's edge as I manoeuvred onto the narrow bench seat opposite. 'Thanks for your help, lads.'

'Where are these creel pots?' I asked tersely.

'Along the coast, barely a mile out.'

'A mile out?'

'Ay, a sea mile out.'

'A sea mile, that's longer than a land mile, isn't it?' There was unmistakable panic in my question.

'Don't worry your head about that for the time being. We'll creep along hugging the coastline at first. Now take up yon rudder and bear starboard keeping us parallel to land.'

'How many pots of yours are out there?'

'Oh, I only shot a score this morning as I knew 'twas you and me alone to do the haling.'

'How many do you usually shoot?'

'Thirty-five to forty,' yawned Jackson. His yawn obviously a comment on the labour involved.

'We must be approximately over the rocks of Scar Shootings where Daniel was spotted with that girl at low tide,' I said with a sudden sense of foreboding.

'Ay, but it's not known as Scar Shootings locally.'

'Why? What is it called then?'

'See that high cliff over yonder?' Jackson gestured with his head. ''Tis where menfolk empty the closet buckets over into the water. We call this stretch Sky Shittings.'

My hand jerked on the long rudder arm as a small wave tumbled beneath the keel-less hull. I was already feeling slightly nauseous without a discussion on Staithes lack of sanitation. I prayed I would be able to see this voyage through without disgracing myself.

'Keep her steady,' commanded Jackson.

'I'm not the world's greatest sailor,' I mumbled. Jackson did not seem to be listening.

'Alus go with the wave when possible, never let 'em take you by surprise. Though there's little enough wind tonight, nothing to either aid or trouble us.' The oarsman powered on, his amateur helmsman could do nothing but marvel at his strength. 'Fix your eyes on something distant, rocks sticking out at Lingrow Knock say, Kettleness even.'

For much of the way I followed instructions, that is until my weather-eye caught something white and fluttering on the periphery, something tempting my curiosity closer to shore – a shore I wished with all my heart to be closer to. A flag or a yacht about to put out with unfurling sail? A seagull's wing perhaps? But there was no wind and for once no seagull. The temptation was too great and my attention turned from Lingrow Knock to the shore of Port Mulgrave. I could see Jackson following my line of interest. He, likewise, saw in an instant it was none of these more obvious things.

Instead of the expected reprimand for not keeping my mind on the job, Jackson screamed, 'God help us, I thought it was a mermaid.'

'No,' I sighed. 'Only Laura Johnson's model shivering in the evening air.'

'I'm not surprised that scant dress hardly covers her. The blood's fair coursing through my veins.'

'Laura must be trying for some effect with the fading light.'

'Ah, Laura is it,' remarked Jackson knowingly.

The model and her white flimsy dress were draped across a rock near the water's edge. Laura had left her easel and was making some adjustment to the model's arm.

There was something very gentle in the way she touched the other young woman, loving almost, a supreme attention to detail. I waved across to the women but they were too engrossed to see me. Laura Johnson in her element, Laura happy. This was one of those moments that would be painted indelibly on my memory. This was an image of Laura I would gladly carry away with me. This was when I first suspected that she, not Rosie or even Harold, would be the one destined for great things.

'Fancy, still out painting at this hour,' said Jackson. 'Well beyond the call of duty, wouldn't you say? Why don't you shout across to them?' he suggested. 'They'll hear you from here.'

I shook my head, feeling a shout would be an intrusion. I turned for a last glimpse of the two women on the rock. The scene of making art was a work of art itself, I was satisfied to leave it at that.

'You are very quiet, Mr Cairn,' said Jackson, after we had rowed on in silence for a while.

'Just thinking, that's all,' I replied evasively. I could have told Jackson that I was suffering from pangs of jealously again. But jealousy and envy are such ugly emotions they are best kept to oneself. All the same, why wasn't I the man back there in Staithes silhouetted against the sunset with Rosie Good?

'Pull hard to port and then straighten up.' Jackson's down to earth voice was a rude interruption into my romantic fantasising. I gave him a mocking salute. 'Keep your hands on that rudder,' he growled.

My fear-induced bravado started to break down once Jackson began stroking directly out into the abyss. The rhythm of my thumping heart was only superseded by the splash of Jackson's oars breaking the water. I held my breath, my nerve had held so far.

'There's this thing troubling me, rolling about in my head all the time, and I've had a mind to ask you about it for a while,' broached Jackson cautiously.

'Go ahead.'

'If it had been my lass spread out dead like that for all the world to see, wouldn't I have felt summat special, different?'

'You mean would you have recognised her as your own?'

'Ay, my own flesh and blood like, even though I'd never set eyes on her living.'

'How can I say for sure?'

'No, no, nothing is for sure but what do you think?'

'It's not beyond the realms of possibility.'

'Ay,' agreed Jackson, maintaining his high stroke rate. The strenuous activity seemed to have loosened his tongue.

'Well, did you feel anything extraordinary?' I asked.

'Nothing, nothing but pity.'

I leant forward over the coble's side. The sea bottom far from being feet deep appeared to be fathoms deep now.

'Ten fathoms deep,' explained Jackson, reading my apprehension. 'Too deep for my pots but don't worry we'll soon get back onto a shallow scaur.'

'How soon?' I asked, leaning over the side once more to scowl down into the depths.

'Over there.' Jackson suspended his rowing and jerked his head round to appraise the way ahead. 'See, my buoys are still in place.'

I saw nothing. The slight sensation of nausea had returned since leaning over the side of the boat. I would take Jackson's word for it, take his word for anything.

'We aren't going out any further then?' I quavered.

'No, no, pull a little to port.'

I swung the rudder arm, the boat turned a little and I could see the buoys now, a whole line of them, two bigger buoys marked the line's beginning and end.

'It's always a wonder to me to find t' pots where I left 'em in all this sea and I've been shooting 'em since a boy. Course once or twice I've shot 'em in fair weather and later a storm's brewed up, and by the time I've got back to 'em they've all been buggered.'

'What storm?'

'Any storm, storms can come at anytime.'

'I wish you'd row me back right away.'

'Don't take on so,' Jackson told me as if he were addressing a child. The fisherman was glowing amid his creel pots like a gambler at the card table. 'You come and sit over here and take the oars, so as I can hale up me pots. If luck will have it a nice little lobster might have crawled through one of t' smouts into the parlour.'

'I am quite capable of hauling,' I objected, irritated by Jackson's demeaning attitude. 'I've hauled myself up and down enough cliff faces in my time.'

Jackson's open palm gestured appeasement. 'If you're doing the haling then, use the natural swell of water. As the coble slides into the trough reach overboard as low down the tow as you can get, when you feel her rise up pull for all you're worth.'

I toiled to get the first two netted cages aboard. They were empty, their stinking bait untouched. The third contained a fair sized crab. Jackson instructed me on how to avoid the creature's pincers while extracting it from the netted parlour and back out through one of the tunnelling smouts. The fourth, fifth and sixth – nothing. It was backbreaking work for so little reward.

''Tis a little early in the season, that's the trouble,' grumbled Jackson, who was rebaiting the pots and heaving them back into the sea on the opposite side of the boat to me.

I worked on, nausea forgotten despite the stench of rotting fish bait. Manning the rudder I had fallen cold, now I felt hot and tracks of sweat were running down my face. The seventh pot did contain a lobster but, disappointingly, Jackson insisted I threw the undersized "nanycock" back into the sea.

A few more small crabs came up in the creel pots to be instantly rejected by a shake of Jackson's head, and returned by a subdued me back into their inky environment. It was not until pot thirteen that a more promising specimen emerged caged from the deep.

'A miffy,' pronounced Jackson after a brief inspection.

'I see, "a miffy",' I repeated none the wiser.

'See, the crab's lost its big claws. Hardly worth keeping.'

Bump! There was a sudden thud against the coble's hull and for a second time I found myself supine in the bottom of the boat, this time legs tangled about the miffy's creel pot.

'What was that?' I asked, too frightened to move.

'Listen,' Jackson put a warning finger to his lips.

A second bump against the lower strakes of the boat.

'Oh God.' The vibration passed through my body – a mechanical shudder – adding to my terror. I pulled myself back onto the helmsman's seat, creel hauling forgotten.

'I'm not sure what's going on,' admitted Jackson, leaning from side to side for a better view.

'Are we sinking?'

'Shouldn't think so.' Jackson's assurance was less than convincing. He still looked mystified.

Bump again. It was as if the coble was a floating door and a giant's hand was thumping for admittance. My arms spread-eagled the body of the boat. I was petrified.

'Something seems to be having a go at us,' said Jackson.

'What something?' I felt close to hysteria.

'Ah, I see it now.'

'See what?'

'A tail.'

'What sort of tail?'

'Shark. A shark is diving beneath our boat, playing with us,' he explained, retaining an interested detachment.

'Will it overturn us?'

'Not if we don't provoke it.'

'You didn't tell me there were sharks out here,' I complained, my voice full of recrimination.

'There aren't many,' he replied coolly. 'Would you believe me if I told you this is only the second shark I've ever seen in my entire life at sea? Look at him, he's come nearer to the surface, he's beautiful.'

'"Beautiful"? When he's eyeing us up and down for a late supper.'

'No, no, you've got it wrong. This is a basking shark, he's not interested in human flesh, in flesh of any kind. He's only curious. We'll just rest here awhile and he'll get tired and go away.'

'But isn't it getting late?' I looked anxiously across to the sun which appeared to be dropping lower by the minute on the western horizon.

'No, plenty of daylight left yet.'

'I can't swim,' I finally admitted.

'Neither can I,' laughed Jackson.

'And I was relying on you to save me.'

'Save you to where out here?'

I looked around and silently acknowledged we were in the middle of a watery nowhere. And as it appeared we were not going anywhere either for the time being, I dared myself to look overboard in the interests of science. The shark was about thirty-five feet long, grey-brown in colour with very long gill slits. Sleek and casual in its movements, it got close enough alongside the boat for me to have stroked its oily skin. Although this fish had reassuringly small teeth, I could not help remembering the sharp teeth of the adult female ichthyosaur I had dreamt about a few days ago. Jackson had implied that the basking shark was a plankton eater, that is why it did not need a set of razor teeth. Nevertheless, many of the skeletal fossils I had seen were the archetypes of modern sea predators akin to this one.

'*Cetorhinus maximus*,' I whispered in awe to myself.

'Maybe the shark will bring us luck, Mr Cairn,' said Jackson cheerfully.

'Maybe,' I replied with little confidence.

We idled away for a few more minutes in the gently lapping waves. The shark made no more attacks on the coble. He or she seemed to have grown accustomed to us before gradually losing interest all together and leisurely making off for deeper water.

'Strange thing about big fish, those that look fierce often aren't and those that look more friendly will bite your hand off,' said Jackson.

'Men can be like that,' I retorted.

Jackson looked away, looked to the more comfortable familiarity of the sea.

'Are you wondering what sort of man I am?' he asked.

'I must admit you are something of an enigma.'

'We'd best finish getting them pots in.'

Exhausted by shark fear, labour and empty creel pots, by pot seventeen I was dead on my feet. I could not have had a better demonstration of the hardships and tough realities of a coble fisherman's daily existence. All we need now is a storm, I thought.

'What have we here?' Jackson carefully unhooked and removed something from discarded pot seventeen, as I tried to straighten my back. 'A good size lobster, all of eight inches from beak to tail, and it's legal and not in berry.' Jackson's strong teeth flashed up towards me. 'This un's yours.'

With all the pots baited and re-shot, a few crabs and my lobster crawling in a sack in the bottom of the boat, we set off for the shore in the fading light. Back at the helm again, I found that some of my earlier adventurous notions about the lot of Staithes fishermen were reawakened.

'Were you truly not frightened by that shark?' I asked Jackson.

'No, I knew he was harmless enough,' he shrugged. 'I'm more worried by creatures that steal the food from my mouth.'

'Hunt like men, you mean?'

'Ay, like men,' agreed a gleaming-eyed Jackson. He pointed to an amber glow high on the cliff top, saying with undisguised pride, 'That's where I get me 'ezzells from.' I stared at him blankly. 'Brigham Hall. Hazel rods for the arches on me creel pots. I've got a permit to cut 'em down from the gamekeeper up there.'

'Isn't that Sir Hugh Parke's place?'

'Do you know him?'

'I've seen his wife once or twice in the village. He was with her at Jacob Fines' funeral. Do *you* know him?' I bounced back the question.

'Should do, shouldn't I?' he laughed derisively. 'I'm one of his... let me get this right ... constituents, isn't that what we're called?' I nodded, but Jackson hardly stopped to take breath. 'But, no, I can't say I'm exactly on familiar terms with Sir Hugh at present though once, before he got too big for his boots, I was better acquainted with him. Now Marlett, his gamekeeper, that's a different matter. Marlett and I go back a long way. Marlett is, as you would say, still one of the boys.'

'And Sir Hugh isn't?'

'Sir Hugh,' pondered Jackson. 'Nobody really knows about Sir Hugh. He rarely shows his face in the village these days. It was his father who made most of their money shipping coal, investments, that sort of thing, well afore Sir Hugh went into government. Can't say either of 'em did anything for us fishermen, apart from allowing us to cut down one or two 'ezzells from their grand estate.'

'You sound bitter.'

'You'd sound bitter, Mr Cairn, if steam trawlers were robbing you of a living and nobody in authority to help.'

'Doesn't being out here in this darkness bother you at all?' I asked, gathering up my jacket collar. The sweat from pot hauling had suddenly turned cold.

'Not as frightened as I am at having to attend that inquest into Alice Jeffrey's death.'

'Tell the truth, that's all.'

'The truth?' he groaned.

'Yes, simply tell them who torched the Robertshaws' cottage, the men involved.'

'If you'll pardon me for saying so, you've no idea, Mr Cairn. I have to live and work in Steers. Whatever we think about each other privately, Steers men never inform against one another.'

'But a terrible wrong has been done,' I interrupted.

'Not deliberately. They only set that fire because the militia men were coming and they wanted to drive the Robertshaws out. It was never intended for someone to die.'

'Nonetheless, a serious crime has been committed.'

'You asked me a moment ago how I felt out here in this darkness. Well, Steers is like this boat and the rest of the world is the sea in darkness.'

'Lane was instrumental in the burning down of the Robertshaws' cottage, wasn't he?' The sudden realisation came to me as if waterborne. Out here in the North Sea was like being on top of a mountain, away from the clutter and clamour of daily life my thoughts had become incisive.

'That old woman's death was an accident, Mr Cairn, however you look at it.' Jackson paused on the oars.

'Lane didn't hold back in making an accusation against you to the police though, did he?'

'He said he did,' shrugged Jackson. 'You can't believe a word that bastard says.'

'You seemed bothered enough about it at the time.'

'That was then, this is now, I thought I'd killed the man. You can't really expect my code of honour to fall as short as Lane's, Mr Cairn?'

'Code of honour?' I was incredulous. I pitied the coroner having to conduct his inquest in such an atmosphere of duplicity. Suddenly I became aware of the wide social gulf that existed between myself and this man. A gulf made all the more real by his increased and aggravating use of my surname. What did I really know about this man? Was he to be trusted? Whatever else there was in his past, he had at least one illegitimate progeny to his name that I knew of. Damn, the evening shouldn't be ending in scepticism like this.

Helmsman and oarsman moved on through the night, one oil lamp and a subtler shaft of moonlight spotlighting our unease, nothing but the splash and lapping of water intruded on our difficult silence.

We strained to pull the coble on its rolling long oars above the high-water mark. Once Jackson was satisfied the boat was safe for the night, he picked up the sack of crustaceans.

'Tell me,' I turned to him as we clambered up onto the staithe. 'If that dead girl, splayed out on here the other day, had been your natural daughter, would you still maintain your silence on behalf of her killer?'

'But it wasn't her.' Jackson pounded his fist against his heart. 'I know from inside, it can't have been her.'

'Whoever she was, would you protect her killer because he was a Staithes man?'

'You are talking about deliberate murder now, Mr Cairn.'

'So, if you were asked to testify, would it be for or against Daniel Robertshaw in the interests of justice?'

'I've already told you, I don't know if Dan Robertshaw did it or not.' Jackson resolutely hitched the sack higher up his shoulder before turning away for Weatherill Street.

'Thank you for my education in seamanship, Jackson,' I shouted after him.

'You are a clever man with words, Mr Cairn,' came his muffled rebuff.

'No, Mr Jackson, I am a careful man with the truth.'

Chapter Nineteen

It was one of those mornings. I woke up convinced that something was terribly wrong. My first thought was that I was leaving Staithes on the afternoon train, back to work gloom. Next, a more overriding melancholia hit me with the realisation that the potting trip with Jackson had ended in failure. Jackson had even walked off with my promised lobster. And finally there was Rosie, Rosie and her man on the beach.

Standing before the dressing mirror, I pushed back my avalanche of fringe and began to examine the first suspicion of a receding hairline. Why, I wondered, did Rosie and I – Jackson and I – never get on an even keel. I watched my reflection smile vacuously. Staithes cobles don't have keels, I mouthed back to myself, just flat bottoms. Perhaps it was something in me that was wrong, something wrong in my general approach to relationships. Those I loved or liked often did not respond to me and those unfortunates who took to me, well, more often than not I lost interest in them. Pathetic really – my fingers deftly fastened my trouser buttons.

After working through Mrs Shaw's son's hurriedly delivered breakfast tray, I took up my spectacles and started to read through some legal papers forwarded by my clerk of chambers, Martin Trotter. An accusation of physical assault during an affray outside a public house in York, a shop theft. I let out a deep despondent sigh – boring everyday stuff – my holiday it would seem was effectively at an end.

'Mr Cairn, Mr Cairn, there's someone come to see you.' Mrs Shaw's piercing voice from below. She must have considered the visitor to be of higher status than Jackson for she was providing no opposition. I merely wished that Mrs Veazey's non-literary double would take the trouble to climb the stairs, knock on my door, and more importantly modulate her voice to a whisper. I stepped out on the landing.

'Who?' I asked. Not Jackson, so who? My heart skipped a beat, Rosie perhaps?

'It's Mrs Fines, whose husband Robert is still missing at sea,' announced Mrs Shaw with all the brutal honesty of Staithes.

'Send Mrs Fines up,' I shouted back, a sinking feeling in the pit of my stomach. Mrs Fines senior and her grief was all I needed to add to my own depressed state. I returned to my rooms completely dispirited.

I recognised the tall woman stooped in the doorway straightaway. She was the woman who had been shrieking the death wail along the staithe. Much of her face had been obscured by a headscarf at her son's funeral, now that exposed face wore the determined fearlessness of someone with little left to lose.

'Come in.' I offered her the most comfortable armchair.

'I'm sorry to trouble you, Mr Cairns.'

'Cairn,' I corrected without much thought, before chastising myself for being so pernickety with this poor widow in all but name.

Mrs Fines took a deep breath and started again, 'Mr Cairn, I am a close friend of Mrs Crooks, at one time landlady to Miss Laura Johnson.'

'Laura … nothing's wrong is there?' I asked, perhaps a little too edgily.

'No, no, nothing's wrong in Steers,' reassured Mrs Fines. 'Nothing that anything can be done about, that is.'

'So, how can I help you, Mrs Fines?'

'This is very delicate matter, Mr Cairn, and I wouldn't like it to go beyond these four walls.'

'I'll keep whatever you tell me in the strictest confidence, Mrs Fines.'

'I've been told you might be acting for Dan Robertshaw regarding that dead girl.'

'As far as I am aware, he doesn't need representation because he hasn't actually been charged with any offence. Though, yes, I will go so far as saying that I am well-acquainted with Daniel and have his best interests at heart.'

'That was Mrs Crooks' understanding and good enough for me.' Mrs Fines' face twitched. A nervous habit, or due to the stress of the occasion, or the trauma of recent events? – I wasn't sure.

'If this has something to do with Daniel and the dead girl, wouldn't it be wiser to tell the police?'

'Bobbies?' Mrs Fines paled and her twitch increased twofold. 'I've no time for bobbies.'

'Along with the rest of Staithes it seems,' I pointed out, forcing an unexpected smile from the widow.

'I have come here this morning, Mr Cairn, at great risk to my present employment,' she told me. Her expression had changed, her smile was gone. 'I have come to you because I've heard you are a decent man and I want to do the decent thing. I have come because I believe that is what my husband would have advised me to do,' she concluded, focusing on her tightly folded hands resting in her lap.

'The information you are about to give me, will it benefit Daniel Robertshaw or go against him?'

'That is for you to decide, sir.'

I reached for my pen and notebook next to the pile of discarded legal papers.

'Although you are reluctant to speak to the police, would you be willing to repeat what you are about to tell me in a court of law?' I asked.

'If matters get that far and my suspicions are right then I realise I may have to.'

'A court needs facts not suspicions, Mrs Fines.'

'If you truly want to help Dan Robertshaw, Mr Cairn, then it is up to you to turn my suspicions into facts.'

'Even if it costs you your employment?'

'We have already lost so much in Steers that once they find ...' Mrs Fines hesitated, became tearful. 'I feel those of us left in my family might soon uproot for work in Hull or Tees-side anyway.'

'Your full name, please?' As soon as I put pen to paper I knew there was no going back. I was making a professional commitment to a drama that had been stalking me ever since I returned here. If needs be, after all this trouble, the Robertshaws had better retain me now. And I'd only come to Staithes to hunt for fossilised shells and ichthyosaurs.

'Maud Fines.'

'Your address?'

'Seaton Garth.'

'Your employment?'

'I'm a kitchen maid to Lady Clarissa and Sir Hugh Parke of Brigham Hall.'

Once Mrs Fines had gone, I tried to pick up where I had left off with my legal papers. But try as I might I could not summon up any enthusiasm for theft and common assault. I was more interested in piecing together the fascinating events that had taken place right here under my nose, possibly resulting in murder.

Glancing at the widow's informal statement, I began to mull over everything she had said. I had to admit that until my interview with Mrs Fines, I believed the dead girl found with Daniel to be the victim of a straightforward drowning accident and that the Staithes public – whipped up with hysteria and ignorance – had made more of the incident than it deserved. Then there had been the second fatality in the Robertshaw fire, pressing the police into action, forcing them to remove Daniel to the Castle at York for his own protection. At least that is how I had read the situation so far. But now serious doubts were beginning to bubble up into my consciousness. Just suppose foul play was involved here. Suppose the circumstances of the girl's life had been as complex as her death. Then there was Clarissa Parke – I had witnessed her odd agitated behaviour on two occasions for myself before writing her off as a hysteric. Was Lady Clarissa the unknown factor in a difficult equation that had been troubling me for sometime? Conscious, unconscious mind, hysteria, agitation, I was beginning to sound like those newfangled Viennese psychopathology chaps.

'Mr Cairn, Mr Cairn.' Oh no, Mrs Shaw's intrusive voice again, ringing through the house like a dinner gong for a glutted man. 'Someone else to see you.'

'I'm busy with something at the moment.' I did my best, resisting from the landing. 'Can't whoever it is come back later?'

'It's Jackson. He's got something for you. Says he won't come in this time. He's waiting on the step outside,' she announced with a hint of victory.

Jackson was on the staithe talking to Nathaniel Nab by the time I had laced up my boots and descended to sea level. Without a word, Jackson thrust a brown paper parcel into my unprepared arms. After our previous night's differences, I remained a little cool.

'Ready to travel, ready to eat.' Jackson's sensual mouth tilted upwards full of bonhomie.

I cautiously unravelled the brown wrapping. It was my lobster boiled and pink. Without thinking I embraced the fisherman, held him close for a moment. Jackson's grin turned to awkward amusement.

'I've seen everything now,' mumbled Nab, shuffling off in disgust. 'No better than them floppy Frenchies.'

'Sorry about last night, Jackson,' I apologised, ignoring the old man's derogatory remark.

'These things 'appen.'

'The inquest, it's none of my business.'

'Maybe it is, maybe it isn't. It was my fault for bringing it up the first place.'

'Do you remember also mentioning the gamekeeper, Marlett, to me last night?'

'Could have done,' nodded Jackson. 'Get me 'ezzells from him.'

'Do you have a lot to do with him?'

'Not so much these days, he keeps to the Hall mainly. Doesn't seem to get down here as much as he used to do.'

'When did you last see him?'

'Must be a week or two back. Why?'

'Just curious. How was he?'

'You and your questions, Mr Cairn.'

'Was he his usual self?'

'Well,' Jackson hesitated, disconcerted by my persistence. 'Come to think of it, Marlett didn't have a lot to say for himself. Usually you can't stop the man bletherin on.'

'Will you do something for me, Jackson?'

'Depends?' grinned Jackson again, his eyes dancing almost flirtatiously.

'Will you keep your ear to the ground for any gossip coming out of Brigham Hall?'

'The Hall,' spluttered Jackson. 'How would the likes of me hear anything from the Hall?'

'Well, in the first place you're acquainted with Marlett and in the second place you're a well-respected and resourceful fellow,' I told him, giving his back a friendly slap. 'And if you do learn anything useful, I'll make it worth your while.' I gave Jackson my card knowing that even if he was illiterate, he would always find some faithful scribe somewhere in Staithes to get word to me in York.

Chapter Twenty

I did my final packing quickly. I had decided to leave Staithes as soon as possible. The next train was not until after lunch but a carrier was leaving for Whitby within the hour and had agreed to take me.

The driver was lean, sunken-cheeked and thankfully taciturn. Perched next to him, I had time to devise my main campaign of the day once we reached Whitby. The morning was fine, very fine, and I began to enjoy the leisurely pace of the horse-drawn vehicle through the flowering gorse countryside. I had only ever sampled the large nut once in my life but I could have sworn the fragrance from the gorse reminded me of the flavour of coconut.

Clip clop – the spark of metal shoes on metalled road, the freedom of the road, the sun warm on my face. All the time in the world to indulge my private thoughts. A gypsy way of life had much to recommend it.

'Sandsend.' The driver nodded to a few houses at the bottom of our steep descent.

Land's end – there it was the glimmering sea again reaching towards eternity. The view of the ocean was inspiring from the Prince's Road. A road built by Queen Victoria's Sikh friend, the Maharajah Dulip Singh, while a guest – or was it hostage? – at Mulgrave Castle. Alas, Dulip Singh proved to be an expensive and passing favourite of the Queen while his large, supposedly cursed diamond was of more permanent interest, somehow finding its way into Her Majesty's crown jewels after its very chequered history elsewhere.

I wondered if the Maharajah on waking had ever looked from his high turreted window and been incensed by the sight of billions of sparkling diamonds out there on the ocean, an elusive reminder of his own mountain of light – the priceless Koh-i-noor.

Dulip Singh was dead. The unavailable Victoria now more available in her Diamond Jubilee year. How feckless and unjust women could be – Rosie had no idea how much I had loved her.

* * * * *

'Could I have a brief word with Inspector Kemp?' Whitby police station was arched and old, musty cellar damp. It had the echoing tiled atmosphere of a Roman bath house rather than a centre for law enforcement.

'The inspector's had to step out for a few minutes. He won't be long, sir,' explained a moustachioed juvenile at the desk.

'I've not got an awful lot of time available myself,' I replied, inwardly recoiling from this callow youth's wispy experimentation with maturity.

'Be good enough to take a seat, sir.' The constable indicated a communal bench along the opposite wall.

I kicked my bags beneath the bench. Five minutes passed. I jingled my watch-chain impatiently.

'Look,' I shouted across to the desk, 'I've a train to catch. Can I leave my card for the inspector? He's detained a friend of mine at the Castle at York and I am merely enquiring how much longer my friend is to remain there without any formal charge being made out against him.'

'And who is this friend?' asked a new voice, not from the direction of the desk but from the open doorway. I immediately recognised Kemp from Jacob Fines' funeral.

'Daniel Robertshaw.'

'The slow lad from Staithes?'

'That's him.'

'And who might you be? Are you family?' Kemp scrutinised me keenly.

'No, I'm not family. As I said, I'm a friend.'

'I must say you are the one and only friend to enquire after Mr Robertshaw's well-being.' Again the copper's unflinching stare.

'His mother ...' I hesitated.

'Ah, you are here on behalf of his mother.' Kemp smiled cynically as if this piece of information explained everything. 'We've not heard much from her either.'

'Her circumstances are very difficult at present,' I began to explain.

'Not as difficult as her son's,' interrupted Kemp.

'Have you identified the dead girl yet?' I asked, grasping the proverbial horns early on.

'You'd best come into my office. We can't stand out here discussing this for all the world to hear, Mr ...?'

'James Cairn.' I offered Kemp my hand. The inspector's grasp was brief, dismissive.

'You'd better bring your luggage with you. Can't be too careful.'

Kemp's office was small. A small office for a small man, I noted maliciously, thumping my bags on the floor.

'Are you a Quaker, Mr Cairn?' asked Kemp. I shook my head. 'I must say you seem a very unlikely friend for the Robertshaws.'

'You haven't told me if you know who the dead girl is,' I said, pushing my luck even further.

'You want to know a lot of details for a man who is just enquiring about his friend's well-being.' Kemp's previous scrutiny had turned into downright suspicion.

'I am simply on my way back to York and decided to pop in here to try and find out how much longer you intend to hold Mr Robertshaw, in prison, without any official charge being made out against him.'

'York?' sniffed Kemp.

'Yes, I live in York.'

'And have you visited Daniel Robertshaw at the prison there?'

'No. I've been holidaying in Staithes for a few weeks and have only recently learnt of Mr Robertshaw's present predicament.'

'But you have met him before?'

'Yes, on an earlier trip to Staithes.'

'Do you holiday on the Yorkshire coast often?'

'As often as possible, I'm a fossil collector and this area is prolific in samples.'

'Perhaps that's what I can smell in your bag then, a fossil.'

'Sorry?' I stared at Kemp askance until I realised he must be able to smell the lobster in my Gladstone bag, ripened no doubt by the warm cart ride. 'I caught a lobster last night,' I explained a little awkwardly. 'You obviously have a policeman's nose, Inspector Kemp.'

'I have a nose for things that aren't as they seem. Is that your profession, a fossil collector?'

'No, no,' I laughed. 'I'm a barrister.' I handed Kemp my card.

'So, what is your true connection with Daniel Robertshaw?' asked Kemp, flipping my card thoughtfully over and over again in his hand.

'He helped me find an ichthyosaur on the beach.'

'A what?'

'The mineralised bones of an ancient sea-going reptile.'

'And you want me to believe that you are going to all this trouble for some retarded village lad who once helped you collect a load of old bones on the beach?' scoffed Kemp, his attitude suddenly more aggressive.

'We actually found a very important specimen.' From my usual standpoint of interrogator, I was beginning to feel that this examination of my motives was not going well. How could I ever get a stupid fellow like Kemp to understand the thrill of a find? – the refinements of this new and challenging science of palaeontology? – the bonding of two men associated with such a find? Daniel had enough remaining intellect to become enthralled by it too, and this Kemp chap had the audacity to call *him* retarded.

'Well, Mr Cairn, I have some up-to-date news for you regarding your client's situation.'

'Mr Robertshaw is not my client at this point in time,' I objected vehemently, 'as I've already gone to great pains to explain to you.'

'Nevertheless, I would have appreciated a little more honesty on your part in respect of your professional interest in this case,' continued Kemp, totally disregarding my denial. 'Especially as Daniel Robertshaw has now been indicted for the murder of the unknown girl.'

'What?' I gulped.

'I think you heard me.'

'On what evidence?'

'Eyewitness evidence.'

'Since when?'

'Since Thursday last at Whitby Magistrates Court.'

'Who was the presiding magistrate?'

'Mr Matthew Wilder. There is only Mr Matthew Wilder. This isn't the city, Mr Cairn.'

'And did Mr Robertshaw have any legal representation?'

'I believe a court appointed Whitby solicitor, name of Scott, was present. But I'm sure he'll willingly hand over the reins to you to deal with *causa causans*. Isn't that how you people put it?'

'Apart from your alleged "eyewitness evidence" have you any new evidence to support your case?' I asked sharply, irritated by the policeman's pomposity.

'If I had I wouldn't be telling you about it first, would I?' smirked Kemp.

'I doubt Mr Robertshaw is capable of such a vile act.'

'He was seen standing right over her, man, out on the rocks.' Kemp was losing his patience. His face was suffused with blood, the veins at his temples were engorged and throbbing.

'But nobody would be foolish enough to murder a young girl in front of an entire village,' I reasoned.

'An idiot would,' snarled Kemp.

'Has anyone else's name been mentioned in connection with this death?'

'Should there have been?'

'No, no, possibly not,' I conceded. It would serve no valid purpose on Daniel's behalf to bring up the accusation made by Lane against Jackson, and certainly not to voice Mrs Fines' suspicions regarding Brigham Hall at this stage.

'It can do no harm for me to categorically state to you that no one has been mentioned or come under the slightest suspicion for this horrendous crime, other than Daniel Robertshaw himself.' Kemp's voice shook; he was obviously struggling to regain his temper, compose himself.

'How did she die, exactly?'

'Official channels, Mr Cairn, apply through official channels for that sort of information.'

I nodded, deciding on an alternative, less confrontational approach. 'Has the poor young lass been buried yet?'

'We're about to. Can't keep her on ice for ever.'

'Will a pathologist see her beforehand?'

'The local doctor's examination was detailed enough for us.'

'For *you* perhaps,' I muttered disapprovingly. 'But will it be detailed enough for a court of law?'

'Doctors are doctors, give me a good old fashioned family doctor every time, never mind all these fancy new titles medics are giving themselves. Specialists in this and that.' Kemp ran the back of his hand under his nose while adding the justifying afterthought, 'We did take the precaution of asking a local photographer to take some detailed plates for both evidence and identification purposes.'

'I don't suppose I can see any of those prints?' I asked, leaping at the bait.

'You know better than to ask me that,' snorted Kemp, laughing contemptuously directly into my face. 'Not without the Crown's permission and not until you are officially involved in this case.'

'If Mr Robertshaw does wish me to represent him, I might well say "yes",' I warned Kemp; Kemp whose foot was pushing my luggage towards me in order to hasten my departure.

'Didn't I overhear you say you'd a train to catch?'

I paused in the open doorway bags in hand. 'I believe you've got the wrong man and given a chance I will prove it.'

'Good day to you, Mr Cairn.'

'Good day, Inspector Kemp.' I noticed the bowing pate below me was flushed with renewed anger.

Chapter Twenty-One

Every time I looked out of my window down onto the street it seemed to be raining, or perhaps because of my low spirits I saw only rain. For once I felt isolated up here in the top chamber of my tall York town house, far removed from the life and transactions being conducted below. I had chosen to live on Gillygate because it was a street of bustling trade and commerce rather than quiet and residential, a man living on his own needed a little human sizzle around him. But what if the sizzle had gone out of the man himself? – the proximity to all that interaction only made his sense of loneliness all the worse, the sizzle itself became an aggravation.

Already I was missing Staithes. Why, in God's name, had I not taken Laura's and Harold's addresses? Then I could have retained some connection with Rosie Good through them. Perhaps Rosie's relationship with Oliver Shepherd might fail yet. And, anyway, Laura and Harold were a couple worthy of cultivating in their own right, so very different from my older, usually married legal cronies. The idea of more lonely bachelor evenings at the Black Swan Inn failed to inspire me. York was flat and boring, Staithes too many boggy miles away even by train. As the river Ouse threatened to burst its banks in these Noah's Ark deluges, I felt the walls of my own heart were at risk. All my life I had swum against the current. The usual flow was south and I had come north. The little family I had left, a mother and a sister, were south. Had I made a mistake?

The bells of York Minister boomed out for a new beginning. This was not the sad, non-resonant tolling of the Whitby bells, this was something far grander and dignified.

The image of another woman's face, not Rosie's face, a Queen's small round face pressed against a turreted window filled my mental frame, a Queen stubbornly soured by loss, her terrible prolonged mourning muffled and indulged in Scottish drizzle. And yet, by a strange twist of fate, it was she who had brought unexpected wealth to a poverty-stricken Whitby coastline. Jet jewellery, the fashion of our age. This was her day, her Diamond Jubilee year, and perhaps now Victoria would finally explode from her shell – and I would explode with her.

Shells, shells, I would go back to Staithes to collect more fossilised shells as soon as possible. And who knows, next year Daniel might be walking along the beach free again and all the artists might have returned. Who knows this time it might be me walking arm in arm with Rosie Good against the sunset, the heroic defence counsel in an infamous murder trial. A seed of an idea began to germinate: if I could win *Regina v Robertshaw*, I might win the woman of my dreams. Dream on counsel, as yet I had to convince my colleagues of the validity of this case. I sighed, my mood as changeable as the clearing light outside.

* * * * *

Drip, drip. Condensation ran like sweat down the walls. *Ping!* Some of the water bounced into his slop-bucket as if the bucket was there only to serve that purpose. Daniel squatted in one corner of the cell, his shaking hands covering his ears. Although it must be summer now, he was freezing cold in his five-by-eight-foot space. *Drip, drip.* He was going mad. On remand and his life-blood was already draining out of him. He could feel it, hear it pumping away until it dispersed somewhere unseen like the water running down the wall and disappearing into that bucket. He would surely die in here.

The only relief in his dungeon gloom was the suggestion of blue through the thick opaque glass window high up the wall. His mam always said she hated blue, perhaps because of its association with the sea, but Daniel loved it more than any other colour. He loved to run and dance beneath a fine blue sky when, on those special days, even the grey water over Scar Shootings turned to blue. Why then had the men come and taken those days away from him? What had he done wrong? Was it the mermaid? Perhaps it was wrong, after all, to find a mermaid.

'Wrong to find a mermaid.' He rocked the phrase to and fro, to and fro, trying the echo there in the corner.

He had exhausted all the cell's other possibilities of play long ago, tired of his hard plank bed being a coble, wearied of the small table under which he tried to cower away from his "pirate" enemies' beating fists.

'Can't you read, can't you read then? Jim, we've got a thee and thou here who can't read a word, would you believe?' The warders punched, taunted, and showered him with his unopened letters – letters he knew must have come from his mam in the mistaken belief that these men would read them out to him. Instead, they called him all sorts of things, things he hadn't heard of before, said he was a monster. They jeered all the more when he said he wanted to go home.

'Wrong to find a mermaid.' To and fro, to and fro.

Snap! The spy-hole in the door opened. Eyes and part of a face peered in.

'Shut it, you dumb beast,' growled the face. Then eyes and part of another face and more growling.

Snap crack – he remembered the excitement of broom pods cracking open in the summer heat, fire crackers exploding all around him as he walked below Roxby moor. And he wondered if he would ever walk there again.

After he had first been bundled out of the van and into the prison building itself, Daniel had cried. He had cried at being strip-searched and forced naked into a cold bath – nothing was ever warm here, not even the weak porridge – now he could not cry.

Snap! He was alone again.

It wouldn't be so bad if he was able to sleep his time away but, despite the rule of silence between inmates at all times, he found prison was a clanking, grating, noisy sort of place.

He'd known hunger at home though nothing like this. In spite of feeling hungry, he just couldn't eat. Gruel, suet and water were the staples offered to him. More often than not he slid the untouched contents of his dish into the slop-bucket. He simply felt too sick to eat.

* * * * *

'Get on with it and stop moaning,' bawled a warder across the exercise yard. Daniel shuffled on doubled over with stomach cramp.

'That's enough, Goater. The lad's ill, needs to see the doctor, can't you see that?'

Good, good, a Good Samaritan at last. Daniel kept his gaze fixed onto the ground. Even he had picked up a little animal cunning in this place – cunning or a clout, day to day existence in the Castle.

'I'll arrange for the doctor to visit the prisoner, myself,' announced the supportive voice.

Daniel dared to glance up. He saw the flutter of a dark cassock vanishing through a doorway into a building beyond. A cassock like that worn by the Hinderwell priest.

'"Needs to see the doctor",' mocked the rebuked warder as Daniel stumbled into earshot. Then in an undertone, 'Bloody chaplain.'

Suddenly the Minster bells pealed out beyond the prison walls. Daniel stopped, panting and transfixed, until he was screamed at to move on.

'The Queen's Jubilee celebrations. You're already celebrating Her Majesty's pleasure though, aren't you, Robertshaw?' sneered the still aggrieved warder, lashing out with his foot as Daniel struggled to complete his final circuit.

* * * * *

The last time I saw him, he had been standing obediently on the sand next to Laura and her easel. His proud grin as open as the backcloth of sea and sky.

'Daniel?' At first I could see nothing the light was so bad. 'Daniel?' I called again. 'Daniel is that you?' All at once I saw that my worst fears were being realised. I turned back to the closed door uneasily. Yes, I really was alone, locked in with this zombie who was curled in the corner in a foetal position making loud sucking noises on his thumb. I had visited many men in here before but never a man I cared for, and never a man accused of such a brutal murder that he was being held in continuous solitary confinement more for his own safety than any risk he might pose to others. The murderers of young girls did not fair too well in a place like this. This was a veiled world peopled by coalescent inmates, a subculture whose only clarity was their own peculiar form of justice. Daniel had the appearance of a man, so he would be judged as a man. Nobody in here gave a damn that Daniel was a man who had never achieved manhood, a man who appeared to have now completely reverted back to infancy. 'Daniel?' I warily crept towards the shape in the corner. 'It's James, James Cairn, remember?' I tried to announce my presence as gently and soothingly as possible. I was a lion tamer fearful of the consequences of startling the wild beast.

The sucking stopped. The shape made something like a choking sound in the back of its throat. Growling, no barking was issuing from the corner.

He's raving mad. I was horrified. I hesitated in my approach, perhaps I was too late, perhaps Daniel had sunk too far into madness to be reclaimed.

'On your feet,' shouted Daniel. 'Didn't you hear me? On your feet, I said.'

I was the one startled now. I nearly jumped out of my skin thinking the command was meant for me, until I saw Daniel staggering to attention, attempting to balance on two discordant limbs, unsteady like a drunk. It was shocking to see how pale and thin he was, he looked jaundiced, the shadows of the bars streaked across his face. He was hardly recognisable as the Daniel I had last seen in Staithes.

The cell stank of faeces. My delicate stomach could not take any more. I retched into my handkerchief.

'I'm very unhappy in here too,' whispered Daniel, disconcertingly switched back into something resembling normality. I felt his comforting hand on my stooped shoulder, a pitying expression in his eyes. 'Thou's come to take me home to the sea.'

'Do you realise the seriousness of your position?' I asked, forcing myself to straighten up.

'I …' Daniel paused. A vacant expression returned to his face.

I started hammering on the cell door. The warder quickly appeared. Tossing my soiled handkerchief into the brimming slop-bucket, I asked the warder if the bucket could be either emptied or removed out into the passageway for the duration of my visit. The warder muttered something unintelligible, almost certainly rude, but acquiesced to my request and warder and bucket disappeared.

'Do you want me to help you or not?' I turned back to Daniel. Daniel nodded in bewilderment. 'Then you'll have to answer my questions truthfully.'

'I want to go home,' he persisted.

My proposed new client might not know a lot but he knows that much, I acknowledged sadly.

'I have a gift for you,' I told him with forced cheerfulness, taking out of my briefcase the vellum envelope containing the seventy-five guineas and passing it across to him. 'It's for finding the stone fish,' I explained. Daniel did not open the envelope but held it up to the high window instead.

Finding it impervious to the trickle of light he abruptly returned it. 'Yes, it's better I keep it safe for you,' I agreed without offence. Daniel's face was blank, apathetic. 'Your mother wanted you to have it.'

'Mam, where's Mam?'

'She's staying with your uncle in Whitby at present.'

'Why isn't Mam here?'

'It's too far for her to travel at the moment.' I watched on helplessly as incomprehension further clouded the face of the child/man of Staithes. 'Daniel, I have to ask you this, did you harm that young girl in any way, the young girl you were seen with on the flat rocks back home?'

'Want to see a sea gull.'

'What?' It was my turn for total incomprehension.

'A sea gull's better than paper, better than that,' said Daniel, nodding to the cream envelope clutched in my hand. 'There's a heart inside.'

This had happened before, once or twice Daniel had expressed a vision that was either metaphysically brilliant or pure gibberish. Matter-of-fact me was now, as then, at a loss to know which.

'Nonetheless,' I said, sliding the envelope back into my briefcase, taking out spectacles and pen, and holding up a fresh sheet of paper before Daniel's eyes. 'It might be that *this* particular piece of paper saves your life.'

'How?' Daniel giggled, another abrupt mood swing.

'Just answer my questions, will you?' I told him. He nodded, intrigued, as I blew dust into the air from the small table and pulled it towards the low plank bed. Making a seat out of the bed, I scratched what must have been for him unintelligible symbols across the top of the paper but which happened to be his Christian and surname. 'On that lovely spring day, the twenty-first of May, the last time you walked out on the rocks, were there sea gulls to be seen then, Daniel?'

'Plenty,' enthused Daniel at this wonderful memory of freedom. 'Always plenty.'

'Was there anything else that caught your attention?' I watched Daniel's tongue loll between his teeth, his mouth slightly open.

'A seal,' he said, looking worried.

'"A seal"?' I repeated surprised, pen suspended above the sheet of paper. I waited patiently as he struggled with the question of whether or not to trust me.

'A mermaid,' he finally admitted.

'And did you speak to this mermaid?'

'She didn't speak.'

'What was she doing?'

'Sleeping.'

'How was she sleeping?'

'Sleeping.' Daniel glared at me for asking something so self-evident.

'Show me how she was sleeping.'

Obediently, if reluctantly, Daniel sunk to his knees on the cold flagged floor. 'Like this,' he said, falling face down and remaining there perfectly still.

'You can get up now, Daniel.' I waited for him to get to his feet, before asking, 'Did you touch or do anything to the mermaid while she slept?' He nodded solemnly. 'What did you do?' I asked, an unwelcome alarm bell ringing in my head. He did not answer. 'What did you do?' I demanded again. 'It is very important you tell me.'

'Tried to see her face.'

I started up from the bed, feeling Daniel's naked toe working its way under my thigh.

'What on earth do you think you're doing?' I shouted, disgusted at the crawling sensation on my skin, outraged at being touched.

'She wouldn't turn over. She had white hair,' explained Daniel innocuously.

'White hair? Like an old person has?' I pressed on, outrage forgotten. He shook his head. 'How do you know she wasn't an old person?'

'Just do,' he shrugged. 'Her hands were so small and they were white too, much younger than Mam's tired hands.'

'Had you ever seen her before?' I asked. He slowly moved his head from side to side. 'Are all the things you've just told me the truth?' He nodded. 'Have you anything else you would like to tell me?' Again he slowly shook his head. 'Will you put your name to this piece of paper then?' He looked aghast. It took me a moment to realise my mistake. 'Look see,' I said, making a diagonal cross with my finger in the remaining dust on the table's surface. 'You can make your mark like so instead.' I handed him my pen, asking,

'Have you ever done this before?'

'The little man who slapped me, made me do it.' The edges of Daniel's mouth sank unhappily.

'What little man?'

'He didn't show me like thee,' said Daniel, ignoring my question, tiring of questions. 'He put his hand on top of mine like this.' Daniel applied considerable pressure to the back of my hand forcing it down on the table, forcing it to make some sort of scrawl.

'Do you know this man's name?'

'Think so,' shrugged Daniel.

'Was his name Inspector Kemp?'

'He had a lot of silver buttons.'

'He actually formed the signature for you? And he slapped you?'

'Like this because of the mermaid.' He raised his hand towards my face.

'No,' I cried. 'No more demonstrations, please.'

'Will thou take me home with thee now?' he pleaded, encircling my waist in his emaciated arms.

'I can't yet, Daniel.' I struggled to break free of his grasp, holding him at bay by the shoulders. 'Maybe some day soon. I'll certainly come and see you soon.'

Daniel's embrace remained embedded in my skin, his weeping face imprinted on my memory. I carried both back out of the prison gates with me. I had lightened the boy's mood only to thrust him back into despair. How unkind was that? But what other option did I have?

I remembered only too well my own father leaving me behind on that first day at Merchant Taylors'. A few years later, following a Christmas holiday, I would never see my father again. James senior was killed in Africa when a Zulu spear penetrated one of his lungs. Killed in action in Africa, the official letter to my mother explained. Bizarre really – why Africa? – what grievance could my tall army officer father have had with an equally proud and tall Zulu warrior? How ludicrous and wasteful it all seemed, how unjust, almost as unjust and ludicrous as Daniel's hero, James Cook, ending his days being hacked to death and partially eaten by cannibals.

As often as not it is service to the Crown that messes people's lives up. Colonialism was indirectly responsible for my own abandonment to school bullies. Bereft and fatherless, lovely-boy James was a target for harassment for most of his formative years, and ever since that unspeakable period of my life I have harboured an obdurate hatred of bullies and possessed an unquenchable thirst for justice.

'Damn that bastard Kemp,' I cursed all the way along Castlegate. That bastard had better watch out for he will get more than his day in court, this I vowed silently and all the more deadly for that.

Chapter Twenty-Two

The walled city of York was ancient and filthy and exciting. Everyday you had to walk with care over the cobbles in case stinking horse dung glued to your trouser bottoms, trousers which were worn long over your boots if you were fashionable. And I liked to consider myself as fashionable, and I loved York on its brighter days, on my brighter days, but I did not like cleaning shit off my trouser hems most evenings, and at such times I yearned for Staithes where, despite a certain lack of sanitation, there was always a clean feel to the place, as if the sea would always eventually come in and cleanse everything anyway. Be that as it may, unless the time ever came when I could hope to make a living out of palaeontology, I recognised that York was the place where I had to earn my bread and butter and over the next few days I would be forced to prepare for another case.

A farmer worker, John Barr, an appropriate name in the circumstances, was accused of being involved in an affray outside the King's Arms public house one Friday night. Friday night was rattle of the till night, rubbing of hands night for the pub landlords of York. Friday night was the night when all the farm labourers from districts around and about deluged the city for a good time. Friday night was known as "animal night" by the non-beneficiaries of this lucrative trade.

My thirty-two year old client was well-known for his brawling skills. He had previous gaol form, and this time faced a heftier prison sentence if found guilty of breaking a Mr Peter Hill's jaw and putting his brother, Mr Robert Hill, in the river Ouse, not to mention the matter of an arresting police officer's nose.

John Barr, like Daniel, was being held at the Castle, but unlike Daniel he was not believed to be dangerous, a fair assumption when Barr was not in drink, and so was allowed to rub along with other inmates from time to time.

'I will do my best for you, Mr Barr,' I tried to reassure him, on my first prison visit to this scowling, scarred tom-cat of a client. 'Though, in fairness, I must point out to you that you are lucky not to be facing a murder charge. It was pure luck that the Ouse wasn't in spate, and the water wasn't too cold, and Mr Robert Hill was a competent swimmer, and Mr Edge, the bargee, was on hand to pull him out at Skeldergate Bridge before he was washed all the way down to the Bishop's Palace.'

Barr raised his huge hand. 'Enough,' he growled. 'Whose side are you on anyway?'

Yours unfortunately, I conceded privately, shuffling through the case papers with my index finger, pretending to be otherwise absorbed.

'What will I get?' asked Barr impatiently.

'It depends how you plead.'

'Dunno.'

'There's a good character reference here from your employer, Mr Walker, says you are a hard worker about his farm.'

'Bloody hypocrite. That 'un treats his beasts better than us.'

'If you want my advice,' I began.

'That's just what I do want,' snapped Barr.

I took a deep breath in an attempt to control my own temper. 'Plead "guilty as charged" and you could get three to five years, if you plead "not guilty", well, you may face a sentence of anything from seven years, seven hard years,' I added forcefully. Barr shrugged. 'The decision is yours, Mr Barr, shall I leave it with you overnight?' Barr nodded sulkily.

The following afternoon I was bustling down Coppergate, on my way to hear Barr's plea decision, when I noticed two women walking arms linked towards me on the opposite pavement. They were Quakers. I should not have been surprised at this as there had been a flourishing Quaker community in York from time *in memoriam* and a Friends' Meeting House stood nearby. But there was something about the older woman, who must have been in her early thirties, that took my attention. She looked familiar to me. The younger woman appeared to be her daughter. There was a peculiar intensity between the two of them, even allowing for the closeness between mother and daughter, they kept gazing into each other's eyes as if afraid of losing sight of one another.

I puzzled over the older buxom woman's identity all the way to the Castle, I could have sworn I had seen her somewhere before recently. But where? – for the life of me I could not remember.

* * * * *

The days ground on between my tall townhouse in Gillygate, my chambers in Bootham and the Castle and the Court House. Despite the demands of *Regina v Barr*, Daniel was never far from my mind and I began to devise arguments to convince my colleagues that his case was a worthy one. No doubt, if successful, it would be a beneficially well-publicised trial, murder trials always are, but, for that very same reason, failure could have catastrophic consequences for our fledgling chambers and for me personally. I did not enjoy the universal approval of all my colleagues and there was always the prospect of being last in, first out.

'Wouldn't pursue that line,' warned Gerald Fawcett.

'What line?' I asked.

'Not without a lot more evidence.' Fawcett handed back my observations on the Robertshaw case which he had studied the previous night.

'I'm not with you.'

'Sir Hugh Parke wields a lot of influence and has many powerful friends in northern England, nay in the country as a whole. Further more, and you can take my word for this, he has enjoyed the hospitality on frequent occasions of one eminent judge who lives not a stone's throw from here. Wouldn't do to have Sir Hugh cutting up rough on us, now would it?'

'But if the Parkes are involved in some way,' I objected. 'Know who the dead girl is for instance.'

'You have to prove it, old boy, and quite frankly your evidence of any implication in that direction is, well, so far and to say the least, flimsy.'

'There's Mrs Fines' statement.'

'You are joking, Cairn? The suspicions of a kitchen maid against the word and denials of Sir Hugh Parke and a friendly judge in tow to boot. Really, Cairn, this could finish up being costly for us, very costly.'

'So class and influence count for more than truth and justice.' I was seething. Gerald Fawcett was my immediate superior in chambers and I had felt it only right that I approach him first. But Fawcett was a prickly and unpredictable character, particularly pompous and overbearing and, more worryingly, I had often found him to be fundamentally flawed in his moral assessments.

'"Truth and justice", come on, old boy,' smirked Fawcett. 'Haven't you learnt that when you're standing there in court it's merely a theatrical performance you're required to give, a game to be won or lost?'

'This case is more than a game to me.'

'Well, I feel sorry for you, Cairn. I hope you haven't made the fatal error of becoming too sympathetically involved with this simpleton, Daniel Robertshaw, because it doesn't look very promising for him. He was seen standing over that girl by two witnesses, dammit, man.'

'You sound like Kemp,' I muttered.

'Who?'

'Kemp, the police inspector who's dealing with the case.'

'Sensible man, Cairn, listen to him.'

'But think of the press interest, the prestige such a case would draw.' I decided to change tack, appeal to Fawcett's selfish flawed morality.

'Only if we win.'

'I think I can win.'

'What? Against those odds?'

'I want to take it on,' I told him, drawing out each word firmly.

'It you want to hang yourself alongside your client, that's your business, but I'll not give you my blessing.'

'Thank you as always for your confidence.' Smarting from ear to ear, I turned my back on Gerald Fawcett.

I needed at least one senior colleague's backing to take on Daniel's case – Daniel's very difficult case, I harboured no delusions about that myself. I had tried the bottom, now I would head for the top.

'Interesting, this Robertshaw case.' The head of chambers, Carlton-Bingham, cornered me in the hallway a day or two later. 'Has a funny feel to it.'

'Can we take it on then, sir?' I asked.

'Quite possibly,' laughed Carlton-Bingham; a convivial bear of a man. 'Quite possibly *you* can take it on, James.'

'But will you be in my corner, sir?'

'I'm always in your corner.' The laugh again and then the decisive afterthought. 'I'd apply for those photographs of the dead girl straightaway, see if they tell us anything.'

I walked on to my room a new man; an inner glow to me now. How different my relationship was with Carlton-Bingham to Gerald Fawcett. There was no doubt that Fawcett was a consummate if bumptious and cynical performer in court, whereas Carlton-Bingham was slow, methodical, but had a deadly instinct for locking onto the vital point that could win a trial.

I had already written to Daniel's court appointed solicitor, Mr Scott, and received a reply from him stating he was more than agreeable for my possible involvement in the Robertshaw case. I now wrote to him and Kemp in Whitby confirming that I had officially taken on Daniel's brief. I added a casual postscript to Kemp's letter, requesting to see some of the prints taken from the original glass negatives depicting the deceased. Much to my surprise, the inspector made no attempt to vacillate and the photographs arrived by return the next day. Did this indicate that he had some additional evidence that indisputably favoured his case against Daniel? No covering reply was enclosed in the envelope.

I examined the images of the dead girl with a magnifying glass from every angle and in various lights. One in particular was haunting: the naked girl appeared to be posed with one finger held aloft like a Laura Johnson model. There was something very sad and unreal about such a young image of death. Everything about Daniel's mermaid was harshly lit, like the glaring brightness of a Staithes fisherwoman's white apron hung out to dry in the sun, all the more a contrast against the toasted sepia bloom background. I rushed the photographs over to Carlton-Bingham's room.

'The detail is exceptionally good. They must have an excellent photographer over there in Whitby,' said Carlton-Bingham, taking his turn to cruise the matt surface with the magnifying glass. 'I wonder what happened to her eyes.'

'Fish, I expect. But what do you think of those, sir?' I asked, squeezing my forefinger between glass and photograph.

'Yes, I've noticed them too.' Carlton-Bingham peered harder. 'Look like some sort of abrasions, don't they?'

'Fingernails?'

'Possibly. A mystery for you to solve, James.'

'I have a medical friend over in Leeds.'

'Excellent,' said Carlton-Bingham, giving me a dismissive little pat on the shoulder. 'When the Barr case is over you'll be able to give this one your undivided attention.'

That lunch-time my heart leaped like Dracula's schooner trying to make Whitby harbour. The headline above an article in the *York Herald* levitated off page three.

QUAKER FIRE
INQUEST VERDICT

An inquest found at Whitby, today, that Alice Rose Jeffrey was unlawfully killed while staying as a guest at her sister's cottage in the fishing port of Staithes. The cottage was set ablaze by a mob on the night of Saturday 22nd May, last. The Coroner, Mr Charles Fenton, said Mrs Jeffrey suffered a terrible death because of the malicious actions of others and through no fault of her own. The Magistrate has been informed and three men are now believed to be held in custody for matters relating to this dreadful incident. Mrs Jeffrey's widower, Mr Roderick Jeffrey, is a jet manufacturer in Whitby and a prominent Quaker.

I sat stunned for a minute or two at my favourite table in the Coffee Tavern in Colliergate.

'He's done it. Jackson's done the honourable thing,' I cried out (I thought only to myself) in exhilaration. I could have taken the floor and spun with joy had I not suddenly realised that many eyes were observing me with silent disapproval round various ornamental ferns. I decided to make a dignified cafe exit before attracting any more attention to myself and getting carted off as a madman to The Retreat.

Chapter Twenty-Three

At my client Barr's first court appearance he had eventually decided to plead guilty and the jury was dismissed. The following day, barrister, solicitor and defendant returned for sentencing. Perhaps out of spite for Barr's previous procrastination and waste of valuable court time, the judge, Mr Justice Brightman, delayed his entrance giving the defence time to gather round the dock and speculate on our client's future.

'Don't fancy another spell inside.' Barr's bellicose comment was not exactly music to my ears, especially as he seemed unable to grasp the reality of his situation. Mr Justice Brightman would be well-versed in all Barr's previous misdemeanours and that he had already served time for similar drunken assaults.

'I think you must brace yourself for that possibility, Mr Barr,' I warned him firmly, exchanging a weary look with Mr Brown, Barr's equally frayed solicitor.

'Locked up with a right load of wankers as it is.'

'Really.' I wondered if Barr's statement was meant figuratively or not. I decided not to enquire.

'Yes, three of the bastards burnt an old woman to death, Staithes way.'

'Really,' I said again, my interest instantly piqued.

'Two fishermen and an ironstone miner. One of the fishermen is a right piece of weasel shit. Lane he's called.' I could not resist a brief smirk at Barr's description of Lane – Lane somehow seemed to be one of those characters who attracted colourful descriptive prose from everyone. Barr rubbed his cuff-linked hands across his nose before continuing, 'Snivels all day to anyone with a mind to listen. Says the old lass's death was an accident. Accident,' he scoffed. 'I'd like to give all three of 'em a taste of this.' He balled up his lacerated but considerable fist. The gyves jingled.

'Mr Barr, please restrain yourself,' whispered Brown, looking anxiously across to where the two complainant brothers were waiting patiently alone on the public benches – waiting for their pound of flesh.

'Well, I for one have no time for fellas that harm women,' protested Barr; a note of accusation directed towards his solicitor.

'That may be so. But you've already given too many men a taste of your fist and see where it's got you,' pointed out Brown, attempting to reach up and shield Barr's offending clenched paw with his own comparative midget hand.

'What's the ironstone miner's name?' I asked Barr, irritated by the trivial banter passing between the other two men.

'Carter, he's called. Babbles on all day that he's got information to trade.'

'There seems to be an awful lot of talking goes on. I thought the Castle prescribed to the rule of silence between inmates,' interjected Brown.

'Puh!' exclaimed Barr. 'Turnkeys can't tell if you're talking or not if you don't move your sodding lips, can they? Doesn't take a numb-yed more than a day to fathom that out.'

'What sort of information does Carter have to trade?' I asked coolly.

'Dunno. He won't tell exact, not until he's spoken to his lawyer. He does say though that it has something to do with an idiot who's also jugged up. Says he always believed this idiot was guilty of a terrible sin and now to his everlasting shame he knows otherwise.'

'All rise,' boomed the clerk of the court. Brown and I returned to our original station adjacent to the prosecution counsel's.

Mr Justice Brightman swooped along his bench with a flourish of robes. Turning, his piercing corn-coloured eyes surveyed the court, a bird of prey selecting his victims whether it be prisoner or counsels. One of the younger judiciaries, Brightman was a man in a hurry for London's more prestigious circuits, and, bearing his future advancement in mind, he deemed it unnecessary to offer an apology for his lateness to these barbarians of one of Her Majesty's more northerly outposts.

'Has learned counsel for the prosecution anything to add to his statement of yesterday?' he asked a circumspect Reginald Humphrey instead.

'Only that we demand the maximum penalty for the vile assaults committed against those two stainless sinless men seated over there, my lord.'

Suddenly finding themselves the focus of the court's attention, the two "stainless" brothers shuffled uncomfortably on the hard wooden bench.

'As always a master of alliteration, Mr Humphrey,' Brightman told the QC sarcastically.

'Thank you, my lord,' grovelled Humphrey. Humphrey, who was a peculiar egg shape of a man, was generally referred to as Humpty Dumpty Humphrey by many of our uncharitable legal peers.

Brightman's bill nose and killer eyes swung in my direction. 'You, Mr Cairn, anything to put forward in mitigation on behalf of the prisoner?'

I bounced to my feet. 'As you heard yesterday from farmer Walker, my lord, Barr is a hard working man. He is a good family man, as well, with a wife and several children to support. Any lengthy imprisonment would cost these dependants dearly.'

'Should he not have thought about that before he set about those two innocent men?' Brightman's wide cuff quivered as he gave a perfunctory wave in the direction of the aggrieved brothers.

I too glanced briefly towards the pair of scowling faces at present fixed aggressively on me. The brothers appeared to be as fight-hardened, fight-scarred as my client though apparently they were not as accomplished.

'Unfortunately, Mr Barr acts out of character when he's the worse for …'

'Drink,' interrupted Brightman. 'Our old friend drink is the evil here, is it not? I seem to recall there was a minor assault involving a constable's nose mentioned in this case too.' Brightman's pince-nez, originally finely balanced, now began to slip slowly further down the acute slope of his own nose as he rummaged through copious papers set before him.

'The nose was not badly broken, my lord,' I pleaded desperately.

'It's always drink with these people.' Brightman impatiently pushing his pince-nez back into position.

Is Brightman a covert Quaker too, I wondered. I had suspected all along that this high-flying judge might be the friend of Sir Hugh Parke mentioned by Gerald Fawcett. Still that was by the by for now, I reasoned, clearing my throat. 'Mr Barr has promised, my lord, he'll not lift another glass to his lips.'

'I see here he has promised that before.' More rustling of papers. 'Several times before in fact. Indeed this man, Mr Cairn, has already been sent to prison several times.'

'Just a matter of months at a time, my lord.'

'For similar offences, has he not?' A glint of sadism flashed in Brightman's eyes. I flopped helplessly down into my seat. 'And you, Barr,' he sniffed.

'Anything to contribute before I pass sentence?' Barr shook his head.

'Barr behind bars,' guffawed one of the brothers.

'Silence!' hissed Brightman. 'You'll hold your tongue in my court or the usher will remove you forthwith.' The judge next turned his icy attention back onto the prisoner. 'John Barr, you have surpassed yourself this time. You have seriously assaulted one man, dared to assault a policeman, and nearly drowned another man. And, although you have pleaded guilty to the charges brought against you, I have to take into account past offences and the considerable risk you pose to the public when in drink. I shall therefore, under such circumstances, be expected to pass the severest sentence that the law allows. Which is in my judgement totally inadequate for such a case as this. The sentence of the court is that you will be imprisoned and kept to hard labour for five years.'

My heart sank.

'Five years,' hissed the court.

'Five years *hard labour*,' clapped the brothers.

'All rise,' – Brightman was already on his way.

If looks could kill … Barr's bared teeth were not directed to the brothers or the court, not even to the disappearing judge, no, his snarl was firmly fixed elsewhere. 'You said,' he growled down from the dock. If looks could kill, I was a dead man.

'I pointed out that five years maximum was a possibility,' I retorted in a whisper, approaching the dock like a penitent approaching the altar.

'I have to admit Mr Justice Brightman's sentence is a surprise to me,' piped up Brown, bravely drawing alongside.

'Not as much as it is to me,' growled our man again. 'It's me what has to walk the treadmill for hours at a time, turn the screw and nothing to show at the end of it, break stones until my back breaks. It's me what has to do these things while my bairns are evicted and starve and you two waddle back to your big houses to service your fat wives.'

One of the warders pressed on Barr's shoulder.

Undeterred by our client's insults as he vanished into the cells below, Brown shouted after him that he would do his best to sort things out with farmer Walker for Mrs Barr's and the children's sake.

* * * * *

The next morning, I hypnotically watched the turnkey opening the lock. I hoped Brown would be as good as his word regarding Barr's wife and children and the tenancy of their cottage, but I could not say I had lost much sleep over my client's incarceration. Barr was self-destructive. I had done my professional best for him and now I was free to concentrate on a case with far more heart to it. I felt myself to be a man with a mission – a man entrusted to prevent a serious miscarriage of justice.

'Up, you,' barked the warder, stabbing Daniel in the side with the toe of his boot.

'Please don't do that,' I told him. If anything Daniel looked more confused and dishevelled than on my last visit. He showed no sign of recognition and remained squatted and cowering in a corner by the bed. 'Are you feeding him properly?' I asked the warder accusingly. 'This man looks to have lost even more weight.'

'Puh, a man is it?' sniggered the warder.

'Yes, *a man*,' I snarled between clenched teeth. 'A man, I would further remind you, who has not been found guilty of any offence to date and should be treated accordingly. Now please answer my question.'

'Breakfast at seven-thirty a.m., cocoa and bread. Noon, one day bacon and beans, another day soup, another day cold Australian meat, and another brown flour suet pudding, with the last three repeated twice a week, potatoes with every dinner, and tea at five-thirty p.m.,' reeled off the warder machine-like. 'That's if the prisoner chooses to eat it of course, sir,' he chuckled slyly.

'Look at him, he's caked in grime. How often has he had access to washing facilities?' Concern fuelled my anger.

Daniel began to cry.

Goater – I had made a point of learning his name – frowned.

'Chaplain tries to visit every day,' he mumbled.

'What has a chaplain to do with hygiene?'

Goater stared at me, appearing to struggle for the connection himself. But it was not that, he already knew the connection he was about to put forward. No, Goater could foresee I was trouble.

'Because the Chaplain is of another denomination to the prisoner, the prisoner refuses to see him, it's the same with water,' he explained with a posturing air of forbearance.

'What are you blathering about, man?'

'Prisoner Robertshaw refuses to wash, sir.'

'Well, listen carefully, my friend. I'm not prepared to have him going into court in this state.'

'I'll see what can be done, sir.' Goater cockily touched the peak of his cap before making a tactical retreat through the iron door.

'Be sure you do,' I shouted after him, adding ominously, 'or I'll be having a word with the governor.' I heard the warder railing against me out in the passageway. The warder did not seem to be of the right calibre to be dealing with a prisoner with Daniel's disability. An obvious bully, he did not seem to be the right calibre of man to deal with anyone in this vulnerable situation. Maybe a word with the governor was not a bad idea anyway.

'Come on, old man, let's have you sitting up on here.' I strained to lever Daniel out of his corner onto the bed.

'Captain Cook came today.'

'Did he really?'

'I am shortly to join him on *The Resolution*.'

'Indeed.'

'Dost thou think I should sail away with him?'

'Why not?'

'Didn't think thou would come today.'

'Well, here I am,' I said with open arms.

Daniel nodded. His face was creased and troubled, his cheeks sunken, his hair thinning. Previously, at Staithes, I had found it difficult to believe that here was a seventeen year old approaching manhood, now, all at once, I was appalled to see how prematurely aged he was.

'What's in those?' Daniel asked, pointing to the brown paper bags damp and twisted in my hand.

'Fruit, I've brought you some apples and oranges,' I explained. Daniel's chin slumped to his chest. 'What would you have me bring?' I asked somewhat taken aback.

'Going home,' said Daniel.

'I can't bring you that yet. But, meanwhile, I am determined to improve your lot in here.'

'Take me out in a bag,' muttered Daniel; his unflinching gaze fixed to a spot on the floor where a cockroach was making its right of way impudently across his shackled foot.

'Freedom in a bag, if only it was that easy,' I sighed. 'Please take the fruit all the same. Your hero, Captain Cook, would be the first to approve. He'd say, if not freedom then health is the next most important thing, and health is fruit.'

Daniel took up the bags from where I placed them on the bed. One at a time he peered distrustfully for the health inside. He took out a shiny red and green apple and examined it carefully, rolling it around in his palm. Finally, he lifted his vacant eyes up for an explanation.

'Scurvy, fruit prevents you from getting scurvy.'

'Scurvy,' mumbled Daniel parrot-fashion.

'Take a bite,' I told him, beginning to feel like Eve though certainly not in The Garden of Eden.

Daniel sunk his teeth into the apple, a flicker of a smile crossed his face as its sweetness must have burst across his taste buds. 'Nice,' he approved.

'Daniel can you just tell me this one thing?' I enquired gently. 'Have you ever had anything to do with a man called Carter from Staithes?'

Daniel nearly choked on the apple. 'No, no, bad Carters,' he spluttered. 'Stay away from bad Carters.' Splutters turned into high-pitched screams.

'Please calm yourself,' I appealed. Worryingly, all my ardent requests were met with louder screams.

Daniel was still screaming hysterically as I banged several times on the door for the warder. I had been shocked at Daniel's physical state now I was gravely concerned about his apparent psychological deterioration.

'I want to see the governor straightaway,' I told Goater out in the passageway.

'Well, I'm not sure …' he prevaricated like a despot preceding the fall. I am certain he must have heard Daniel's screams long before he opened the door to let me out. No doubt he thought at first it would do this clever barrister some good to be left alone with a madman for a while. Now I could see Goater was not so convinced he had made the right decision.

'Immediately,' I told him emphatically.

Chapter Twenty-Four

I walked along the platform, along the tail of the train to its head where serpent steam hissed and spouted angrily into the airless roof. I loved living in this age of steam – loved the immediate power of it all – journeys that had taken days by road now only took hours by train. I would be in the new city of Leeds in a trice.

I always emerged from a train journey somehow expecting to find the world irreversibly changed. It was therefore something of an anticlimax to discover my location had most certainly changed but never the world.

Leeds station – Leeds streets – if York was ancient and filthy, Leeds certainly had a contemporary feel to it but her streets and buildings were filthier.

I clutched my briefcase under one arm as if my life depended on its contents, a smile of derision crossing my face. *Brief* case, normally and actually just that but not today.

Leeds had boomed from a small woollen into a wealthy woollen town under Victoria's patronage. Standing in front of the town hall, opened by the great lady herself several years before I was born, I could see how the imposing building had already begun to turn black with soot and muck – the industrial alchemy for money. Leeds success was everywhere to be seen, there was a vibrancy about the place. From the station I had fought my way through arcades and shops and markets clinking and chinking with exchanging currency. I had been forced to dodge the horse buses and cabs which clanked and squealed in criss-cross patterns across the city. Leeds, created a city only four years before, already appeared to be carried away with itself. Barges chugged along the canals to and fro between ports east and west; citizens gorged on products from the agricultural plains north and east, while earning their keep from that old staple, wool, south and west.

In the past Leeds, like most other English towns and cities, had endured bad times too. Plague and civil war had left their mark on an otherwise smiling face. But, whatever the circumstances, the town guardians had always had the foresight to embrace people with a contribution to make. In the fourteenth century they had welcomed Flemish immigrants who started up woollen manufacturing, centuries later East European and Russian Jews help to hone the clothing trade to greater heights. Leeds was not York or Staithes – Leeds was cosmopolitan – Leeds was the industrial revolution.

One of the town hall's reposing lions snarled contemptuously down on me. Unsure of my liking for Cuthbert Brodrick's architectural concept anymore, I moved quickly on up Oxford Place.

The General Infirmary in Great George Street struck me as grand and reassuringly Gothic. I stood waiting and absorbed in the hospital's high-ceilinged echoing foyer as a porter rushed off to find my friend from university days, Richard Tate. It was at least a comfort to know that I was not there to anguish over a sick friend or relative as many must have done under this roof over the years.

'Dick.' I reached out my hand to the approaching swirl of white coat.

'It's been a long time.'

'Too long.'

'Really good to see you. How are you, James?'

'Fine, just fine. And yourself?' Much vigorous shaking of hands before the slightly self-conscious mandatory release and withdrawal.

'Must say I was both intrigued and surprised to receive a telegram from you after all this time.'

'If the technology is there, why not use it?'

'Indeed. Though I never saw you as an upholder of innovation, James. But why the sudden urgency, old friend?' asked Dick suspiciously.

'Might I say your equally speedy reply was very much appreciated in the circumstances,' I prevaricated, not ready yet to reveal all.

'You've got me all hot and bothered now,' laughed Dick. 'I just love secrecy and mystery.'

'I require your expertise.'

'Well, I never.'

'I've got something I want to show you.'

'I'm not sure I want to see.' The years had obviously not curbed Dick's sense of humour.

'Something in here.' I patted my briefcase.

'How exciting. Come with me and let's take a dekko.' He ushered me towards a wide staircase. 'What do you think?' he asked, making a sweeping gesture with his hand towards the spacious building.

'I like it very much. But I hope you'll forgive me for saying this, Dick, I am reminded of a train station.'

There was a long silence as our leather soles slap slapped up the stone steps.

'St. Pancras perhaps,' suggested Dick.

'St. Pancras exactly,' I confirmed.

'What about the Albert Memorial then?'

'Sorry?'

'Same architect, dear friend. George Gilbert Scott designed all three. Though his original plan for this building was influenced by none other than Florence Nightingale herself. She made the addition of pavilion style wards.'

'Very impressive. And I bet it wasn't designed in a Hull attic like your town hall.'

'Brodrick was something of a young genius though, don't you think?'

'I expect he was,' I gasped, pausing before ascending the final few steps. 'But I'm not as convinced.'

'What, not fit?' chuckled Dick. 'You'd better let me take a listen to that chest of yours before you leave.'

'Oh, no,' I baulked. 'You're more used to this stairway than me, that's all.'

'I don't attend as many stuffy law dinners either,' jibed Dick, stroking his enviable flat stomach. 'Should have followed your heart and gone in for architecture and stayed thin.'

I decided not to rise to the taunt. I always felt slightly apprehensive in the company of medics. Perhaps it was an awareness that they knew your physical inner workings better than you did yourself. I found medics had a directness, an earthiness about them as if they'd seen it all – and of course they had. It was only in court, on my territory, cross-examining some medical worthy that I felt any sense of being on a par. I would watch barristers, such as Gerald Fawcett, tearing into medical witnesses with a particularly malevolent relish, and I would wonder if their malevolence was born out of the same sense of uneasy awe I strived to control in myself. Then again, perhaps it all merely came down to the petty and historical politics for supremacy between the two professions.

'Hello Charles, are things going well?' Dick stopped a tall moustachioed man walking towards us along the passageway. 'Charles, here, is helping to develop the art of X-ray photography in Leeds. He is an ardent disciple of Herr Roentgen, are you not Charles?'

Charles nodded watchfully, as I baulked again under the direct gaze of this doctor who with his machine could literally look right through me.

'This is an old Cambridge friend of mine, James Cairn,' Dick continued with the introductions.

'Pleased to meet you, sir.' I bowed. Charles remained distant.

'You might be needing him, Charles, if you kill one of your poor, old unsuspecting testees with all these skin burns I've been hearing about,' resumed Dick unabashed. 'James is a barrister.'

'Pity a brilliant pathologist like you, Tate, fails to recognise that radiology is not an *art* form but a diagnostic tool. I guarantee that in the years to come my X-ray room will save more lives than all the other departments in this hospital put together,' retorted the radiologist before striding arrogantly away.

'Not today though, Charles, and not tomorrow either,' Dick roared after him.

'What's all that about?' I asked disconcerted.

'A little ethical difference. The man's just a pompous idiot. Nothing for you to bother your head about, James. Now come in here and let's see what you have to show me.' Dick pulled me into a neat sterile office which actually did smell of hospital and disinfectant.

'I must impress upon you, Dick, a trial is pending and what I'm about to show you …'

'Strictest confidence,' pre-empted Dick, a finger to his lips.

I flipped open the strap on my briefcase.

There was a harmonious snap as Dick switched on his new electric desk lamp. The Swan bulb magically burnt sharp and bright in the already well lit room. Dick carefully lifted the photographs out of their protective sleeves and examined them before the lamp. He picked each one up and put it down thoughtfully but without comment – no longer Dick the abrasive joker but Dick the scientist.

I watched the pathologist's long fingers manoeuvring the image of death this way and that. I began to relax with the dawning realisation that I had not made a mistake consulting this man after all, this man knew his business.

'Who took these?' asked Dick, still holding one of the photographs up in front of his face.

'A photographer over in Whitby.'

'The detail he's got on this one is amazing.'

'That's what Carlton-Bingham said.'

'Who the hell is Carlton-Bingham?'

'My head of chambers.'

'Well, your Mr Carlton-Bingham knows what he's talking about,' said Dick, still engrossed with the one photograph. 'With definition like this we hardly need post-mortems.'

'The police seem to agree with you. Believing they've already got enough evidence against my client to secure a conviction, they felt it unnecessary to conduct one. I think they'll have buried the girl by now.'

'I didn't say I wouldn't have done a post-mortem, I was merely expressing my admiration for this photographer's work. There's only one man I know of in our part of the world who is able to reproduce images like this, and he is a Whitby man.'

'Who?'

'A chap called Wilfred Thornton. Ever heard of him?'

I shook my head, asking, 'Do these photographs give you any indication whether or not foul play was involved in this girl's death?'

'Almost certainly, and because of that I feel the police have been negligent not to hold a full post-mortem.'

My spirit fell. 'You don't think death could have been caused simply by drowning then?'

'You didn't tell me she'd been in water, though I see that for myself now.'

'I deliberately didn't tell you anything in case it influenced your findings. But yes, this young woman was fished out of the sea at Staithes.'

'Salt water, eh? See the wrinkling of the skin there, the hands of a body immersed in water for a few hours or more takes on what we call "a washerwoman's appearance".'

'Her hands seem manicured though, don't they? Those hands haven't scrubbed many floors.'

'No, I agree with you there.'

'A gentlewoman's hands perhaps?'

'Quite possibly.

'Her eyes have gone. Could fish be the cause of that?'

'An eye is the easiest piece of anatomy for a fish or crustacean to attack. On the other hand, there might be a more sinister explanation for her condition.'

'I don't understand.'

'Murderers sometimes fear the accusatory stare of their dead victim. They are often incapable of accepting the death of "the thing" they've tortured to death.'

'You are absolutely sure this young woman has been murdered then?' I asked him, both fearful of and desperate for clarification.

'Eighty per cent certain.'

'This doesn't exactly help my client's case, the fact that she's been murdered.'

'Tell me about your client. What sort of chap is he?' asked Dick, eyeing me with curiosity.

'He's regarded in Staithes as the village simpleton. But I've always found him to be a nice, helpful sort of lad. After years of dealing with society's dross, I think I can recognise rogues and murderers when I see them.'

'And you don't see this simple lad as a murderer then?'

'The police have witnesses who actually saw him standing over her on some rocks as the tide came in. But by the time a rescue party was assembled and reached my client, the girl had been washed out to sea. Her body was recovered a short time later.'

'A short time, you say. How short a time, hours, days?'

'I haven't received any exact information on that yet.'

'Although this body has not been immersed in the sea for long, it must have been floating around for more than an hour or two. See, there's no swelling in the face or neck yet, though there is wrinkling in the feet and hands. Was any kind of weapon found on your client?'

'Not to my knowledge.'

'Tell me, have you noticed if he wears a belt or a neckerchief even?'

'A belt? A neckerchief? I'm not sure.'

'There are bruises around this unfortunate young woman's throat and neck that are as numerous as they are confusing. And there is something else that puzzles me, something I would like confirming before I commit myself further.'

'Confirming, how?'

'If you are agreeable, I would like to consult a man whom I regard as one of the most experienced authorities in the land on forensic medicine and toxicology, my old mentor Thomas Scattergood.'

'You are acquainted with Thomas Scattergood?' I asked impressed.

'You obviously have read his medico-legal case book.'

'I found it fascinating. Both volumes.'

'Thomas retired from lecturing some time ago and is not in the best of health at present. But if you leave these photographs with me, I can consult him about them tomorrow. His home in Park Square is only a short walk from here.'

'I really appreciate this, Dick.'

'I hope your client has been wrongly accused, James. Because in contrast to your experience, mine is that some evil bastards are good at concealing their true natures.'

'Just a gut feeling,' I confessed.

'By the way,' said Dick, escorting me to the door. 'The back of each one of these photographs should be inscribed with the deceased's name.'

'That's just it,' I shrugged. 'She hasn't got a name, nobody has claimed her to date.'

'I think we should apply for an exhumation forthwith,' proposed Dick forcefully.

'You did say "we",' I checked.

'Leave the science to me and I'll leave the law to you. And I only hope that big gut of yours doesn't let both of us down, Cairn.'

Chapter Twenty-Five

To kill two birds with one stone – I was back on Bram Stoker territory.

KILL. KILLING. KILLER – chilling words on a warm muggy August day. Dick Tate seemed sure the Staithes girl had been murdered by someone. But by whom, if not Daniel?

With short reluctant strides, reminiscent of a Shakespearean schoolboy, I made my way once more to Flora Robertshaw in Grape Street.

'Madam is expecting thee, sir. Can I take thy coat?'

'No, I'll not be staying long enough for that.'

'Very well, sir.' The same buxom maid who had previously opened the door disapprovingly on me in holiday attire seemed to have undergone an attitude change confronted by my black morning coat and striped business trousers. 'Your hat then, sir?' she suggested.

'Thank you,' I agreed, dabbing a handkerchief across my sweating forehead.

The maid almost purred over the relinquished silk top hat. 'Mr Cairn,' she announced as Flora Robertshaw rose to greet me as before in the heavily draped drawing-room. The maid hovered before asking, 'Any tea, madam?' Flora Robertshaw looked to me. I politely declined, and the maid withdrew closing the heavy oak door gently behind her.

Click – a double-take – I remembered.

'Please be seated, Mr Cairn.'

I bowed and flicking back my summer tails sank thankfully into the nearest chair.

'How's poor Daniel?' Mrs Robertshaw asked straightaway.

'How long has that woman been with you?' I asked, deflecting her enquiry.

'Why? What's wrong with her?'

'I could have sworn I saw her in York recently.'

'That could be so. Susannah is entitled to go where she wishes on her day off.'

'Susannah, you say?' Flora Robertshaw nodded a little suspiciously. 'And what is Susannah's surname, might I ask?'

'Thou might ask, Mr Cairn, but whether or not I tell thee is a different matter. Pray, why such concern over our maid?'

'Oh, there is nothing personally meant by it, ma'am,' I explained, flushing with the sudden realisation that my inquisitiveness might be misconstrued. 'I am merely curious at seeing her again in such different circumstances.'

'And what were the circumstances of thy previous encounter?' Flora Robertshaw's own curiosity was now aroused.

'I was walking along Coppergate when your maid, in the company of a much younger woman, passed me on the other side of the street.'

'So, 'tis the younger woman who has captivated thee then?'

'No, no,' I denied vehemently, my cheeks on fire again.

'It appears to be thy habit chancing upon ladies in the street?'

So she did see me that time in the market square when she had been on Roderick Jeffrey's arm. I nodded politely but thought it imprudent to comment further.

'Mott, our maid's surname is Mott.' Mrs Robertshaw's shrug was dismissive.

'And do you know how long she's been in service here?'

'She must have been …' Mrs Robertshaw paused to metaphorically scratch her head. 'I remember my sister telling me they'd just employed Susannah, yes, she must have told me that only hours before …'

'She died in the fire?'

'Indeed,' agreed Mrs Robertshaw, shuffling nervously in her chair. 'Now, as I've told thee all there is to know about our maid, will thou be good enough to tell me how my son fares?'

'He is as well as can be expected. The block he is housed in is not all that old. I have spoken to the governor, face to face, and drawn his attention to Daniel's vulnerability. He has assured me that given Daniel's particular circumstances, he will do his best to improve his conditions and assign a more empathetic warder to his cell.'

'Art thou saying he has already been subjected to some cruelty?' picked up Mrs Robertshaw instantly.

I remembered Goater.

'A little bullying perhaps,' I admitted. Flora Robertshaw looked horrified.

'Do you know what would really help Daniel?' The widow shook her head not wanting to hear, avoiding my gaze, knowing the answer. 'You do not feel able to visit him then? Not yet at least,' I added hopefully.

'I …' Again she shook her head.

I crossed my legs, allowing her time before asking, 'Do you know of an ironstone miner called Carter who must have lived near you on Cowbar Bank?'

'Would that I could forget that villain and his entire family. He was in the mob that set fire to my home and killed my sister.'

'Was Daniel aware of Carter's involvement in the tragedy?'

'Could have been,' said Mrs Robertshaw, her expression suddenly circumspect.

'But Carter's involvement was only revealed at the inquest, was it not? And Daniel is kept in solitary confinement so it is unlikely that he could have gained access to that piece of information in prison.'

'Who knows,' commented Mrs Robertshaw vaguely. 'Maybe he saw him on that terrible night with a flare in his hand or heard him shouting outside.'

'Maybe,' I pealed in doubtfully. 'But what have you got against the rest of the Carter family, Flora?'

Mrs Robertshaw did not react to my familiar use of her Christian name, asking instead, 'Why art thou pursuing this, Mr Cairn?'

'You just told me that you wished to forget the entire Carter family. Now why would you want to do that unless they were all involved in the fire?' Mrs Robertshaw closed up like a flither shell, a posture I had confronted many times from witnesses in the box. 'What are you holding back, Flora?'

'Believe me, Mr Cairn, some things are too shameful to discuss.'

'What, more shameful than your son being hanged for a crime he didn't commit?'

'But this has nothing to do with the girl on the rocks.'

'Let me be the judge of that, Flora. Daniel became hysterical when I mentioned the name "Carter".'

'All right, I'll tell thee the whole story if it will help.' Mrs Robertshaw held up her hand in appeasement. 'Jed Carter has three sisters, all of them run wild. A few years back they cornered Daniel on the empty beach.' I watched with professional detachment as tears of anger and humiliation began to fill Flora Robertshaw's eyes. 'They pulled his breeches down and played with him like a toy till he screamed out in pain and fear. Holding him down each of 'em pulled up their skirts and took it in turn to flop down on him. Exhausted from the struggle, he eventually manage to wriggle free and escape onto the flat rocks sobbing inconsolably. Although we don't believe in drink, Mr Cairn, if it hadn't been for the Cod and Lobster landlord raising the alarm I believe our Daniel would have been sitting out there to this day.'

'Or drowned,' I ventured poignantly. 'That sounds to be a serious sexual assault, whether committed by a man or a woman. Didn't you send for the constable?'

'Send for the constable? Much use he was. The Carter girls denied it of course, said it was Daniel who made all the running. Daniel who hasn't a clue. Nobody in the village believed them. Even before they assaulted my lad they were generally referred to in the community as "drunken papist whores".'

'The Carters are a Catholic family then?'

'Yes, they are, and having suffered from religious discrimination in Staithes myself, I, personally, never held that against them. But they treated Daniel ill, and it was the lies of the three of them against the word of my lad. It was all conveniently hushed up and apparently forgotten, only Jed Carter didn't forget, and when his sister Grace fell with child shortly afterwards he blamed Daniel.'

'And could Daniel have been the father?'

'Him and a dozen others. And now look what's happened. Poor Daniel's fated for trouble.'

'This might sound strange but perhaps it's even more important, the crucial reason for my visit in fact, has Daniel ever worn a belt or neckerchief say?'

'A belt, neckerchief?'

'Ay, either or both?'

'Sometimes braces, more often string, but never a belt, and certainly never a neckerchief. We were too poor for such refinements, Mr Cairn.' The flow of conversation was suddenly interrupted by a knock on the door. 'Come in,' snapped Mrs Robertshaw irritably.

'Sir wishes to inform thee, madam, that he is returned home and in his study.'

'Very well, Susannah.' Mrs Robertshaw visibly tensed. Susannah curtsied and left.

'I must be wending my way too,' I announced getting to my feet.

'What so soon?'

'I have another appointment in Whitby today.'

'Well, I must not delay thee further. It's good of thee to call, Mr Cairn, and I cannot thank thee enough for pursuing my son's cause with such diligence.' Mrs Robertshaw bobbed her head in acknowledgement. Remaining seated, she took up a small hand bell from the nearby table and tinkled it delicately in her work-worn hand.

I marvelled at how easily the captain's wife had slipped back into gentility after all those years living in a hovel on the Cowbar. Perhaps old habits do die hard.

'Madam, thou rang?' Susannah stood framed in the doorway again.

'Please be good enough to show Mr Cairn out, Susannah.'

Old habits die hard – another double-take on the Jeffrey maid – and then a thunderbolt of an idea stuck me. Susannah Mott was particularly eloquent by any standard of household but unusually so for a manufacturer's home. Even in the best Yorkshire houses most servants would refer to their employers as "master and mistress", not "sir and madam", unless instructed otherwise.

I took my hat and pausing on the threshold turned back to the maid and asked, 'Where were you previously employed?' Adding, after taking in her ringless state, a belated 'Miss Mott.' Susannah Mott stared back at me completely flummoxed although I had tried to make my enquiry sound casual. 'It's all right, my dear, I'm merely impressed by your …' I stumbled for the right word. 'Refinement.'

'I thank thee for the compliment, sir. Though I thrived on schooling, I was born of lowly folk until fate placed me in a situation where refinement was an obligation.'

'And where was that, Miss Mott?'

Rather than mistrustful, Susannah now appeared to be flattered by my keen attention. 'Why, Brigham Hall, in the service of Sir Hugh and Lady Clarissa Parke.'

'Is that so?' I swallowed hard.

'Art thou acquainted with the Hall, sir?'

'A little,' I replied, trying to reorganise my thoughts, remember what Maud Fines had told me. Before asking, I knew the answer to my next question. 'Tell me, Miss Mott, what was your exact employment at the Hall?'

'I was nanny there.'

'So, why are you here in Whitby now?'

'My employment was terminated.'

'Suddenly?'

'How dost thou know that?' Susannah Mott's manner abruptly swung back to mistrust.

'I guessed.'

'Art thou a policeman?'

'Certainly not.'

'All the same, I think I have already said too much.'

'On the contrary, soon I think you will have to say much more,' I said, handing her my card and raising my hat.

* * * * *

The church clock struck noon. I waited for my appointment in the churchyard of dead mariners. The eerie sea-fret I had imagined all those weeks ago, seated on this same bench, was actually rolling in today. Common to the east coast – frequently turning warm humid days cold – a fret was never regarded as anything exceptional by Whitby locals. Nevertheless, I felt uneasy as if I was being enveloped by the unknown, touched and caressed by a multitude of insistent clammy hands. I had got so far as thinking these were the hands of dead mariners when Jackson arrived.

'Thank goodness,' I told him. 'I was afraid the postmistress might not have passed on my reply.'

'Glad you got my letter too,' said Jackson, rubbing his hands together for warmth.

'So, you decided to tell the truth at the fire inquest after all. Read it in the *York Herald*, can't tell you how pleased I was to see that.' I gave Jackson's jacket a friendly tug. 'Sit yourself down, man, next to me.'

'Why, for God's sake, did we have to meet here?' asked Jackson, looking nervously from tombstone to tombstone.

'It's where Bram Stoker hatched a fantastic plot.'

'Bram who?'

'Never mind,' I laughed. 'So, what's this all about?'

'I've been told something, something I think might be important.'

'Told by whom?'

'By a man called Thompson.'

'Thompson? I've heard that name mentioned before.'

'Yes, you might well have done, he's the odd-job man at the Hall.'

'Is his word to be trusted?'

'Well, there's no doubting he was far the worse for drink on t' night he spoke to me, but that isn't anything unusual for Thompson. Though beer surely loosened his tongue that don't mean his information is unworthy of investigation, do it?'

We remained huddled together there on the bench for another quarter of an hour. Two spies plotting our next course of action in the swirling mist. Dracula might not have risen from under a tombstone that day but another equally sinister possibility was beginning to emerge.

Chapter Twenty-Six

A prolonged, strangled blood-curdling screech rent apart the still night air.

'What was that?' I whispered, swivelling and wide-eyed.

'Barn owl,' explained Jackson calmly, placing a reassuring hand on my arm.

'Umm! Barn owl of course,' I shrugged, my subsequent smile unconvincing.

I could see the flickering glow of candle-light in the great house a hundred yards across the expanse of close-cropped lawn. I wondered how long it would be before Brigham Hall's chandeliers sparkled with electricity. Not long, I suspected, the rich always had the capital to invest in the latest discoveries first. That is, unless something catastrophic were to happen that changed their fortune.

'We're almost there,' said Jackson, guiding me carefully down a difficult zigzagging path that ran from the top garden down towards the sea. He suddenly stopped and squatted down to light the oil lamp he was carrying. He had not dared risk the light until we were hidden from the Hall.

'How do you know about this place?'

'I told you I got me 'ezzells for t' creel pots off this estate. What I didn't tell you was that me and Marlett have a little private enterprise going on from time to time. We shoot the odd deer and an occasional brace of pheasants when the fishing isn't good down in t' village come wintertime.'

'I'm not hearing this,' I said, covering my ears with my hands. 'You mean you poached them.'

Jackson nodded solemnly. 'We store the meat down in t' cave afore a boat arrives to collect it. Come I'll show you.'

The cave that Jackson referred to was not a cave at all. At least if it ever had been a cave it was now fully converted into a stone-rendered ice-house cut well back into the cliff. We crawled through the narrow arched entrance into a large cellar. Jackson swung the lamp towards the ceiling where several hooks dangled down like tools of the Inquisition.

'I expect you hang your illegal venison from those before transportation,' I snorted disparagingly.

I liked Jackson very much but I could not abide stealing. Jackson's eyes gleamed back at me in the lamp light, they posed a question of their own: how could I pass judgement on others when I had never known the desperation of real hunger? Without a word passing between us, Jackson had conveyed his meaning.

'No, not up there, up there is too obvious for quarry,' he explained, still without a hint of contrition. 'See, through here.'

I followed him and the swinging lamp into a further cellar. This one darker, smaller and mustier than the first. My skin prickled with the fear of imaginary insects. I irritably dashed away fragments of gossamer gliding across my face like the tips of moth wings. Jackson indicated more ceiling hooks.

'Thompson told me this is the place, this is where he found it.' Above us, down through the crust of earth came the distant but penetrating howling of big dogs. 'The Hall's wolfhounds,' muttered Jackson. 'We must be quick.'

'Wait a minute,' I interjected. 'If we do find something how do I know it hasn't been planted here?'

'You'll just have to trust me, Mr Cairn,' affirmed Jackson with a weary tolerance.

'And do you trust Thompson?'

'He's all we've got so far.'

'But how come this Thompson is so well informed?'

'I don't know,' cried Jackson, his aggravation finally bouncing from wall to wall. 'But he told me that dead lass certainly wasn't my daughter. Said he'd been drunk and asleep behind a fish cart the night Lane and I started arguing outside the Cod and Lobster. Said he overheard Lane telling me that vicious lie, saw me hit him. Thompson said there was no way she was my daughter because she came from here. Said he'd found …'

'Keep you voice down,' I warned him. 'Or we'll have the entire staff of the Hall arriving. Wolfhounds and all.'

'Here, you use this then.' Jackson relinquished the lamp. 'And take a look for yourself.'

I began to systematically comb the floor. Hands on hips, Jackson watched on. At first I saw nothing, until I caught a glimmer of silver in the corner of the cellar where the north and west walls met. Was this merely the beginning of a snail's thin trail perhaps? All the same, I decided to investigate closer and lowered the lamp. Sinking to my knees, I reached out and carefully retrieved a few fine silk strands, then I found more, draping them all across my other wrist.

'Look,' I exclaimed, offering them to Jackson.

'Just like Thompson said "white hairs from the witch girl",' gasped Jackson.

* * * * *

Almost too neat, too perfect, too propitious, I acknowledged back in my Gillygate room. The spy-glass shook in my hand as I examined and re-examined the contents of this tissue wrapped gift of evidence. I roughly estimated a hundred strands of hair, a good deal of hair. A lovelock perhaps? But silvery white, how on earth could this be from a young girl's head? Nevertheless, it was unmistakably fine human hair. But something other than the hair and its colouring was troubling me – it was this man Thompson – Carl Thompson, the odd-jobman. How involved was Thompson in this gruesome business? He must have wanted, needed to tell someone about the hair. Was it a matter of conscience? Guilt? Was it the desire of a murderer to be ultimately caught? Thompson must have had a good idea that a man like Jackson would go and investigate the ice-house, would not just let that sort of information rest. It did not make sense, none of it made sense. My owl-hooting visit to Brigham Hall with Jackson the other night had felt unreal like an act from the contemporary melodrama showing at the theatre down the road. As if to emphasise the fiction factor of the other night, I became aware of the hustle and bustle of Gillygate rising up through my open window. It was business as usual down there on the street, yet nothing seemed usual to me high and alone in my tenement.

I ran the hair through my fingers – to think a man's life might in reality hang on these thin threads.

I knew I should really hand over this piece of new evidence to the officer in charge, but Kemp's mind was already closed against any possibility of Daniel's innocence. Moreover, I regarded Inspector Kemp as being at best stupid and at worst corrupt. And unless I could get the hair authenticated as belonging to the dead girl, it wouldn't be a worthy court exhibit anyway. Despite Kemp, despite the hair's questionable validity, my attention was firmly focused back on the Hall. I felt in my gut that someone there knew the answer to this mystery. If need be I would subpoena the entire household to attend court.

* * * * *

Help finally landed through the letter box in a pile of prosaic mail. Flipping through the envelopes, it was the appallingly written address on one that caught my eye. Indeed, I was so impressed that this piece of correspondence had reached me at all, I decided to open it immediately.

I struggled to decipher the date. I struggled all the way through.

10th August 1897.

My dear James,

I am delighted to inform you that an exhumation order has been granted to us by the Whitby coroner, Mr Charles Fenton, for the day after tomorrow. My esteemed colleague, Mr Scattergood, has agreed to assist me at the post-mortem. We will be gathered in Whitby churchyard at the young woman's unmarked grave at 6-30 a.m. prompt.
I remain,
Yours Truly,
Dick.

God, Dick's writing was terrible. So the girl had been there all the time in her unmarked grave among the mariners. She could have been listening, heard me and Jackson plotting her right to a decent headstone. So near and yet so far … I was determined to be at that graveside the next day no matter what.

Chapter Twenty-Seven

The grave was in a corner of the churchyard well away from the rest – a sinner's grave, a pauper's mound, alienated. She should not really have been here at all, this particular cemetery had been closed for burials long ago. But where else could an unknown be placed in Whitby with no kin to pay for a headstone? If aware, how could anyone allow their sister/daughter to be buried in such a manner? – anonymous –unmourned. Was this poor creature as isolated in life as she is in death, I wondered.

A six-thirty Thursday yawn. Half a dozen reluctant early morning policemen stamped their booted feet like stallions eager for the off, eager to be anywhere but here. Kemp scowled as he recognised me and looked away in disgust. He had already placed the blame for this unnecessary and farcical procedure.

Several of the policemen began to construct a makeshift canvas screen round the grave to ward off the curiosity of the press and public and to give the exhumation some dignity. Already in place was a large bell-tent, no doubt the venue for the post-mortem. The tent resembled a piece of army surplus from some forgotten war, possibly the same African war my father had fallen in. Still on a military theme, I noticed two gravediggers stood waiting stiffly at attention, gripping their shovels tightly like bayonets. Their trade, usually performed in privacy, was now in the spotlight and they were about to embark on celebrity.

In contrast Dick, followed by a fussy little fellow and an older, hunched taller man, looked relaxed, everyday, as he emerged from the tent and strode across the path towards the police activity.

'James, glad you could make it.' Dick extended his hand. 'This is Mr Gaunt who is the sexton of St. Mary's, and I'd like to introduce you to my colleague for the day, Mr Thomas Scattergood.'

Mr Gaunt's handshake was perfunctory, tall Mr Scattergood's more genial and firm.

'Good to meet you, James.' Scattergood's shaved top lip curved into a smile above a mass of white beard. The beard appeared to be in compensation for his hairline which must have receded into the smooth backwaters of his cranium many years ago. His face was sallow, deep lines splayed from his eyes, but the eyes themselves glowed with a youthful joyful interest. I was disconcerted by this doyen of forensic medicine and toxicology, this expert on the darker world, because my initial impression of Scattergood could be described as nothing other than "jolly".

'Let's get to work, men.' Kemp's growl rudely interrupted any other niceties. The two gravediggers still deferred to Mr Gaunt who gave them the nod.

I kept my hand clamped over the mouth of my jacket pocket. I did not want to lose any possible coign of vantage at this stage. Throughout the excavation, I could not rid my mind of the description of a similar scene that had haunted my imagination since childhood. I remembered it was my sister who first told me the true story of how the poet and painter, Dante Gabriel Rossetti, had exhumed his wife's body to retrieve a book of poems. It was said that Rossetti's agent, Charles Howell, had to cut Lizzie's luxuriant auburn tresses free from the manuscript because even after death they had grown around it.

With rolled up shirt sleeves the gravediggers laboured on. Their steel spades occasionally flashing in the light of the rising sun. From a cold start it looked as if the cloudless day would turn out to be a hot one. The two men stopped their digging once or twice to rub the sweat from their foreheads – sweat and dirt mixed – their frowns marked like Cain.

Crunch! – the uncomfortable grating sound of steel striking wood.

'Careful now,' instructed Mr Gaunt, leaning forward over one of the gravediggers to get a better view.

I shivered at this very macabre rendition of find the buried treasure.

Ropes were sent for. After the gravediggers had struggled to secure them under the coffin, which had all the brittle and cheap consistency of an elongated orange box, the policemen hauled the deceased to the surface with as much ceremony as I had shown hauling Jackson's creel pots up from the North Sea.

This was Dick's cue to take over command from Mr Gaunt. He ushered orange box and policemen into the bell tent.

'Coming?' Scattergood beckoned to me.

'No, no, I'll wait out here if you don't mind,' I replied, reaching into my jacket pocket. 'But would you be kind enough to do me a great favour and find out if this belongs to her?'

'What is it?' Scattergood gazed curiously down on the tissue wrapper placed into his large palm.

'Hair. I want to know if this is her hair.'

'That shouldn't be much of a problem.' Scattergood spun slowly round on his heels and stooping disappeared into the tent.

'Too soon after breakfast, eh, Mr Cairn,' jeered Kemp, quickly following Scattergood through the canvas door and out of sight before I could think of a suitable reply.

My only prayer now was that Scattergood would be discreet about the possible match of hair and conceal the entire process from a vengeful Kemp.

Kemp appeared a quarter of an hour later. Kemp appeared too soon. Seated on my favourite bench overlooking the sea, I was confronted by the seething inspector.

'This is all a waste of time, a waste of police time, even *your* doctors have had to confirm that she was strangled and didn't die from a drowning accident. Dr Allanby's original finding wasn't good enough for the likes of you, was it, Cairn? You had to meddle, make trouble, give the council extra expense. Well, I hope you're satisfied. The girl was strangled and I will see that your client, Daniel Robertshaw, hangs for it.'

'Even if someone else strangled her?' I snapped back. I did not know what I had actually expected from Dick's post-mortem but I had expected more than this.

Lost for words, Kemp flung his hands akimbo in exasperation before finally screaming, 'Why can't you get it into your bloody head, there isn't anyone else? There's not one other single person under suspicion.' With this he stormed off.

'Temper,' I muttered sarcastically after the retreating back. Nevertheless, I remained on the bench for a good half-hour or more gloomily mulling over the facts of the Robertshaw case and Kemp's final statement. "Not one other single person under suspicion", could that really be right? Eventually, getting to my feet, I steeled myself to go over to the bell tent and ask for confirmation of the post-mortem results.

'You've decided to brave it,' laughed an aproned Dick, squatting to clean his hands in a bucket of soap and water in the far corner. 'Good timing, we've just finished.'

I nodded grimly, quickly taking in the various glass sample jars, buckets, and a small fold-up table displaying a microscope and an array of other scientific paraphernalia. I detected a slight, sickly-sweet odour, death mixed with earth and grass inside the tent.

'Of course there's been some deterioration since the photographs were taken. Almost impossible now to pick out any petechiae but on the whole the police did a good job at refrigeration,' announced Scattergood heartily, glancing up from the centre-piece – the post-mortem table. Nonetheless, out of a sense of decorum or sensitivity to my nervousness, the eminent old surgeon obligingly drew a white sheet up over the girl's remains. Though not before I had seen the leering, shrivelled, almost mummified mask of what had once been a vital young woman. And not before I had seen the long white tresses flowing down from the head of the table, still flowing exposed from beneath the matching covering sheet.

'Kemp's told me that you've only been able to confirm she was strangled.' I cleared my dry throat.

'*Only that?* Is that what he's told you?' asked Dick.

'From Thornton's photographs alone, it didn't take a genius to deduce strangulation,' put in Scattergood.

'The good inspector should have stayed a little longer, should he not?' said Dick, winking across to his colleague.

'Fella didn't seem to have much of a stomach when we rolled up our sleeves for the more serious detailed business,' sniffed Scattergood.

'Why, what have you found?' I asked, like a curious schoolboy striving to be in on the big secret.

'Where do we begin?' Dick once more appealed to Scattergood.

'First and foremost one doesn't accept strangulation at *face* value,' explained Scattergood, hesitating for his witticism to take root with all the panache of a man about to impart great wisdom in his beloved lecture theatre. 'I always told my students never to lose sight of these three principles when conducting an investigation into a capital offence: manner, method, motive. For example what sort of ligature has been used, how much force has been applied? Is this an act of suicide or murder? Which finger imprints belong to the victim or to her killer? Allow me to demonstrate to you, James, the scratches normally made by the victim herself. Get behind me and pull this scarf tightly round my neck.' I took up the ends of the specialist's tendered silk scarf and begrudgingly obliged without applying too much pressure. Scattergood's mottled hands clutched and jerked and tried to loosen the noose round his throat as he theatrically rasped, 'Can you see how I attempt to alleviate the pressure?'

'Is that what she did?' I asked horrified, still uncomfortable in my role as the venerable Mr Scattergood's strangler.

'Hardly any sign of her own fingernail scratches at all. Her strangulation was rapid, efficient and unexpected.'

'Despatched professionally, one might say,' added Dick.

A flicker of hope – Daniel, professional? – I could not imagine Daniel being capable of despatching anyone or anything efficiently, the poor lad was too clumsy.

'Have you any idea yet exactly what sort of ligature was used?' I asked.

A cunning twinkle of pleasure passed between the two medics.

'You've really hit upon an intriguing question there,' enthused Scattergood.

'If you brace yourself and come over to the table, we'll show you exactly what we mean,' said Dick.

I took a deep breath and manfully stepped forward. Obligingly, Scattergood arranged the sheet so that only part of the corpse's face and neck were visible. He held a magnifying glass over a specific area and invited me to bend closer and take a look.

'There's some sort of thick strap mark there, see?' indicated Dick. 'It reaches round both sides of the victim's neck lifting slightly to the lower jaw. We've measured it at about an inch and a half wide. Below that indentation note the other mark, possibly from a sliding buckle.'

'And observe there,' pointed out Scattergood, his long index finger extending to another position beneath the glass. 'These are the marks that we believed would give us our best results all along, right from our preliminary inspection of Wilfred Thornton's excellent photographs. There are faint impressions at either side of them but those two central ones are very much clearer.'

'They look like letters, an M and possibly an A,' I ventured.

'Let me show you,' said Scattergood, leading me gently by the arm away from the table. Behind me, I heard Dick flick the sheet back over the dead girl's head. I watched transfixed as Scattergood tore off a plain piece of notebook paper and copied the two symbols I had just seen inscribed in the victim's neck. Scattergood then carefully drew two more symbols next to them and again invited me to take a look. 'What do you see now?' he asked.

'You've inverted both letters. The A is obviously not an A but an R. The M remains the same. A mirror image of course.'

'Anything stamped will always produce this reverse effect.'

'But why would anyone want to … to brand her?'

'Unintentionally, old chap, of that I can assure you.' Scattergood smiled indulgently at my naive assumption. 'I think you will find the perpetrator of this crime owned or owns some sort of belt or strap with embossed metallic lettering. He used it to kill her.'

'We've found something else,' piped up Dick again.

'What?' I gasped.

'The very thing you've been looking for. Apart from identifying our killer's strange taste in fashion accessories, we think we've found his motive.'

'Which was?'

'There are one or two more tests and calculations I have to do regarding the accuracy of this piece of evidence, and it's so important that I think you will be better served reading my finished report.'

'And if all this isn't tantalising enough,' resumed Scattergood, breathless now with excitement. 'Dr Tate and I suspect this young woman suffered from a very unusual and rare condition. A hereditary condition I've heard about but personally never encountered.'

'Nor have I,' stressed Dick. 'Although my experience is of course more modest than Thomas'.'

'The lack of eyes didn't help, did it?'

'But the hair…'

'Surely, if we're right, this must eventually lead to a positive identification of the victim.'

'Can I be included in this conversation?' I butted in.

Dick and Scattergood solemnly shook their heads. I laughed, thinking this was another medical tease.

'We're not ready yet to put forward any positive conclusion regarding this rare condition and the victim, not until an expert in the field has examined the samples we've taken today.' For once Dick's serious expression did not crack.

'What samples?'

'Skin, hair. I've stored away two phials of them in my sample box ready for transportation. And you'll never guess where and to whom they're bound.'

'How could I?' I was beginning to feel slightly aggrieved, disgruntled. It was I, after all, who had first promoted this investigation. And now the experts were taking over and not telling me things.

'You've met him. Charles Ambler-Smith, the X-ray man, remember?'

'I thought you didn't get on.'

'We don't. Ambler-Smith's one of the rudest bastards I've ever met. However, that doesn't mean he isn't the country's leading authority on the reactions of skin to light, pigmentation, that sort of thing.'

'Yes, Ambler-Smith is definitely the man to sort this one out,' agreed Scattergood.

'What about the hair I gave you?' I asked him. 'Is it hers?' I nodded across to the tiny hillock of sheet.

'That sample is also interesting. Where did you get it from?'

'I'd rather not say.' I could be cagey too.

'Well, we'll let that pass for the moment, come over to the microscope and take a look yourself. I've already placed a small sample of the victim's existing hair alongside yours on the slide. Although "existing" is perhaps an inappropriate term to use here,' chuckled Scattergood.

Ignoring the forensic specialist's inveterate black humour, I pressed my eye to the microscope's eye-piece and fiddled with the magnification. 'It looks the same to me.'

'Oh, it's the same all right,' confirmed Scattergood. 'But it hasn't been pulled out of her scalp during her murder, if that's what you've been thinking.'

'How can you tell that?'

'Look again, your sample's on the right. If that hair had been forcefully removed from the victim's scalp one would expect to see more matrix stuck at the end of each shaft. Further more, this is what we call a contaminated specimen.'

'Contaminated?'

'See, there's a lot of fluff mixed up and clinging to the hairs themselves. Although you feel unable to tell us where it actually did come from at this stage, I'd hazard a guess that its origins were a bedroom.'

'You've lost me now.'

'Fluff, man,' said Scattergood.

'What Thomas is trying to tell you is that from the neat alignment of the end of the hairs in your sample, he suspects they've been deliberately cut and kept in a dusty bedroom drawer somewhere,' Dick contributed tactfully.

'A love-token perhaps,' suggested Scattergood.

'Or a lock of hair planted on purpose?' I whispered in dismay.

'You alone know the likelihood of that,' said Scattergood.

'It's been a long and rewarding day for all of us,' said Dick yawning, bringing any further speculation to an abrupt conclusion.

'It certainly has,' agreed Scattergood readily.

Overwhelmed with all this prima-facie evidence, I was not sure what sort of day it had been for me. It was my job now to assemble all this new information and see how it panned out in respect of my client's defence. Perhaps only then would my true debt to Dick and Thomas Scattergood be fully realised. Nevertheless, I thanked them both profusely.

'Think nothing of it, old boy, it's our job when all is said and done,' responded Dick, beginning to clear the surface of the fold-away table. 'I'll be in touch as soon as I can with my final report and Ambler-Smith's findings.'

'I think I already know what Ambler-Smith's findings will be,' I said.

'Well done, old boy, but let's make sure first, shall we?' said Dick.

'By the way, can I keep that contaminated sample of hair?' I asked Scattergood.

'Of course.' He replaced the hair carefully in its tissue wrapper and handed it back to me. 'Not for use in court I hope, counsel?'

'Who knows,' I shrugged.

The guard's whistle paralysed the station. Immune, my confused thoughts continued to tick away as I boarded the train. I struggled to fit all the pieces of the dead girl's story together as the York express clattered and knocked hypnotically across the sleepers. But sleep would not come for me, not even in the comfort of my own Gillygate bed. I wrestled and tossed questions about in an exhausted, semi-delirious state. Some small detail was eluding me over and above the rest. *MA – RM – RM –* a scorpion of memory was clamped to my brain and would not let go. A belt with an embossed badge, I was sure I had seen one somewhere recently.

Chapter Twenty-Eight

At first he thought it was some sort of ghostly aberration like the visions his mother had had of his father and brother long after they were gone. But no, the shimmering figure kept coming on across the moor, kept getting closer, gathering speed. A knight in shining armour, he could be nothing else, was about to enter Daniel's insular world.

He watched the knight slowly descending the cleft of the valley that eventually ran out into the sea – the same cleft that hid and protected Daniel's village – a village that did not welcome strangers. The boy on the hillside could not take his eyes off the iron clad man. With lolling tongue, mesmerised, he followed his clanging progress.

'Pots and pans,' shouted the knight. 'All sizes, all kinds.' Pots and pans hung and swung from his waist, his shoulders, dangled down his back as he reached the cobbled High Street.

'What's your name, lad?' asked the knight in a thick Irish brogue, turning quickly on Daniel. Daniel didn't understand, didn't attempt a reply, didn't have time for a reply.

'Come see this,' someone shouted from a tavern doorway. 'Bloody idiot's brought a filthy gyppo into Steers.'

'No need for that sort o' talk, gentlemen,' objected the knight gently as drunks spilled out around him. 'I am only here to sell.'

'Steal and sell our wives and daughters, more like,' jeered Marlett, down from the Hall, unusually drunk for him and spluttering beer into the air.

'What wife, what daughter?' guffawed a fisherman, poking his elbow into the bachelor Marlett's side.

'All the same Marlett's right,' put in Jed Carter, cool and sober, a man Daniel both feared and detested.

'Yes,' screeched an old bitch with sores on her face. 'Let's drive the gyppo out.'

'There's no need ...' began the knight. But it was too late for either the blarney or a reasonable retreat now.

Clang! The first stone was thrown hitting the knight's armour. Hands over his ears, Daniel ducked down behind the wheel of a cart as a rain of stones and curses followed. *Clang*! He jumped up from the plank bed.

'Hello,' he said blinking, trying to blink away the picture of his beautiful knight's dancing curls turned deep red and matted with blood.

'Hello, yourself,' I responded, unsure at first if Daniel had recognised me. His shirt looked cleaner, his lank brown hair looked washed. Daniel rubbed both hands down the front of his breeches before shaking mine. 'Is he behaving himself?' I turned to the most benevolent looking warder I had ever seen, certainly in this prison. Goater had obviously been assigned elsewhere. The governor had been true to his word.

'Prisoner Robertshaw isn't doing too badly, sir, though it's near impossible to get him into the bath tub. We're forced to wash him down as he stands,' complained the warder.

'Why is that, Daniel? Why won't you get in the bath tub for this gentleman?'

'Drown,' said Daniel.

'Drown?' I repeated troubled, wondering if Daniel's aversion to water had something to do with the fate of his father and half-brother or even more recent events out on the rocks. 'Would you be good enough to allow me a few minutes with my client alone?' I asked the warder. Without further ado, the man nodded solemnly and backed out into the corridor locking the heavy door behind him.

'Have you come to take me home?' asked Daniel immediately.

God, I thought, however improved his circumstances are that's the one question he never fails to ask.

'They'll kill me, won't they, if I go back?'

'I …' I hesitated, surprised. 'Who told you that?'

'Just know,' shrugged Daniel, hand in pocket.

I took the tissue wrapper out of my own pocket, feeling that this was becoming almost ritualistic, and carefully opening it out on the small table asked, 'Do you know what this is?'

Daniel stared at the wrapper's contents for a second or two. 'Mermaid hair,' he acknowledged guilelessly.

'I want you to think about this next question very carefully, it's very important. Do you own a strap or belt with letters on it?'

This time seconds ran into minutes as Daniel slowly ground the question round and round in his head. 'Do you mean like Mr Farnborough's?'

'Who is Mr Farnborough?'

'Mr Farnborough stands on the platform,' proclaimed Daniel, brightening instantly at this more pleasurable memory of home.

I sensed my own colour draining in contrast: of course that decrepit old porter at Staithes railway station. I had seen him wearing that same ostentatious shoulder strap myself. No wonder Daniel remembered, remembered the gleaming silver buckle mounted with the large railway badge. 'Can you tell me what the letters are on Mr Farnborough's badge?'

'Letters?' asked Daniel mystified.

'Doesn't matter for now,' I reassured him, upbraiding myself for the stupidity of asking a man who cannot read or write to interpret letters.

* * * * *

MONGOLISM First recognised by John Langdon Haydon Down, circa 1866, Medical Superintendent at Earlswood Asylum for Idiots, Redhill.

Idiots – an unkind word to use – an idiot to me is some unfortunate, often gifted, unconventional sort of boy made to stand in a corner for hours with his back to the rest of the class. I smarted in the comfort and protection of Bootham Chambers at a distant memory of one such school friend's humiliation. Garth Rothbury – exhibitioner and now don in English at Oxford – if Garth was an idiot where did that leave me? Idiot or not that morning I had armed myself with various publications from The Retreat library and was now settling my feet on a footstool to swot up on Daniel's condition in full. I amused myself with the notion that far from being my old biology master's dunce, I had recently developed into something of an expert in both forensic and psychological medicine. Humour apart, I knew it was vital to be acquainted with my client's mental impairment in order to defend him properly.

LANGDON-DOWN SYNDROME is characterised by a broad flat face; short neck; up-slanted eyes, sometimes with an inner epicanthal fold; low-set ears; small nose and enlarged tongue and lips, sloping underchin; poor muscle tone; mental retardation.

I smarted again, this time on Daniel's behalf like an outraged mother. I had to allow that this could be regarded as an accurate description of my client physically, but its cold clinical detachment missed the very essence of the man. Or was I being oversensitive, too involved, as Gerald Fawcett had implied?

The mental retardation seen in persons with this condition is usually moderate, though in some it may be mild or severe.

So is Daniel moderate, mild or severe? Just as I was pondering this question, my clerk of chambers, Martin Trotter, knocked on the door to tell me a lady was waiting outside who wished to see me.

'Her name, Trotter?'

'Susannah Mott, sir.'

'Send her straight in.'

'I must say I've been expecting you.' I kicked away the footstool and rising to my feet bowed curtly to Roderick Jeffrey's maid.

'I've been visiting in York.'

I gestured to a chair. 'Yes, I've seen you here in the city before.'

''Twas madam who finally persuaded me to come,' she admitted, ignoring my sighting reference. Somehow Susannah Mott managed to slump even in the straight-backed chair. Her usual high colour was pale now beneath a head of burnished gold curls poking beneath her Quaker bonnet.

'Flora Robertshaw is a good woman.'

'The best. I knew her long before I worked in her sister's house,' said Susannah before falling silent. Never taking my eyes off her, I waited patiently. In her agitation the maid's fingers twisted and gripped and wrung out part of her skirt. Then the words began to tumble, 'Thou hast to believe me, Mr Cairn sir, I had no idea that madam's lad had been accused of murder, and that a dead lass had been pulled from the water beyond Staithes, not until she unburdened herself to me the other day.'

'The dead girl, do you think you know who she might be?' I asked, getting down to business straight away. Again silence. 'I can actually see for myself, Susannah, that you are wrestling with your conscience. Would it not be better to tell me all you know, here, in the privacy of this room?' Still silence, still the wringing fingers.

'She taught me to write,' swallowed Susannah.

'Who did? Mrs Robertshaw?'

'No, no, Clarissa Parke.'

'You liked her?'

'She was very good to me in her way.'

'So what has Lady Clarissa to do with this?' I asked feigning surprise.

'Thou cannot know how frightened I am, Mr Cairn sir, they're such powerful people.'

'So is the law,' I said, taking up pen and paper.

'*He's* such a powerful man,' rephrased Susannah desperately.

'And you are a religious woman who is about to do everything in her power to prevent another young woman remaining in a pauper's grave, and an innocent man going to the gallows for her murder.'

'Pauper's grave,' whispered Susannah in disbelief. I would not have believed it possible but Susannah appeared to slump further down in the upright.

'That is why you are here, is it not?' I pressed.

'Yes indeed, sir. But I hardly know where to begin.'

'When did you start working for the Parkes?'

'About fifteen years ago.'

'In what capacity?'

'I was employed as a wet-nurse at first for their newly born child. Madam having no inclination to feed the poor wee thing herself.'

'That must have been the child who died.'

'No, no, the child lived right enough, sir, though she always remained delicate and sickly. I became her nanny. Despite all Estelle's infirmities I loved her as if …' Susannah stopped in mid-flow.

'"Estelle", you say?' My pen bit deeper into the paper.

'That was her name, sir.'

'And what of your own child?'

'My own child was stillborn,' Susannah volunteered quickly, too quickly.

'The whole truth,' I reminded her.

'My daughter was a love-child, loved by me but unloved by my family, dragged from my arms at only two days old. 'Twas Mrs Robertshaw who encouraged me to find her through the Whitby Friends. She is in service to one of our brethren here in York. Happily, we are reunited again.'

'And the father?'

'Lost to me years ago.'

'How did you come to leave such an excellent position at Brigham Hall?'

'Sir Hugh told me that they had sent Estelle away for treatment and my services were no longer required.'

'So, in effect, you had lost two daughters?' Susannah nodded; her quivering bottom lip the only indicator of the real cost. 'Treatment for Estelle, you say, why treatment?'

'As I have already told thee Estelle was unwell. She wasn't allowed out during the day, she couldn't see in sunlight.'

'Her disorder made her something of a prisoner in her own home then?'

'Very much so, sir,' nodded Susannah. 'Moreover, Sir Hugh didn't like her venturing out anywhere without him. He seemed to regard feeble-mindedness as part of her malady but Estelle wasn't that, certainly not that.'

'What did she look like? Was she ugly, pretty?' I remembered the leering shrivelled mask of death and quaked inwardly.

'White, everything about her was pure white. Lady Clarissa, who never had an inkling of fashion, not even for herself, would buy the most expensive fabrics in inappropriate pastel shades for Estelle's dresses and have them cut from such childish patterns.'

'As if she couldn't stand the thought of her child growing up,' I suggested.

'Although Estelle was often unhappy, many's the time we would laugh over her mother's lack of taste. Sir Hugh was just as bad as her ladyship for trying to stunt Estelle's growth into womanhood. But what can thou do against the whip hand?'

'There's something you can do for me.' I took out the tissue wrapper from my desk drawer and passed it across to Susannah. 'Please open that out and tell me if you recognise the contents.'

''Tis all too late, is it not, sir?' she moaned, squinting down on the silver strands before lifting them up and pressing them against her cheek.

'Are you acknowledging that is some of Estelle Parke's hair?' I asked, forced to seek positive confirmation. Susannah nodded, preoccupied. 'I'm sorry,' I told her.

'I knew, I knew. I think I knew from the moment he told me she'd gone away, gone away and no "goodbye" for Susannah.'

'You said a moment ago that Estelle was often unhappy. Did she ever confide in you the reasons for her unhappiness?'

'She didn't have to.'

'No?'

'No, she never enjoyed good health and then there was …' Susannah eyes filled with tears.

'"The whip hand"?' I helped out.

'What could I do, Mr Cairn?' appealed Susannah. 'If I set up too much resistance against him, he'd just have sent me away earlier. And where would Estelle have been then?'

'And I expect it was Sir Hugh who secured you a position in the Jeffrey house, was it not? A job for your silence?'

When she lifted her head, Susannah Mott's eyes were dry of tears. 'No, as a matter of fact it wasn't. Lady Clarissa gave me the introduction.'

After she had gone, I was again left pondering over my contaminated hair sample. One of Susannah's tears remained glistening on the tissue's non-absorbent surface. I stared down at the tear long and hard for several minutes willing it to disappear. The fact alone that this hair had been deliberately planted in the ice-house of Brigham Hall was evidence of a sort in itself. If the scene of the girl's murder was firmly fixed at Brigham Hall, if the murder victim was the daughter of that house, why on earth would someone want to draw attention to the place by planting such an incriminating clue? Something had to be done quickly. Jackson, Thompson would have to be interviewed. Even the decrepit porter's shoulder strap would have to be examined, though for the life of me I could not envisage that poor old soul being physically capable of committing such a crime.

I riffled through Susannah's statement. To whom should I pass on all this evidence? Not to Kemp, I could not stand sending anything to Kemp. Kemp would thank me for my possible identification of the victim, but say this didn't change the fact that Daniel was seen standing over her and had killed her. No, I needed someone with a more developed social conscience than Kemp, someone in authority.

Dick was professionally bound to send his post-mortem results back to the Whitby coroner. I decided I, too, was honour bound to furnish both the Whitby coroner and magistrate with my suspicions as to the dead girl's true identity. I still held onto the faint hope that it might not be too late to prevent Daniel having to go through the ordeal of a trial. Nevertheless, I was not about to lose sight of the Lenten Assizes – the biggest test of my career – looming large on the horizon in six months time.

Chapter Twenty-Nine

Five days later I had a reply. The envelope was thick and rich, the magisterial seal impressive, the letter inside disturbingly guarded and vague. It stated that there was no record of the birth of an Estelle Parke, or any other formal registration for anyone of that name. Despite this, and because of the gravity of the discovery of human remains near Staithes, a local investigation would be launched forthwith.

Oh no, I cringed, not Kemp? Not Kemp interviewing Sir Hugh Parke?

The letter was signed with an impersonal, I am, Sir, Yours Faithfully.

'Damn! Damn!' I exclaimed, bringing a concerned Martin Trotter in at a rush. 'You know those letters I had you send to the Whitby coroner and the magistrate a few days ago?' The still frowning Trotter nodded. 'Well, one of the buggers has just washed his hands of the whole affair and passed it back to Kemp. And you know what Kemp will do with it?'

'Very little, sir, from what you've said about him.'

'Too damn right!' I roared again.

'Might I see the offending communication?' asked Trotter soothingly; a parent about to kiss and make everything better.

'Well, I don't want it,' I said, sliding it across my polished desk in disgust.

'Do you think this Mr Wilder might have some connection to Sir Hugh Parke?'

'Well, thank you, Trotter, that serves to only reassure me more. It seems the whole bloody county is beholden to Sir Hugh Parke.'

'Sorry, sir, but it's best to be forewarned.'

'Have you been talking to Gerald Fawcett about this?' I asked suspiciously.

'Certainly not, sir.' If Trotter was offended by my accusation of a breach of loyalty and confidence, he did not show any sign of it. He stood by waiting patiently as I picked up my pen and scribbled a brief note.

'For Seth Jackson, care of the post office, Staithes. And, Trotter, cancel all my appointments for next week,' I snapped. 'I'm going to Staithes myself.'

'Very well, sir,' bowed Trotter unfazed, wearing his usual constrained eastern potentate expression.

* * * * *

'Can I take your bags, sir?'

My investigation began the moment I set foot on the station platform. The decrepit Staithes porter dressed exactly as before, sporting his shoulder strap with its showy buckle and railway badge, instantaneously materialised as before. I was confused by this piece of immediate good fortune having anticipated that I would have to seek the porter out. But then why wouldn't the old fellow be here to meet the train? – it was his job, and his job would concur with the train timetable.

'What an interesting strap.' I tried to make the remark sound casual.

'From my days as a guard, sir.' The porter fluffed and preened himself. I had lit the touch-paper. 'The company let me keep the strap on my retirement because I'd worked for them for so long.'

'Might I take a closer look?'

'Of course, sir,' agreed the old man eagerly; no one had shown him this much attention in years.

I stroked the railway badge, frowning. I felt like some mischievous uncontrolled child fingering a priceless piece of art. 'YNMR,' I spelt out slowly, disappointedly.

'Anything wrong, sir?' asked the aloof station-master gingerly stepping up, his curiosity finally getting the better of him.

'No, nothing,' I reassured him, pulling back from my examination of the porter's shoulder strap. But that was a lie – there was something wrong – although from memory the two forensic marks on the dead girl's neck were almost identical in shape and size, the badge's central letters of NM were not.

'Yes, sir,' said the porter, polishing my finger-marks from his silver wear with his sleeve. 'York and North Midland Railway, the best. I worked for 'em nigh on thirty-five years and never a day missed.'

'Do you know of a railway company with the letters RM in their abbreviated title?' I threw the question into the air for either man to catch.

With little hesitation the station-master was first to respond. 'Of course.'

'Why "of course"?' I asked.

'WRMR, Whitby, Redcar and Middlesbrough Union Railway Company, the company who first started building the line to this station,' replied the station-master, incredulous that anyone could be so ignorant of such a fact.

'Finished by the North Eastern in eighty-three if my memory serves me well,' added the porter with a predilection for detail.

'That's about fourteen years ago,' I calculated quickly.

'That's right, and it took a long time to build it too. The Marchioness of Normanby inaugurated the work to begin to link up Staithes with the rest of the network in seventy-one. Poor lass never lived to see its completion,' said the station-master.

'Do you know of anyone in Staithes having a guard's shoulder strap similar to Mr … ?' I racked my brain to remember the surname Daniel had used.

'Mr Farnborough,' filled in the porter.

'To Mr Farnborough's here?' I confirmed. 'But with a Whitby, Redcar and Middlesbrough Railway badge?'

'You must be a collector then?' fished the station-master.

'No, just an interested amateur,' I assured him vaguely.

'Haven't I seen John Raw with summat similar hanging in his cottage?' suggested the station-master to the porter.

'No, no,' disagreed the porter. 'That was his father's. NER, his father worked North Eastern same time as I worked North Midland.'

Station-master and porter conferred for a minute or two further before shaking their heads pessimistically.

'You know of nobody then?' I asked disheartened, my mind awash with abbreviated capitals.

'Whitby, Redcar wasn't the most successful railway company but someone might own its strap and badge for old times sake, might even have worn it from time to time for a bit of devilment like. Just because we don't know of anybody, doesn't mean there isn't somebody,' offered the station-master in consolation.

'That's right,' agreed the porter.

'Of course I'm right,' said the station-master.

'Can I take your bags now, sir?' asked the porter, turning to me.

'Thank you,' I consented wearily. 'Just out to the street, mind.'

The station-master bowed, the porter beamed, and somehow I knew in this instance I had made the minutiae of a move towards achieving justice.

'I hope you find the right strap, sir,' the station-master shouted after me.

'Oh, don't worry, I will,' I confidently predicted before addressing the accompanying porter more quietly. 'Mr Farnborough, if need be might I ask a big favour of you?'

'Depends,' replied the old man.

* * * * *

There was no room at the inn, any inn. Jackson had left instructions at the post office for me to take up lodgings with Mrs Crooks, Laura Johnson's old landlady. The room in Mrs Crooks' house was the last possibility at such short notice as I had expressed my unwillingness to stay with Jackson himself: Jackson, who might be a principal witness in the impending trial.

'Pardon me, I've had a bad chest all summer long. Can't seem to shake it off,' wheezed Mrs Crooks as she heaved her way up the steep staircase. 'I hope you'll be comfortable here, sir.'

'I'm sure I will,' I replied. Mrs Crooks' cottage in Church Street (confusingly called Weatherill Street by Jackson who lived only a few doors higher) was well-known for being clean and traditional if not luxurious. But then, where in Staithes was luxurious?

'Miss Laura and Mr Harold are not in Steers at present,' pointed out Mrs Crooks as she flung open the door to my room. Was she telling me this believing it might be relevant to my stay?

I shrugged indifference and asked instead, 'And your friend, Mrs Fines, has she remained in Staithes?'

'Her husband and t' other lad's not been washed up yet. And to tell the truth, I doubt they'll find 'em now. But still Maud stays on. It's my opinion she'll not leave, not now. Steers is all she's ever known.'

After Mrs Crooks had gone, I took in the scene through the open airing window.

Though there was not much of a view of the sea, I rather liked the jigsaw effect of the red pantile roofs below. Extremely exhausted by all the prior arrangements I had had to make back in York for this rushed visit, I flopped back onto the iron bedstead testing it, testing if I really minded that "Miss Laura and Mr Harold" (and presumably Miss Rosie) were not in Staithes.

* * * * *

My knuckles felt cold on the door as I gave a few sharp raps.

'Jackson, I thought you weren't in there for a moment.'

'So you've arrived.' The greeting was unmistakably frosty.

'Yes, all a bit of a rush, I'm afraid. But I'm glad you got my note, care of the post office, and thank you for recommending Mrs Crooks,' I told him, my eagerness unabated. Jackson's expression remained sullen, uninterested. He stood, hands in pockets, staring down on me in the well of his yard as if I was some unwelcome pedlar. 'Don't worry, I've not come to sell you anything.' I tried a little humour. Jackson did not laugh. A group of flither pickers, in their pea jackets and erotically revealed blue petticoats, made some wayward flirtatious comments to us both in passing. Still Jackson did not laugh. 'Aren't you going to invite me in then?' I asked, finally defeated by this sea-change in demeanour of a man I had begun to regard as a friend.

'What do you want exactly?'

'It's certainly not something I wish to discuss on the doorstep for the whole of Staithes to hear,' I told him, an edge to my voice now. Perhaps the odd uncertainty I'd felt about Jackson in the past had some justification to it after all.

'Best come inside then.' Jackson reluctantly stepped aside as I, stooping under the door's lintel, brushed past him.

We stood facing each other in the low-ceilinged cottage room, adversaries weighing up enemy potential, fighters waiting for the handkerchief to drop.

'What's wrong with you?' I made the first probing jab.

'Folk can see you coming in then, although I'm not good enough to stay with.'

'I can't stay with you, don't you see? You're too connected with this case.'

The unblinking Jackson appear unimpressed by my legal argument. 'Expect you've come to interrogate me over that dead lass again then?'

'I'm not aware I've ever interrogated you over anything.'

'No, but you think I'm involved in some way, don't you?'

'Do I? What on earth makes you think that?'

'Your attitude.'

'*My* attitude.'

'Yes, your attitude all along. You've never quite trusted me, have you?'

'It's my job. Trust has to be earned. I'm a barrister, God damn it!'

'Well, I think I've already done enough to earn yours. The mistrust you showed towards me at Brigham Hall was enough to make any man spit blood.'

'My mistrust wasn't directed towards you. I do admit, though, I was suspicious of finding that lock of hair so easily and conveniently placed in the ice-house like that.'

'"Placed"!' exploded Jackson. 'There's a perfect example of how far you trust me. The police not trusting me is one thing, but you, James, I thought you and I were mates.'

How ironical that Jackson should finally choose to use my Christian name under these circumstances. And what was even more ironic, I suddenly realised, was that Jackson – arguably the most respected man in Staithes – had no real friends, needed my friendship.

'I never said you placed it there. And it isn't you I've come to interview.'

'Who then, Sir Hugh Parke?' scoffed Jackson.

'No, not him either.'

'I thought not.'

'Not yet, anyway.'

'Well, if you're not prepared to tell me what business you do have in Steers …' Jackson indicated the door.

'Tell me about this man, Thompson,' I said, ignoring Jackson's dismissive gesture and lowering myself onto a chair. 'Your father saved his life after the *Daniel* sank, didn't he?'

'How do you know about that?'

'It's part of village folklore, is it not?' I had no intention of revealing one source of information to another.

'It entailed a little more than folklore,' muttered Jackson to himself.

'Then surely, Thompson must have remained on good terms with the son of a man who risked his own life to save him?'

Jackson nodded cautiously. 'Carl's a little on the odd side though I've never had any trouble with him personally.'

'So you believed him about the hair in the ice-house?'

'As I think I told you before, I'd no reason not to.'

'And you get on with him fairly well?'

'As well as I do with most men.'

'Could you arrange a meeting for me with him?'

'With you?'

'With me,' I repeated before delivering the punch line. 'That's why I'm back here in Staithes, to meet Mr Thompson.'

* * * * *

The man with the grey neckcloth gawped as Jackson introduced me to him. Carl Thompson evidently was not expecting Jackson to bring along a friend – a toff, at that, carrying a Gladstone bag.

The top pub, the same pub in which my client had been questioned by the constable three months earlier, was filled with men anaesthetising themselves against memories of their day's employment and a beckoning more of the same tomorrow. Many of these men wore wide belted trousers round their skinny girths, and from their soiled hands and clothes appeared to be Grinkle ironstone-miners. But despite their comprehensively emaciated appearance, the thirst of these men was something to behold.

BELTS – one belt – a wide leather belt – not a miner's belt like the ones worn by these men but a railway guard's badge and shoulder strap belt biting into a young girl's soft neck. The image jerked me back into the reality of why I was here.

'Drink anyone?' I asked Thompson and Jackson.

'A pot of ale for me,' said Jackson.

'A small glass of brandy would be nice.' Thompson screwed up his eyes, reminding me immediately of Lane. Let the toff pay, I read in those eyes, but the toff was not the only one about to pay that evening.

I walked quickly across the dimly lit room turning to smile pleasantly back at my two seated companions, put them at their ease. Unlike the Cod and Lobster this ale-house had nothing of the aura of fishermen and the sea about it. With its tobacco-stained walls it could have been a working man's pub in any industrial area, in any city, in England. I did not care for the rough smoky atmosphere of this place at all.

'Now,' I said, putting the drinks down before my two companions.

'Your health,' chuckled Thompson, wrapping his right hand firmly round the glass.

His left hand remained on the table. I noticed two of the fingers on that inert hand were missing.

'Your health,' echoed Jackson and I.

We kept Thompson talking about this and that, nothing too controversial, nothing too alarming, until the odd-jobman was fully relaxed puffing on his clay pipe, sipping at his fourth-in-quick-succession brandy. I studied Thompson's face, the lines around his mouth remained drawn tight, hard. I took to this man as much as I did to Thompson's drinking den. Could this man be responsible for allowing Daniel to be incarcerated all this time for a murder he knew he hadn't committed? He had a possible motive. Thompson, once the mate on the *Daniel*, must have lost considerable prestige in his community by becoming a landlubberly servant of the Hall. And wasn't there talk that he'd sustained some kind of head injury at the time of the shipwreck? Yes, Carl Thompson could imagine he had reason enough to make Daniel – *delicta maiorum immeritus lues* – though guiltless, expiate his father's sins.

'Carl,' piped up Jackson through the blue fug. 'You know that lock of hair you told me you'd found in the ice-house at the Hall, is it still there?'

'Gone,' mumbled Thompson, more interested in the swirling contents of his oval glass.

'Gone, how do you know it's gone?'

'Went to see of course.' Smiling Thompson gave a rattling laugh at something so self-evident. Another look, a more hostile look passed between Jackson and me.

'You went to see if I'd taken it, you mean,' said Jackson.

'I never …' Thompson looked stunned for a moment.

'Why, if you truly believed that dead girl fished from the sea belonged to the Hall, haven't you ever thought fit to report it to the authorities?' I interrupted abruptly.

'"Authorities",' spluttered Thompson. 'There's only one authority in this part of the world.'

'Your employer,' I sighed. Down every avenue of this case, I always came to the same brick wall – Sir Hugh Parke.

'Ay, him,' agreed Thompson. Thompson who was now scrutinising me with peevish curiosity. 'Are you some sort of authority yourself, Mister?'

'You planted that hair for me to find as if I was some kind of gullible fool, didn't you?' The offended Jackson came to my rescue.

'No, no, you've got it all wrong there,' objected Thompson vehemently. 'He used to take her into t' cavern after dark and afterwards she'd comb her hair with a brush like this.' Thompson began a ludicrous female impersonation. Some of the miners at the bar picked up on it, nudging each other and jeering, nodding in the odd-jobman's direction.

'Who took her there?' I asked bluntly, unperturbed. Thompson shook a refusal.

'Come on, Carl, get it off your chest,' coaxed Jackson more gently.

'Sir Hugh Parke took his own daughter into that ice-house at night, is that what you are asking us to believe?' I observed Thompson aghast.

'Listen, Mister, I'm not asking you to believe anything. Who are you to be asking all these questions anyway?' Thompson decided to turn defence into attack.

'James is here to help, Carl,' explained Jackson. 'He's a barrister representing Flora Robertshaw's boy.'

'Daniel, poor Daniel.' Carl Thompson lowered his maudlin head. I was unsure whether Thompson's lament was for Daniel the man or *Daniel* the boat or perhaps they were one and the same in his present drunken state.

'I don't believe that amount of hair could simply come from a brush,' I announced firmly, struggling to pull meandering Thompson back on course.

'Believe, believe, don't you know no other word, Mister?' slurred Thompson.

'How about *liar*,' I suggested.

'Now look here.' Thompson wriggled in his chair in an attempt to pull up to his full height before slumping back.

I reached down into my Gladstone bag, resting by one of the table legs, and withdrew Mr Farnborough's loaned shoulder strap. 'Ever seen one of these before?' I asked Thompson.

Thompson flinched at first as if the strap was a cobra about to leap forward and bite him. Then he laughed saying, 'Course I have, that's that silly old bugger Farnborough's shoulder strap. Hell's teeth, what are you doing prancing about with that? Nearly frightened me to death there for a moment.'

A strap like this actually strangled that young girl to death, I thought of replying but immediately thought better of it.

'Mr Farnborough's strap is the only one of its kind that you are familiar with then?' I asked Thompson instead, unable to hide my disappointment.

'What have I just told you?' retorted Thompson irritably.

'You did not actually say it was the only one you've ever seen,' I persisted.

'Well, it is, Mister, and there's an end to it.'

But it was Jackson's attention, not Thompson's, that remained fixed on Mr Farnborough's strap as if it was some sort of weapon dangling from my fist. He looked preoccupied and puzzled as the banter ebbed and flowed between the odd-jobman and myself.

'He's cost me the best part of a bottle of brandy,' I complained to him as we stepped out onto the pavement together, leaving Thompson drooling over a fifth glass. 'But hopefully Thompson will have such a thick head in the morning, he'll not remember much of this.'

'Memory isn't Carl's strongest point in or out of drink,' pointed out Jackson.

'That could work for us now and against us in court.'

'What was all that about the railway guard's shoulder strap anyway?' There was a certain strained exactness in the way Jackson phrased the question that made me look at him.

'Are you aware of someone else owning one in Staithes?' I asked him intuitively. 'Someone other than Mr Farnborough or a fellow called John Raw?'

'Was it a shoulder strap like the one you've just shown us in the pub that strangled the life out of that poor young lass?'

'Yes, very much like Mr Farnborough's strap but with the letters WRMR on its badge instead.'

'Whitby, Redcar and Middlesbrough Union Railway Company,' translated Jackson. 'I might not have been too good with reading and writing but I know that much. Us lads would regularly truant from school to spend days watching them laying the new track to Steers, dreaming of driving our own train along it one day. But better than that, the real high point of any given day, was when a train would pass on the existing line and the guard at the back would throw us down a shower of farthings to catch. I can see that scattering bronze shower now, and the white steam from the train disappearing into the distance, and us scrabbling up the bank after them coins.'

'But what reason did the guard have for doing that?'

'Charity begins at home, is the voice of the world.'

'Sir Thomas Browne, I'm very impressed. Nevertheless, I have to know which friend's relative threw those coins off the train.'

'And the shoulder strap?'

'You know if there is one, I have to see it.'

'First I'll get that strap if I can and then, if necessary, I'll give you a name.'

'You do realise if a forensic examination proves the strap to be the murder weapon, you'll be forced to testify who the owner is in court.'

Like a retreating tide, Jackson's outdoor swarthiness suddenly deserted his face. 'You're turning me into a spy, a traitor and now a thief, Mr Cairn.'

'I think you might have been the latter all along, Mr Jackson,' I replied, placing a friendly arm round Jackson's shoulder.

Chapter Thirty

The early winter of 1898. The river Ouse was frozen in places. The honking of the Canada geese occasional and more subdued than in summer months as their webbed feet slipped and slid on adjacent ponds. Beyond the river's banks, in the water meadows, even the sheep munched on the abrasive frosted grass in complete silence. Things were in a sorry state, especially when that essential – eating – was not so much fun anymore for these fluffy, white polled lowland sheep used to a better living. Immured from the life and death struggle going on outside, the archbishop in his draughty palace further down stream armed himself against the cold with an excess of spirituality and a double layer of woollen drawers. Despite these precautions, the York Primate's nose remained a stubborn and seasonal blue above his kaleidoscope of silk vestments whenever he ventured forth into society.

I consoled myself and my chilblain feet with the one personal plus in these arctic conditions – that bane of my life, horse dung, which tumbled in steaming piles onto the streets from its prolific hosts' backsides all the year round, now froze hard in minutes and so failed to adhere to my trouser hems.

'Would you be kind enough to take a cab right away to meet the twelve fifteen from Leeds? Here is a card with the gentleman's name on it. Please bring him straight back to me here in chambers.'

'Right you are, sir,' nodded Trotter; a keen allotment man whatever the weather, he loved fresh air.

'By the way, before you go.' I fluttered the page of a letter in the air. 'I've just received another missive, this time from the Whitby coroner. And surprise, surprise, he tells me here that Kemp and the magistrate are finding Sir Hugh and Lady Clarissa Parke less than helpful regarding the dead girl and most of their staff are actually being obstructive.'

'Really, sir?' Trotter faked surprise.

'Afraid of losing their jobs more like.'

'Possibly, likewise Inspector Kemp and the magistrate,' suggested Trotter smiling.

'Why do I keep getting the impression that you know more about this case than me, Trotter?'

'I certainly do not, sir, as I believe I've already assured you.'

I scrutinised the clerk's face closely, aware that I was becoming increasingly paranoid about Gerald Fawcett's warning.

'Thank goodness we've got Susannah Mott at least,' I muttered as Trotter began to disappear through the open doorway.

The framed Trotter turned, hesitated a moment before speaking. 'You think she'll keep to her story then, sir?'

'What is this, Trotter? You seem to be doing your best to undermine my confidence at every turn.' I tightly balled up the coroner's letter in agitation.

'No, sir, I'm merely aware of the ways of the world,' sighed the clerk of chambers. 'And they're not always how they should be,' he added, closing the door quietly behind him.

I stared long and hard at that closed door. Was Trotter really on my side or was he a Fawcett man? Maybe I should be more discerning in future as to how much information Trotter was privy to. Could it be that Sir Hugh's long tendrils had infiltrated Bootham Chambers itself? Could there be an enemy within as it were? Would Susannah Mott stick to her story? Would Jackson? Would any of them? Would I be able to get either of the Parkes to co-operate beforehand or have to break them down in court? Ultimately, would I be able to save Daniel from the gallows?

* * * * *

'It's cold enough to …' Dick Tate paused, laughing, rubbing his gloveless hands together, taking stock of my room.

'To what?' I asked.

'Oh, just an unfortunate crude expression I picked up from some antipodean, old boy. Most unsuitable language to use in a barrister's chambers.'

'I think the language already used within these four walls would shock even you, Dick,' I informed him reaching out my hand. 'It's good to see you, it really is.'

'That looks interesting. A paper weight?' Dick pointed to the large brownish grey pebble on my desk. The pebble was imperceptibly split and parting the two halves into each palm I offered them to Dick.

'A perfectly prepared ammonite if I say so myself, *Amaltheus stokesi*, I found it in the ironstone cliffs of Penny Nab,' I explained proudly.

'*Amaltheus stokesi*, sounds like a disease. And where for heaven's sake is Penny Nab?'

'Staithes, where my client comes from, remember?' Dick gave the two ammonite pieces closer scrutiny.

'It's beautiful, wherever it comes from.' For once Dick spoke with hushed admiration. 'So intricate.'

'See that acute keel there and the smooth ribbing. Not many fossils have such fine longitudinal ridges like this one either.'

'This pebble is like the Robertshaw case to you, isn't it?'

'How do you mean?'

'Split it open and see what's inside.'

'The truth, hopefully.'

'Ah, the truth. Philosophers are forever telling us there are many truths.'

'But you're a scientist, Dick.'

'Indeed,' agreed Dick with a smidgen of regret.

'Anyway, for the time being, I'll settle for proving just the one truth.'

'And what might that be?'

'That my client, Daniel Robertshaw, didn't murder Estelle Parke out there on those flat Jurassic rocks off Staithes on the twenty-first of May last.'

'A tall order.'

'Another order, let's get out of here and I'll treat you to lunch in Colliergate.'

'But I thought we ...'

'Don't worry we can discuss things over lunch.' I herded Dick briskly down the steps of Bootham Chambers. 'The city beckons,' I laughed as the cold air nipped at our faces.

'Not very busy in here, is it?' said Dick, leaning forward in his window seat to peer doubtfully round a piece of Coffee Tavern foliage.

'The weather, I expect,' I reassured him. 'Still, a little privacy suits our purpose, does it not?'

'I feel like something warming,' Dick announced bluntly, too cold to be immediately drawn into one of my intrigues.

Dick was well-versed in my infatuation with plotting and spying at university. I would pore for hours over articles describing foreign anarchists creeping down the alleyways of London with explosive grenades in their pockets. Indeed, I had been so obsessed with anarchism for a time that I am sure some of my fellow students must have suspected me of being a sympathiser. But then, Cambridge was a hive of tittle-tattle and intrigue itself. Dick must have realised that I had chosen my profession well – the dramatic theatre of law – though Dick would have to wait a while longer to see how well his old college mate performed.

'Soup?' I suggested. 'They do an excellent French onion soup here.' Dick nodded and I called the waitress over.

'Do you do Welsh rare-bit as well?' he asked the girl, silently appraising the dark ringlets bubbling down from under her cap.

'We do, it's Cook's speciality.'

'I'll have some then, thank you.'

'And anything else for sir?' the girl asked me, as I cast a discerning eye down the menu.

'Who's written this?' I asked, ignoring her impatience to take our order and be gone.

'Mrs Hubie has started to make out all the lists herself,' said the girl uneasily.

'Mrs Hubie?'

'The manageress.'

'Look, Dick.' I handed him the menu. 'What's your opinion of this?'

'Excellent.'

'Please give Mrs Hubie our compliments on her excellent hand. This menu is a work of art in itself,' I said, reaching across the table and snatching the sheet, student-fashion, back from Dick. 'And I'll have a plate of cold pig's chap with onions and bread and butter.'

'That'll do nothing for your waistline,' warned Dick, obviously feeling it was professionally incumbent on him to voice his disapproval.

'Maybe not, but it'll keep me warm in this polar bear weather,' I retorted, a little hurt.

'Not bad, eh?' said Dick, nodding towards the retreating waitress' dancing ringlets and curvaceous backside.

'Suppose so,' I replied without a second glance. My previous exuberance suddenly flipped to gloom. Pretty though the waitress was and frequent my visits had been here of late, I realised not once had I noticed any of the staff. How could I begin to explain to Dick that I had eyes for no other woman than Rosie Good? Rosie Good whom I felt sure was soon destined to become another man's wife.

'Well, not long to go now,' said Dick, clearing his throat.

'To go now?' I repeated, staring vacantly at Dick and wondering for an instant how the hell he could know that.

'The trial date.'

'Oh, yes, the trial,' I sighed. 'It starts the twenty-first of March.'

'You said in your reply to my telegram that you'd something urgent to show me too.'

'Certainly I have, but I have no intention of getting it out in here. It's down by my foot right now.'

'What in that Gladstone bag thing?' asked Dick horrified. 'I hope it's cleanly wrapped or Thomas will be getting very upset again. And you'd better make sure no one steals it from under the table.'

'Stop fussing, my boot toe's through the handle.'

'A determined thief might take your boot, foot and leg as well,' roared Dick; his weather-nipped face thrown back and growing more florid until he almost fell backwards off his chair.

'Dick, it does my spirit good to see you, it really does,' I told him, grazing the back of his hand with my own. 'How is Mr Scattergood?' I asked, embarrassed by this sudden need for nostalgic chumminess.

'Thomas is doing well enough for a man in his seventy-third year.'

'Will he be fit enough to attend the trial, do you think?'

'God willing.'

The soup arrived and we fell silent apart from the odd slurp of satisfaction. Staring at the bottom of Dick's clean, bread-scrubbed dish, there was no need to ask if he had enjoyed it.

'Very French?' I could not resist a subtle enquiry.

'Very *chic*,' responded Dick with a three fingered kiss.

'The Parkes are still being unhelpful,' I said with an apologetic back to business groan.

'I know. I've been in touch with the Whitby magistrate and Charles Fenton, the coroner, recently myself.'

'Oh,' I exclaimed surprised. 'I thought you'd already informed them of your findings.'

'Something else has cropped up. Something very important. That's why I've come over to York in person to explain it to you.'

'Nothing that will damage my case, I hope?' I failed to conceal the note of apprehension in my voice. Nothing lately had gone smoothly in the Robertshaw case, a labyrinth of twists and turns, positives and negatives – and the Parkes.

Dick stared back at me short on humour himself now.

'Remember that sample of hair you showed us?' he asked. I nodded. 'Well, as you know, Thomas and I had already formed our own supposition at post-mortem regarding the victim's general colouring and now Ambler-Smith has as good as confirmed it.'

'So, what are you telling me?'

'I'm telling you that our victim was ill-fated from the start. The hair and skin samples I took from Whitby to show Ambler-Smith proved pretty conclusively that she was badly affected by albinism. Of course, had we been able to see her eyes that would have been additionally helpful.'

'Her eyes?'

'Yes, the irises of sufferers from albinism often appear to be pink, while the pupils themselves seem to be red from light reflected by blood in the unpigmented choroid. In the living, vision abnormalities are common, rapid oscillation of the eyes and extreme sensitivity to light.'

'She couldn't see in sunlight,' I echoed Susannah Mott's words.

'Most probably not,' picked up Dick. 'What's more the briefest exposure to the sun's strong rays would burn her skin red raw.'

'What would she look like, her appearance in general?'

'Rather odd, I'd say.'

'She'd stand out in a crowd as odd then?'

'Most definitely.'

'So, in this case, rather than fear of the evil eye, the murderer could have removed the victim's eyes in an effort to hide her identity?'

'Forgive the pun but it looks that way. Although there were signs of minimal shrimp infiltration, Thomas and I noted the otherwise clean condition of her eye-sockets at the time of post-mortem but, because of your squeamishness, we chose not to draw your attention to them then. We are convinced that our young victim lost her eyes well before any nibbling sea life took an interest. If you read my original report more carefully you will find a note to that effect.'

'And you will be willing to testify in open court that her eyes were deliberately gouged out?'

'No, not gouged, never gouged,' refuted Dick forcefully. 'This is the really fascinating bit, her eyes were removed by precise surgical scoops.'

The waitress arrived with Dick's steaming Welsh rare-bit and my cold dish. Dick smiled up at the young lass and told her flatteringly that with her dark looks she could be Welsh herself.

'It seems almost certain now that the murdered girl and the absent Estelle Parke are one and the same,' I continued when the waitress had gone.

'The story fits, doesn't it?'

'No matter who she is or was, I still have to prove that my client didn't kill her.'

'Of course. But it will help knowing it was Estelle Parke, won't it? Don't worry, I believe official acceptance of that fact shouldn't be too long in coming now, not with the coroner finally on board,' said Dick, tucking into his rare-bit with gusto.

'Is he really?'

'Really,' confirmed Dick.

Despite this piece of promising news, a sudden revived dread overcame me. Somehow my cold pig's chap did not look quite so appetising anymore.

'Cuthbert Henge is standing against me,' I informed Dick.

'Cuthbert Henge,' spluttered Dick. 'Why, the man's a buffoon,' he added unconvincingly.

'But a good barrister with a formidable record for convictions, almost ninety per cent last year.'

'As high as that?' gulped Dick. I nodded gloomily. 'Well, look at it this way, old man,' continued Dick, regaining all his usual glowing optimism with every warming cheesy mouthful. 'Did anyone see blood on the clothing of your client out there on the rocks?' I shook my head. 'Once in custody did the police surgeon examine and find any blood or semen on the clothes your client had been wearing at the time of the alleged offence?'

'Well no,' I admitted. 'Although this argument might prove to be contentious as most of Daniel's clothes were blackened with soot and burnt off his body, a day later, following an act of arson against his mother's property.'

'Was a knife ever found in his possession?' asked Dick. Again I shook my head. 'Well, I think you have a good case, counsel.'

'Thanks for the vote of confidence. You say Charles Fenton is on our side regarding Estelle Parke's identity but will her parents ever admit the dead girl is their missing daughter? – that there is a missing daughter at all?'

'The nouveaux riche cannot afford to admit to anything less than perfection, although in this case they might have to.'

'"Nouveaux riche", I knew that the Parkes had inherited some industrial wealth but are you telling me they weren't originally from landed stock?'

'His family most definitely was not. But don't underestimate him for all that, he still enjoys all the influence of the gentry with perhaps more money to spend. Let me see, I think it was Charles Fenton who told me that Sir Hugh's father made a killing investing in a short-lived venture, known as the Whitby, Redcar and Middlesbrough Union Railway Company, before selling out.'

Chapter Thirty-One

'Here, cheer up, I've brought you this.' I draped my frock coat round the seated Daniel's bowed shoulders. I had heard of people drooping from heat but Daniel appeared to be drooping from cold. He did not get up to greet me as usual, hardly acknowledged me. He looked as dishevelled as when I had first visited him. Unfathomably, the neck of his shirt gaped wide open in the freezing cell. 'Come on, old man, this will not do,' I chivvied, aware of the circles of my own breath disappearing like smoke signals into the cold atmosphere.

'Mam came to visit a day past,' Daniel mumbled almost inaudibly down onto his exposed hairless chest.

'Sorry, I didn't quite catch that,' I said, seeking confirmation of what I thought I'd heard, on what would be a very surprising piece of news.

'Mam came with another lady t' other day.' Daniel was shouting now.

'Oh, how lovely,' I enthused.

'Mam cried a lot.'

'Well, she'll have been a little distressed seeing you in here like this.'

'She wouldn't take me home with her either.'

'She couldn't, though I know she would have liked to.'

'Really?' A glimmer of hope rose in Daniel's eyes.

'Of course.'

'Well, unless she comes to take me home, I don't want her to visit again,' said Daniel emphatically.

'What was the lady with her like?' I asked, curious and wishing to move the subject on.

Daniel made a wide curving gesture from his chest, adding for good measure, 'She had curls like flames all around her face.'

'Susannah Mott,' I acknowledged quietly to myself. Susannah Mott whose testimony might help save Daniel from the gallows. I observed my client thoughtfully for a moment, Daniel's mood fluctuated from one extreme to another with all the capriciousness of a child. Was he aware of the seriousness of his position? Had he any idea that at this very moment his life was resting in the balance?

'I liked her.'

'Sorry, who?'

'The lady with curls, I liked her.' Daniel gave (what I judged to be at the time) a discreet little cough. 'She'll do right by me and Mam.'

I reassessed my previous opinion. Perhaps not Daniel the child, more Daniel the senile relative who one assumes has taken in very little but at some level shockingly understands all.

* * * * *

Unfortunately, though, Daniel's little cough did not remain discreet for long but soon got much worse. And when he broke out in a fever, in reparation for my previous medical naivety, I immediately hired an independent doctor to attend him.

'Pneumonia,' pronounced the pin-striped apothecary.

'Is he going to be all right?' I asked, deeply concerned.

'That depends.'

'Depends on what?'

'Depends if he gets through this acute stage of his illness or not.'

'You mean he could die?' I stared down on my inert client in horror. Beads of sweat were pouring off Daniel, drenching the plank bed like a rain storm.

'Patients with this sort of retardation often succumb to pneumonia.'

'"Succumb"?'

'Yes, they seem to be susceptible,' shrugged the doctor.

'But he's due to stand trial for murder in four weeks time.'

'Well,' chuckled the talking down his nose, thick-set, middle-aged doctor. 'It will save the council the hangman's wage.'

'Ever heard of innocent until proved guilty.' I was tempted to punch this older man on his already congested rhinophyma nose.

'All you legal fellows say your clients are innocent,' scoffed the doctor.

'Innocent or not, aren't all you doctors morally obliged to treat your patients with equal care and respect?' I snapped back.

'Only if we are paid,' smirked the doctor.

'You'll get paid, don't worry. Because this poor chap,' I nodded towards the moribund Daniel, 'happens to be a good friend of mine.'

'Indeed,' grunted the doctor, before turning his attention towards a distasteful appraisal of his patient's surroundings. 'Well, if you really want to get this man to court, I suggest you begin by hiring some round-the-clock nursing care to keep him hydrated. In the meantime, I'm going to start him on a dose of calomel followed by a saline purgative.'

'Will you be coming back to see him?'

'Of course,' said the doctor, adding a withering, 'and I hope this friend of yours is worth it, Mr Cairn.'

'You're not the first to express that sentiment.' I turned away as the doctor supported Daniel's enfeebled head in the crook of his arm, coaxing and cajoling him like a baby to swallow the medicine. Daniel groaned that his head was falling off before giving in to a shuddering gulp and falling back into semi-consciousness.

'Now we pray,' said the doctor.

'Will he live?' I forced myself to ask.

'Now we pray,' repeated the doctor.

* * * * *

I sent desperate word to Flora Robertshaw of Daniel's illness, asking her if any of the Friends in York might be prevailed upon for twenty-four hour nursing care. I then made an appointment to see the governor to explain that Daniel was too sick to be moved, too near the crisis to be hospitalised, and would he, the governor, kindly allow Daniel the private nursing care that I had already begun the process of negotiating.

'Seriously ill, you say?' The powdery skin around the governor's mouth dropped.

'Gravely ill,' I emphasised.

'But bringing outside nurses into prison is most irregular. I've already accommodated your request for a change of guard for Robertshaw and now this. And who will be accountable for the nurses' safety, tell me that?'

'I'll take responsibility.'

'No, Mr Cairn, it is I who am ultimately responsible for everything that happens inside this place.'

'I think if you saw him now you would agree that Mr Robertshaw poses absolutely no threat to anyone in his present state.'

'But this prisoner is, I believe, on remand for a heinous crime against a young woman.'

'At the moment Mr Robertshaw can barely raise his head from the pallet let alone hurt anyone. He is incapable of feeding himself and supplying him with nursing and medical care out of my own pocket will ensure he and his illness remain in isolation.'

'Tell me truthfully, Cairn, is Robertshaw's illness contagious? Because if it is, such fevers can spread through a prison population like wildfire,' twittered the governor.

'A little, not very. He has pneumonia.'

'Oh dear, that is serious.'

'Mainly for him,' I said pointedly; thinking this man is a fool dithering over one of his charges succumbing to a bout of pneumonia when a good percentage of his prison population is already infected with syphilis. I knew this to be a fact on the good authority of Dr "rhinophyma" Williams, who happened to be a personal friend of the prison doctor, who had in turn furnished Williams with graphic details of his mercury treatment. Sounds little short of torture, I remembered commenting with an involuntary shudder.

'You say you've already had an independent medical assessment made of Robertshaw, Cairn?' asked the governor. I nodded. 'Ah, well, I expect I should be grateful for anything that relieves the Prison Service's dwindling funds.'

* * * * *

First impressions sometimes can be misleading: as I walked across the Castle yard early one morning towards Daniel's cell, I was surprised to see the seemingly indifferent Dr Williams ambling back towards me.

'How is he?' I asked. I hated sickness, hospitals, anywhere where the news was uncertain and might be bad.

'Holding his own,' replied Williams, with all his usual nonchalance though his brow was furrowed with tell-tale concern.

Here is a man who through continual exposure to other people's pain has become totally inept at expressing his own feelings, the sudden insight struck me uncomfortably.

'Have you been able to increase his medicine?' I asked him a little more solicitously.

'No, one dosage is enough. The persistent use of purgatives can prove injurious in his present condition. I'm trying him on a little quinine today instead, in an attempt to lower his temperature.'

'What is his temperature?'

'One hundred and three.'

'One hundred and three degrees, that's very high isn't it?'

'Very. I wouldn't normally give a patient quinine yet but in his case, well ...'

'Well what?' I demanded, fearing the answer.

'By the way, that little girl you've got nursing him is lovely,' said Williams, changing the subject, his puckered brow falling smooth. 'Quaker, isn't she?' I nodded, although I had not met her or the other promised girl yet. 'I say,' winked Williams with a leering smile, 'forget mercurial preparations, forget quinine, when Daniel is able to focus clearly on that fair countenance, I'll guarantee a dramatic improvement in his health.'

'I hope you're right.' I walked on.

Williams was indisputably right about one thing, about the young female delicately mopping Daniel's brow – her slender fingers intermittently wrapping round a glass of water to slake his fevered thirst – the girl was "lovely" in both manner and appearance. Wisps of golden hair escaped beneath her bonnet, yet there was an outdoor swarthiness about the girl, a glow not exactly fashionable in today's pale ladies' salons but which suited her and her penetrating blue-grey eyes well enough. Then again, she was not anything like the robust country lasses either who stooped and hoed the fields around York, her bending waist was tiny. Here was a very different breed of creature if ever I had seen one.

Apart from the girl herself, I saw that there were other light feminine touches here and there transforming Daniel's gloomy cell. Small jars of primroses and other early flowers had been placed cleverly and strategically to catch the meagre light.

'What is your name?' The question caught in my throat, affected by the girl's gentle attention to Daniel.

'Elizabeth Mott, sir.' Her voice was hardly a whisper.

'Then you must be Susannah Mott's girl.' I should have guessed, though of a much finer build she had all her mother's beauty.

'I am.'

'And I am Daniel's barrister,' I explained.

'Pleased to meet thee, sir.' Elizabeth motioned a half-curtsy without leaving her chair.

'You are not unlike your mother,' I told her. Elizabeth wrinkled her nose at this, with pleasure or youthful distaste? – I wasn't sure. 'And I have seen you in her company once before.'

'Oh, where was that, sir?' Her eyes lifted with interest for a moment from Daniel.

'You were walking arm in arm along Coppergate.'

'My mother is well-known to thee, sir?'

'No, no, I was first briefly acquainted with her while visiting Mrs Robertshaw.'

'And this is *her* son,' said Elizabeth with meaning, dabbing at the continuous beads of sweat erupting on Daniel's forehead. 'Strange isn't it, sir, how things seem to come round in full circle?'

'Your own employers have no objection to you attending to this poor fellow then?' I asked, deciding now was not the time to pursue Elizabeth's philosophical observation.

'They have gladly released me from my usual duties for Daniel is a Friend in dire circumstances.' *Dire* – on cue Daniel vomited into Elizabeth's outstretched bowl. After each convulsion, she meticulously wiped his mouth clean. 'It's terrible to see healthy men kept in these conditions, let alone the sick.' She gave the cell a brief pejorative valuation.

'How old are you?' I hovered over the administering Susannah Mott's daughter with a sense of awe and helplessness, knowing I could not possibly deal so skilfully with Daniel's basic needs myself.

'I am sixteen, sir, next month.'

'Can you read and write, Elizabeth?'

Indignation flashed in the blue-grey eyes. 'I most certainly can, sir.'

'Will you be able to get word to me at either of these two addresses, whatever the hour, when Daniel reaches his crisis?' I placed my business and home cards on the small table.

'That will not be a problem, Friends come enquiring after him regularly,' nodded Elizabeth. 'I will inform thee and Dr Williams straightaway if there is any change.'

'Dr Williams?' I asked surprised.

'Ay, I have his card too, here in my apron pocket.'

'And the other girl?'

'She has been instructed the same.'

'What do you think of Dr Williams, Elizabeth?'

'He is not a godly man, sir, but he is kinder and better than he would have anyone believe.' Elizabeth Mott smiled a strong perfect set of teeth.

* * * * *

Daniel's crisis was not long in coming. The next morning at breakfast time I heard persistent knocking on my Gillygate door. I knew instantly what the knocking meant. My heart skipped between fear and cowardice before I plucked up courage to ring for Kate, the maid, who would be unaware of the caller at the front of the house as she was preparing toast in the back kitchen.

'Is this the house of James Cairn, Esquire?' asked the apparition waiting on the doorstep, completely nonplussing Kate.

'Ay,' she gasped, trying not to linger too obviously on the buttoned breeches, Quaker collar, large rimmed hat, all apparently balanced and resting on a black walking-cane.

'Will thou be so good as to tell thy master he is urgently required at the Castle?' The large rimmed hat raised an inch.

'Ay,' gasped Kate again. 'Ay, right away.'

Still in a state of bewilderment, she passed the descriptive doorstep scene and Quaker's message on to me in the breakfast room.

'Why, I thought it was George Fox himself standing there, sir, truly I did. George Fox in the flesh and resurrected,' she giggled, unaware of the seriousness of the man's request.

* * * * *

Daniel was delirious when I got to the Castle. Dr Williams was already there preparing various juju on the bedside table. The night nurse, whom I had never met, remained mopping Daniel's forehead with a linen cloth smelling of vinegar. Elizabeth hovered eagerly behind her, desperate for the other girl to relinquish her position, eyes appealing to me to endorse the shift change. Even the prison governor had braved a cursory visit, crowding the small cell further.

'If my treatment has been effective at all, his temperature will level out. If not his fever will burn him away,' sighed Williams, the worried frown back on his face.

'Literally?' I asked horrified; I'd heard of these cases of spontaneous combustion before.

'No, figuratively, you fool,' retorted Williams with scathing superiority.

Elizabeth Mott flashed me a look of sympathy, a look that said Daniel's barrister should not be addressed like that. But I was too concerned about Daniel to put any value on my own injured feelings, and, anyway, I was dependent on Williams to pull my client through this crisis.

'What's that he's saying?' I asked, leaning closer to the sick bed as Daniel began to moan random words.

'Something about mermaids and signals on shore,' sniffed Williams. 'Been jabbering rubbish like this off and on since daybreak.'

'Hot sun and glass like gold,' moaned Daniel defiantly. 'High on t'big cliff.'

'The big cliff?' I repeated, struggling to understand.

'They always talk nonsense when the crisis has really taken hold,' said Williams, again dismissive.

'But he must mean Boulby Cliffs. Boulby Cliffs are huge. Boulby Cliffs, near Staithes, where Daniel comes from.'

'The result of a fevered brain, I tell you. I'd not read too much into what he's saying at present, Cairn,' advised Williams, carefully sculpting a linseed meal poultice round Daniel's heaving chest.

Chapter Thirty-Two

The day was uninspiring – a Monday in early spring – a day that seemed to provide no diversion, a perfect day for legal focus, otherwise a very ordinary sort of day.

At 10 a.m. Daniel stumbled across the square from the Castle to the courthouse sandwiched between two warders. After his imprisonment and illness his cheeks were sunken, his skin pale and as bland as the day itself. He was wedged between two accompanying hulks, who were almost carrying him along, his body was so willowy thin.

Ringing with chains, Daniel kept blinking up to the leaden sky, leaden but wonderful to a worshipper deprived of the width of sky for so long. His mouth gulped from time to time as if attempting to suck it all in at once. Who knows, after all he had been through this might be his last chance to experience all this again.

I had been studiously reviewing Daniel's case notes with the help of his Whitby solicitor, Mr Wilson Scott, when I suddenly became aware of an unease around me and looked up. Daniel appeared relieved that I had finally noticed him and gave a pathetic little wave across the floor. I waved back but I could have cried instead. This child in a man's body had no idea why he was being goaded forward in such a way.

He struggled on feeble wasted legs up the final step to emerge in the corralling dock with the courtroom beyond. Those in the know – legal men, pressmen, courthouse clerks, men with background knowledge – thought here is a man saved to most probably die.

Though I had been convinced of my client's innocence from the outset, proving it was a different matter.

'A lamb to the slaughter. Tough, ain't it,' muttered Cuthbert Henge QC callously to his colleagues seated at the prosecution table, muttered loudly enough for me and my defence team to hear.

'Wasn't it Wilde who said "It often happens that the real tragedies of life occur in such an inarticulate manner that they hurt one by their crude violence, their absolute incoherence, their absurd want of meaning, their entire lack of style"?' I retorted equally loudly to Duncan Wallbridge; an intense and brilliant junior barrister who had recently joined Bootham Chambers and been seconded at the last moment by Carlton-Bingham to assist me in court with the Robertshaw trial. Wallbridge's presence was another imperative for me to do well, he could easily be my replacement should I fail.

'Bugger didn't win though, did he?' chortled Henge.

'Wilde also said "All trials are trials for one's life". Perhaps it might be wise, gentlemen, to keep our minds on that as this is indeed a trial for that poor fellow's life over there,' pointed out Wallbridge compassionately.

'And what tambourine do you shake, dearie?' mocked Henge; his sycophant table exploding into appreciative laughter.

'A professional one, I hope,' responded Wallbridge, measured but outraged.

'I can tell you've not been playing long though, have you, dearie?'

'Enough,' I warned Wallbridge. 'Save all this for later.'

'All rise,' shouted the clerk of assize, as Mr Justice Sledgemore made his quiet and unremarkable entrance.

10-30 a.m. and at last all the players were in position. A tingle of excitement ran the length of my spine, knowing, without a doubt, that the curtain was about to rise on the world's greatest theatre. And in this respect, this respect alone, I had to grudgingly concede that Gerald Fawcett had a point.

Carlton-Bingham had done his best to fill me in on Sledgemore's credentials. Sledgemore had a very long and distinguished career as a prosecuting counsel behind him before finally making the bench. More ponderous and not as sharp as say Brightman, Sledgemore was credited as having far greater experience.

'He's a better bet for this case,' Carlton-Bingham had reassured me, before adding a precautionary, 'though one can never tell for sure of course.'

'Daniel Robertshaw, you are charged on indictment that on the twenty-first of May, 1897, you murdered Estelle Parke. Are you guilty or not guilty?' asked the clerk of assize.

Estelle Parke. I crossed my arms with satisfaction: here at least was my first small victory.

Meanwhile my client was surveying the room of strange faces. Daniel looked bewildered. Mr Justice Sledgemore was, in turn, looking him up and down doubtfully.

'Daniel Robertshaw …' began the clerk of assize all over again believing the prisoner had not heard.

'One moment,' intervened Sledgemore. 'Would senior counsels be kind enough to step up to the bench before we continue?'

Oh no, I thought, moving forward in reluctant slow-motion.

'Look,' said Sledgemore *sotto voce* to me and Cuthbert Henge, motioning to the dock. 'Do you really think the prisoner is of sound enough mind to continue with these proceedings?'

'This is unprecedented, your lordship,' blustered Henge. 'The man was about to make his plea.'

'Unprecedented or not, Mr Henge, this man appears obviously and seriously mentally deficient,' responded Sledgemore calmly.

'My client is just recovering from pneumonia, my lord, and has been kept in solitary confinement in a dark cell for months. These three factors have greatly contributed to both his pallor and his confusion,' I explained. Adding a more feeble, 'Normally, he appears more robust in body and mind.'

'Pallor and confusion are hardly valid reasons for a man not to stand trial,' blustered Henge again. 'Why, the courts would be empty that being the case.'

'I would like to draw counsels' attention to the Rules of Mc Naughton which might be applied here if the prisoner is of unsound mind. Then again, *actus non facit reum nisi mens sit rea.*' Sledgemore's Latin was immaculate.

'*Mens rea*, of "wicked mind",' I put in gloomily, my stomach tightening. I had my own principled reasons for fearing a cessation of this trial. 'I can assure your lordship, my client has neither a wicked mind nor a wicked thought in his entire body. Though I believe he is aware of what it means to act under such evil influences. But he is innocent of this charge and his only wish is to clear his good name.'

Daniel's only wish was to be free, or hanged, rather than to endure further incarceration in prison or in some terrible lunatic asylum was more the truth of it. After many sessions of gentle probing, following his recent recovery from pneumonia, I was convinced that this was Daniel's deepest desire and a good barrister must always follow his client's best interests.

'I must point out to you, Mr Cairn, that the law can be merciful if there is proof of imperfection of understanding.'

'My client proclaims he is innocent while remaining sensible to the capital charge brought against him. He wants to be heard.'

Henge took a step back at this, obviously prepared for a defence plea of diminished responsibility.

'A medical man, Dr Shaw from The Retreat, has already examined the prisoner and says he is cognisant of the difference between right and wrong,' he butted in unknowingly helpfully. 'Of course I realised, your lordship, that the question of Robertshaw's diminished intellect might be raised, but the onus of proof one way or the other regarding this surely rests with the defence?'

'Mr Cairn?' asked Sledgemore, raising his prolific eye-brows.

'My client understands perfectly,' I insisted. 'And we would like to proceed, your lordship.'

'Very well.' Sledgemore nodded to the clerk of assize to repeat the indictment.

'Daniel Robertshaw ...' began the clerk, this time wearily.

Again Daniel did not answer, his eyes wandering the court in confusion.

'Are you guilty or not guilty of the charge brought against you?' snapped Sledgemore impatiently.

'*Not guilty*, say *not guilty*,' I mouthed.

Finally, Daniel fixed on me.

'Not guilty!' He beamed, pleased with himself, pleased that he had remembered, beaming for a pat on the back from James for remembering.

Still not completely happy, Sledgemore hesitated a moment before instructing the jury to be sworn in.

'So it begins,' I muttered over my shoulder to Martin Trotter, who was sitting errand-boy-ready directly behind our table.

The clerk of assize drew up his shoulders in defiance of any more false starts. 'Members of the jury, the prisoner at the bar, Daniel Robertshaw, is indicted and the charge against him is murder in that on the twenty-first of May, 1897, at Staithes in Yorkshire, he murdered Estelle Parke ...'

This is the biggest examination of my career, I reminded myself, looking across to Daniel in the dock. Daniel who, head cocked to one side, was still beaming happily at the grave and sallow-faced clerk of the court.

'Upon this indictment he has been arraigned: upon his arraignment he has pleaded that he is not guilty and has put himself upon his country, which country you are. It is for you to inquire whether he be guilty or not and to hearken to the evidence.'

Awed by the historical preliminaries not a sound could be heard, not until Cuthbert Henge got to his feet. A lumbering elephant waking on the edge of the peaceful savannah. I felt at that moment as if a thousand birds had hatched in my stomach and were fluttering for escape.

'May it please your lordship, members of the jury, until her death in the spring of 1897, Estelle Parke resided at Brigham Hall, near Staithes. She was the fifteen year old daughter of Sir Hugh and Lady Clarissa Parke. From the day she was born, Estelle was an extremely delicate and sickly child who enjoyed vigilant and constant care within the loving bosom of her family. True to say, Estelle lived a rather secluded life because of her various medical infirmities, her parents fearing the mortal consequences of any contagion from other children, but she was provided with a personal and devoted nanny and her father and mother took upon themselves much of her education. Miss Parke had books, needlecraft, in short, being a young lady from a privileged background, she wanted for very little.'

A small cry broke out from the body of the courtroom. Cuthbert Henge broke off. I traced the interruption to a woman swathed in a dark waterproof cape – it had to be Clarissa Parke – nobody else dressed like that.

'Please be good enough to continue, Mr Henge,' nodded Sledgemore.

'I repeat, Miss Parke came from a privileged background whereas the prisoner over there certainly did not. Somehow, despite her parents' vigilance and unbeknown to them, a friendship developed between these two unlikely young people a couple of months or so prior to Estelle's death. I use the term "young people" advisedly for although Miss Parke was just fifteen, I am well aware that the prisoner is a nineteen year old man. Nonetheless, contrary to Robertshaw's adult physique, I am sure that bright Miss Parke would have been more than a match for him upstairs as it were.' Here, Henge jabbed his forefinger against his temple.

Some ignoramus in the public took this as licence for a joke and bellowed loudly, 'What about downstairs though?'

'Silence!' Sledgemore's face turned puce inside his wigged frame of cream curls. 'Any more outbursts like that and I'll have the public benches cleared immediately.'

'Indeed,' resumed Henge undaunted, 'it could have been the prisoner's mental vulnerability that first attracted the kind attention of this physically vulnerable and socially naive young lady.'

Unable to contain himself any longer, Daniel's solicitor leaned across to me. 'What is he going on about? They didn't know each other at all, did they?'

'Not to my knowledge,' I retorted quickly, fearful of missing a word of Henge's opening statement.

'So what is he getting at then?'

'If we listen, we might find out,' I whispered irritably back.

'In his first two statements to a local police officer the prisoner didn't deny being with the girl on the rocks though refused to say more or give her name,' blared Henge. 'Despite his lack of co-operation, we have evidence supplied by the senior investigating officer, Inspector Kemp, of the violent nature of Robertshaw's relationship with Miss Parke. You will hear from another witness where and how the prisoner engineered these meetings between himself and this innocent and unfortunate child. You will hear evidence from the same witness that while seemingly offering friendship, in reality, the prisoner bore a deep grudge towards Miss Parke because of her social superiority, and because his own family had from being once moderately comfortably off since fallen into reduced circumstances.'

'What witness is this?' Wallbridge asked me.

I moved a dithering finger down the list. 'The name must be here somewhere but I can't imagine who it might be.'

'Though the prisoner's diminished intellect is apparent to everyone, you must bear in mind that he has the body and desires of an adult man. And without any regard for social proprieties those desires can turn into the lust of a beast.' Henge paused here for maximum impact. 'The Crown maintains that the prisoner, despite his mental retardation, cunningly set out to systematically seduce and rape an innocent underage girl to satisfy his own wicked carnality. Until,' Henge raised his finger demanding a silence that was not threatened. 'Until,' he repeated dramatically, 'the twenty-first of May last when, out there on the flat rocks off the shore at Staithes, Miss Parke informed the prisoner that she was expecting his child.'

'What?' A gasp ran through the courtroom, especially through the assembled pressmen. The trial had hardly started but already this was great copy, sensational headlines for the evening editions.

Cuthbert Henge smiled, he had got their attention now, the king was holding court right enough now. 'You will hear from two witnesses how, on the twenty-first of May at midday, the prisoner was actually seen stooping over Miss Parke on the rocks. So strange was his behaviour that one of these witnesses, a Mr Fletcher Warrington, observed him in detail for sometime from Boulby Cliffs with his telescope.'

Hot sun and glass like gold, and Dr Williams had said it was merely Daniel's fevered nonsense. I could have kicked myself for not pursuing this line further once Daniel had recovered. Too late now, I'd have to see what came out in cross-examination.

Cuthbert Henge's reverberating gravelly presentation continued regally, mesmerically, he was encouraged by our defence frowns. 'You will hear how a party of Staithes men waded out to the rocks to rescue the pair as the tide was rapidly coming in. Four brave men risked their own lives, fearing that the prisoner and the young lady with him would soon drown unless they took expedient action. Alas, by the time the men got to the rocks, Miss Parke had already floated away, strangled and despatched by the prisoner. One of those men later reported that the prisoner was in a confused and dishevelled state, the buttons of his breeches were undone in two places.'

I jumped to my feet. 'Your lordship, I really must object to the last comment as being both provocative and …'

'Mr Henge,' Sledgemore interrupted me turning to the QC. 'Do try to keep your opening speech more factual and less graphic. We will be hearing your witnesses' observations in due course.'

'As your lordship pleases.' Henge gave one of his most practised and sarcastic smiles. 'Put simply the Crown's case is this, at sometime between eleven and twelve a.m., on the twenty-first of May last, a tryst out there on those flat sea rocks at Staithes went badly wrong and turned into a scene of murder.' Henge turned directly to the jury and a little warm water travelled over the gravel as he moved his opening address smoothly to its conclusion. 'I have spared you a great deal of detail which it will be necessary to call before you later, but there you have a brief outline of the incidents leading up to the tragic death of Miss Parke. We, the prosecution, ask you to say that the prisoner is guilty of this brutal murder and with the assistance of my learned friend, Mr Arthur Brougham, I will call the evidence before you.'

A murmur as to the merits or weaknesses of Henge's opening statement rose in court, only to fall into silence with the clatter of Fletcher Warrington's riding boots beating a path across the wooden floor. If senior counsel for the Crown lumbered about elephant-like, the Crown's first witness, despite his girth, strutted more in the manner of one of his own golden cock pheasants back home.

'The evidence I give …' Fletcher Warrington repeated the oath clearly, precisely, as if he was savouring every moment of his appearance, and an appearance it was – as glittering as the gold buttons on his fancy waistcoat proclaimed.

'Mr Warrington, as a gentleman and landowner of Staithes, are you acquainted with the prisoner in the dock?' asked sleek and slick Brougham.

'Wouldn't say I'm exactly acquainted with the fella,' bellowed Warrington pompously. 'Seen him round and about, if that's what you mean.'

'Please try and keep your answers to a simple "yes" or "no" to learned counsel's questions whenever possible,' interrupted Sledgemore, staring fixedly down on Fletcher Warrington and his dandy attire with an expression bordering on abhorrence.

'Mr Warrington, is it true that on the twenty-first of May last, you were standing on Boulby Cliffs and observed the accused out on the flat rocks at Staithes?'

'I did.'

'With this?' asked Brougham. Fletcher Warrington nodded his agreement, and the QC spun round holding up the witness's brass telescope for all the courtroom to see as if it was already a winner's trophy.

Deep in thought, my eyelid twitched. My brain cells tussled to organise themselves into recalling where and when I had last seen a telescope like that before.

'You had a very good view of the sea and flat rocks from the cliff then?' continued Brougham.

'Excellent. The sun was shining, visibility was perfect.'

'The court does not require you to give a weather forecast, Mr Warrington. A simple "yes" or "no" will suffice,' Sledgemore informed him.

'Well, yes,' responded Warrington slightly crestfallen.

'Would you be good enough to tell us what exactly you saw the accused doing on that fateful day, Mr Warrington?' asked Brougham huffily, annoyed by the judge's pernicketiness.

'I saw Robertshaw standing over something on the rocks. It was a young woman and he appeared to be flapping his arms about in frustration.'

'Really, my lord.' I leaped up, this time with great indignation.

'I hear you, Mr Cairn. Perhaps it wasn't frustration at all,' suggested Sledgemore, turning back to Fletcher Warrington. 'Perhaps you merely observed the prisoner attempting to impersonate a sea gull.' The court erupted. Fletcher Warrington's normally weathered cheeks flushed an even deeper red. 'Silence!' Sledgemore's icy voice once more quickly re-established gravity into the proceedings. 'Please try not to give your own interpretation of the prisoner's state of mind, Mr Warrington.'

'What happened next?' resumed Brougham sharply. Suddenly all his witness's previous ebullient confidence appeared to be deserting him. 'What happened next?' repeated Brougham, his voice high-pitched with desperation.

'Yes,' said Warrington, struggling to collect himself, his brain grinding away to salvage something from a performance that had unexpectedly gone awry. 'I saw him stoop down over her, pulling her about. Then he lay on top of her and, yes, then I'm sure I saw him kiss her.'

'You saw him *kiss* her?' A note of triumph imbued Brougham's voice.

'Yes, sir.'

'Against her will, would you say?'

'My lord, my learned friend is leading the witness,' I complained.

'Mr Brougham, please refrain from asking the witness to elucidate on the subtleties of attitude when he was obviously a good distance from the event,' censured Sledgemore.

'I do apologise, my lord, but Mr Fletcher Warrington is such a reliable and honourable witness that I have been trying to glean as much information as possible from him.'

'Perhaps in this instance a little too much,' quipped Sledgemore.

Brougham bowed to the judge before returning to Fletcher Warrington. 'You, with three others, bravely risked your life in an attempt to rescue the couple from the rocks, isn't that so?'

'Yes.' Warrington looked relieved to be finally asked a question that would show him in a valiant light.

'But when you got there only the accused remained?'

'That is correct.'

'No further questions,' concluded Brougham, receiving a welcoming smile from Henge as he sidled down next to him.

'Have you any questions for this witness, Mr Cairn?' Sledgemore raised his eyebrows once more in my direction.

'You said you saw the accused flapping his arms about, Mr Warrington?' I cautiously got to my feet.

'Yes.'

'Have you ever seen Mr Robertshaw displaying that same mannerism before?'

'I can't say that I have.'

'Isn't that mannerism merely born from the frustration caused by the accused's inadequacy to express himself rather than the sexual inference you've put upon it?'

'I can only say what I saw.'

'No, sir, as his lordship has already demonstrated to you in a most vivid fashion, you have made your own interpretation of what you think you saw. Could not Mr Robertshaw's flapping arms have been a sign of his great distress at finding something beyond his comprehension?'

'My lord, I must object,' intervened Brougham. 'My friend is asking this witness to give yet another interpretation of the prisoner's actions when his own original one was rejected as unreliable. And isn't the question of the prisoner's mental inadequacy now inadmissible?'

'Mr Cairn?' asked Sledgemore.

'I am merely trying to elucidate what the witness might in fact have really seen,' I explained.

'I think, Mr Cairn, we are all trying to do that,' sighed Sledgemore. 'Nevertheless, please keep your questioning factual.'

'Mr Warrington,' I turned briskly back to the witness. 'Did you actually see sexual congress taking place, out there on the rocks at Staithes, between Daniel Robertshaw and Estelle Parke on the twenty-first of May last?'

'Well, I wouldn't go as far as saying that.'

'And is it your habit to spy on couples with a telescope? Are you actually hoping to see intimacy taking place between them?'

'My lord?' appealed Brougham horrified.

'Well, if they are out there cavorting for all the world to see,' huffed and puffed a belligerent Fletcher Warrington, before the judge had a chance to rule on Brougham's objection.

'But that's just the point, isn't it, Mr Warrington?' I sped on without drawing breath as Sledgemore waved away Brougham's objection. 'Would anybody be rash enough to indulge in the sort of behaviour you have described out there on those exposed rocks, let alone risk committing a murder in clear view of the whole of Staithes?'

'But Robertshaw's a simpleton,' exclaimed Warrington.

'Sir, it has just been made perfectly clear to this court by my learned friend over there,' I pointed across to Brougham, 'that any mental deficiency Daniel Robertshaw might suffer from is no longer an issue in this trial. That not withstanding, the statement made by my other learned friend, Mr Henge (now scowling), that Miss Parke was an extremely bright young lady remains uncontested by anyone. So, I ask you, would this same bright young lady have agreed to go out there on the rocks, alone with the accused, to cavort?'

'Robertshaw must have dragged her out there.'

'Must he? What, kicking and screaming? Have you forgotten, Mr Warrington, your village lies in a bowl of echoing cliffs?'

'Of course not.'

'Then did you hear her screams?' I asked. Fletcher Warrington sagged limply in the witness box. 'Did anyone?'

'Please answer counsel,' Sledgemore told Warrington firmly, interested now to follow this flow of cross-examination himself.

'No, sir, I did not hear her scream.'

'My lord, I must object.' Brougham bounced back onto his feet. 'Staithes is a place of screaming gulls, particularly in May in the nesting season. I've been there myself.'

'And did you have a good holiday, Mr Brougham?' enquired Sledgemore sarcastically, playing to the appreciative gallery, before turning his attention back to the witness box. 'Are the screams of an anguished young woman discernible from the mating calls of sea gulls, do you think?' he asked Warrington bitingly.

The public benches shuddered into silence, unsure of his lordship's sense of humour this time. Warrington hovered over the question as if he was being asked to explain the origins of the universe.

'Mr Warrington?' prompted Sledgemore.

'A local man like myself should be able to tell the difference,' he admitted reluctantly.

'Warrington is being undone by his own vanity,' Wallbridge muttered in an undertone.

'Do you want to continue your examination of this witness, Mr Cairn?' asked Sledgemore.

'You have said under oath that you saw the accused kiss a young woman out there on the rocks at Staithes and that you did not hear her scream, is that correct, Mr Warrington?' I smiled patiently. Fletcher Warrington nodded impatiently.

'Answer "yes" or "no"?' snapped Sledgemore yet again.

'Yes,' simpered Warrington, his lower lip jutting out like a spoilt child's.

'That is all for now, my lord.' I bowed.

'Then I think a break is called for at this juncture, gentlemen. Mr Cairn and Mr Brougham, I would like to see you both in my chambers at one forty-five prompt before we resume this afternoon.'

I swung round and passed a note back to Martin Trotter. 'See Jackson gets this message before he sets out on his journey here,' I told him quietly. 'Send it by telegraph or if necessary a private courier.'

Chapter Thirty-Three

A more chastened Brougham and I waited for his lordship's arrival back in court. Despite Fletcher Warrington being a poor witness, Sledgemore had privately warned us that he considered our form of questioning that morning had been emotive, manipulative and our casual asides down right improper at times, and he would not tolerate any more of it. It was a new Mr Justice Sledgemore who reappeared for the afternoon session, his mouth set in a severe straight line.

Leaning forward, Nathaniel Nab rested his hands on top of the witness box. He perused the court as if he were on sea-watch. Between his outstretched arms his mane of beard dangled long and unkempt.

'It's Neptune himself,' said the *Herald's* man to one of the nationals. A deep belly laugh rumbled along the press benches.

'Nathaniel Nab you are a retired fisherman of Staithes, are you not?' began Brougham.

'I didn't quite catch that, sir,' complained Nab, cupping his ear.

'You are a retired fisherman, sir?' bellowed Brougham, hoping his lordship did not interpret his increased volume as over zealous questioning.

'I am that,' agreed Nab proudly.

'And you are a Quaker as indeed the prisoner is over there in the dock, and he is well-known to you, is he not?'

'He is that, and his father afore him, God rest his soul.'

'Did you see him stooping over a young woman on the rocks at Staithes on the twenty-first of May last?'

'Yes, he was certainly stooped over summat.'

'And as the tide was coming in, it was you who first raised the alarm, was it not?'

'I did.'

'Fearing for two young lives?'

'Yes.'

'But when you got to the rocks with your companions, Robertshaw was alone and in a state of some distress, is that correct?'

'Yes.'

'Thank you, Mr Nab, no more questions from me for now.'

'Mr Nab, you've just told the court that the accused was stooped over something. How sure are you that *something* was a young woman?' I probed.

'Sorry?' Nab's hand cupped his ear again.

I shouted out the question once more. Laughter from the gallery. A cry of "silence" from his lordship.

'It looked like a female body to me,' muttered Nab ponderously.

'A body, you say? A dead or an alive body?'

'Um, 'twas difficult to tell with the naked eye.'

'I hope your naked eye is better than your hearing, sir,' I said, pausing momentarily to see if Sledgemore would let this off the cuff remark slip through. 'I see here, in your original statement to Police Constable Jonathan Sleightholm, you said that some time before this incident on the rocks you'd seen the accused walking on his own along the staithe, is that so?'

'"Staithe"?' queried Sledgemore.

'The staithe, my lord, is a wooden walkway or landing by the sea in the village of Staithes,' I explained.

'All very confusing,' muttered Sledgemore, penning a reminder to himself.

'Did you see Daniel Robertshaw walking alone shortly before going out onto the rocks, Mr Nab?' I asked, happy to rephrase the question.

'Yes, sir, there was no one with him at first.'

'And, later, did you see any movement at anytime from the body on the rocks with Mr Robertshaw?'

'I object, my lord,' exclaimed Brougham.

'On what grounds?' asked Sledgemore.

'My learned friend's controversial use of the word "body", my lord.'

'I must overrule you here, Mr Brougham, as the witness himself has already referred to the person with the prisoner out on the rocks as "a body".'

'Mr Nab, did you see the accused kiss or lay on this body in a sexually explicit manner?' I asked.

'As I've just told thee, sir, with the naked eye it can be difficult …' Troubled, Nab hesitated, looking wildly about the court for inspiration.

'"Yes" or "no", Mr Nab?' Not Sledgemore's but my turn to request the definitive answer.

'Then no, sir. Some might say they saw such things but not me.'

'By "some" you mean Mr Warrington, don't you?'

'Yes, sir,' mumbled Nab.

'Constable Sleightholm recruited you, along with two other men, to guard the accused at his mother's cottage, on the evening of the twenty-second of May last, following the recovery of Estelle Parke's body from the sea, did he not?'

'Ay.'

'Did you see that cottage torched to the ground?'

'I did. There was nothing we could do, too many of 'em.'

'Is there much religious discrimination against your faith in Staithes?'

Nathaniel Nab looked about the room once more, nonplussed. ''Tis better to keep thy own counsel on such matters,' he mumbled down into his beard.

'I must remind you that you are in a court of law and must answer all questions put to you concisely,' interjected Sledgemore.

'Put it this way, Mr Nab,' I coaxed the old man more gently. 'At the time of the fire Daniel Robertshaw had only been questioned regarding the young girl's body, had he not?'

'Yes, sir.'

'He'd not been arrested or even accused of killing her, then?'

'No, sir.'

'So would his cottage have been burnt to the ground, at this stage of enquiry, if he had been say a Wesleyan?'

'This really is too much, my lord,' cried out Brougham. 'My friend's cross-examination is inflammatory in itself.'

'Mr Cairn?' Sledgemore raised just the one bushy eyebrow. 'Is this line of questioning really pertinent to your case?'

'I am simply demonstrating to the court, my lord, that in a tight-knit community such as Staithes, my client's unusual religious affiliation, along with other more apparent differences, make him an easy target for any unjust charge.'

'But Mr Nab is here to tell us what he saw taking place between Miss Parke and the prisoner out there on the rocks last May,' protested Brougham. 'Not to give us his opinion on religious attitudes in Staithes.'

'But it was my learned friend who first brought to the court's notice that Mr Nab is a practising Quaker,' I retorted.

Meanwhile, amid legal argument, Neptune remained subdued and rooted to the spot.

'Do either of you two gentlemen have any more constructive questions to put to this witness?' requested Sledgemore.

'What more can you ask, when you've made your point brilliantly?' uttered Wallbridge softly as I bent forward over the table to re-examine my notes.

'I have just one more constructive question to ask, my lord.' I gave a brief meaningful glance across to the glowering Brougham. 'Mr Nab, did you ever witness Daniel Robertshaw being persecuted or bullied because of either his religious affiliation or obvious defencelessness in the village of Staithes?'

Nathaniel Nab thought long and hard, weighing the implications of the question and his answer this way and that, before replying, 'Ay, sir, plenty of times.'

'My lord.' Henge was on his feet now. 'Though Mr Nab is a fellow Quaker, he came here today to make it absolutely clear to this court that he saw the accused stooping over a person, who turned out to be Miss Parke.'

Nathaniel Nab nodded compliantly in the witness box.

'I think that fact is well established, Mr Henge,' said Sledgemore. 'Is that not so, Mr Nab?'

'Yes, your lordship,' agreed Nab, wishing he were home.

'No more questions from me.' I took my seat.

It had been an entertaining day so far. The buzzing public adjusted their buttocks on the hard wooden benches waiting for the next witness to be called. A hushed expectancy fell as the sound of chains could be heard dragging through the rustling bureaucracy of barristers and clerks on the floor of the court.

The same cunning face; the same jaunty walk despite being shackled between two warders; the same hooded eyes casting about the court; the same slight figure, made slighter in coarse but thin prison cloth, seemed to elbow its way to the box.

Well, well, Lane in chains, I grimaced, hoping upon hope that Lane's pride would not demean itself by revealing that he had been in a scuffle with defending counsel.

'Job Lambert Lane, you are an ex-fisherman of Staithes and at present enjoying Her Majesty's pleasure in this city, is that correct?' asked Henge.

'I am, sir, though I am an innocent man,' whined Lane.

'Just answer counsel's question,' sighed Sledgemore, obviously wondering how many more of the Crown's rustic, now villainous, witnesses the court would have to endure.

'I do beg your pardon, sir,' toadied Lane.

'*My lord*,' corrected Henge.

'My lord,' repeated Lane like an ABC schoolboy.

'You are one of the four men who rescued the accused from the rocks and encroaching tide at Staithes, a day before the body of Miss Parke was pulled from the sea?' resumed Henge.

'I am, sir.' Lane attempted to puff out his narrow chest.

'And what condition was the accused in when you rescued him?'

'Bad, sir, very bad. Muttering to himself and suchlike.'

'"Suchlike"?' enquired Sledgemore.

'He was humming like, me lord,' explained Lane.

'Humming what? A tune?'

'More a dirge, me lord.'

'A dirge, I see,' said Sledgemore, not seeing at all.

'Was the accused fully dressed when you got out to him on the rocks?' came in Henge again.

'He was dressed, sir, but I noticed his breeches' buttons were undone.'

Wilson Scott looked to Wallbridge, Wallbridge to me – mystery solved – it was Lane who the prosecution had dragged out of prison to give this piece of colourful invention.

Damn good, I thought, a sour taste in my mouth. Lane of all people.

'And what did you think to that?' asked Henge.

'Not a lot at the time,' replied Lane with a shrug of indifference.

'And later? Tell the court what occurred to you later?'

'My learned friend is leading the witness, my lord,' I objected.

'Would you please rephrase your question, Mr Henge,' suggested Sledgemore helpfully.

'I'll try my best, my lord,' bowed Henge. 'Job Lane, did anyone put the possibility to you, following the unhappy events of the twenty-first and twenty-second of May last, that Robertshaw might have raped and murdered Miss Parke?'

'Yes, Fletcher Warrington, sir.'

'Fletcher Warrington seems to be orchestrating much of this affair,' muttered Wilson Scott in a low aside to me.

'I've not finished with that gentleman yet,' I vowed.

'And, during this same conversation, did you and Mr Warrington discuss the state of Robertshaw's undress at the time of the incident out on the rocks?' Henge asked Lane.

'We did, sir.'

'And did you further report your observation of Robertshaw's gaping trousers to an Inspector Kemp at Whitby police station?'

'Yes, sir.' Lane almost saluted, apparently already institutionalised by the Castle's penal regime.

'I have no more questions for this witness.' Henge folded back into his chair as we, the defence, rummaged desperately through various documents.

'Mr Lane,' I acknowledged, papers in hand, my false smile sickly-sweet. Lane flinched back uneasily, chains ringing. 'You have just told this court that you reported the accused's state of undress to Inspector Kemp, isn't that so?'

'Yes,' replied Lane edgily.

'I can see no mention of this button observation in your original statement taken by Police Constable Sleightholm and dated the twenty-first of May, 1897, the day of your rescue attempt. Why is that?'

'Didn't think it was important then.'

'But it was important enough to mention to Mr Fletcher Warrington later?'

'We were just having a jar and a jaw, you know how it is.'

'Yes, I know how it is,' I agreed still smiling sweetly. 'Can you tell me, did you notice if the accused's buttons were actually undone or just missing?'

'Undone, I'd say.'

'You must have looked at the accused's flies closely?'

More sniggering from the press and public.

Lane was insentient, insisting, 'I recollect they were unbuttoned in two places at least.'

'Surely, we have the prisoner's breeches in evidence,' interrupted Sledgemore, addressing the prosecution table.

'Unfortunately, my lord, they were destroyed in the fire at the prisoner's home,' explained Henge.

'That is unfortunate,' agreed Sledgemore genuinely dismayed.

'Convenient too,' I murmured maliciously, before asking Lane loudly, 'Speaking of the Robertshaw fire, you are embarking on a life sentence for the manslaughter of a woman in that fire, are you not?'

'Is this relevant, my lord?' asked Henge, flouncing to his feet with sudden and surprising agility.

'The accused's home was burnt to the ground in an unlawful act of revenge before he was even charged with this offence, as has already been stated at this trial, and the woman who died in that fire was my client's aunt. I'd say the fire is very relevant to our case, my lord,' I retaliated with equal vigour.

'Go ahead, Mr Cairn,' nodded Sledgemore.

'Is it not a fact, Job Lane, that you never mentioned the accused's state of undress to the police until your arrest for arson and murder?'

'I can't remember.'

'See, here, your first reference concerning the accused's state of undress was made in this deposition signed and dated the seventh of September, 1897,' I pointed out as the usher presented the document to Lane. 'Some three and a half months after Estelle Parke's body was found. Did Inspector Kemp put some pressure on you to validate this incriminating observation or did you merely offer it up, invent it, in the hope of avoiding the more serious capital charge of murder?'

'My learned friend is making a serious allegation here,' blustered Henge.

'Let me see that.' Sledgemore ignored Henge's objection and held out his hand for the usher to furnish him with Lane's deposition.

'Well?' I asked, my smile a distant memory.

'Can't recall exactly when I first told the police, but I am sure I saw Robertshaw's buttons undone,' affirmed Lane.

'No more questions,' I concluded.

'With a good deal to dwell on already from today's proceedings, I think we'll take the opportunity for an adjournment,' announced Sledgemore acidly.

My expression remained hard and unflinching as I watched the wiry figure of Job Lane clumping and ringing out of court between his minders. The cockiness of the man finally gone – a broken man – a man facing the rest of his life in prison without the hope of a pardon.

Chapter Thirty-Four

A bushel of March dust is worth a king's ransom – the second day of the Assizes was dry and windy – a good day for tillage but an unnerving day for standing on trial for your life.

Outdoors at Staithes, Daniel had been indifferent to climatic change, had revelled in hail, rain and sunshine without distinction. Indoors now, bored and in the dock again, today there was no self-conscious grin, no making faces at the court, no poking tongue directed towards the press, no jerky little wave for me. Daniel was acting like Queen Victoria on one of her bad days.

'Jonathan Sleightholm, you are the local police-constable covering the area of Staithes, are you not?' opened Brougham.

'Yes, sir.'

'And can you tell us what happened on the twenty-first of May last?'

Constable Jonathan Sleightholm's big hands nervously opened up his black leather bound notebook. Daniel slumped forward in the dock, remembering the book and the dark uniform and contrasting silver buttons. This man had heralded his incarceration. Daniel watched on even more grumpily.

'I was called in the afternoon to a public house in Staithes to interview the prisoner, Daniel Robertshaw, as some local men had seen him in the company of a person on rocks nearby.' Sleightholm's fingers shook as he read down the page. 'Four of these local men had been forced to mount a rescue operation as the sea was threatening to engulf the prisoner and his companion. By the time they reached the rocks only Robertshaw remained, and his companion was feared drowned. Robertshaw was unable to name this other person. At four p.m., the following afternoon, I was sent for to go down to the staithe as the body of a young woman had been recovered from the sea by fishermen.'

'Where in the sea had she actually been found?' asked Brougham.

'A few miles from Scar Shootings.'

'Otherwise known as Sky Shittings,' I could not resist muttering impishly into Wallbridge's ear.

'What?' Junior counsel's eyes danced, eager for fun.

'Never mind, I'll explain later,' I told Wallbridge, grinning back broadly.

'Has counsel for the defence some joke he would like to share with the rest of the court?' asked Sledgemore.

'Indeed not, my lord,' I replied with a bow. 'I do apologise.'

'Despite our decrepitude, Mr Cairn, we are all not as hard of hearing as you might suppose,' admonished Sledgemore.

Obviously irritated by the interruption from our table, Brougham made a vigorous adjustment to the lapels of his gown before returning to his examination of Constable Sleightholm. 'Scar Shootings are the rocks on which Miss Parke was last seen with the prisoner, is that not so?'

'Yes, sir.'

'Do you think you can tell me approximately how many miles the body was found from those rocks?'

'I understood from the coble fishermen who recovered the body, it was about three miles south of the rocks,' replied Sleightholm.

'Would that be towards Whitby?'

'Yes, sir, the normal current flows north to south.'

'Pray continue with your report.'

'I ...' Sleightholm struggled to find the place where he had left off. 'I sent for the prisoner and asked him again if he could identify the dead girl. He denied knowing her. When asked if he had anything to do with her death, he denied that he had.'

'And did you have any reason to think otherwise?' enquired Brougham.

'Yes, sir, Dr Allanby was unhappy about some faint marks around the girl's throat.'

'You took the precaution of putting a guard on the prisoner's cottage on Cowbar Bank that night, did you not?'

'Yes, sir.'

'Can you clarify to the court why you deemed it necessary?'

'For fear of a reprisal, sir.'

'Because of the prisoner's Quaker faith or mental impairment?'

'No, no, sir. Robertshaw needed protection because the entire village believed he had something to do with the young girl's death and was set against him.'

'And such was the local feeling against the prisoner that during the night of the twenty-second of May you were forced to call out the Whitby militia, isn't that so?'

'Alas, sir, they arrived shortly after the Robertshaw cottage had been torched.'

'Thank you, Constable Sleightholm,' smarmed Brougham.

Damnation, I thought, knowing Henge, not Brougham, was really behind this counter move.

'Aren't you going to challenge him?' asked Wallbridge, bursting with indignation. 'Puh, the militia arrived too late.'

'The militia always arrives too late,' put in Wilson Scott blandly.

'Isn't it a fact that the militia's arrival acted as a catalyst, provoking the crowd to torch the accused's house as they ran off?' I asked Sleightholm.

'That I couldn't say, sir.' Sleightholm looked perplexed.

'The spark as it were?' I resumed my seat with a flourish.

'Ask him about originally assigning only three men to guard Daniel's cottage,' begged Wallbridge.

'Anything more I say at this point will merely work against us.' The dismissive wave of the hand I gave him was born out of my own exasperation.

Without further challenge a frowning constable stepped down as a hesitant general practitioner stepped up.

'Dr Peter Ernest Allanby are you a medical practitioner in Staithes?' The main man was on his feet again.

'I am, sir.'

'And did you attend a body on the staithe, at Staithes, on the twenty-second of May last?' asked Henge, pretending to consult notes he already knew off by heart.

'Yes, I did, sir.'

'A body who turned out to be young Miss Parke?'

'Indeed, sir. Though I didn't know it at the time.'

'Can you tell us how you believe Miss Parke died?'

'From either drowning or strangulation.'

'Come, come, my lord, can't the witness be more specific when giving such a vital piece of evidence?' I piped up again.

'Which is it to be, Dr Allanby?' asked Sledgemore.

'Because of some abrasions round her neck I suspected she had been strangled and then thrown into the sea.' Allanby nervously ran his fingers across a poor attempt at a beard.

'No more questions, my lord,' said Henge, smugly flouncing down next to his colleagues.

'That was short and sweet,' uttered Wallbridge in amazement.

'Too short, and too sweet,' I elaborated suspiciously.

'Mr Cairn, any questions for this witness?' asked Sledgemore, knowing only too well that I must be champing at the bit to get at Allanby.

'You only suspected, sir, that Miss Parke was strangled to death prior to her body entering the water?' I asked cautiously.

'Strongly suspected,' emphasised Allanby.

'Dr Allanby, how long have you been in general practice?'

'I joined my father's practice some seventeen years ago.'

'You have just told this court, and I see here from your deposition to the Whitby magistrate, Mr Matthew Wilder, that you had no idea who the girl was when you first examined her there on the staithe.'

'Yes,' agreed Allanby guardedly.

'So you had no idea that some sixteen years ago Dr Allanby senior, your late father, attended a difficult birth at Brigham Hall?'

'Well, I did …'

'Did what, sir?'

'After I had examined the body on the staithe, I did wonder …'

'Wonder what?' I decided Allanby's wispy beard was in fact there to hide a weak chin.

'From the deceased's fine silk dress, I wondered if she belonged to the upper class.'

'And would you consider the owners of Brigham Hall as belonging to the upper class?'

'Well, yes, I suppose so.'

'And are there many upper class families living in or around Staithes?'

'Not many.'

'No, not many.' I pondered this statement a second or two before asking, 'Tell me, did your late father ever mention that the child born at Brigham Hall had a very peculiar appearance?'

'Well, he might have done.'

'Come, come, Dr Allanby, are you telling me that your father wouldn't have mentioned to his junior medical partner, and son, something as unusual as the delivery of a child with pink eyes?'

'Pink eyes?' gasped Sledgemore, the pupils of his own eyes narrowing. 'I do hope you're not bringing creatures from outer space into your argument now, Mr Cairn.'

The court exploded like never before over this surprising piece of insensitivity which must have just flipped unthinkingly off his lordship's tongue.

'Silence!' insisted Sledgemore with only himself to blame.

'Silence!' screamed the clerk of assize, blaming both myself and his lordship for incitement to riot.

'No, my lord, my examination is well within the boundary of our own galaxy,' I replied coolly. 'I am merely informing this court that Dr Allanby's father helped to deliver Estelle Parke. And that Miss Parke had an obvious and very rare defect at birth, involving a pink-eyed appearance that would have interested any medical man let alone his newly qualified son.'

'I did know some of the unusual details of Miss Parke's birth,' finally squeaked Allanby.

'Yet faced with a young girl's body dressed in silk and of the same age, you failed to put two and two together?' I asked incredulously.

'She was badly disfigured.'

'How exactly?'

'Her eyes had been eaten away.'

'Had they? By what?'

'Fish, crustaceans.'

'Then she must have been in the water for quite some time, wouldn't you say?'

'Perhaps.'

'Longer than the twenty-four hours or so from the tide rushing in onto the rocks, where she was seen with the accused, and her final recovery from the sea, wouldn't you say?'

'I am not an expert in these matters.'

'No, you certainly are not,' I affirmed ruthlessly. 'And what is more I suggest from the lack of hair and skin pigmentation alone, you could have made an educated guess at the body's true identity.'

'I am a man of science,' retorted Allanby arrogantly.

'No, sir, you are a man who is afraid of getting involved, of upsetting those you consider to be your social superiors.'

'Mr Cairn,' cut in Sledgemore. (I flinched, sure I was about to be admonished again.) 'Does Miss Parke's rare condition have a name?'

'Yes, my lord. I intend to call a medical expert who is prepared to explain the complications of her disorder in detail.'

'Have you any more questions for this witness then, Mr Cairn, because if you haven't I'd like to suggest a lunch adjournment?' Sledgemore's domed forehead wrinkled morosely over his morning's note-taking. His lordship was obviously still cross with himself for making the flippant outer space comment.

Gathering up my own papers, I glanced up to the public gallery. The woman in the dark waterproof cape was still there. Clarissa Parke's face was crumpled in grief and anxiety as it had been all those months ago on the staithe during the storm. The time would not be long in coming when I would be forced to confront her in the witness box.

Chapter Thirty-Five

Jackson, who was due to attend the Robertshaw trial in a day or two as a witness for the defence, arrived early after lunch as a sleuth.

'Well?' I asked him quietly in the echoing corridor of plotting and power outside the courtroom.

'I did as you asked,' replied Jackson.

'Good news then.'

'Yes, good news,' affirmed Jackson, handing over a brown parcel.

We remained huddled to one side of the corridor discussing his covert operation for a few minutes more. I saw a nervous tic beginning to leap up his cheek. Jackson obviously did not like this building, this corridor, very much. He must have felt too restricted here, confined.

'This all looks very cloak and dagger,' shouted Wallbridge; who, seemingly fortified with a good lunch, was quickly bearing down on us with Wilson Scott in tow.

'Mr Jackson is one of our key witnesses,' I explained.

'Of course.' Wallbridge warmly shook Jackson's hand. Jackson recoiled a little at Wallbridge's Black Swan bonhomie. 'We've been laughing like hell over yesterday's choice comment.'

'And which one was that?' I asked.

'Yours about Lane observing Daniel's unbuttoned flies closely,' explained the irrepressible Wallbridge. 'Made him out to be a right little poof.'

'Not given you too much cause for mirth and celebration this morning though,' I pointed out a little dispiritedly.

'Yesterday we had the testimony of a convict, today we merely have had the meanderings of the village bobby and a local quack,' chimed in Scott supportively.

I, who had not lunched at the Black Swan, suddenly noticed that Jackson seemed to have curled even further into the wall, curled into himself.

'Anything wrong?' I asked him, after Wallbridge and Scott had disappeared back into court.

'What did Lane say about them buttons?' frowned Jackson.

'He said two of Daniel's trouser buttons were undone when you got out to him on the rocks. He was lying of course.'

'No, he wasn't. I thought no one else had noticed.'

'What?'

'I saw 'em undone too.'

'For God's sake, Jackson!' I cursed. 'You could have warned me. Why have you waited until today to tell me this?'

'I thought too much might be read into it at the time. A lad like Daniel might go about all day long with his breeches unfastened.'

'But to say nothing.'

'To be absolutely honest with you, them buttons went clean out of my head.'

'Well, it's too late now. We'll have to let that piece of information ride.'

The downcast Jackson retreated with fellow bachelor, Martin Trotter, back to Trotter's York home. House-proud, garden-proud Martin Trotter lived near the onetime gatehouse and barrier in the old city wall named Fishergate Bar. Trotter, who liked word puzzles, made an immediate connection with his visitor's occupation but, with Jackson in his present mood, thought better of drawing his attention to such frivolity.

'There's no pleasing that bloody man,' muttered Jackson.

'Know what you mean,' agreed Trotter; further blackening my name, he admitted later.

* * * * *

As Inspector Malcolm Kemp was being sworn in, I threw my client a worried glance. I need not have been concerned, Daniel appeared more absorbed with the gyve marks round his wrists than the bullying police inspector's presence in court. It was then that I was struck by a terrible possibility: suppose I had been blinkered against Daniel's darker side all along, suppose Daniel had actually committed this horrendous crime.

'You are a police inspector in the North Riding Constabulary stationed at Whitby, are you not?' Henge asked Kemp.

'Yes, sir.'

'And it was you who finally obtained a signed confession from the prisoner to the charge of murder during his remand at the Castle prison, was it not?'

'Yes, sir.'

'Which he now refutes?'

'He does, sir.'

'I draw your lordship's and the jury's attention to Exhibit Five.' Henge wafted Daniel's confession high above his head. 'And it was also you, Inspector Kemp, who was able to establish the identity of the murdered girl as Estelle Parke?'

'Yes, sir.'

'You are to be commended for your diligence. Thank you, that will be all from me for now.'

Seesaw fashion, I bounced up as Henge bounced down. Faced with cross-examining this self-satisfied little runt of an inspector, my niggling doubt regarding my client's innocence was put on hold.

'You did well to discover, single-handed, that the dead girl was Estelle Parke,' I began out of pure devilment.

'Well, the magistrate …'

'Ah, so it was Matthew Wilder who first drew your attention to the possibility, was it?'

Kemp tossed his head back defiantly before muttering, 'Yes, it could have been.'

'And had Sir Hugh and Lady Clarissa Parke already reported their daughter missing then?' Kemp shook his head. Without pressing for a verbal response, I quickly asked, 'Did the Parkes tell you why they'd never informed the police that their fifteen year old daughter was missing?'

'They thought at first she'd just gone off.'

'Gone off, where?'

'Maybe to stay with a friend's family.'

'But as far as I can gather Miss Parke didn't have any friends, did she?'

'I wouldn't know about that.'

'Miss Parke didn't officially exist either, did she?'

'You'd have to ask Sir Hugh and Lady Clarissa about that,' shrugged Kemp.

'Oh, I will, Inspector Kemp, I will. But didn't you?'

'No, I was more interested in conducting a murder investigation.'

'But wasn't Estelle Parke the central figure in that murder investigation, indeed its victim?'

'Well, yes, at it turned out.'

'So, wouldn't any detail of her life have proved important to your inquiry?'

'Not all of them, no.'

'Inspector Kemp, why do you think you were able to obtain a confession from Robertshaw when PC Sleightholm was not?' I asked, suddenly switching track.

Kemp looked nonplussed for a moment.

'It's a matter of experience,' he explained, leaning conspiratorially forward in the witness box.

'Experience, I see,' I laughed, one experienced man to another. 'My lord, might I take a look at Exhibit Five?' I asked turning to Sledgemore.

Sledgemore nodded to the usher and Daniel's signed confession was handed to me and then to the witness.

'I see there that the prisoner has made an attempt at some sort of doodle. D. Robertshaw, is that right?'

'There nothing wrong with this signature,' insisted Kemp. 'It's perfectly legal and binding.'

'Yes, sir, it certainly seems to be,' I agreed.

Henge bounced up at this. 'Would my learned friend get to the point, if there is a point to be made, instead of prevaricating?'

'Your point being, Mr Cairn?' enquired Sledgemore, a little impatient himself.

'If legal, that signature obtained by Inspector Kemp is in itself something of a miracle, my lord and members of the jury.' It was my turn for a little theatrical fanning of the air. 'Because my client, Mr Robertshaw, is barely capable of making his mark let alone signing his name.'

A general hiss of interest fizzed round the courtroom.

'Can you supply the court with any proof that the prisoner is unable to write his signature, Mr Cairn?' asked Sledgemore.

I picked up a pile of papers from my table and the usher deposited them beneath Sledgemore's nose.

'These are all legal papers taken to the Castle prison by me during Mr Robertshaw's months of confinement there. You will see, my lord, they are all signed with a cross. A symbol I had to demonstrate each time with my finger in the dust on his cell table, and which he then laboriously transcribed in ink against his name.'

I waited, giving Sledgemore time to flick through the dozen or so papers. Removing his steamed up spectacles, Sledgemore wiped them clean thoughtfully. He then turned his attention to Kemp, who was visibly squirming in the witness box.

'Can you explain to me how Daniel Robertshaw wrote this signature?' I asked angrily across the court to Kemp. 'Daniel Robertshaw who has never had a day's schooling in his entire life and is unable to make his cross without an example to copy from?'

'I ...' Kemp shrugged once more and fell silent.

'I'll tell you how,' I offered, as Kemp's fingers clamped down harder on the top railing of the witness box, a man on the verge of falling out of his chariot. 'One of those two hands of yours pressed Daniel Robertshaw's illiterate hand into its own scrawling service.'

Henge watched on as if paralysed – Sledgemore watched on impassively – Kemp was out there in the arena alone.

'You forced Mr Robertshaw to sign that confession, didn't you?' I dropped my head, ashamed at having to articulate such a disgusting scenario.

'I might have had to help him a little. You said yourself he was incapable of ... Just look at him over there with his tongue lolling out. Look see, your lordship, he's sticking his tongue insolently out at me. Surely, he shouldn't be allowed to do that, not here in a court of law.'

'I have no more questions for this witness,' I announced contemptuously.

'Mr Henge?' asked Sledgemore, studiously ignoring Kemp's tirade against the prisoner.

'No, my lord, the prosecution has no more questions for this witness either,' said Henge, with a brief flash of admiration in my direction.

'Inspector Kemp.' Sledgemore turned back to the witness, his tone slow and measured and all the more intimidating for that. 'To physically force a man into signing a confession is an offence according to law as I am sure you are well aware. I, therefore, have no other option than to refer this serious allegation made against you in this court to the appropriate authorities. You are dismissed.'

Kemp had had his day in court and I had honoured my self-imposed obligation. I watched without regret or pity as another tearful bully stumbled out of my world forever.

'Hugh Osbert Parke, do you swear …' If Fletcher Warrington had made an entrance and Kemp exited in disgrace, Sir Hugh Parke remained resigned and quietly noble as he took the box.

'Sir Hugh, the question has been raised why you failed at first to report that your daughter was missing?' Henge launched in.

'My wife and I had been aware for some time that Estelle had become frustrated with her ill-health and the restraints it put on her freedom. We thought she might have just taken herself off to stay with relatives.'

'And not informed you?'

'Well, yes.'

'Did you contact any of these relatives?'

'Yes, we'd begun making enquiries when a police inspector arrived and told us of the body found at Staithes.'

'And you'd heard nothing about the goings on at Staithes until this police inspector informed you?'

'Well, actually no.'

'Police inspector? What police inspector? Doesn't he have a name?' remonstrated Sledgemore.

'Inspector Kemp,' acknowledge Henge with distinct embarrassment.

'Of course, it would have had to be,' groaned Sledgemore.

'Now, unfortunately, I have to ask you this question, sir. Did you or your wife know that your daughter was pregnant until informed by the police?'

Sir Hugh faltered, looking down the full length of his long body to his shoes. 'We'd no idea, it was a terrible shock,' he mumbled.

'Can you speak up? I can't hear your reply,' complained Sledgemore, showing not the slightest deference to rank.

'We had no idea that our daughter was with child, my lord,' rallied Sir Hugh with the vaguest hint of annoyance.

'Having been made aware that she was, had you any suspicions as to who the father might have been?' asked Henge.

'We could only think she had been forced.' Greying side-whiskered Sir Hugh returned to an appraisal of his shoes.

'You knew of no men friends then?'

'None.'

'Was she familiar with any of the servants say?'

'Certainly not.'

'But she walked the grounds of Brigham Hall freely enough, did she not?'

'No, Estelle was only able to take the air after dark because of her skin. She was extremely sensitive to sunlight, you see.'

'Alone?'

'Sorry?'

'Would she walk out of doors alone at night?'

'Very infrequently. I made it my duty to escort her whenever I could. It wasn't an easy situation for any of us.'

'But she could have been taken advantage of during an occasional nocturnal walk on her own in the grounds, could she not?'

'It's possible,' sighed Sir Hugh.

'Thank you, sir, for coming here today, and might I extend my deepest sympathy to you and your wife.' Henge gallantly tossed up the tail of his gown before resuming his seat.

'Is the man standing over there in the dock known to you at all, Sir Hugh?' I asked, pointing to Daniel – Daniel who was by now benumbed and expressionless.

'Robertshaw looks like one of my wilting lettuces in summer.' Brougham smiled across to Henge. Henge, listening intently to my cross-examination, did not smile back.

'No, I've never seen him before,' replied Sir Hugh.

'Not even down in the village?'

'No. Not so far as I can recollect.'

'Approximately how many months was it between your daughter going missing and Inspector Kemp telling you of the discovery of the girl's body at Staithes?' I began to mentally close in on the witness box.

'Living such a busy public life, one tends to lose track of time,' apologised Sir Hugh; one lifted index finger checking his moustache.

'What? Five, six months of time?'

'All time,' sighed Sir Hugh again, this time extremely wearily.

'Did you originally tell Inspector Kemp that you believed your daughter might be with a friend's family?'

'No, relatives, we thought she might be enjoying a temporary stay with relatives.'

'Inspector Kemp testified that you said "a friend's family".'

'He was mistaken.'

'Then, sir, can you tell this court why you dismissed your daughter's nanny and companion, Susannah Mott, if you believed your daughter's absence was only a temporary one with relatives?'

'Yes, I most certainly can. As I explained to Susannah, we had arranged for Estelle to undergo an extensive period of treatment for her various conditions abroad. Indeed, we privately thought this might have been another reason for her running away.'

'But I understand from Miss Mott's statement that you failed to tell her that Estelle was missing?'

'Estelle and Susannah were very close. I didn't want to distress Susannah any more than was necessary.'

'"Necessary"?' I hissed in disbelief. 'But you were in the process of dismissing the young woman after years of faithful service, were you not?'

'Yes, and that was upsetting enough,' affirmed Sir Hugh calmly.

'Very plausible, isn't he,' I heard Scott whisper to Wallbridge.

'Too bloody plausible,' moaned Wallbridge. 'The fellow's an adept politician.'

'There is just one minor point that still mystifies me, Sir Hugh,' I said. 'Why wasn't your daughter's birth ever officially recorded?'

'Oh, that's easy,' laughed Sir Hugh. 'Estelle was so poorly at birth, her mother too, somehow that whole procedure thing got overlooked.'

'It wasn't that you were ashamed of your daughter then?'

'Why should I be ashamed?'

'Her ...' I hesitated tactfully. 'Estelle's appearance was a little unusual, was it not?'

'She looked like an angel.'

'You must have loved her very much.'

'Don't all fathers love their daughters?'

'Some more than others, Sir Hugh.' My gaze remained welded to the baronet's as I announced, 'I have no further questions for this witness at present, my lord, but would like to recall Fletcher Warrington.'

'Sir Hugh's lying through his back teeth,' muttered Wallbridge, as I sank down to the table to await Fletcher Warrington.

'I know, I know,' I agreed, suddenly feeling exhausted. 'But failure to register a less than perfect child, out of vanity, is hardly in the same league as murder.'

'Loved her though! How can he have the nerve to say he loved her when he kept her in a cloth-covered cage all those years? Possessed, is more the truth of it.'

'You could be right but this is not the way. Keep your voice down or you'll have us both in trouble,' I warned the apoplectic Wallbridge, as we watched a somewhat cowering Fletcher Warrington bow to Sir Hugh Parke on crossing paths with him.

'Remember you are still under oath,' Sledgemore reminded the landowner, whom for some reason he still appeared to dislike acutely. Perhaps it was the riding boots.

'Let's redeem something here,' I told Wallbridge appeasingly, springing to my feet. 'Mr Warrington, we have recalled you here today to clarify one or two points.'

'Of course, if I can assist in anyway …'

'To get to the truth, the whole truth,' I filled in obligingly.

'Well, yes.' Fletcher Warrington stared back at me blankly. He did not want to be here again. He had suffered enough humiliation the first time.

'Good, good,' I pondered. 'Now you've already told this court that you were standing on Boulby Cliffs on the twenty-first of May last, have you not?'

Fletcher Warrington nodded suspiciously, only too aware that I was anything but his friend.

'Those cliffs reach a height of six hundred and sixty feet, the highest cliffs on the entire English coastline, are they not?'

'I believe so,' mumbled Warrington still looking for the trick.

'Speak up!' cackled Sledgemore.

'Yes,' exclaimed Warrington loudly before exhaling a despondent sigh.

'And where were you standing exactly on those cliffs when you saw the accused kissing the girl now known to be Estelle Parke? Can you remember?'

'I think I was directly above the old alum works.'

'Boulby alum works? But aren't they at least a couple of miles away from the flat rocks at Staithes?'

'I had my telescope.'

'Ah, your telescope. It was one like this, wasn't it?' I unwrapped Jackson's brown paper parcel and the usher presented Warrington with the exact replica of his own optical instrument. 'Same magnification, same specifications, the same?' I asked.

Warrington examined the telescope carefully before agreeing 'yes'.

'Well, Mr Warrington, I have had a younger man than you, a man with excellent eyesight, standing at the highest point on those cliffs with that instrument, and he could barely pick out a fisherman's figure standing on the Staithes rocks let alone the detail of a man kissing a girl.'

'I might have been a little further down the cliffs closer to the village.'

'But wouldn't the Cowbar have then obscured your view of the spot where Daniel Robertshaw and Estelle Parke were said to be?'

'I hope your collaborator in Staithes is going to appear before the court to validate this new geographical evidence, Mr Cairn?' intervened Sledgemore testily.

'Yes, my lord, he is one of the fishermen who, along with Mr Warrington, rescued the prisoner from the rocks.'

'I see you have it all in hand,' acknowledged Sledgemore, his eyes peering wickedly over his spectacles.

'Mr Warrington,' I continued. 'I further suggest to you that you didn't see the accused flapping his arms from the cliffs but when you later waded out to him?'

'No, I …' Warrington became flustered.

'And that at no time did you see the accused kissing Estelle Parke?'

'I did.'

'You can't have done. Not with the limited magnification of a telescope like that one. I further suggest to you that you invented these details merely to enhance your own reputation in Staithes, and that you have wasted this court's time?'

'My lord, that's not true,' appealed Warrington to deaf ears.

After indicating his wish for the telescope to be deposited on his bench, Sledgemore appeared to be more interested in the weight of the instrument than Warrington's denial.

I retired, Henge shook his head, his shoulders hunched in grim acceptance of the dismantling of yet another star witness.

'Look at Henge,' crowed Wallbridge.

'Beware the wounded tiger,' I cautioned.

Another titter rang through the court, not over my startling cliff revelation but because Mr Justice Sledgemore had begun to survey the court through the telescope like an aged Captain Ahab.

'Captain Cook!' shouted Daniel in sudden delight from the dock, flinging out his hands in recognition until restrained by a warder.

'Silly old fool,' grumbled Henge to himself, scrabbling to his feet. (Brougham was fairly confident his principal meant the judge rather than Warrington.) 'I would like to call my next witness, Francis Edward Marlett, my lord.'

'Call Francis Edward Marlett,' cried the clerk. 'Francis Edward Marlett, Francis Edward Marlett,' reverberated through the courtroom and down the corridor. Francis Edward Marlett was slow in coming; a slow powerful countryman in gaiters crossing the floor; his gaiters worn in a defiant statement of who and what he was.

'Mr Marlett, you are a gamekeeper employed on Sir Hugh Parke's estate, are you not?' Fired, it seemed, with a successful barrister's eternal optimism, Henge was not beaten yet.

'Yes, I am.'

'Do you know the accused, Daniel Robertshaw?'

'I do.'

'Will you be good enough to point him out to us?'

'Over there.'

'How long have you known the accused?'

'All of my life, his as well.' Marlett spoke as he walked: slow, deliberate, obdurate.

'Have you ever seen the accused in the grounds of Brigham Hall?'

Marlett's hand pushed back his already slicked back dark hair. He pondered the question carefully before replying, 'Once or twice last year.'

'Didn't you tell him he shouldn't be there, that he was trespassing?'

'Ay, course I did. It was my job to tell him.'

'And what was his reply?'

'Said as how I couldn't stop him as he was meeting someone from the Hall.'

'Did he tell you who that person was?'

'Her, Estelle.'

'And where had he actually arranged to meet her?'

'In the cave.'

'What cave?'

''Tis really an old unused ice-house known as the cave.'

'Did he tell you any more about those meetings?'

'No, but Carl Thompson, who also works at the Hall, showed me a clump of Estelle's hair lying on t' floor of the cave. So, they must have been there, mustn't they?'

'A clump you say?'

'Yes.'

'By that you mean a considerable amount?'

'Ay, he must have dragged it from her head in a handful.'

'I draw the jury's attention to Exhibit Seven.' Henge tendered to the court Estelle Parke's hair still in its pathetic tissue wrapper.

'Bloody cheek!' said Wallbridge. 'That's our exhibit, isn't it?'

'Are you telling this court, Mr Marlett, that you believe the accused yanked out a considerable amount of Miss Parke's hair in a fit of rage or as part of some appalling frenzied sexual attack upon her?'

'Yes, he was always complaining about the Parkes. How much money they had whereas he and his mam had nothing, his father being a drowned sea captain and all. How Estelle wore such pretty silk dresses when his own mam had to go about in rags, that sort of thing.'

'Did other people overhear him expressing such sentiments?'

'He was forever spouting off to anyone with an ear and the time to listen.'

The atmosphere in the stunned room had become thick and airless. Nobody dared draw breath.

'My lord,' I appealed – too late, the damage had been done – the terrible picture already painted in the jurors' minds, the lustful satyr and an innocent young maiden.

'Mr Henge, please try to keep your form of questioning away from hearsay and closer to the relevant facts of this case,' reprimanded Sledgemore lamely.

'But, my lord, surely the fact that the prisoner was both jealous of Miss Parke and hostile to her family is relevant to this case,' retaliated Henge fiercely.

'Mr Henge, you know perfectly well what I mean.'

'And Exhibit Seven is actual physical evidence of the violence the prisoner must have used against Miss Parke.'

'Has this hair actually been established as belonging to Estelle Parke?' Sledgemore asked Henge.

'No, my lord, not as yet in this court though I believe my learned friend for the defence has medical witnesses that are about to do so.'

'Is that so?' Sledgemore turned to me. I gave a perfunctory and furious nod of the head.

'Then I have no more questions for this witness, and that, my lord, is the case for the prosecution.' Henge's timing was perfection.

I stared open-mouthed at my client, stared up to the public benches to see what effect Marlett's evidence was having there. At first I saw no one but young Elizabeth Mott in her Quaker bonnet, before seeing the older woman weeping silently next to her – Flora Robertshaw – so Flora Robertshaw had again defied her brother-in-law. But alas, she had made the long journey a second time only to hear this damning piece of evidence given against her son. I looked away as Elizabeth wrapped a comforting arm round Flora's shoulder. I dared not look at the impact Marlett's evidence was having on the twelve men and true. Sensing a flutter at my own table, I saw Wallbridge and Scott frantically flicking through their notes.

'Did you know about this?' Wallbridge asked Wilson Scott. 'Did you know Daniel had been to Brigham Hall?'

'No, did you?' retorted the solicitor aghast.

'This is a disaster,' I muttered.

Cuthbert Henge smiled across at us and winked.

'It's just a bloody game to him,' swore Wallbridge.

'Perhaps it is the best way to treat it,' I said, bitterly recalling Gerald Fawcett's advice.

A terrible silence fell across the courtroom, a silence that was deafening apart from a delicate scratching sound from the dock as Daniel's fingernails fidgeted after a piece of fluff on top of the railing. Not once had he glanced up at the man accusing him.

Hopeless, I acknowledged quietly to myself, a lost cause. Daniel is impervious to the happenings around him, cocooned in his own private world like a …

Chapter Thirty-Six

A small grub of an idea had buried itself into my mind and for better or for worse I was the host for its emergence. I did not sleep well that night.

Early the next morning, before the trial resumed, I was lying-in-wait for Daniel in the cell below the dock as the warders escorted him in from the Castle across the way.

'Do you know what silk is?' I asked, before my client had crossed the threshold.

'Silk?' repeated Daniel, shaking his head, wondering if this was another test he had to pass. He was getting really tired of all this. He was beginning to wish people would just leave him alone back in his cell, in peace.

'Worms make silk.'

'Do they?' Daniel looked a little more interested.

'Well, moth caterpillars to be precise. And to your knowledge you've never seen a garment made of silk?'

Daniel shook his head again. He could see I was angry but he was not sure why.

'What was Estelle wearing when you were with her on the rocks?'

Estelle, they kept saying the word "Estelle" in court. Daniel stared at me blankly.

'What was the mermaid wearing on the rocks?' I elucidated. To my shame, Daniel's simple-mindedness was beginning to pall.

'Pretty dress,' grinned Daniel, happy to be helpful at last.

'Made of ...?' I waited. Daniel's grin faded. My anger began to abate. 'Daniel, have you ever been to Brigham Hall at any time?'

'Brig ... am,' Daniel struggled with the word.

'Yes, Brigham Hall, the Hall?' I asked crossly.

'Ah, the Hall.' Recognition slowly registered across Daniel's face.

'Yes, the people living there are Quaker like you. Have you ever been there?'

'No,' replied Daniel solemnly.

'Do you know a man called Marlett, the man who was in court yesterday?'

'Yes,' admitted Daniel, lips pouting, head sinking to chest.

'Do you like Marlett?' I asked suddenly curious. Daniel shook his head. 'Why don't you like him?'

'Bad man,' said Daniel.

'All men are bad to hear you speak.'

'Yes,' said Daniel.

'Why is Marlett, in particular, a bad man?'

'He threw stones at the knight.'

'Talk sense, for goodness sake!' My sense of hopelessness and agitation returned. 'Anyone can throw stones into the night.'

'No, no, they said he was a gypsy but I knew he was a knight.'

'Not night that comes after day, you mean a warrior knight?'

'Yes, yes.' Daniel rubbed his hands together in glee, thinking I had just made a splendid joke.

'And Marlett threw stones at him?'

'Yes, yes. Ping off his armour.' There was no stopping Daniel's excitement now, eyes twinkled with animation. 'Pots and pans,' he shouted.

'That's enough,' growled one of the warders.

I drew back, studying my client's face, his eyes.

'Is that why you refused to look at Marlett yesterday?' I asked, comprehension suddenly flooding in. 'Marlett who would have us believe that you described Estelle as wearing pretty silk dresses while you're own mother went about in rags.'

'Yes, bad man,' stressed Daniel.

But it's only your word against his, I acknowledged disconsolately to myself.

* * * * *

'Are you proposing that Daniel answers these accusations?' was the first question Wallbridge asked me back in court.

'You can't even be contemplating it, not after Francis Marlett's damning evidence.' Wilson Scott was staring at me in disbelief.

'As a defendant, Sledgemore will not allow Daniel to give evidence under oath anyway. So, for the time being I intend to let others speak for him,' I announced with an air of calculation.

'I hope they do and you're right,' said Wallbridge doubtfully.

'So do I,' I said.

'All rise.' Across from me a glowing Cuthbert Henge rose. I could see the man loved the dressing up, the pomp of all this. He sniffed the air scenting victory, victory made him youthful, was what he loved best of all. The rest of the court got to its feet with less enthusiasm following the night's adjournment as Sledgemore made his own shambling arthritic return.

'Members of the jury, you must be satisfied that the prosecution has proved that Daniel Robertshaw killed Estelle Parke there on the rocks, known as Scar Shootings, within view of his entire community.' I began my opening statement with the considered zeal of a man seeking only the truth. 'You must be sure beyond any reasonable doubt that she was alive when the prisoner found her, and that he despatched her there and then by strangulation. Although the infamous crime of rape has been mentioned several times by my learned colleagues acting for the Crown, I must remind you that rape is not included in the indictment made against Daniel Robertshaw, as there has never been any physical or forensic evidence found to support such a crime ever having taken place. Nonetheless, it has been mentioned as a possible motive, and I intend to provide you with proof that will negate the possibility of the prisoner's involvement with such a foul violation, let alone the heinous crime of murder. My learned friend himself, in his opening statement, pointed out that Estelle Parke would have been more than a match for Daniel Robertshaw "upstairs". I ask you to consider then, would such a bright young woman have put up with an abusive relationship with the prisoner for any length of time?'

No response from the sea of faces staring exclusively my way – a terrible feeling.

'My lord, members of the jury, with the assistance of my learned friend, Mr Wallbridge, permit me to call the evidence for the defence before you.'

'Bugger's conveniently overlooked the victim's pregnancy as an additional motive,' Henge muttered to Brougham.

I coolly sat down as my friend, Richard Tate, made his usual enthusiastic bouncing progress across the floor to give evidence.

'Dr Tate, you have an MA honours degree from Cambridge, are a Fellow of the Royal College of Physicians, and work as a pathologist in The General Infirmary at Leeds?' Wallbridge's smile sought clarification.

'That is correct.'

'And on the twelfth of August, 1897, were you called to perform a post-mortem examination on an exhumed body in Whitby cemetery?'

'I was, and I was accompanied by a colleague, Mr Thomas Scattergood.'

'Can you tell the court your findings?'

Dick opened out a wad of papers. 'The body was that of a young woman, whom I estimated to be between fourteen and seventeen years of age. The body was in a surprisingly good state of preservation as I understood she had first been interred almost three months earlier.'

'I refer the jury to Exhibit Twenty-three.' Wallbridge nodded to the court usher and the jury was presented with a body length photograph of Estelle's remains taken by Dick before he performed the post-mortem.

Pink faces soon drained of colour. Most members of the jury did not dwell on the photograph for long before quickly passing it down the line.

'Can you tell the court why the body was in such a good state of preservation?' asked Sledgemore.

'Yes, my lord, I believe the police had refrigerated this young woman's corpse for some weeks before burial. The body would then retain that frozen state for a few days under the ground. Also, the soil in Whitby cemetery is well-drained and is made up of finely bedded grey shales topped with a lighter sandstone, here is a composite of certain salts and minerals that would further assist in the preservation process.'

'Thank you.' Sledgemore was beaming for the first time in a long time: a succinct professional witness at last.

'Exhibits Twenty-eight and Twenty-nine.' Wallbridge wafted two of Wilfred Thornton's photographs of Estelle's body prior to burial towards Dick and the jury. The room was hushed. The photographs next swished and crackled in the court usher's hand as he carried them across to the witness box. 'Dr Tate, have you had an opportunity to examine these two photographs taken shortly after Miss Parke was found?'

'I have.'

'And from them have you been able to form any conclusion as to how long she was immersed in the sea before being pulled out?' asked Wallbridge.

'Many hours.'

'How many? More than the twenty-four hours from her being reportedly seen on the rocks with the accused and her retrieval from the sea by boat?'

'Nearer two to three days, I'd say.'

'Two to three days?'

'Yes. Possibly longer, possibly four days. The cooler the water the better the state of preservation.'

'Let us get this perfectly clear, Doctor, are you saying it is your considered opinion that Miss Parke must have been dead long before the accused came across her on the rocks?'

'Yes,' confirmed Dick.

The constrained court bubble hissed again.

'Did you discover anything particularly unusual about this young woman's body?' resumed Wallbridge after a suitable pause.

'I did. She was about eight weeks pregnant.'

More affronted gasps. Henge half rose to remind the court that Estelle's fecund state had already been well-established by the prosecution, but was summarily waved down by Sledgemore.

'Two months with child – will the members of the jury please note that important fact? Anything else, Dr Tate?' asked Wallbridge.

'Her eyes were missing.'

'Due to the fish and crustacean damage as already described to us by Dr Allanby, who conducted the initial examination of the body?'

'No, I don't believe so,' replied Dick with an air of humble dignity. (I could not help a flicker of amusement passing across my face at my old Cambridge chum's newly acquired mien.)

'So what do you believe happened, Dr Tate?'

'I believe the deceased's eyes were deliberately removed by someone who had expertise in dissection.'

'Like a surgeon perhaps?'

'No, I would say the perpetrator lacked a surgeon's delicate skill.'

'More like a butcher then?'

'Yes, someone like that. The muscles of the eyeball, the Recti superior, inferior, medialis, lateralis had been deftly cut. The Obliqui superior and inferior likewise. The Bulbus Oculi itself had by then probably been punctured and collapsed.'

'The Bulbus Oculi being the eyeball, I take it?'

'Yes, who ever did this had enough knowledge to scoop round the eyeball in order to prize it out and sever the tethering optic nerve behind.'

'And what was the incision like across the optic nerve, is it a difficult thing to cut through?'

'No, not particularly, in this case the nerve had been severed obliquely. I think the perpetrator had made two attempts at it in the right eye, the incision marks weren't quite aligned leaving the nerve with a somewhat ragged appearance.' Dick chopped his hand twice across the air at an angle.

'Thank you, Doctor, a chilling demonstration. So the right eye was possibly the first eye to be attacked, a trial run as it were?'

'Yes, I'd say so.'

'Do you think you can tell us what sort of knife would have been used to perform this gruesome task?'

'Maybe something like a hunting knife with a curved end.'

'A hunter's knife?'

'Yes, possibly.'

'Do you think the accused would possess the dexterity to perform such a dissection?'

Dick stared ironically across at Daniel who appeared to be chopping with his hand in imitation. 'I doubt it very much.'

'Do you think the person performing this vicious act would have got blood on their clothing?'

'Yes, that is highly likely.'

'And at the place of such barbaric butchery?'

'I'd expect to find a small amount of blood there too. The dead can still bleed.'

'My lord,' appealed Henge. 'By the time the fishermen had waded out to the prisoner, the rocks would have been washed clean by the sea of any traces of blood, if that is the place my friend is referring to.'

'But the sea wouldn't have washed all traces of blood from the prisoner's clothing,' retorted Wallbridge. 'And I don't recall one prosecution witness mentioning any sign of blood on Daniel Robertshaw or his clothes.'

'Nonetheless, I must uphold counsel for the prosecution's objection regarding the obliteration of blood on the rocks,' said Sledgemore.

'Tell me, Dr Tate, why, in your professional opinion, would anybody remove another person's eyes?' asked Wallbridge.

'Some murderers imagine their victims are staring at them, but in this case it was more probably an attempt to hide Miss Parke's identity.'

I looked towards the public benches wondering what effect Dick's forensic evidence would be having on Clarissa Parke. Thankfully, for some reason she did not appear to be in court that morning.

'Exhibit Seven,' Wallbridge nodded across to the usher. 'Do you recognise this hair sample, which I believe was found in the ice-house at Brigham Hall?' he asked Dick.

'I do.'

'Would you say it is Estelle Parke's hair?'

'Most definitely. We matched it perfectly at post-mortem with the hair of the deceased.'

'And its bleached appearance is in keeping with a young person suffering from Miss Parke's rare condition?'

'Yes. I believe the hair's fine texture and lack of colour is consistent with albinism.'

Confusion on the floor of the court, confusion in the press gallery, the jurors looked one to another askance. Albinism – no one had mentioned this before, not even the victim's father.

'Order,' shouted Sledgemore. 'Order and we might get some clarification.'

'Dr Tate, would you be so good as to acquaint the court with the condition of albinism?' asked Wallbridge.

'Yes, it is a disorder that affects the pigmentation in skin, hair and eyes because of an inherent inability to produce melanin,' explained Dick. 'If a Negro child has the disorder, for example, it can appear to be white.'

'And a white child whiter?'

'Exactly.'

'And do you think this white hair of Estelle Parke's was *yanked* from her head during some kind of frenzied sexual attack as earlier theorised at by my learned friend for the prosecution?'

'No, the end of the hair shafts are too clean. They appear to have been cut straight across by a pair of scissors.'

'Someone might have kept the hair as a love-token then?'

'Yes, Exhibit Seven has a lot of fluff on it as if it could have been kept in a bedroom drawer for example.'

'Not the sort of fluff you'd find in a ice-house then?'

'Certainly not,' confirmed Dick.

'Perhaps there was someone at the Hall, who really believed Miss Parke to be an angel,' offered Wallbridge satirically as he took his seat.

'Might I venture just a little further into the evidence you have given that disputes Dr Allanby's, a respected medical practitioner and the first man on the scene?' asked Henge bitingly.

'Please go ahead,' nodded Dick, satisfied, in control.

'Are you absolutely sure, Doctor, that a dead body floating about in the sea wouldn't have been immediately attacked by fish? That nibbling fish or crustaceans couldn't have excised Estelle Parke's eyes in the same dreadful manner you have just described?'

'Yes, I am sure, on the whole the cuts were too neat and uniform. Although I do admit that we did find a suggestion of sea life damage in her right and more particularly her left orbital cavity.'

'Nonetheless, you can conclusively differentiate between knife cuts and the nibbles of prawns?' snorted Henge.

'Yes, I can,' replied Dick confidently.

'Then you are in agreement with Dr Allanby that this poor young woman was murdered before she found her way into the sea?'

'Yes, if she had died from drowning I would have expected to see some evidence of ballooning of the lungs, possibly water in her stomach, we found none.'

'Well, it is good that you medical men can agree on something,' grunted Henge. 'Tell me, Doctor, would poor Miss Parke have been dead when her eyeballs were plucked from her head?'

'I sincerely hope so,' replied Dick frowning.

'Must have been the act of a madman, wouldn't you say?' Henge turned from Dick to stare directly across at Daniel.

'Or, alternatively, someone who is very shrewd.' Dick Tate held his ground, Wallbridge stayed put.

'But you are not qualified to make such a supposition, are you, Doctor?'

'Then, sir, you shouldn't have asked me the question.'

'I'll ask you whatever questions I choose,' retorted Henge reddening. 'That's what you are here for, to answer my questions.'

'So what *is* your question for this witness, Mr Henge?' intervened Sledgemore, like a weary referee who appeared to have missed the low punch but actually had not.

'Dr Tate, would you really have us believe that some highly dangerous person, other than the prisoner over there, is still at large butchering young women with a hunting knife?'

'Yes, it is possible that the person who mutilated Estelle Park is still at large,' replied Dick, quietly, deadly, to the deadly hushed court.

'Who then?' appealed Henge dramatically to all and sundry with open arms. 'Please tells us who he is because as far as I know no other young female has come to grief since Robertshaw has been in prison?'

'As you say, there have been no reports of any similar crimes against women being committed in our region recently,' Dick hesitated thoughtfully. 'But then, Mr Scattergood and I have never come across a case like this one in our combined careers. The pattern of this crime is unique, the forensic evidence multifaceted. The perpetrator, in all probability, has never killed before and might never kill again. That makes him a very difficult man to catch.

'Or do you think he could merely be a figment of your imagination, Doctor?' scoffed Henge. Without giving Dick the benefit of a reply, he announced, 'I have no further questions for this witness.'

Clickety-click – tall Maud Fines in her high-laced boots and widow's weeds was next to enter the arena. Despite her mourning clothes, Mrs Fines was fuller of face, her whole demeanour less drained by loss than when I had last seen her.

'You were employed until recently in the kitchen of Brigham Hall by Sir Hugh and Lady Clarissa Parke, were you not?' Wallbridge attempted to make himself appear accessible, less menacing, to this tragic woman who had already been through so much.

'Yes, I was,' she replied without a waver. Wallbridge needn't have bothered with his soft approach, rigid and toughened by an environment that was beyond most people's imagination, Maud was not about to be fazed by this mild ordeal.

'Tell us what it was like working at the Hall.'

'Eerie, I'd say.'

'What do you mean "eerie"?'

'There was an air of secrecy about the place.'

'Really, my lord, is all this irrational concentration on Brigham Hall absolutely necessary?' asked Henge, still smarting from his confrontation with Dick.

'We, the defence, feel that Brigham Hall is of vital interest to our case and this trial, my lord. It is the place of Estelle Parke's birth and possibly the scene of her murder,' argued Wallbridge.

'A preposterous claim,' barked Henge.

'Nevertheless, go ahead, Mr Wallbridge. I'm interested to see where this is going myself,' instructed Sledgemore.

'And this strange atmosphere permeated as far down as the kitchen itself?'

'Yes.'

'Did you know the Parkes' daughter, Estelle, well?'

'I didn't know her at all. As far as I knew her ladyship's only child had died at birth some sixteen years before.'

'And you'd been part of the household for how long, Mrs Fines?'

'A good twenty years, sir.'

'Twenty years,' Wallbridge exuded surprise. 'Surely you knew Estelle Parke's nanny and companion, Susannah Mott, though?'

'Hardly ever set eyes on her. Didn't recognise her until someone pointed her out to me in the corridor just now.'

'How could that be?'

'The lady, who I now know to be Susannah Mott, kept herself to herself.

Oh, rumours abounded at the Hall about her right enough, rumours of sightings and noises coming from the attic rooms in the east wing late at night. But you see, sir, the east wing had its own entrance and was out of bounds to all other servants.'

'Are you asking this court to really believe that Miss Mott and Miss Parke lived entirely separate lives in that east wing from the rest of Brigham Hall?'

'Yes, sir, I am. Nobody knew about Miss Parke at all during my time at the Hall.'

'But Sir Hugh, himself, told us his daughter took the air in the Hall grounds?'

'Then those excursions must have been late at night, and very few in number, and well away from the house.'

'What do you mean?'

'The only inkling I ever got of the existence of another person, other than Miss Mott herself of course, was Marlett's ghost.'

'Marlett's ghost?'

'Ay, Francis Marlett flew into the kitchen, late one evening, saying he'd seen a ghost.'

'Though Mr Marlett has already appeared before this court as a witness, would you be kind enough to refresh us all on his position at the Hall?' interrupted Sledgemore.

'He is the gamekeeper, your honour,' replied Mrs Fines, arms clasped beneath her ample bosom.

'And when did he report seeing this ghost?' resumed Wallbridge.

'A year or two back. She was arm in arm with the master. The master threatened Marlett with instant dismissal if he ever walked that way again, or breathed a word of what he had seen to anyone.'

'So why did he tell the entire kitchen?'

'He didn't, he was telling Cook mainly. He and she were very close, working regularly together as they did over the game he caught. I've never seen Marlett in such a dither as he was that night. Marlett and Carl Thompson, the odd-jobman, maintain to this day that some sorcery was afoot.'

'*Sorcery*, really my lord,' exclaimed Henge.

'And why, my dear, did these two men think sorcery was involved?' asked Sledgemore, kindly if indulgently.

'Because the woman with Sir Hugh looked ghostly. Marlett said her face was as white as snow and her eyes showed up pink and wandering in his lantern light.'

Pink eyes again – Sledgemore shied back.

'You just mentioned a Carl Thompson, what had he to do with this?' put in Wallbridge quickly.

'Only what Marlett had told him, I believe.'

'Thank you, Mrs Fines.' Wallbridge smiled gratefully.

Henge in contrast was scowling when he got to his feet. 'Mrs Fines, you are a widow, are you not?'

'Yes, sir, I lost my man and two sons at sea some seven months ago.'

'Perhaps due to your state of bereavement and living alone you could have imagined much of this testimony?'

'I do not live alone, sir. I live with my remaining lad.'

'A good deal of what you have told this court today is merely servants' tittle-tattle, is it not? Hearsay?' Henge gave his lordship an accusatory glare.

'I have only told what was impressed upon me as the truth.'

'But you are no longer dependent on Lady Clarissa and Sir Hugh Parke for your livelihood, are you?'

'No, sir, I help my lad and a cousin with the fish.'

'Thought so,' muttered Henge cheaply, skulking down into his seat.

Chapter Thirty-Seven

A minute or two before the afternoon session got under way, I had a word with Susannah Mott outside the courtroom door. Susannah was due to take the oath next. I could see she was very apprehensive and I welcomed the chance to try and steady her nerves.

'It is good to see your Elizabeth supporting Mrs Robertshaw in court through this terrible ordeal. Elizabeth is a wonderful girl for her age, so mature.'

'Dost thou have children?' Susannah asked me.

'No, no, I'm not married,' I replied smiling.

'Thou dost not have to be, remember?' retorted Susannah, the hint of a sad reciprocal smile playing on her lips. 'True enough no mother could wish for a better daughter than Elizabeth, though her incessant questions tries my patience cruelly at times.'

'Questions? Questions about what?'

'She's begun to press me as to who her father is, and why we never wed. For some reason she has suddenly grown curious on the subject.'

'So why not tell her?'

'Because I want my lass to know of only the righteous road. I do not want her to take a wrong turning too. How dost thou warn a sixteen year old girl against overriding passion, Mr Cairn?'

'Is that what it was, overriding passion?' I asked intrigued.

'I wasn't a woman to lose my chastity over nothing, Mr Cairn. But how can I explain that to her?'

'Well ...' I stopped, aware that I was not the most experienced person to give advice on this subject. 'Would you be against her meeting her father if it ever became possible?' I asked instead.

'If she persists, and it is her dearest wish, not at all. He was a good man. He was ...' she swallowed deeply. 'He was the most handsome man I'd ever seen.'

'If I can help in any way,' I offered, doing my best to control an inexplicable pang of jealousy for this "most handsome man".

'Thou will forgive me for saying so, sir, but life has taught me that on such matters the best help comes from within,' announced Susannah with a startling mix of worldly and spiritual conviction.

'But friends surely …?' I enquired, aware through the open door that the court beyond was rapidly filling up.

'Not even those Friends,' she said, shaking her head.

* * * * *

'I swear that …' began Susannah who had never sworn in her life. Her already high colour was now poppy red. Her fantastic corn-in-sunset curls modestly tucked out of view under her bonnet.

I stared at her long and hard across the court as if seeing her for the first time. In an instant, I realised I could not even conjure up the face of Rosie Good anymore. It was no longer thoughts of Rosie Good that inspired me to make my name, produce a brilliant defence in a seemingly impossible case, no, it was more the woman now standing before me. These feelings for Susannah Mott had come on me by stealth, taken me off guard, and suddenly I found I was in the lion's mouth. This would not do. I struggled to collect myself and re-establish a semblance of professionalism.

'Miss Mott, you were once nanny and companion to Estelle Parke, is that correct?' I asked in a different voice, different from my empathetic corridor voice, this voice was firm and formal.

'Yes,' whispered Susannah.

'Could the witness please speak up, my lord?' Post-luncheon Henge appeared to be more bullish than ever.

'Yes,' repeated Susannah more forcefully.

'How many years did you work at Brigham Hall in total?' I asked, disconcertingly formal again.

'Must have been for a good fifteen years, sir.'

'Did you find your working conditions at the Hall abnormal?'

'Abnormal, sir?'

'You and your young charge, the daughter of the house, were kept in isolation, were you not?'

'For myself it suited but in respect of Estelle I often felt it was unkind.'

'Why did you stay in this unkind situation then?'

'Because without me, Estelle would have had no one.'

'So, under what circumstances did you eventually leave?'

'I was asked to leave by Sir Hugh.'

'What reason did Sir Hugh give?'

'He said they had sent Estelle away for treatment.'

'What sort of treatment?'

'He didn't specify but Estelle had many medical complaints.'

'And was Estelle's relationship with her father a good one, would you say?'

Susannah stalled, appeared uncertain, before asking rather than replying, 'How dost thou mean exactly, sir?'

'Well, was the affection between father and daughter warm, would you say?'

Once more Susannah hesitated, carefully weighing up the question as if fearing to say the wrong thing. 'Sometimes Sir Hugh seemed cold and indifferent towards Estelle, at other times he appeared to be almost ardent.'

'A-r-dent,' I repeated, stressing each syllable. 'Like a suitor, would you say?'

'Objection!' screamed Henge. 'My learned friend is trying to draw out of this witness a most scurrilous insinuation, without a shred of factual proof, against an upstanding member of society and a grieving parent to boot.'

'Mr Cairn, I must uphold counsel's objection, please refrain from leading the witness,' reprimanded Sledgemore with some severity.

'Miss Mott, did you know that Estelle Parke was pregnant?' I continued, unconcerned, aware that whatever Henge or Sledgemore said I had already planted the seed.

'I began to suspect she was.'

'Why did you suspect she was?'

'Estelle complained that she did not bleed any more and her breasts appeared to be swollen.' Susannah flushed right down to her concealed hair-roots at having to inform a mixed court of such intimate details, eventually adding more calmly, 'And she started to be regularly sick on rising.'

'Did you confront her with this possibility?'

'I did. I told her if I hadn't known any better I'd have said she was having a baby.'

'How did Miss Parke react?'

'Nothing, she said nothing. Thou has to understand Estelle was so innocent. The poor child didn't deserve any of this.' Susannah eyes welled with tears.

'So, in reality, you thought Miss Parke's departure from Brigham Hall might have had something to do with a possible pregnancy?'

'Yes, sir, though I had no proof.'

'Thank you, Miss Mott.' I flipped down into my seat.

'You have little real proof of anything, do you?' snarled Henge, prowling this way and that behind his table. 'Little proof and plenty of innuendoes. What is more you have cynically led this court to believe that Sir Hugh Parke, a loving father, treated his daughter with total inconsistency, isn't that so?'

'No, I …'

'Further more, you have conjectured in open court that Sir Hugh's affection for his daughter was verging on the unnatural, isn't that so?' asked Henge, giving Susannah no time to respond to his previous question.

'Well, yes, I …'

'These allegations of yours are all pique, are they not? Pique at being dismissed from a lucrative employment.'

'No, that's not so,' Susannah managed to retaliate.

'Don't you think you are showing an abysmal lack of loyalty to a man who housed and fed you for fifteen years?'

'Objection, my lord.' I was on my feet again. 'What sort of loyalty did Sir Hugh Parke display to the witness by dismissing her, without notice, after all those years of faithful service in the most trying and abnormal circumstances?'

'I think both counsels have made their point. Pray proceed, Mr Henge, with a little more caution and a little less intimidation.'

'Miss Mott,' wailed Henge, shrugging off Sledgemore's ruling as if it was no more than the buzz of an annoying fly. 'Wasn't the real reason for your dismissal from Brigham Hall your repeated failure to secure the doors in the east wing, which eventually and disastrously resulted in Miss Parke's fatal meetings with the prisoner?'

'If that was the case, I was never reprimanded for it, not once,' replied Susannah in astonishment.

'No more questions,' retorted Henge, crumpling back into his seat and throwing an expression of sarcasm towards Susannah Mott whom he had finally reduced to flowing tears.

'The keys were ultimately my responsibility but I was never commissioned to be Estelle's keeper. I am telling the truth,' sobbed Susannah, turning to the judge for support.

'I know, my dear, you can step down now,' said Sledgemore, relieved himself that Henge's grilling of this attractive young woman was over.

I noticed one or two men on the jury shuffling nervously from one buttock to the other, made uncomfortable by the QC's overt bullying tactics. Although my heart went out to Susannah and her distress, I forced myself to look at her performance with the objectivity of a barrister. Nothing was lost: Henge's onslaught on Susannah had merely won her the sympathy of most of the court and, perhaps, Sledgemore's too, although it was difficult to tell with Sledgemore.

Grace Mallaby was next to walk across that "mile" of intimidating space to the witness box. Striding Grace Mallaby, heavily pregnant with her second child though she carried it well, like Maud Fines showed not the least sign of being about to be intimidated by anything or anyone. She wore the stout boots and pea jacket of a Staithes flither picker. Her face was long and hard, a sour-milk face.

Henge will never reduce this one to tears, I noted with satisfaction. I stared across at Daniel to see the effect on him of Mallaby's entrance. It was catastrophic – forget his surprising indifference to Kemp, forget Marlett and all the others – Daniel watched every twitch of muscle in Grace Mallaby's formidable frame, his face transfixed with fear.

'They say people with Daniel's disability don't have feelings, don't remember things,' said Wallbridge as Mallaby was being sworn in. 'But just look at him now.'

'I know, I know,' I sighed. 'It can't be helped. I had no other option than to call her. As I explained to Flora Robertshaw, this woman might be the one witness who can spring Daniel from this appalling situation once and for all.'

'We are ready, Mr Cairn,' prompted Sledgemore, as I stood lingering over my notes.

'You are recently married, are you not?' I lifted my head towards Mallaby.

'That I am.'

'To the father of your two children?'

'Ay, Mallaby made me an honest woman last year.' Grace Mallaby smacked her lips over what was obviously for her a rewarding fait accompli.

'Your maiden name was Grace Carter, was it not? And you are the sister of Jed Carter who is in prison for his part in the arson attack on the Robertshaw property?'

Mallaby nodded. ''Twas Jed that finally made up me mind to come here and tell.'

'But you are here entirely of your own volition?'

'Ay, in all conscience I had to come.'

'You are one of the few practising Catholics in Staithes, are you not?'

'I am that, and proud to be so.'

'Although you might find the task of telling the truth to his lordship and members of the jury a daunting and embarrassing experience, you are a woman who, I understand, has reaffirmed her faith and is now well used to the confessional box?'

'Indeed I am.' More smacking of righteous lips.

'Then you are aware that you are under oath and will treat this court accordingly?'

'I will.'

'And Cairn like a bloody priest,' side-mouthed Henge to Brougham.

'Is it true, Mrs Mallaby, that a few years ago you and two of your sisters decided to have a little fun with the accused on the beach at Staithes?' I pressed on, regarding Henge's remark as beneath contempt.

'Ay, to our everlasting shame.'

'And as a result of that "fun", for a long time afterwards, your brother, Jed Carter, believed Daniel Robertshaw to be the father of your first child?'

'He did, and I said nothing to put him right.'

'Why didn't you put your brother right?'

'Because Mallaby was t' bairn's real father, and the first Mrs Mallaby was ill but still alive.'

'So your first born was the result of an adulteress affair?'

'Ay, if you choose to put it that way.'

'And not from any sexual congress with Daniel Robertshaw on the beach?'

'No,' sniffed Mallaby scornfully. 'Though I led my brother Jed to think otherwise.'

'You preferred your brother to think Daniel Robertshaw fathered your child rather than Mr Mallaby?'

'As you just said it was adultery with Mallaby, a grave sin. Jed would have killed us both for the shame we were bringing on our two families.'

'Is that why you tried to seduce Daniel Robertshaw?'

'No, as you just said, it all started as a bit of fun at first between Dan and my sisters. Though it didn't take long to dawn on me that here could be the answer to my troubles, an easy conquest as it were.'

'Did it work out that way?'

'No, iced fish landed from Greenland have more life to 'em than he.' Mallaby pointed to Daniel cowering lower in the dock.

'But in the event, Jed did try to kill Daniel Robertshaw because of your fictitious allegation?'

'No, no, not entirely. Jed torched the Robertshaws' cottage mainly because he believed Dan had done away with that lass.'

'That lass being Estelle Parke, who was also pregnant. Do you think the accused was capable of fathering her child, any child?' I pointed across to Daniel. Daniel, who was now propped up between the two warders, watched on, flushed and in tears from a remembered and all too vivid humiliation.

'Him, over there, wouldn't know how to thread his cock into a lobster smout let alone get a lass into trouble.' Mallaby gave a perfunctory little chuckle at her own wit. No one else joined in. Too shocked to titter, the court fell into a heavy breathing silence – a salacious spectator peering down the naughty nude stereoscope. 'Believe me, Mister,' she continued, 'me and my sisters tried ever trick we knew.'

'You are making that more than apparently clear, my dear,' said Sledgemore giving a little censorial cough.

It was then that Daniel rebelled, attempting to lever himself forward out of the dock. He called Grace Mallaby something to the effect of "a wicked woman", or it could even have been the adjective "wanton" that he used – I did not quite catch it all. The two warders guarding Daniel pulled him back, restraining him by pressing down on his sloping shoulders.

'Be silent! If you are not then we will continue this trial without you,' Sledgemore warned him.

'Perhaps the prisoner might be permitted some water, my lord,' I suggested. 'Mrs Mallaby's evidence has been very trying for him. See, he is drip white.'

'Very well.' Surprisingly, Sledgemore obliged and requested the usher to deliver water to the man in the dock.

I rearranged my wig, and waited until I was sure Daniel was settled, before lifting my volume to maximum. 'Are you telling this court, Mrs Mallaby, that Daniel Robertshaw is impotent?'

'Never met a fella more so.'

'And I bet that one's met a few,' muttered Brougham to Henge.

'Not half,' replied the QC; his large frame slumped, his expression despondent. 'Nevertheless, this foul-mouthed bitch has ruined any sexual or parental rejection motive we might have planted in the jury's mind against Robertshaw.'

I finally asked Mallaby the question I had previously agreed with her to ask for her appearance without a writ, 'And do you feel any regret for your unprovoked attack on the prisoner?'

'I do, and me and my brother, Jed, want to publicly apologise to the poor soul for any mischief we might have caused him and his family.'

'Thank you for that at least, Mrs Mallaby.' I retired behind my table.

'Any questions, Mr Henge?' dared Sledgemore; a hint of wry amusement infusing his voice.

'No, I have no questions for this *lady*,' spluttered Henge.

Ladies, it seemed, were falling thick and fast upon the ground. But the next witness was the real thing, a titled lady, Lady Clarissa Parke summoned deliberately at the last moment by me for her impromptu interrogation. I studied her closely as she flowed into the witness box. Her black cape seemed to engulf the entire structure. She was the antithesis of Grace Mallaby.

Leaning forward over my table, closing in on that lined face, I was not looking forward to doing what I knew had to be done. The trial, at this stage, had become like the tennis game of doubles I had watched men playing on the West Cliff at Whitby while staying with Mrs Veazey. There was something I had learnt during that late summer afternoon as a tennis spectator – when the going gets tough always pick on the weakest opponent on the other side of the net – I was about to blast a ball from close range.

'Lady Clarissa, did you know that your daughter Estelle was pregnant before she disappeared?'

'Yes, it had become apparent.'

'Did you know who the father was?'

'She refused to say.'

I regarded Clarissa Parke thoughtfully for a moment. I had to admit I was taken aback by her calm assurance and the beautiful modulation of her voice. A real shock to the system after Grace Mallaby.

'Did your husband know of Estelle's condition?'

'Somehow he got word of it.'

'"Somehow he got word of it". How?' I asked.

'Well …' Clarissa gave the first indication of being slightly flustered.

'You do realise, Lady Clarissa, that your husband denied under oath knowing that your daughter was pregnant until informed by the police? Are you now telling us he perjured himself?'

'This is a very serious allegation to make, Lady Clarissa,' interrupted Sledgemore stony-faced. 'If found guilty of perjury your husband could face a very lengthy prison sentence.'

'He knew she was with child.' Clarissa's reply was suddenly emphatic, unapologetic.

I looked to the judge for direction. Sledgemore was scribbling like mad but nodded for me to continue my examination.

'How did Sir Hugh know Estelle was pregnant?'

'That I cannot tell you.'

'Can't or won't?'

'I really don't know.' Clarissa's left shoulder gave an involuntary twitch.

'But you didn't feel it was your duty to tell him yourself?'

'I was afraid to.'

'Anyway, that became irrelevant as he already knew, didn't he?'

'Yes.'

'So what did you and your husband propose to do about your daughter's unwelcome condition?'

'My husband had arranged a boat ticket for Estelle to go to France.'

'Just before she went missing?'

'Only days before she was missing.'

'Did Sir Hugh choose France so that Estelle could have the child in secret?'

'No, he knew of a doctor there.'

'A doctor to look after her?'

'No, a doctor to get rid of the child.'

'An abortionist, you mean?' This was news to me. I had not expected this, had not expected this amazingly cool piece of frankness from Clarissa. The court snorted and sniffed its puritanical disgust.

'Yes, I think that is what they are called,' said Clarissa vaguely, seemingly unperturbed by the waves she was creating around her.

'My lord, I intend to show Exhibit Seven to Lady Clarissa.'

Sledgemore nodded to the usher to retrieve Exhibit Seven.

'Lady Clarissa, do you recognise that lock of hair as belonging to your daughter?' I asked.

'Yes, yes I do,' admitted Clarissa, at the same time refusing to physically take up the offering of her dead daughter's hair.

'Have you ever seen it before?'

'Yes, my husband kept those few strands in a drawer in his dressing-room.'

'Approximately a hundred strands,' I corrected. 'So how did they finish up in the ice-house?'

'I cannot say, but Carl Thompson told me my husband regularly walked Estelle there.'

'How did you feel when he told you that?'

'Nothing.'

'Lady Clarissa, were you jealous of your husband's relationship with Estelle?'

'No, why should I have been?'

'Their closeness?'

'Nonsense.'

'Did you feel at anytime that your husband was having an incestuous relationship with your daughter?'

'Objection!' screamed Henge. 'This is outrageous.'

'Overruled,' Sledgemore informed him quietly.

'No, no.' Lady Clarissa's denial quivered on her tongue.

'Why do you think Sir Hugh was so adamant that your daughter should have an abortion then? You believed he could have been the father of Estelle's child, didn't you?' My pursuit was relentless.

'No,' denied Clarissa breathlessly. 'He said Estelle wasn't strong enough to endure a pregnancy, said he was afraid Estelle's disfiguring condition might be passed on to the child. He said the scandal would bring shame on the family name.'

'Ah, the family name,' I repeated with a long sigh.

'Yes.' Clarissa's quasi-aristocratic chin fell.

'But an abortion was very much against your own religious convictions, wasn't it?'

'Very much.' Finally shaken, Clarissa was barely audible now.

'Do you believe your husband murdered your daughter?'

'I don't know.' Clarissa's left shoulder twitched again.

'Is that why you had a servant plant Estelle's lock of hair in the ice-house to incriminate your husband?'

'Sir Hugh has always been such a bully.'

'That doesn't necessarily mean he is a murderer.'

'He was prepared to murder an unborn child.' She stared directly into my eyes, appealing for understanding.

'Your father-in-law, Lady Clarissa, had business connections with the Whitby, Redcar and Middlesbrough Union Railway Company, did he not?'

'Yes, I believe he did but that was a very long time ago,' she replied, bewildered by the change of emphasis.

'Did you ever see a shoulder strap belonging to that company in your house?'

'I can't say …'

'Similar to the one worn by the porter at Staithes railway station?' I prompted.

'I think I might have seen something of the sort somewhere, but where and who it belonged to I couldn't tell you.'

'Thank you, Lady Clarissa, for coming here today under such trying circumstances and allowing the court to hear your account of events leading up to your daughter's disappearance.' I could be gallant, too, once I had driven in the telling wedge.

Chapter Thirty-Eight

The Parkes were not the only ones to experience a miserable evening together
– Jackson received a death threat. Somehow an anonymous note had found
its way under Trotter's Fishergate door addressed to my key witness. Trotter
was pale as he handed me the threatening note, the following morning, at
Bootham Chambers. He said he felt responsible, cursed himself for failing
to catch the malicious postman.

'Never mind that now, who knew Jackson was staying with you?' My
tone was unmistakably accusatorial.

'I,' gasped Trotter. 'I told no one.'

'Who has Jackson been speaking to then?'

'That is a question for him to answer, sir.'

'And it will be asked,' I snapped.

'Have you not considered, sir, that Jackson and I could have simply been
followed from the courthouse the other day?'

'Did you notice anybody trailing you?'

'If I had, I would have said.'

'I hope so,' I replied absent-mindedly, re-examining the note.

JACKSON,

    IF YOU GIVE EVIDENCE IN THE ROBERTSHAW

    TRYAL TOMOROW. YOU ARE A DEAD MAN.

'This scrawl has hardly been penned by an educated man. But who would
know Jackson is due to appear today?' I passed the note back to Trotter.

'Your bet is as good as mine, sir,' said Trotter, staring dismally down on
the soiled cheap piece of paper. 'Perhaps someone saw you in conversation
with him. But don't you think it's best to keep an open mind as to whether

the author is educated or not? They could have deliberately written badly and thrown in the odd misspelling here and there in an attempt to hide their identity. Strange, don't you think, they can spell "Robertshaw" and "evidence" correctly but not "trial" and "tomorrow"?'

'Is Jackson shaken by this?'

'Hard to tell with him. Says he'll not let you down though. I could see he couldn't read a word of it, had to drag the page off him and read the awful thing out loud to him myself.'

'Of course, you would have had to. That is the one thing Jackson has always been good at concealing.'

'Whoever sent this note can't know Jackson is illiterate then, can they, sir?'

'There's a good chance whoever sent this note is Estelle Parke's murderer.'

* * * * *

'Mr Scattergood, you were a lecturer in forensic medicine and toxicology at Leeds School of Medicine and are the present Dean of the now amalgamated Faculty of Medicine at the Yorkshire College, are you not?' I asked before a packed morning session.

'Yes.'

'You are also the author of various medico-legal books?'

'I am.'

'Throughout the country you are regarded as an expert in your field, an eminent man?'

'I hope I enjoy the respect of a few of my colleagues,' replied Scattergood, his tall frame stooped with age and academia.

'I know that is very much the case, Mr Scattergood.' My gratitude was heartfelt for this distinguished old man who had put himself out to appear in court in person. 'Now, sir, would you be kind enough to examine Exhibit Twenty-five, another plate taken by the photographer, Mr Wilfred Thornton, concentrating on Miss Parke's face and neck? Perhaps you might explain the marks shown there to his lordship and members of the jury?'

'I must admit this is one of the most intriguing cases I have ever been involved in. There is the suggestion of petechiae there and there.' Thomas

Scattergood held up Thornton's twenty by twenty-four inch enlargement to the court. 'Although at post-mortem they had faded too much to be physically visible.'

'Petechiae?' asked Sledgemore.

'Yes, my lord, tiny petechial haemorrhages caused by the rupture of small blood vessels commonly associated with asphyxia.' Scattergood turned the photograph towards the judge and pointed to Estelle Parke's left eyebrow and cheek.

'You mean those little spots there?' squinted Sledgemore.

'Yes, petechiae, my lord, first described by a French police surgeon, Tardieu, and otherwise known as Tardieu spots.'

'And is there any sign of finger-marks round the deceased's throat or neck?' I asked feigning ignorance.

'Yes, a cluster of four faded fingernail impressions are just visible at the front of the left side of her lower neck, and we found a further thumbnail impression on the back of her neck at post-mortem.'

'A large hand then?'

'Yes, a very large left hand restrained the victim from behind, the tips of the assailant's fingers biting into her flesh while the right hand pulled on a ligature.'

'A right handed man, would you say?'

'Yes, I'd definitely say so.'

After Sledgemore had hummed and hawed over the photograph for a minute or two, it was passed on to the jurymen bracing themselves to stare death in the face again.

'Along with these fingernail impressions did you find any other bruises, Mr Scattergood?' I asked.

'Yes, a thick band of bruising.'

'From the ligature used to strangle Estelle Parke?'

'In my opinion, yes.'

'I would like to draw the jury's attention to a post-mortem photograph, Exhibit Twenty-six, concentrating on the right side of the deceased's face and neck. Can you tell us what you found there, Mr Scattergood?'

'I was able to discern a complex pattern of bruising on her neck. A pattern totally new to me despite many years of involvement in forensic medicine.' Scattergood turned demurely to the judge. 'If my lord will allow, I would like to demonstrate with the aid of a diagram?'

'Please.' Sledgemore gestured to the usher to fetch Scattergood's prearranged diagram and easel. At my request it was placed on the jury side of the witness box and Scattergood was supplied with a long cane.

'You will see I have drawn an outline of the deceased's head and neck in profile,' began Scattergood. 'Right here, my colleague, Dr Richard Tate, and I found these two strange marks.' Scattergood had drawn a huge insert of two symbols. 'You can see they represent some sort of distorted lettering. Now, with the help of a large mirror, they will become clearer to you.'

On cue the usher next struggled in with a large wall mirror.

'Perhaps, my lord, members of the jury might be permitted to take a closer look,' I suggested.

Peering forward over his bench, Sledgemore nodded his tacit agreement. The jurymen trooped out of their box two by two as if emerging from the ark.

'See,' said Scattergood, pointing towards the insert and then the mirror with his cane. 'The letters have clearly become an R and an M in the mirror.'

The jury trooped back absorbed but confused. I whispered a further request to the usher as he removed Scattergood's visual aids. Those in court who had been unable to get a good view of the demonstration muttered their frustration.

'Exhibit Seventeen, my lord,' I announced, as the usher handed me a parcel. This was the same parcel I had hidden, months ago, under the Coffee Tavern table to be taken back to Leeds by Dick for further examination. I removed the outer wrapping slowly.

'Lunch perhaps,' joked Henge, loudly to his colleagues, before his face fell on seeing me unfurl the contents.

'What on earth is it?' Brougham leaned over to Henge.

'God! It's reminiscent of the deadly moray eels I saw being removed by Maltese fishermen from their nets in Valletta.' Henge remained glued to his seat.

'Valletta?' enquired Brougham.

'Yes, Pa was on diplomatic service out there.'

'Mr Scattergood, do you recognise this shoulder strap?' I asked as the usher draped the strap over the expert's wrinkled hand.

'Yes, it is the one I examined with Dr Tate under a microscope at Leeds.'

'On the strap is a badge bearing the embossed letters WRMR, an abbreviation for the Whitby, Redcar and Middlesbrough Railway, am I right in thinking?'

'I believe so.'

'The middle letters being RM?'

'Yes.'

'Do you think this shoulder strap or one like it could have been used as a ligature to strangle Estelle Parke to death?'

'Yes, I do. Although only the middle two letters of the strap's badge left a clear imprint on the surface of the neck.'

'Like a printing block in reverse?'

'Yes. And, interestingly, the killer must have inadvertently buckled or twisted the strap inside out, nap uppermost, to make such an impression.'

'Confused by his own dastardly act, no doubt. Was there anything else about this strap?'

'Yes, we found small traces of blood here and there, though I suspect some attempt had been made to wipe it clean.'

'And where has this shoulder strap actually come from?' asked Sledgemore, pen poised.

'Staithes, my lord,' I informed him vaguely. 'Exhibit Seventeen has been undergoing a forensic inspection, and is a recent entry, but it will be there on your lordship's list.'

'Where exactly in Staithes?' he brayed despairingly.

'I intend to call a witness shortly, my lord, who will explain precisely where it was found.'

'I'm relieved to hear that counsel is inveterate in his pursuit of corroborating testimony.'

I decided not to waste breath on Sledgemore's longwinded, backhanded compliment. 'One final question, Mr Scattergood, is it possible to estimate how tall Estelle Parke's killer might be?'

'The impression made by the ligature round her neck rises to one side. So Miss Parke's assailant was either much taller than she was, or he had forced her to kneel during strangulation.'

'Known as the execution position,' I concluded, with a nod of thanks to Scattergood.

A pin could have been heard to drop as Henge warily crept out of his seat to confront Thomas Scattergood – a different approach to the one he had adopted towards Dick Tate – Henge and Scattergood had clearly locked horns once or twice before.

'I must confess I am always a little in awe of the medical profession,' announced Henge still in grovelling posture.

'But our knowledge is so specific, Mr Henge,' retorted Scattergood with game amusement.

'Now tell me, Dr Scattergood …?'

'Mr,' corrected Scattergood quickly. 'I was appointed honorary surgeon to the Hospital for Women and Children in 1863, sir.'

'I do beg your pardon, *Mr* Scattergood. I overlooked the medical profession's sensitivity regarding these slight matters.'

'Nothing slight about it, Mr Henge. Certainly not if someone is about to open up your belly and he isn't a "Mr".'

The gentlemen of the press in particular appreciated this exchange.

'Silence!' Sledgemore's headmaster cry was beginning to lose a little credibility among the naughty boy ranks of journalists.

'How is it that these fingernail and other impressions were so easily identifiable by you and not by Dr Allanby who originally examined the body?' Henge asked Scattergood more firmly.

'In fairness to Dr Allanby, it can take some time for bruising to become apparent after death. And, although the petechiae shown on Mr Thornton's photographs had faded, it was at post-mortem that we were able to confirm most of our findings by examining the pressure marks from different angles.'

'How long after death do bruises begin to appear?'

'It can be several days, depending on how much pressure was applied and the tissue involved.'

'So Dr Allanby was somewhat at a disadvantage faced with a newly discovered corpse?'

'Possibly.'

'A corpse only twenty-four hours old?'

Scattergood smiled slyly. His smile said, "you'll have to do better than that, Mr Henge", while his old hoarse voice croaked, 'I understand from the police that Mr Thornton's photographs were taken at least a day after Dr Allanby's preliminary examination. And all the signs indicate that the deceased's body had been immersed in sea water for several days before even Dr Allanby came across it.'

'But that's what I'm trying to get at, man. Why wasn't all this bruising visible to Dr Allanby if Estelle Parke had been dead for a good deal longer than a day?' asked Henge. Henge in open attack now, openly hostile.

'Objection, my lord, my learned friend is trying to bully the witness. Mr Scattergood has already explained in some detail how bruises often only become apparent *several* days after death.' I intervened, angrily shaking some papers in my lifted hand. 'And if my learned friend examines his notes more thoroughly, he will see that Dr Allanby did in fact testify that he found some abrasions round the deceased's throat. I suggest, though, it takes a man of Mr Scattergood's extensive forensic experience to be able to translate these abrasions, one from another.'

'And again in fairness to Dr Allanby, photographic lighting, and the fact that the deceased suffered from a condition where her skin was extremely pale, helped enhance any unnatural colouring that happened to develop subsequently,' added Scattergood generously.

'Pity Mr Scattergood isn't eminent enough to be able to tell this court the owner of those finger impressions.' Once more Henge gave Daniel the long hard stare.

'As we speak the London police force is conducting experiments into finger-printing techniques. And allow me to reassure you, sir, these new procedures will be in general use only a few years from now. Though, alas, not on soft surfaces such as skin but on polished leather surfaces such as a WRMR shoulder strap perhaps.' Scattergood grinned broadly at the astounded QC.

'You'll be telling us next who bleeds,' scoffed Henge.

'If only I could but I'll not see that kind of science in my lifetime,' replied Scattergood calmly, remaining the unruffled perfect gentleman. 'You see, if

I was able to tell you that, I could say unequivocally that the small traces of blood found on the leather, on the badge, on the buckle and pin of Exhibit Seventeen belonged to Estelle Parke.'

'Repeat after me …' Jackson clutched the bible tightly. At least he did not have to read anything, all he had to do was mimic the clerk of assize. He had been here before, in a box like this before, standing before all these staring people. He had been forced by conscience to give evidence against Lane and Carter at the Robertshaw fire trial, and now he was having to relive that ordeal.

'Mr Jackson, you are a fisherman?' I solemnly examined my notes.

'Yes, yes, I am.'

'And you were one of the four men who rescued the accused from the rocks at Staithes on the twenty-first of May last?'

'Yes.'

'Speak up.' Sledgemore shuffled irritably on his seat of power.

'Did you see any blood on Daniel Robertshaw's clothing?' I asked.

'No.'

'You are also the owner of this?' I lifted up the replica telescope to Warrington's from the defence table.

'Yes, sir, that is mine.'

'And with this piece of equipment I understand you went up to the highest point on Boulby Cliffs, the other day, to assess how much detail you could pick out on the rocks at Scar Shootings. The same rocks on which Mr Fletcher Warrington testified he'd seen Daniel Robertshaw kissing Estelle Parke, isn't that so?'

Jackson looked on as my fingers caressed the telescope. I expect he saw me in an entirely new light. He must have realised that this courtroom was my boat, this was my sea, and that opposing counsel was waiting somewhere out there to pounce with all the poise, strength and assurance of an arch-predator. It was Jackson's turn to feel out of his depth.

'Answer counsel's question.' Another shuffle of irritation from Sledgemore: this was proving to be a long trial and a long sitting.

'I could barely make out the figure of what I took to be a rod and line fisherman on the Shootings.'

'Could you see his expression or if he'd caught a fish and kissed it?' My sarcasm provoked a snigger here and there.

'No, I couldn't even see him casting out.'

'Objection!' cried Henge. 'Who is to say this man's eyesight is as good as Mr Warrington's?'

'He is a very much younger man for one thing,' I countered. 'But as I know from personal experience just how good Mr Jackson's distance vision is, I suggest my learned friend satisfies himself with a simple experiment, my lord.'

'Go ahead, as long as it's not too convoluted.' Sledgemore nodded.

'My lord, I'm not sure the Crown wishes to take part in a defence experiment without any prior warning,' protested Henge.

'But I recall it was you who challenged the validity of this witness's eyesight,' pointed out Sledgemore.

Meanwhile, I was scanning the room for assistance. 'Mr Brougham is of a similar age to Mr Jackson. If he will be good enough to stand over there by the witness box and you, Mr Henge, remain at your table and choose one of these seven letter cards.'

Henge, muttering something to the effect of "childish games", nonetheless snatched a card begrudgingly out of my hand and held it up.

'This letter is about an inch and a half in width and height,' I explained to the jurymen. 'Mr Brougham, you tell us which letter it is first?'

Brougham stared hard towards the card in Henge's slab of hand before pronouncing, 'It's a D, D for David.'

'Do you agree, Mr Jackson?' I turned with a prayer to my witness. My witness who I had already established knew the letters of the alphabet if not how to string them together into words.

Jackson shook his head, saying with uncharacteristic certainty, 'No, sir, it's a B.'

'Mr Henge?'

'B,' admitted Henge. 'B for bast …' He only just stopped himself swearing in the nick of time before flinging the offending letter onto his table in disgust.

'Well, I thought it was an O,' said Sledgemore blinking. 'O for oh dear.'

'With respect, my lord, you are a little older than the witness,' I responded delicately before refocusing on Jackson. 'If the prosecution is satisfied that I have demonstrated this witness's keen long sight enough, perhaps I might be permitted to continue my examination of him.' Henge scowled across ungraciously as I grinned further encouragement to my witness. 'Now, I understand you tried moving further down the cliff closer to Staithes, proposed by Mr Warrington as another possible explanation for his grandstand position of the goings on between the accused and Estelle Parke. Can you tell this court what you were able to see from there?'

'Nothing. The spot where we found Daniel on the rocks was completely blocked from view by Cowbar Nab.'

'No more questions from me for the moment.' I had a real bounce to my step now.

'A very impressive display of local knowledge,' Henge complimented Jackson smarmily. 'As you are such an observant chap perhaps you can confirm to this court the accused's attitude when you reached him out there on those rocks?'

'Bad, he was bad.'

'I know he *is* bad,' tee-hed Henge. 'But how did he generally strike you?'

'Really, my lord!' I objected.

'This court requires facts not general impressions, Mr Henge. And might I further remind you that I'll not tolerate any more of your witticisms at the expense of the accused or witnesses,' admonished Sledgemore.

'How did he greet you?' asked Henge, unabashed.

'He didn't.'

'What? You'd risked life and limb to rescue this man and he offered no greeting?'

'No.' Jackson of few words, flummoxed by this legal world of words, shook his head.

'Was he happy or sad?' persisted Henge.

'He looked *bad*,' repeated Jackson, beginning to smoulder.

'Are you trying to tell his lordship and members of the jury that the prisoner's emotional state appeared to be bad?'

'Yes,' sighed Jackson, teeth clenched.

'So, we've touched upon the prisoner's emotional state,' reflected Henge, hovering thoughtfully. 'What was his state of dress? Can you tell me anything about that?'

'Jackson isn't the only fisherman in town.' Trotter's breath (or was it his observation) sent a cold shiver down my back.

I watched on helplessly as the colour drained from Jackson's honest face. His knuckles were white, too, as he gripped the edge of the witness box.

'Well?' insisted Henge. 'Remember you've sworn an oath on the bible.'

My frown deepened, Henge sensing blood was really going for the jugular on this one.

Jackson stared back at the QC horrified. 'Two of his breeches' buttons were undone,' he confessed in a reluctant muffled undertone.

'Can you repeat what you've just said? I'm sure his lordship won't have quite caught it.'

'I said two of his breeches' buttons were undone. But a lad like Daniel doesn't always trouble about things like that.'

'No, I expect he doesn't,' snorted Henge, praying for a lunch-time adjournment, wishing the curtain to fall on his intuitive master-stroke.

God and Sledgemore seemed to be listening. The judge left the court still in a rather restive mood, whereas Henge and his team were almost celebrating victory as they collected up their documents. In contrast, our defence team was about to embark on a gloomy meeting in Bootham Chambers where Wilson Scott went as far as proposing a change of plea.

'Not that *bad*, things aren't that *bad*, surely?' Wallbridge looked round for some appreciation of his ironic impersonation of Henge.

'Bad being the operative word of the day so far,' I confirmed miserably, until, in a sudden flash of inspiration, the sun passed from beneath the cloud for me, and I glimpsed for the first time what I believed to be the truth regarding Estelle Parke's murder.

BAD – such a drab word to detonate explosive colour.

Chapter Thirty-Nine

Carl Thompson stood in that same retained imaginary arc of light as I squared up to him that afternoon, stood with the same grey neckcloth he had worn when I had interviewed him in the ale-house. Carl Thompson was my last throw of the dice.

'The evidence I shall give ...' Thompson, holding the bible in his good right hand, swore an oath over gospels he had long since failed to believe in.

'Mr Thompson, you are employed as a general manual worker at Brigham Hall?' I asked, giving not the slightest indication of any previous meeting between the two of us.

'I am,' confirmed Thompson, slightly unsettled by my impersonal approach.

'And you are an ex-fisherman who once sailed with the accused's father, Captain Robertshaw, until his boat the *Daniel* went down?'

'Yes.'

'You were the mate aboard that sinking vessel and, despite sustaining serious injuries, you were the only crew member to be saved, is that correct?'

'It is,' murmured Thompson.

'I see you have lost two fingers on your left hand, was that due to the accident?'

'No, sir. I lost 'em gutting fish as a youngster.'

'Just hours prior to the loss of the *Daniel*, did you not suggest to Captain Robertshaw that the yawl put into Whitby, a safer harbour?'

'Who says I said that?' smouldered Thompson.

'As reported by your rescuers in the newspapers of the time.'

'What is this?' Henge burst out in indignation. 'A murder trial or a maritime inquest?'

'Mr Cairn?' Sledgemore's raised brow.

'I'm just trying to establish this witness's relationship to the prisoner.'

'Well, I'd have thought you would already know that, he is your witness,' barracked Henge.

'Mr Henge, I'm warning you, I'll not suffer any more of your facetious comments. As you are well aware, it is counsel for defence's job to acquaint the jury with facts already known to him and not to them.' Mean-lipped, Sledgemore turned back to Thompson and instructed him to 'please answer the question'.

'Did you or did you not suggest that Captain Robertshaw put into a safer port?' I asked again.

'Might have done,' admitted Thompson sulkily. 'One minute we were becalmed, the next … The sea's a cruel mistress and only those who sail upon her know just how cruel.'

'Yes or no?' insisted Sledgemore.

'Yes, I think I suggested we should make anchor at Port Mulgrave or turn back for Whitby.'

'And would you say you held Captain Robertshaw ultimately responsible for the loss of life on the *Daniel* and your own injuries?'

'Partly. Though allowing for that one doubtful decision the man was the finest skipper I ever sailed with.'

'Do you have an opinion why Captain Robertshaw didn't put into a safe harbour when the storm began to blow up?'

'He wanted to get home to her, didn't he, his new bride.' Thompson nodded disparagingly up to the public gallery.

'Who do you mean?' interrupted Sledgemore.

'Widow Robertshaw of course,' snapped back Thompson, as if the judge was an imbecile. 'She was pregnant with him.'

'Let it be noted that the witness is pointing to Mrs Flora Robertshaw and the prisoner,' Sledgemore instructed the court reporter.

'Would you say this tragedy has affected your attitude to the Robertshaw family?' I asked Thompson, with a discreet little bow to his lordship in apology for my witness's ignorant outburst.

'Don't know,' replied Thompson guardedly.

'Let me put it this way, do you have the same respect for Daniel and Flora Robertshaw as you had for Captain Robertshaw?'

'Can't say that I do,' mumbled Thompson.

'What did he say?' asked Sledgemore, hand to ear.

'He said he does not have the same respect for the prisoner and his mother as he did for the deceased Captain Robertshaw, my lord.' Under these circumstances, I was, as always, more than happy to indulge in a little reiteration for his lordship.

'Um,' muttered Sledgemore. 'Don't know why witnesses bother turning up to court if they aren't prepared to make themselves clearly understood.'

'Sometimes they have no choice, my lord, as in this case,' I replied, glad to draw the jury's attention to Carl Thompson's possible hostility.

'I know, I know,' moaned Sledgemore, waving off my literal interpretation of what was meant to be a light aside.

Lives, a life, can be changed in a fraction of a second by a runaway horse or something as innocuous as a nodded request to the court usher.

'Exhibit Seven,' I announced. With all the deference befitting the handling of a body part, the usher lay the exhibit on the table before me. I lifted up Exhibit Seven, unravelling it from its original tissue wrapper which was by now in tatters. 'Do you recognise this?' I asked Thompson.

'I can't rightly see,' squinted Thompson.

I gestured for the usher to take Exhibit Seven across the floor to the witness box. 'Do you recognise it *now*?' I asked, as the usher dangled the exhibit directly in front of Thompson's face.

'Yes,' replied Thompson, staring in horror at Estelle Parke's lock of white hair floating alive in his own exhaled breath.

'Whose hair is this?'

Lives, a life, can change in an intake of breath.

'Mr Thompson?' I persisted impatiently.

'Miss Parke's,' murmured Thompson.

'How do you know it is when you've told other servants at the Hall that you never set eyes on her?'

'Guessed.'

'Wasn't it you who told another witness, Seth Jackson, that you'd found this same sample of hair in the Hall's ice-house?'

'Suppose I did?'

'Answer "yes" or "no",' commanded Sledgemore, now dangerously close to losing his temper too.

'Yes,' hissed Thompson between clenched teeth.

'So how do you know it belonged to someone you've never seen?' I spelt out once more. Thompson shook his head from side to side. 'Did the gamekeeper, Francis Marlett, tell you it was Estelle's hair by any chance?' I asked quickly, inspirationally, robbing Sledgemore of his chance for another distracting intervention.

'Lady Clarissa told me,' finally admitted the increasingly subdued Thompson.

'What, when she asked you to plant it in the ice-house?'

'Ay, I was only obeying her orders.'

'Do you always obey orders, no matter what they might be?'

'Yes, always.'

'So, if someone asked you to commit murder you'd do it then?'

'No, I …' Thompson abruptly crawled into his mental shell liked a poked snail.

'Objection!' shouted Henge. 'My friend is harassing the witness.'

'Upheld,' confirmed Sledgemore. 'Although I must point out to you, Mr Henge, this is rather a case of the pot calling the kettle black.'

Smiling at his lordship's fondness for cliché, I asked Thompson, 'Did you tell Francis Marlett that you'd found this lock of hair in the ice-house?'

'Can't remember.'

'He testified that you did.'

'Then I must have done.'

'Or, more precisely, did you admit to your close colleague, Marlett, that you'd planted it there on behalf of Lady Clarissa Parke?'

'Yes, I think I did tell him it was her as put me up to it.'

'So why did Marlett recently tell the court that this hair exhibit was proof that the accused met Estelle Parke there?' I slipped in slyly.

'I don't know anything about that.' More vigorous shaking of the Thompson head.

'Why did you tell Lady Clarissa that Sir Hugh regularly walked their daughter to the ice-house?' My eyes lifted with expectation. Thompson fell mute again. 'As stated by Lady Clarissa herself.'

'Don't recall saying anything about that.'

'Lady Clarissa told this court that you did.'

'Marlett told me he'd seen Sir Hugh with the girl there.'

'But you didn't have to tell Lady Clarissa that, not unless you wanted to cause trouble.'

A long thoughtful period of silence ensued on the part of Thompson.

'Exhibit Seventeen.' I gestured to the court usher again. 'Do you recognise this?' I asked, unravelling the shoulder strap towards Thompson as I had done Estelle's hair.

'I said afore that's Farnborough's down at the station.'

'No, it isn't. Look closer, WRMR is the insignia on this badge. WRMR for Whitby, Redcar and Middlesbrough Railway. And there is blood on this strap.'

Thompson peered forward over the box, staring towards the strap in disbelief.

'Mr Thompson, I remind you that you are under oath and ask you again do you recognise this strap?'

'It's nowt to do with me.' Thompson stared round the room, stared anywhere as long as it was not at the dangling strap, stared across at Daniel who was staring pathetically back at him. They were both in the dock now, the same boat now.

'Does this strap belong to you?' I finally asked in exasperation. Thompson gave the briefest of glances up towards the public benches. I did not miss it. 'Mr Thompson?' I prompted again.

'No, it's not mine,' said Thompson, sounding dry-mouthed, suddenly jerked back into the reality of his situation.

'I'll ask you once more, do you know the true owner of this strap?'

'No, I've said "no" and I mean "no".'

'Exhibit Seventeen was provided for inspection by the previous witness, Seth Jackson. If you will not tell us who this WRMR shoulder strap belongs to, I shall have to recall him to confirm its ownership.'

'You must do as you think fit,' shrugged Thompson.

'A man's life is on trial here,' I reminded him.

'I cannot tell you any more.' Carl Thompson was stubborn, his old instincts had fallen into place, the odd-jobman was still at heart a crewman who did not tell tales.

'No more questions for this witness at the moment, but I would like to recall Seth Jackson.'

'Do you wish to cross-examine Mr Thompson before he stands down, Mr Henge?' asked Sledgemore.

'No, not at present, my lord,' replied Henge, intrigued, alert and biding his time.

Jackson and Thompson crossed without a word. Thompson's dark brown eyes were empty, fathomless. I was still clutching Exhibit Seventeen as Jackson took the box. I held the long strap in a noose, like the hangman's rope itself.

'Mr Jackson, you were a reluctant agent in the appropriation of this shoulder strap with its incriminating Whitby, Redcar, Middlesbrough Union Railway badge, were you not?'

'Yes, sir.' Jackson did appear hesitant, shy almost.

'Can you tell the court why?'

'Because I remembered it was part of a guard's uniform worn by a Staithes man many years ago, a man who is long since dead.'

'But why such reticence, Mr Jackson, if this man is no more?'

'He was the father of a boyhood friend.'

'And you feared this boyhood friend might have inherited the shoulder strap and be involved in the murder of Estelle Parke?'

'Yes, I did.'

'And, although a man of conscience, you didn't want to get a friend into trouble unless it was absolutely necessary?'

'That's right.'

'I take it that your childhood friend isn't the man standing at present in the dock? Isn't the prisoner, Daniel Robertshaw?'

'No, sir.' Jackson looked across at Daniel and gave him a quick reassuring smile. Something of the gravity of this moment must have impinged on Daniel because he didn't respond to Jackson's smile, but continued to stare fixedly at him.

'Well, a complete understanding of this situation is absolutely necessary now, Mr Jackson,' I announced into the pin-drop silence. 'Where did you get this shoulder strap from?'

'Brigham Hall,' came Jackson's slow measured reply.

'Where in Brigham Hall?'

'An empty lodge in the grounds where I pare me 'ezzells down.'

''Ezzells?' asked Sledgemore.

'Hazel sticks used as arches in the making of crab and lobster pots, my lord,' I explained.

'I can see you are something of an expert on the fishing industry, counsel,' quipped Sledgemore.

'Not at all, my lord, it takes a lifetime to learn such crafts,' I replied, before returning back to Jackson. 'Is this hut used for anything else, do you know?'

'I believe Carl Thompson keeps one or two of his things there, but it is mainly used as a hunting lodge. Marlett hangs game and venison there before butchering it.'

'Francis Marlett, the gamekeeper?'

'The same.'

'What tool does Mr Marlett use in butchering game?'

'A knife of course,' laughed Jackson.

'What sort of knife? Can you be more precise?'

'A hunting knife, I believe,' confirmed Jackson, reverting to his previous apprehensive state.

'And who is the deceased person that the shoulder strap belonged to originally?'

'Marlett's father. He was a guard on the Whitby/Middlesbrough line. In more recent years, Marlett sometimes used the strap to hang hare from the beams.'

'What? He used his father's fine shoulder strap for hanging hare?'

'Hair?' queried Sledgemore.

'Hare, as in mad March hare, my lord.' I could not resist a hint of irony.

'Hare, as in *Alice's Adventures in Wonderland*,' chorused Henge's table more overtly.

'Marlett never thought a lot of his father or the strap, said his father used the strap to whip him with once too often.' Jackson struggled on as if he was trying to resolve something within himself. 'Said the silver buckle and badge cut him up something rotten.'

'Just one moment,' interrupted Sledgemore; a finger raised in the air. 'If this strap was used for hanging meat, couldn't the blood on it be from that rather than from Miss Parke. And if Mr Marlett's father used to regularly beat him with it, couldn't some of that remaining blood be Mr Marlett's own?'

'As I think Mr Scattergood pointed out we have no way of telling one person's blood from another, not even one animal's blood from another, my lord,' I replied.

'Nor the freshness of the blood?'

'Not as yet, my lord.'

'Pity,' said Sledgemore.

'Although, as Mr Jackson has just testified, the strap was used in the hanging rather than in the butchery process, my lord. Further more, that does not negate the evidence that part of the badge's WRMR insignia was imprinted on Estelle Parke's neck.'

'Indeed, indeed,' agreed Sledgemore, writing more copious notes.

'Mr Jackson, could you tell the court how exactly you obtained this strap?' I asked.

'I just took it from the lodge when Marlett went off to feed the pens.'

'We are having to listen to thieves now,' mutter mutter from Henge's table but no formal objection.

'In the months that have followed has anyone approached you for its return?' I asked Jackson.

'If they guessed that it was me who took it, they've never come after me.'

'Perhaps they have to Fishergate Bar,' I whispered quietly, before reverting to my normal courtroom decibels. 'In the last few days you have been threatened not to appear at this trial, isn't that so, Mr Jackson?'

'Yes, that is true, Mr Cairn, sir. I was warned off in an anonymous note.'

'You have painted a picture of Francis Marlett being an abused and rather lonely figure, am I right in thinking?'

'I suppose he could be seen like that.'

'Does Marlett have time for anybody else other than himself?'

'That I couldn't properly say, though I've seen him in Thompson's company from time to time.'

'Thank you, Mr Jackson. No more questions from me.'

Jackson looked relieved until he saw Henge taking the floor.

'Mr Jackson, have you ever seen anyone else in Staithes with a uniform strap like Exhibit Seventeen?' asked Henge.

'Similar but not the same. This is the only one I know of with the letters WRMR on the badge. I have never seen another one like it in my life,' added Jackson for good measure: he wasn't having this fancy York lawyer getting the better of him a second time.

'And do you make a habit of stealing your friends' possessions?' asked Henge.

'Here we go,' moaned Wallbridge. 'Henge desperate and on the attack.'

'No, sir, I do not.' Jackson's head gave a toss of defiance. His black curls danced for a moment above his reddening face and neck. 'A young lass had been plucked from the sea in mysterious circumstances close to my village. There was a lot of local speculation that she'd been strangled. Then, following up something said to me by Mr Cairn, I realised I might know the whereabouts of the possible murder weapon. In the interests of justice, I felt it was my duty to secure that piece of evidence.'

'Most commendable, I'm sure. Do you have children yourself?' asked Henge.

Oh no, I thought, sure now Henge did have a sixth sense or failing that a superb spy network. The black curls remained still but Jackson's face was distorted with revised pain.

'I ...' Jackson fumbled with the question, fumbled to shape a coherent answer. 'Yes, sir, I have a daughter though she is unknown to me.'

'You have a daughter but she is "unknown" to you?' repeated Henge, wide-eyed with derision.

'Really, my lord,' I broke in. 'Is this relevant?'

'I think members of the jury have a right to some background knowledge regarding the moral calibre of such an important witness,' responded Henge.

'The Crown on this occasion has a point,' agreed Sledgemore.

Henge smirked at being given the judicial go-ahead for once.

'I had a daughter, but I was not allowed to marry her mother because we were of different faiths,' announced Jackson, before Henge had a chance to resume his licensed intrusion. 'I understand our child was given away at birth.'

'No more questions,' said Henge; knowing he would gain little capital and possibly lose some sympathy pursuing this line of cross-examination any further.

Jackson grinned as the QC flopped into his chair. He was reminded of a fat bull seal retreating to the island safety of Lingrow Knock.

'You proposed marriage to the lady in question but her Quaker parents wouldn't hear of the match, isn't that right?' I asked, angry at Henge's low attempt to besmirch the reputation of a man who had been so valiant and helpful to Daniel's cause. I, for one, had not finished with the subject of Jackson's worthiness. 'And for many years you've lived alone and not once entertained the possibility of marrying anyone else?'

'No, sir, I've never been so taken with a lass again.'

'Thank you, Mr Jackson.' I turned to Sledgemore. 'I would like to recall Carl Thompson, my lord.'

Jackson had moderated his Staithes dialect in court, honed it with a slow Yorkshire precision. The man passing him seemed incapable of honing anything, certainly not his emotions, he snarled something inaudible across to Jackson.

'Mr Thompson, I am sorry I have to ask you a few more questions,' I apologised.

'All right,' snorted Thompson gracelessly.

'Has the witness been advised that he is still under oath?' interrupted Sledgemore with a nervous cough.

'Ay, I know I am.' Thompson nodded curtly to the judge.

'Mr Thompson,' I began again, exasperated by Thompson's rudeness. 'Are part of your duties at Brigham Hall the upkeep of water pipes, external and internal maintenance, that sort of thing?'

'Ay, what of it?' Thompson glowered around the court, hostile to anyone and everyone at that moment, and especially hostile to this man in his face.

'Do you have a set of master keys for most of the locks at the Hall?'

'Ay.'

'Do you have a key for the east wing?'

'Ay, I expect I might have, though Sir Hugh told me never to try the locks there unless advised by him alone.'

'Where do you leave this set of keys when not at work?'

'In the lodge, in a drawer in the lodge.'

'The same lodge used by Francis Marlett for hanging game?'

'The same.'

'Do you ever help Mr Marlett with the butchery of that game?'

'Occasionally.'

'Is he dextrous with a knife?'

'Dextrous?' baulked Thompson.

'Handy?' I interpreted.

'Seen no better.'

'Are you?'

'Am I what?'

'Good at butchery?'

'Now look here,' objected Thompson, finally scenting danger.

'Just answer the question,' rasped Sledgemore.

'I can use an Arkansas toothpick as well as any man, if that's what you're getting at,' admitted Thompson aggrieved.

'Did you say an Arkansas toothpick?' My ears prick up at this.

'Ay, that's what Marlett calls it.'

'By an Arkansas toothpick, do you mean some sort of a knife?'

'Yes, Marlett's special American knife for skinning and gutting.'

'Do you know where that knife is now?'

'No, come to think of it, I've not seen it around for some time. Marlett is usually never parted from that knife. It's the same knife that he used to cut the black horse free at the Robertshaw fire.'

'Were you at that fire, Mr Thompson?'

'No, I was not.'

'But Mr Marlett was there?'

'Yes, he told me he was watching on when the aunt's horse began to panic.'

'Mr Marlett's Arkansas toothpick, isn't it better known as a bowie knife?'

'Ay, it's exactly that. It has a curved end.'

'Mr Thompson, when I asked you earlier if you recognised the guard's WRMR shoulder strap, Exhibit Seventeen, you denied ever seeing it before, did you not?'

'Yes,' agreed Thompson cautiously.

'How can that be, Mr Thompson, when Francis Marlett kept it hanging up in the lodge you shared with him?'

'I …' Silence, another Thompson stony silence as he calculated the outcome of various possible responses.

'Was it you, Mr Thompson, who took down that strap and strangled the life out of a young girl?'

'No, I couldn't do such a thing.'

'Are you saying that Francis Marlett did it then?' I asked, adding scathingly, 'Mr Marlett, who loves horses?'

'Just because you love horses, doesn't mean you love women,' muttered Thompson, still engrossed in various computations of his own.

'Do you love women?'

'I was married once. She died.'

'I didn't get the impression that you liked Flora Robertshaw very much.'

'She turned the captain's head,' said Thompson thickly.

'So when a lovely young creature like Estelle Parke came along on her nightly ramble, she wasn't going to turn your head?'

'She wasn't lovely,' sneered Thompson.

'But how can you form that judgement if you've never seen her?' I asked. Thompson gave another brief glance, an appeal almost to somewhere up on the public benches. 'So, she wasn't lovely, in your opinion, but she was vulnerable and easy to overpower for your own beastly gratification, isn't that so?'

'No! No! It wasn't like that.'

'So what was it like?'

Thompson's head started to ache. He stroked the top of the witness box as if it was the wooden railing of the *Daniel* before she went down. He was bewildered, in a bad dream.

* * * * *

'Abandon ship! Abandon ship!' Captain Robertshaw was almost hysterical, life and death now. One by one the men clambered down to the seaman already manning the coble, orderly enough but not quick enough for Robertshaw. 'Here, take my son.' Robertshaw passed young Daniel carefully down into the sinewy embrace of his mate. Thompson saw the captain's lips still moving above him, though he could not make out his words, each syllable was being broken up by the deafening roar. But Thompson did not feel this was a leave taking, did not feel the captain intended to go down with the ship, he felt sure Robertshaw was about to follow.

Clasping the captain's son to his shivering chest with one arm, he reached up his other arm beckoning the father to hurry. Too late – the big wave came, the wave they all had dreaded might come, a wave sucking them into it, curling them up in it, a freezing womb of a wave.

Carl Thompson felt the boy wrenched from his grasp, felt the ice water burning his ears, heard his own failing heartbeat. A terrible stillness fell on the other side of the mountain.

* * * * *

'Mr Thompson!'

Thompson could feel Daniel's brother slipping from his grasp and he could not let it happen again. He hung his throbbing head there in the witness box. He had failed Captain Robertshaw's first son, he could not fail a second.

'Mr Thompson!' I repeated even more forcefully. 'Will you tell this court what you know about the murder of Estelle Parke?'

'It was Marlett who saw her first with Sir Hugh.' Thompson sighed relief; an almost cheerful, nothing could get any worse sigh. 'I remember Marlett swore she was a white witch, properly shook him up it did. After much speculation between the two of us, we decided from the master's defensive attitude that the witch was more likely to be some powdered trollop he'd picked up in a town somewhere. Then, months later, Marlett and me were out late watching for deer poachers – must have been an autumn evening because I remember plenty of leaves and breaking twigs scrunching beneath our boots – that's when we both saw her again, she was running along the lake, her skirts ballooning about her like sails in a fair wind. We joked and Marlett said "what about a little sport with the white witch?" I said "maybe she'll cure my bad heads with a spell".'

'You waylaid her?'

'Yes, sir, we did. It wasn't hard either. Marlett can trap almost any animal in flight.'

'Go on.' I was barely able to contain my disgust. The contents of my stomach lurched as they had done on the opening day of the trial but for a very different reason now.

'That's when things began to go wrong, got out of hand. We had only intended a little fun, sir, as we pushed the lass one to another. I'm not sure if she was still giggling or screaming then, but somehow the bodice of her dress got torn. I could see her breasts, the whitest breasts I'd ever seen. They looked like magnolia flowers at dusk – ghostly. Saw her paps and everything. It was then that Marlett suggested we see if she was really a woman or a witch. You have to understand, sir, it had been a long time for me. I'm only human.'

'Are you?' groaned Sledgemore.

'Yes, sir, I am,' replied Thompson with an amazing degree of indignation.

'You raped her?' My question was as much a cold statement.

'We thought she was just one of Sir Hugh's whores.'

'You think that is mitigation?' asked Sledgemore incredulous.

'Both of you raped her?' I was fully committed to the truth now.

'I'll never forget her standing there stripped naked, pale in pale moonlight, shivering and pleading for her dress. It was then that Marlett said something was wrong, the lass wasn't behaving like any whore he'd known. I said I didn't care and pressed my hand over her mouth and pushed her down into them leaves. It wasn't easy, she wasn't easy. She fought and scratched like a cat. But before I got properly started, it was then that I felt Marlett's hand on my shoulder, pulling me back off her, said it wasn't right. I thought the bugger only wanted her for himself. But afterwards, when she'd got back on her feet, stunned like she was, he helped her into her dress and wrapped his coat about her because she was trembling so much.'

'What?' I exclaimed. 'You expect this court to believe that?'

'Yes, sir, I do, because it's the truth.'

'You both let her go?'

'Not before she'd screamed blue murder, screamed she'd tell her father, and Marlett had jeered what father, and she had said Sir Hugh was her father. We both feared for our jobs then and more, but Marlett whispered to me that he would take her back to the Hall and make things right.'

'How could he make things right?'

'Beats me, sir, but Marlett has a way with him. Somehow, between the lake and the Hall, he befriended Estelle, won her confidence. Of course she never liked me after that. And we never did find out how she got out that night, maybe Sir Hugh himself forgot to turn the lock, but on one or two subsequent nights it was me who supplied Marlett with the key to the east wing.'

'Are you saying Marlett had an affair with Miss Parke?'

'Well, I don't know if you'd call it that. They had a tumble now and again in the lodge, according to Marlett. He said she was a needy little piece, said he wasn't the first, said her papa was the first.'

The belly of the court groaned. Sledgemore groaned again, before asking Thompson if he had carefully considered the repercussions of repeating such a serious allegation.

'Ay, I have right enough. When Estelle told Marlett she was expecting, Marlett asked me how could he be sure if the bastard was his and not Sir Hugh's. Marlett said Estelle was threatening to tell Sir Hugh about them. He said she was putting pressure on him to run away with her before ...'

'Did you really believe Marlett when he said he'd had sexual congress with Miss Parke?' I cut in.

'I didn't know what to make of it to be honest. Marlett enjoys a good boast about women from time to time, same as any other fella. But, I'll say this much for him, if he did have her, I don't know how he dare, she being Sir Hugh's daughter and all.'

'That didn't stop you trying to rape her.'

'No, it didn't, but that was afore I knew who she really was.'

'And if you'd known, that would have made all the difference in the world, wouldn't it?' I asked scornfully.

'Of course,' admitted Thompson, oblivious to the contempt he was drawing upon himself.

'So you thought Marlett might have been lying when he said he'd possibly got Miss Parke pregnant, did you?'

'I got the feeling that Estelle was just another bird with a broken wing to Marlett.'

'I ask you again, Thompson, did you kill Estelle Parke or were you an accomplice in her murder?'

'No, I was not.'

'Do you know who murdered her then?'

'Yes, sir, I think I do.'

'Who?'

'When Estelle first went missing, I thought the master might have despatched her himself.'

'Are you saying you thought Sir Hugh had sent her away?' interjected Sledgemore with apparent (or was it assumed?) naivety.

'No, killed her,' replied Thompson bluntly. 'Then I got to thinking that I'd heard of fathers having a fuck with their own daughters, killing 'em even, but never putting their eyes out as I believe it's been alleged by gentlemen here in court.'

'I'll not allow you to express one further base obscenity in my court, there are ladies present.' Sledgemore's eyes bulged with rage. If his lordship disliked Fletcher Warrington, he had begun to dislike Carl Thompson even more if that were possible.

'A good deal's gone through my mind, lately,' murmured Thompson, seemingly unaware that his previous utterance could possibly be the cause of any real offence. 'I remember something struck me as very odd, just before Estelle's disappearance, Marlett started asking me all about the tides in detail, said he fancied a spot of fishing.'

'And was Marlett capable of handling a boat on his own?' I asked.

'Ay, the Hall owned a small boat and Marlett was a strong oarsman but he lacked a fisherman's knowledge of high and low water times, currents and suchlike.'

'But wasn't the deceased's body eventually retrieved from the sea under the cliffs not far from Brigham Hall?'

'Exactly,' exclaimed Thompson. 'Be sure your sin will find you out, isn't that what religious folk say? Any regular old salt might have taken the lass up the quiet north coast but would never have dumped her body so inshore as to float back home.'

'Are you telling this court that whoever disposed of Miss Parke cannot have been an experienced seaman?'

'I am,' replied Thompson confidently.

'And Marlett fits within that bracket,' I reaffirmed.

'Maybe Estelle *was* bearing his kid all along, and, as he said, she was about to tell her father,' suggested Thompson with a sniff.

'My lord, this is all conjecture, opinion, with no basis in fact,' shouted Henge.

'Mr Thompson, do you truly believe Francis Marlett murdered Estelle Parke?' My insistence swept across Henge's appeal, across the silent courtroom.

'It must have been him.'

Out of the mouths of babes and sucklings, out of Daniel's mouth, now out of Thompson's mouth – Marlett is a very bad man.

'He's lying! Can't you see he's lying?' A desperate scream from the public gallery. Sledgemore gestured to the usher and a policeman to sort it out. 'Don't you see, Thompson killed her himself?'

Locating the source of the uproar, I shouted back, 'Not so, Mr Marlett. An expert medical witness gave evidence that four finger tips from the murderer's left hand pressed into Estelle Parke's throat as his right hand tightened the strap. Lift up your left hand, Mr Thompson. See, this man has only two fingers on his left hand.'

One card has wavered and the whole house is about to tumble, I realised in bewilderment. Just like that, just as simply and suddenly.

'Really, my lord, this is merely accusation and counter accusation,' whimpered Henge desperately.

'Nevertheless, I've seen and heard enough. An innocent man has been put through enough.' Then and there, Sledgemore instructed the jury to bring in a verdict of not guilty. 'The accused is in your charge,' he told them. 'Please confer among yourselves and choose a foreman.'

Pencils were held expectantly over press notebooks, the suspense in the public gallery was palpable.

'Not guilty!' announced the foreman. Not guilty was returned by the twelve men and true without retirement and with very little hesitation.

The courtroom exploded. Flora Robertshaw and Elizabeth Mott jumped up from their seats. Not guilty, could it be true? Was Daniel's trial really over at last? Was this trial finally at an end for everybody? Flora's tears spilt onto the swart cloth of Elizabeth's narrow but stalwart shoulder. Daniel reacted with the same equanimity as he did to all things in his life – he gave a little conciliatory wave up to his mother – what was all the fuss about anyway?

'Take that man away and hold him in custody.' Sledgemore's manner was icy, intimidating, as he wagged a finger up towards Marlett who was struggling violently with the policeman and the usher. Sledgemore commandeered two further officers to sort out the affray. 'Quickly now!' he shouted to them. 'Before my court degenerates into a scene from the Wild West.'

'Let me speak, let me go.' Marlett's voice alternated between screams of desperation and pleading sobs. 'He made me do it, ordered me to do it. Said otherwise he'd have me put away for ever. Said he'd tell 'em it was me that raped her. Said it would be his word against mine. Please, please listen.'

The court watched on with a mixture of pity and embarrassment, although nobody was really listening, not after my spectacular rejection of Marlett's initial accusation against Thompson.

A stunned Thompson remained in the witness box as his former friend Francis Marlett was dragged away through the public gallery door by the usher and three very big constables.

'Thank you,' Thompson shouted across to me.

'Don't thank me,' I replied quietly, now free to approach the witness box for the first time. 'You'll still have to answer for tampering with evidence, aiding and abetting the concealment of a serious crime, and anything else the police can think of throwing at you. Do you realise you were on the point of allowing that man, over there, to hang for a crime he didn't commit?' I gestured towards Daniel. Daniel, who from being mildly alarmed by Marlett's tussle in case it spilt down on his head, was now smiling beguilingly round to everyone and anyone because everyone and anyone was smiling at him.

'I tried to convince myself it didn't matter so much because it was him, because he is lacking.' Thompson winced at his own weak attempt at justification.

'It's you that's lacking,' I told him scathingly. 'Daniel's a far finer person than you'll ever be.'

'Much better as it turns out,' agreed a jaded Thompson.

'But tell me this, if you can, to make some amends for what you've put my client through, what did Marlett do with his American hunting knife?'

'The sea, I expect,' sighed Thompson. 'There's always the sea.'

'All rise.' Mr Justice Sledgemore slid out of court as he had slid in, though perhaps even his lordship had gained something from the past few days, perhaps there was a little more assertion in his stride.

'We've defended our client and got the guilty man at the same time,' crowed Wallbridge.

'Yes,' celebrated Wilson Scott.

'The hangman hasn't got the wrong man, that's the important thing for us,' I said, with a reserve that seemed to surprise both Wallbridge and Scott.

'Congratulations.' Henge gave a pugilistic wink across the divide, the wink of a fellow professional. 'Get you next time, my friend.'

I acknowledged Henge's begrudging capitulation. But, uneasily, I sensed a few more dramatic notes were waiting to be played.

Stepping from the courtroom – the partitioned scene of victory – I saw to my astonishment that the long corridor outside was transformed into a family party of hugs and handshakes all round.

'Fancy, you've won. I knew you would all along.' A beaming Jackson was the first to welcome me.

'Sorry about your ordeal with the anonymous note,' I said, allowing myself and the fisherman the briefest of manly embraces.

'The sea you can fight, men you can punch, but paper ...' laughed Jackson. 'Looks now as if Marlett must have sent it.'

'Yes, it certainly looks that way,' I sighed; an element of fatigue setting in.

'I'm so pleased for you, and especially for Daniel,' said Jackson, his mouth close to my ear, his large calloused hand still gripping mine. Like Wallbridge and Scott, a minute or two earlier, I could detect Jackson was a little baffled by my reticence.

'Well done, yourself. If you'd been unable to obtain that shoulder strap we might not have got an acquittal,' I responded, trying my best to force a little matching enthusiasm. I did not have to try for long, suddenly I felt Jackson's grip slacken and the warmth of him abruptly fall away. Jackson was staring down the corridor wide-eyed in disbelief.

Jackson did not blink, could not move, could not speak. Here amid all the wigs and gowns and all the complex paraphernalia of law was the Loftus maid in all her wonderful simplicity. She was just as he had first seen her on Cattersty Sands, all those years ago. But this time, she was coming towards him arm in arm with someone else.

It was my turn to be captivated, fascinated by this world outside my world. Susannah Mott and Jackson did not kiss each other, did not touch, did not even greet each other. Limpet-eyed they just stared, drawn, locked in an age old dance. Despite all that had happened, all the lost years without contact, they were immediately reunited, irreversibly bonded one to the other.

'I guessed you were my father as soon as I heard you speak in court this afternoon.' It was only Elizabeth who could claim Jackson from her mother's powerful physical spell.

'Our daughter,' explained Susannah.

'But she's so grown, so …' Jackson choked. 'So beautiful like you.'

When Flora Robertshaw eventually arrived with her restored son, she found Elizabeth, Susannah and Jackson wrapped together as one. Daniel giggled, happy again to see all this love around him. Disconcerted, Flora looked to me for an explanation.

'I'm afraid you've lost your maid,' I told her, with a shrug of envy towards the reunited lovers and their daughter.

'I'd no idea. Never mind, thanks to thee, I, too, have regained my own.' Flora glowed, smothering, mothering a wriggling Daniel.

When he was still, I took out of my briefcase the vellum envelope containing the ichthyosaur money and handed it across to him. 'I nearly forgot this, Daniel, perhaps you'd like to keep it now.'

Flora gently tugged it from her confused son's grasp and tried to pass it back to me, saying, 'For expenses.'

'No,' I said, shaking my head vehemently. 'Daniel should never have had to stand on trial in the first place. And, secondly, winning such a prestigious case will be invaluable publicity for my chambers. I want him to keep this for finding the stone fish.'

'Find stone fish again.' Daniel wrapped his arms round me and kissed me wetly somewhere on the cheek, somewhere near my mouth – *somewhere,* because I was so taken aback by my client's sudden expression of affection I was unable to say exactly where I was kissed.

'Someone loves you, Cairn,' teased Henge in passing.

Susannah was the first to break from the love-wrap and go over to Daniel and his mother.

'I helped bring thee into the world the night of the big storm,' she told a blushing Daniel, giving him a hug. 'I held thee in my arms when thou were small enough to fit inside a flither basket.'

'You knew about this all along, didn't you?' Jackson asked me with a husky mix of suspicion, emotion and gratitude.

'Some of it.'

'This is my daughter,' he told me proudly, keeping his arm tightly wrapped round Elizabeth's waist.

'We've already been introduced.' I laughed, winking at Elizabeth.

'She's sixteen today would you believe,' said Jackson.

'It's a new beginning for everyone,' I replied, my gaze shifting back to Susannah. I had tasted victory, now I was tasting the sweetest of defeats.

Chapter Forty

The next morning, in Bootham Chambers, Trotter announced that I had a visitor.

'You,' I exclaimed in astonishment.

'I had to come to offer my congratulations in person.'

'But how did you know?'

'Harold and I have been following the case closely. I have even sat in court once or twice but I expect you never noticed the shadowy figure at the back of the public gallery making the odd sketch.' Laura Johnson handed me a brown paper parcel. Inside was a mounted crayon sketch of my gowned back as I examined Sir Hugh Parke. 'Just a little memento to celebrate Daniel's release.'

'You always believed in his innocence, didn't you?' I asked. She nodded smiling. 'Thank you. Thank you so much. I'll keep it with *The Fossil Collector*.'

'I thought you might. Now how's Daniel?'

'Well, he's extremely well. And Harold?'

'Harold is Harold,' she smiled. 'Working too hard as always.'

'And Rosie?' I dared to ask.

'Still more in love with the idea of being an artist than the industry involved.'

'And "Gorgeous Pompey"?'

'Still around.'

'Ay,' I said, the dream finally vanquished.

After Laura had gone, I examined her drawing in detail. She had captured Sir Hugh in a few lines. The set of his jaw, his angular posture. Neither she nor I knew then that this was a rehearsal for a more sinister mid-twentieth century encounter, and Nuremberg, not York, would be the venue.

But for youth, the present is all. And the tower of mundane paper work waiting on my desk was real enough. I felt certain I would sail through it that day, sail through anything, my life had finally moved into a period of calm. I thought of Captain Robertshaw becalmed before the storm. And, in abrupt contrast to all my previous optimism, as my pen scratched out my looping signature, a recurring doubt painfully took shape. Had I really got to the end of the Estelle Parke affair?

As the morning dragged on towards noon, I tried to slough off this niggling uncertainty. Why did I feel so flat when I should feel elated? – after all I had done my job, I had got Daniel off. By mid-afternoon, only half-way through the paper work, I had had enough, could not concentrate a minute longer, a change was called for. High tea in the Shambles would make a welcomed break.

The Shambles, one of the oldest streets in town. A way stomped out by Roman legions. A street which once rang out with the bartering cries of furred Angles and Danes. A Norman Conquest street lit up by the glow of torched fields to the east.

I looked up to the twisted Tudor roofs, overhanging peaked gables, walls leaning with age, so narrowly spaced in places across the street that leaning neighbours could reach out and shake hands. It would only be later that I would muse on the fate that had drawn me to this particular street on that particular day – drawn as Susannah and Jackson had been to each other – but this time, unlike them, the moth would be drawn to the flame with singeing and lasting consequences.

But first Indian tea, or China tea? The Indian was strong and good. I shook my head at the creamy temptation offered on the cake trolley. Dick would have been pleased with my new resolve.

Walking slowly back along the Shambles, I felt both light and healthy but fortified as I enjoyed the lively jostle of fellow passers-by. It was not until I approached the sign of the Eagle and Child that I saw my way ahead was partially blocked as people spilled out of the pub onto the street and began to congregate. My previous good spirits sank. There was something about the crowd's attitude that reminded me of the wake outside Jacob Fines' ironstone cottage. I hoped I was wrong.

'What's going on?' I asked one disgruntled looking fellow with a floppy crimson cravat.

'Some bloke's topped himself.'

Another man with obviously better descriptive powers was more forthcoming, sparing no one within earshot the lurid details, spouting off with all the relish of a habitué of public hangings. 'Cut his wrists with a bowie knife, it's a right old mess up there, I can tell you, pools of blood all over the bedroom floor.'

A life that must have been in shambles, I thought with ironic detachment. I took a step towards moving off. 'Did you say "a bowie knife"?' I asked, swinging round on the habitué.

'Ay, I did that.'

'Landlord's spitting blood over the scene, right now,' black-humoured someone else. 'Said he should have seen it coming, the police having only just arrived to serve the nob with a warrant for his arrest or summat in the public bar.'

My heart skipped a beat.

'Ay, Billy told me the nob went quietly upstairs to the bedroom, a bedroom he'd hired from Billy the previous day. "To collect some of his clothes", the nob told him. They posted some useless bobby outside the room, and that's when he did it,' pealed in a woman.

'York's full of lunatics these days,' concluded an older man with a dismissive neurotic shake of his head.

'And stupid bobbies,' added the humourist.

'I just wish they'd hurry up in there, I've left a full glass of ale on the table,' complained the man with the floppy crimson cravat.

'Well, you'll not have to wait long,' pointed the older man.

'Look, they're bringing him out now,' gasped others in the crowd.

I watched on with the rest in stunned silence. Marlett had said "he made me do it, ordered me to do it", and everyone had assumed he was still referring to the previously maligned Thompson. But "made me, ordered me" – what, Thompson *ordering* Marlett? I did not really need to see the litter borne waist high by sombre-faced policemen, the long draped sheet covering the long body, the vague outline of a fine nose and arrogant chin protruding like a snow covered mountain range from a once distinguished face now drained of life. I did not really need to see these things because, walking away from the Eagle and Child that afternoon, I knew that only a few minutes earlier a form of self-administered justice had taken place somewhere up there in the lonely rented bedroom.

Author's Note

Friday 9th June, 1865. Charles Dickens's boat train carriage dangles precariously off a Kent bridge, as James Cairn takes his first intake of smoky London air.

1879, fourteen years later, in the northern fishing village of Staithes, another child, Daniel Robertshaw, sucks desperately at life. In adulthood these two disparate men will form an alliance for justice against overwhelming odds. Queen Victoria has been widowed for eighteen years. Lord North, who has an uncanny resemblance to George III and is related to the diarist Samuel Pepys, is her Tory prime minister. Earlier in the decade, North has had to contend with an attack by the Spanish on an English garrison at Port Egmont on the Falkland Islands – little changes in the affairs of man. The Americans are rebelling against British rule across the water, and during this year the Zulus rise up against colonial rule in South Africa.

Although Staithes might be considered by many to be a small dot on the map of empire, between 1750 and 1880 the village folk own one hundred and seventy merchant ships between them. A hundred more fishing vessels use its harbour. The rich fish stocks in the sea along its coastline have turned the port into an important commercial enterprise.

On 23rd January, 1897, James Cairn's great rival Sherlock Holmes is exploring the fictional corridors in the *Adventure of Abbey Grange*. A month later, in France, Marcel Proust is in reality firing his duelling pistol at the journalist Jean Lorrain for giving his book a bad review and accusing him of homosexuality. On 18th May, as Oscar Wilde is freed from Reading Gaol, the Irish novelist Bram Stoker's *Dracula* is given its first public airing on stage at the Lyceum Theatre in London.

During June of the same year, Queen Victoria celebrates her Diamond Jubilee. But unlike her eighty-six year old descendant Elizabeth II, at seventy-eight Victoria's poor mobility precludes her from climbing the steps of St Paul's Cathedral and the service has to be held outside. The distant and reserved Robert Gascoyne-Cecil, another Conservative prime minister, is serving a third term. During her reign, Victoria has already seen ten British PMs come and go.

The train has come to Staithes. The train that takes the fish out to all the major industrial cities of the north has brought the artists in. This northern outpost has become a mecca for painters such as Harold and Laura Knight (née Johnson) and many others who will become known as the Staithes Group. They are attracted by the east coast's tough breed of expressive fisherfolk and her rocky shores. Unfortunately though, apart from the vagaries of the sea, there are ominous specks riding the horizon. Steam trawlers have begun to drag their nets across the ocean floor.

Sir Joseph Wilson Swan has invented the incandescent light bulb. Sir Francis Galton and the police are experimenting with finger printing techniques. A year before, in 1896, Wilhelm Conrad Roentgen is honoured for discovering the X ray – the birth of radiology. This is an age which sees the embryonic science of forensic medicine springing to life. In Leeds the genial Thomas Scattergood is one such pioneer with his medico-legal case books. Whether revered in their time, reviled or forgotten – these often unsung innovators are the people to admire – they are the bedrock of today's society.

Acknowledgements

I am extremely grateful to all the friends who have kept me company on this long journey, especially my soul-mate, Paul, without whose support and encouragement this book would never have been written.

Special thanks go to Rosamund and Tom Jordan, whose knowledge of the Staithes Group of painters is legendary, and who gave my first literary foray a wonderful launch at two of their art exhibitions.

I am indebted to The National Maritime Museum, Greenwich; Arthur Credland MBE of Hull Maritime Museum; Reg and Anne Firth of the Staithes Heritage Centre; Whitby Archives; Whitby Public Library; Whitby Museum and Whitby Literary & Philosophical Society; The Sutcliffe Gallery, Whitby; Michelle Petyt of The Castle Museum, York; The National Railway Museum at York; York Reference Library; Leeds Reference Library; Briony Hudson of The Royal Pharmaceutical Society; Leeds Medical School Library and all the numerous medical publications recommended by them.

I cannot overstate my gratitude to His Honour Judge John Altman and His Honour Peter Charlesworth for their efforts in improving my knowledge of court procedure. Andy Brown, GP, for his medical guidance on eyes and albinism.

I have gained great insight into the lives of the seafaring folk of Staithes through the late John Howard's excellent book *Staithes*, and Jean and Peter Eccleston's *A History and Geology of Staithes*. Peter Osborne's *The Floating Egg* was as much a pleasure to read as a research tool. Likewise Peter Frank's informative *Yorkshire Fisherfolk* and Andrew White's *A History of Whitby*. Janet Dunbar's *Laura Knight* was a great help as was Laura Knight's own book *Oil Paint and Grease Paint*. I found Richard Ellmann's *Oscar Wilde* a fascinating insight into this nineteenth century literary giant.

Finally, I am appreciative of those who have courageously raised their heads above the parapet to offer constructive criticism – not least among them my new publisher, Jeremy Mills.

Now available in the same series

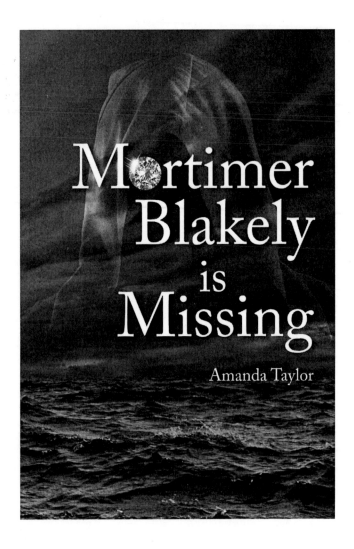

Mortimer
Blakely
is
Missing

Amanda Taylor

'*Mortimer Blakely is Missing* is a wonderful read. It is compelling
story: gripping, original, accomplished and challenging.'

Gervase Phinn

Author Profile

Educated in Leeds, Amanda Taylor did some magazine work and won a National Poetry Prize. She played squash for Yorkshire for nine years. Despite living in the middle of a grouse moor, about as far away as you can get from the sea, Amanda completed a successful relay swim of the English Channel and maintains that working out her plots helps the tedium of all those training miles.

Visit her website: **www.amandataylorauthor.com**